D1257597

MONDAY MORNINGS

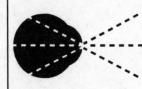

This Large Print Book carries the
Seal of Approval of N.A.V.H.

MONDAY MORNINGS

SANJAY GUPTA, MD

WHEELER PUBLISHING
A part of Gale, Cengage Learning

GALE
CENGAGE Learning·

Detroit • New York • San Francisco • New Haven, Conn • Waterville, Maine • London

GALE
CENGAGE Learning®

Copyright © 2012 by Sanjay Gupta, MD.
Wheeler Publishing, a part of Gale, Cengage Learning.

LIBRARY OF CONGRESS CATALOGING-IN-PUBLICATION DATA

Gupta, Sanjay, M.D.
  Monday mornings / by Sanjay Gupta, MD.
    pages ; cm. — (Wheeler Publishing large print hardcover)
    ISBN-13: 978-1-4104-4908-5 (hardcover)
    ISBN-10: 1-4104-4908-4 (hardcover)
    1. Surgeons—Fiction. I. Title.
  PS3607.U5484M63 2012b
  813'.6—dc23   2012009084

Published in 2012 by arrangement with Grand Central Publishing, a division of Hachette Book Group, Inc.

For my beautiful wife Rebecca and our three wonderful daughters — Sage, Sky and Soleil. Be lifelong students and also wise and patient teachers. Remember to "see everything, overlook most and correct a little."

Also, for all the healers out there who continuously strive to perfect the "practice" of medicine.

To the staff and faculty at the University of Michigan hospitals, and the residents of idyllic Chelsea.

And finally, for Dr. Julian T. Hoff. I thought of this book many years ago when you took on the task of training me. Thanks for all the lessons, inside and outside the operating room.

ACKNOWLEDGMENTS

Bob Barnett is my lawyer, and also my friend. He has made my writing career a reality, and I am honored to have his guidance. Jamie Raab is the "boss" at Hachette, and has never hesitated to publish one of my books. Thanks so much for the opportunities. My editor Deb Futter skillfully guided my editorial process, prodded me just enough to stay on schedule, and cheered loudly along the way. Dianne Choie made the whole process hum along, even at times when it seemed as though the end would never come. And thank you to the countless editors who internalized *Strunk and White* in a way I didn't think possible and allowed me to benefit from their skills. Thank you for your dedication.

Dan Barrow is the chairman of neurosurgery at the Emory Clinic. He is the boss in my medical world, and my friend. Thank you for all your guidance and wisdom. I hope this book honors some of the medical and surgical traditions we have discussed.

The indefatigable Roni Selig runs our medical team at CNN and manages an incredibly productive and busy unit of a couple dozen producers. Her constant support and encouragement is priceless. Thank you for listening to my ideas and helping focus them.

And finally, most importantly, thank you to my friend and fellow writer David Martin. For decades, David has been the kind of writer I hope to be one day. Simply put — this book and many of the projects I do on television would not be possible without him. Thank you, David.

CHAPTER 1

The EMTS crashed through the swinging bay doors of the emergency room. Wearing bright blue polyester jumpsuits with a yellow insignia on the left front pocket and standard-issue black boots, they were moving fast. It was impossible to miss the concern, and also the soot, on their young faces. Wherever they were, there had clearly been smoke, probably a fire. Between them was a woman on a gurney, in a silver reflective thermal cocoon. An IV bag, slowly dripping into plastic tubing connected to her arm, swayed wildly on a pole as they wheeled her toward the center of the crowded emergency room.

It was only when you saw the ER from the top that you understood the ingenuity of the layout. It was not a single room, but an apparent maze designed like a large round tire with a series of spokes. There were rooms around the periphery; patients were placed closer and closer to the middle depending on how critical they were. This woman was coming to the epicenter.

"I got an attempted suicide. Single vehicle into a telephone pole." The EMT's voice carried across the ER, above the urgent voices of doctors and nurses, the moans of patients, a crying baby, the beeping monitors, the adjoining waiting room's blaring television.

Dr. George Villanueva was the man who lived and worked in the center of the ER, and his eyes were on the woman even before the words reached him. Villanueva was a gargantuan man who sat on a swivel stool that was barely able to contain his significant girth. He gave the impression of an elephant in the circus — or perhaps a supernova at the center of a solar system. He had followed the patient as soon as her small prone form came into his ER. From his perch, Villanueva immediately noted that her face, immobilized by a slightly crooked, hard plastic neck brace, was unlined. He guessed her age as twenty-five. She was pale. Her lips were almost bluish in tint. Her nose looked as though it might have been broken by the air bag, and deep bruises were beginning to bloom below the orbits of both eyes. "Raccoon's eyes," he muttered to himself.

It was an indication that the base of the young woman's skull had been smashed. He quickly counted the number of drips from the IV bag. "Too slow." The paramedics repeatedly squeezed a bag connected to a breathing tube, forcing air into her lungs. "Also too slow," he mumbled.

"Trauma Bay Eight," Villanueva shouted, sending the patient to the trauma bay near the center of the ER. The doctor's small brown eyes locked on the woman, his massive, watermelon-size head pivoting on his even more massive torso like some sort of giant Claymation figure. As the EMTs veered past Villanueva, he continued to make mental notes. He noticed that her eyes were open but pointing in slightly different directions, with one pupil a little larger than the other. She was weakly moving both her arms beneath the foil blanket. He glanced down to the catheter bag, draining the young trauma victim's bladder. It was nearly empty. Her heart monitor beeped too fast. Villanueva calculated 124 beats a minute.

"What'd you say happened?" Villanueva called to the paramedics.

"Tried to flatten her Camry into a telephone pole. No skid marks. Didn't even try to stop. Suicide by car, without a doubt," the EMT answered without stopping, sweat

11

dripping from his brow.

"Like hell," Villanueva said. He launched his 350-pound frame off his stool and caught up to the fast-moving EMTs. He moved with an extraordinary grace for such a big man, and the speed at which he crossed the tile floor was startling. There was still the glimpse of the agility that had made him the Detroit Lions second-round draft pick out of the University of Michigan. Now he strode step for step with the EMTs as they raced toward the trauma bay. Villanueva looked as though he were leading a sweep. He'd lasted four years in professional football before his relatively diminutive 275 pounds became a liability. By the time he left the league, even high schools had three-hundred-pounders on the offensive line. Of course, Villanueva's weight was now well into the acceptable range for an NFL offensive lineman. But instead of a helmet and pads, he wore size XXXL scrubs that strained to contain his midsection, which had grown to enormous proportions in the twenty-two years since he had left the NFL. Often the scrubs failed, and a small rim of belly was visible beneath his shirt. Villanueva's scrub pants were so tight that many of the nurses found them obscene. He usually had the decency to wear his white coat, which was the only thing big enough to cover the large man and all his parts. But today, the coat was lying bloodied and crumpled in another trauma bay. It was the casualty of an emergency resuscitation a few hours earlier.

As the paramedics slid the injured woman from the gurney to the examination table, Villanueva and an ER nurse converged on the spot. Villanueva reached down and quickly adjusted the woman's neck brace so it was perfectly straight, then glanced at the closest EMT.

"Turn up her oxygenation, increase her ventilation, get her some more fluids, and call the neurosurgeons. This wasn't a friggin' suicide attempt. She just had a bomb go off in her head! Stop screwing around. Let's go!"

The nurse hesitated for a split second, considering whether to deny that she was screwing around, thought better of it, and began moving around the injured woman, turning a large valve to increase the flow of pure oxygen through a clear mask.

The paramedics looked at each other and shook their heads in wonder as though they had just seen their favorite magician performing another mind-bending trick. Then they began retracing their steps through the emergency room, their radios squawking, and their black laced-up boots leading the way.

Villanueva's impulsive diagnoses were the stuff of legend around Chelsea General. His quick thinking and physical agility earned him the nickname El Gato Grande — the Big Cat — or simply Gato. Dr. George Villanueva himself spoke only a smattering of Spanish, and he hadn't gone by his given name, Jorge, since he was six and started school. Still, the Gato Grande nickname stuck.

Earlier that same shift, Villanueva had been on his stool watching the actions of two emergency room doctors in a close-by trauma bay. They were arguing back and forth when their patient's blood pressure started to plummet. If you had been watching Villanueva closely, you would've seen a flush appear on his cheeks and a nearly imperceptible squint in his eyes. It was vintage Villanueva, and not a look you would ever want directed at you. A second later he'd had enough and burst into the room while the two emergency room doctors were unsuccessfully trying to revive a man in his sixties. One of them had his mouth to the patient's ear and was shouting, "Sir, can you open your eyes?"

"No . . . he can't . . ." Villanueva angrily mumbled as he strode toward the slumped man, almost gliding on the balls of his feet. He grabbed a bottle of iodine in his left hand and an enormous sixteen-gauge Cook needle in his right.

He told the ER doctor to "please step aside" and when the man didn't react fast enough, Villanueva swept the MD aside with his forearm, the way he might have handled a defensive back in his previous career. Before the doctor could protest, Villanueva had pulled the patient's shirt open and was squirting iodine onto his left chest to sterilize the area. A second later Villanueva plunged the needle deep into the man's chest. A faint smile crossed his face as the needle found its mark. He pulled back on the plunger, and the syringe started to fill with bright red blood.

"Cardiac tamponade," he said to no one in particular. "Five. Four. Three. Two. One." Villanueva paused. Nothing happened. He gave another squint to the monitor next to the patient. "One half." Suddenly the patient's blood pressure and heart rate normalized as the pressure was relieved around his heart. The patient's skin started to pink up. "Zero."

Villanueva turned and walked away.

15

The other doctors in the room were stunned. They had missed the problem, almost costing the man his life.

"There was nothing to suggest this man had a tamponade," the ER doctor stammered to the receding Gato Grande. Villanueva didn't look back, instead tearing off his now-bloodied white coat and throwing it into a passing bin of laundry.

The jacketless Villanueva strutted back across the emergency room toward his stool, his head held high as he passed the nurses admitting, the kid getting his head stapled, the group of obstetricians trying to coax a young fetus to stay in its mother's womb, the drunk who fell off his roof, and a businessman in a suit who had been complaining of chest pain. A medical student who looked as though he'd be much more at home in the library stacks than the ER caught up to Villanueva. The student carried a clipboard and a quizzical expression. He was now rapidly turning his head back and forth between the young woman Villanueva had diagnosed with "bomb in head," and Gato himself.

"But how?" was all the med student could muster. He pulled his pen from his pocket and prepared to write. Villanueva abruptly

16

grabbed the pen and the clipboard, and even loosened the student's tie for good measure before stopping and facing him.

"Don't write. Listen and learn from the master," he said. He winked at an attractive nurse standing at the station. "I knew she needed more oxygen because her skin was pale and her lips were blue, that's an easy one." He was in full professor mode now, standing tall and upright, using his entire six-foot-two frame to project across the emergency room. As intimidated as all the students were by him, he was the reason the best of them from all over the country chose to come to Chelsea General. In the world of medicine, it is tough to call anyone the "best" at anything, but that wasn't the case here. Villanueva was the most celebrated trauma chief in the country, hands down.

"Always remember to look at the Foley catheter bag," he instructed the medical student. "These patients should be making plenty of urine. If they aren't, it means they need more fluid." The med student looked for something to write with before remembering Villanueva had his pen and clipboard. "Don't worry about writing this stuff down," Villanueva said again, reading the student's mind. "Just immerse yourself in this situation and you will never forget."

The med student nodded like a true believer.

"By the way, how old is this woman?" Villanueva asked. The med student scurried over to Trauma Bay 8, checked the chart, and returned.

"Twenty-six," he said. Squint. "No wait, her birthday's in December. She's twenty-five." Villanueva smiled to himself.

"Now, I bet you're wondering how I knew this little lady had a bomb explode in her brain," Villanueva called for all to hear, enjoying his moment center stage. Truth was, a lot of people who pretended to be disinterested in the bombastic Villanueva were craning their necks trying to garner a little of his amassed wisdom.

He quickly grabbed a penlight from the student's jacket. Villanueva himself never carried anything — no stethoscope, no tongue depressors, nothing to write with, certainly no penlight. He just grabbed what he needed from the closest victim. The penlight was simple white with no pharmaceutical advertising on the outside. Everyone knew how Villanueva felt about freebies from Pharma companies. "No such thing as a free lunch," he had once shouted across the ER at an attractive woman drug representative as she scurried out of the ER. A single bright light emerged when he pushed the button, and he pointed it at the woman's eyes.

"This young lady has a ruptured cerebral aneurysm. See here, a little disconjugate gaze," he said.

"Disconju— what?" the med student replied.

"It means her eyes aren't quite lined up." Another squint. "Jesus, what are they teaching you these days? You think between the sensitivity training and the financial investment classes, they could teach you some medicine." The med student blushed. "Oh, and her pupil on the right is larger than the one on the left. It means the aneurysm was pushing on one of the nerves in her brain that controls eye movements."

"Oh, I get it." A light went off in the med student's brain. "The aneurysm ruptured while she was driving. Rendered her unconscious. That's why she crashed her car . . ." He trailed off.

"Yes!" Villanueva shouted. "Like I said, she had a bomb go off in her head. Speaking of which, did anyone page Neurosurgery?"

"Yes, Dr. Villanueva," an unseen female voice answered from across the room.

"Well, where the hell are they?"

"On his way," the same faceless voice said.

"Which one of those overpaid and underutilized guys is it this time?" Villanueva asked.

"Dr. Wilson."

Squint.

"Oh boy! I am surprised all you nurses haven't already run to the powder room to doll up your hair and put on some lipstick," Villanueva bellowed. "Oh, Dr. Wilson, can I help you, anything at all . . . really, Dr. Wilson . . . anything at all." He had an alarmingly good falsetto.

The nurses giggled and shook their heads.

"Hey," Villanueva said to the medical student. "Since I taught you all that, why don't you go and get me a sandwich?" The student looked around, trying to figure out if Villanueva was joking or not. To no one in particular, the doctor called out, "And will someone please page pretty boy Wilson again?"

In a darkened call room, Ty Wilson sat, eyes closed, motionless and very still. There was a window cracked, and the smell of freshly fallen leaves wafted through the air. In the distance, the ripple of the Huron River could be heard. Other than that, the room was absolutely silent. His scrubs were a

20

deep shade of blue, seemingly designed to match Wilson's eyes. They also fit him perfectly, with no extra folds or wrinkles. He was on his knees, with his back straight as a dead man's EKG. The neurosurgeon visualized his breath as he inhaled. In through the nose and then around the sinuses. First the maxillary and then the ethmoid sinuses, followed by the frontal sinuses. He visualized the breath going down the trachea, anterior to the esophagus. "About fourteen millimeters anterior to the esophagus," Wilson had told his therapist.

"I don't think you necessarily need to go into that level of detail," the therapist had replied. "Actually . . . I do," Wilson said.

Now he visualized the breath making its way into the progressively smaller bronchioles and then slowly getting absorbed into the bloodstream. It was his form of relaxation. Meditation didn't really fit with his image of being a neurosurgeon, which was why Wilson mainly practiced it in the solitude of the call room. His beeper went off again. *Gato needs you. Now.*

Wilson opened his eyes, stood and walked out of the room. A minute later, when he pushed through the ER's swinging doors, he looked every bit like a USC quarterback in to run the two-minute drill and win the game. He was tall and fit, with wavy dark hair and those blue eyes, which had a hypnotic effect on nurses, patients, just about anyone locked in his gaze. Villanueva, as it turned out, was an exception.

"Trauma Bay Eight," Villanueva called to him. Villanueva glanced down at his beeper, which had just gone off. It said simply, *311. 6.*

The medical student had returned with his sandwich and was peering over Villanueva's shoulder at his beeper.

"What do all those numbers mean?"

Villanueva quickly crammed his pager back on his scrub pant waistband.

"What are you, a spy or something?" Villanueva took the sandwich and started eating, garbling a thank-you through his full mouth.

"No, just trying to learn," the med student answered. "From the master," he added, laughing.

Villanueva cackled. "Good, kid, I like that." He thought about it for a second. "Those numbers represent an invitation to the most secret and best-guarded meetings that ever take place in a hospital," he whispered. "Every few weeks, a select group

22

of surgeons get together and discuss mistakes."

The student's eyes widened. "What kind of mistakes?"

"All kind of mistakes. Morbidity and Mortality, some call it. Others call it Death and Complications. I call it the Someone Effed Up Conference. Capiche?"

"Can I come?" the student asked.

"You one hundred percent, absolutely, without a doubt can*not* come," replied Villanueva. "Did you not hear me when I said this was a secret meeting? Strictly invitation-only. No other doctors, no administrators, and certainly no friggin' lawyers! This conference is for us, and us only."

In the Trauma Bay, Wilson assessed the situation in just a few seconds. As he started to examine the young woman, he agreed with everything Villanueva had said. It was a classic case of chicken-and-egg in the world of neurosurgery. Doctors at many hospitals around the country would have heard the woman's story and deduced in a matter of moments that the blood in her brain was a result of the car accident. They would also deduce that since she'd been in a single-car crash into a telephone pole, she was trying to kill herself. The truth was far different.

The aneurysm, a small blister on the surface of an artery, had suddenly let loose, spraying blood throughout her brain. She had likely felt a sudden thunderclap headache, and within seconds was rendered unconscious. That was why she'd crashed her car. In this case, the aneurysm was the chicken. The car accident was the egg. The science of deduction, and Ty knew there was no one better at it than Villanueva.

Ty's beeper went off again. Like Villanueva's, it read *311. 6.* He took the message like a punch, sucking in air involuntarily. Tomorrow morning, he was going to be where no doctor at Chelsea General wanted to be. Ty forced himself to breathe out slowly, then caught Villanueva's eye across the room. He wanted to see if the trauma chief had gotten the page. One glance at Villanueva's expression of near pity, and Ty knew he had. *Damn,* Ty thought. The last thing he wanted was the fat man feeling sorry for him.

Villanueva muttered to himself, "Poor bastard."

CHAPTER 2

In the neurosurgery offices up on the twelfth floor of the hospital, a single light still shone along the long hallway, leaving the beautifully framed pictures of neurosurgeons present and past adorning the walls in subtle darkness. The names were all giants in the world of surgery: Edgar Kahn, Richard Schneider, Lazar Greenfield, Bob Bartlett, and Julian T. Hoff, who was widely credited with building Chelsea General into the powerful institution it now was. His nickname BUZZ was engraved under his name. The last picture was of Harding L. Hooten, the current chairman of surgery. Underneath the beautifully engraved wording of his name was his simple nickname: THE BOSS. There were also several museum-worthy paintings Hooten had requested through old-boy connections in the art world, also in shadows at the late hour.

Right outside his office was one of his

favorites, Mark Rothko's *Untitled 1964*, which was on loan from the National Gallery of Art. The abstract painting consisted of a large black rectangle with a dark gray rectangle inside. No one knew why the Boss liked it so much, but no one dared ask. There was a large Cy Twombly abstract and a David Hockney photo collage, also on loan, and a couple of John James Audubon prints Hooten brought from home. One showed a yellow-crowned heron, the other, a South American scarlet ibis. This particular ibis was one of the few birds Hooten had never seen with his own eyes, and he had spent a lot of his life hunting for the bird around the world. Most people who saw the art either had no idea of the works' gilded provenance or assumed they were reproductions. The air smelled of the expensive cologne that seemed to linger around Hooten's office.

Amid the grit of Chelsea General, Neurosurgery was far from the norm. Many other departments were so strapped for decorations that doctors would frame their children's artwork and hang that up, or order the type of forgettable prints of generic landscapes or flowers more at home in discount hotels — anything to distract. Neurosurgery was so atypical that several faculty members were embarrassed by the appearance and often took pains to see their patients in other areas, instead of the museum-like atmosphere of their own department. Few things killed rapport with patients more than the impression that the doctor was getting rich treating them.

Inside one of the more modest offices near the end of the mostly dark hall, Dr. Tina Ridgeway sat next to a tired-looking junior resident holding a bag of microwave popcorn, a whiff of melted butter in the air. There were a few framed pictures on the bookcase in the corner. One was of a couple of young girls in cheerleader uniforms. Another was a wedding picture of a very pretty Tina and her new husband. There was a picture of the whole family crouched around a young girl in a wheelchair. Everyone was smiling, almost laughing in the picture, including the girl in the middle. They sat on a couch across from Tina's desk, peering at Michelle's book of neuroanatomy lying on the coffee table. The picture showed the two lobes of the cerebellum, and all the various blood vessels that supplied blood to the back of the brain. There were a lot of nonsense scribbles on the page, in typical doctor's bad handwriting.

"C'mon Michelle, I'm not leaving till I'm sure you understand this," Tina said. While Michelle slouched on the couch with a few kernels of popcorn sitting in her lap, Tina sat up straight. She looked crisp and in command. "Tell me again, what are the different types of posterior fossa tumors in children, and how you would manage each one?"

Michelle nervously adjusted her glasses. "Uh . . . medullo . . . uh, something like that." She stammered something incomprehensible. Then she just sat, dejected and embarrassed.

Tina offered the younger woman some more popcorn as though that might fuel a burst of understanding. Michelle Robidaux was a resident pretty much everyone in the department had given up trying to help. She'd failed the boards twice, and all the faculty members were waiting for her to either quit or be fired. They ignored her during teaching rounds and hardly called her name when they needed a resident to scrub in on a case. They even asked senior residents to take extra call so Michelle was never allowed on call by herself. That served to alienate her even further from her colleagues. What they hadn't counted on was Dr. Ridgeway's unfaltering support for the young woman. The neurosurgeon had convinced all of her colleagues to give Michelle one more chance and allow Tina herself to mentor her. Some of her colleagues were sure Tina felt sorry for Michelle more than anything else. After all, Tina had grown up with everything, and Michelle, by all accounts, had been brought up on the wrong side of the tracks. This type of extra help was unheard of, considering Tina's packed schedule as well as her husband and three children at home. Still, here Tina was teaching long after her family ate dinner, again, without her.

The contrast between the two women was striking. Aside from the fifteen-year gap that separated them, Dr. Tina Ridgeway was gorgeous in a way that went beyond her flawless skin, high cheekbones, and the kind of lips lots of women were paying lots of money to replicate. She carried herself in a way that somehow suggested elegance and grace, unheard-of commodities in an urban hospital like Chelsea General. Even though Tina always wore her hair pinned back and was rarely found in anything but scrubs, male residents from all over the hospital could be found furtively walking the hallway in front of her office for no apparent reason. They called her Chelsea-Lina, given her resemblance to the famous movie actress. Anyone spotting Dr. Ridgeway outside the hospital might guess that she was in the fashion business, or maybe a politician or community leader. She was the kind of woman who seemed to attract attention without trying.

Michelle Robidaux, on the other hand, was a face in the crowd. She was slightly overweight, medium height, with bad posture, stringy hair, and skin pocked by teenage acne. She always looked tired and besieged, even after the rare full night of sleep. Still, her story was remarkable. She was from a small town in Louisiana, where most of her family lived under the thumb of relentless poverty. Her parents raised chickens and grew vegetables and sugarcane, eking out a living on the small patch of land south of I-10 between Lafayette and Lake Charles. Michelle's father had quit school in eighth grade to help his own father with the farm. Her mother made it through high school, but college was out of the question. Michelle's grandfather was a mechanic who fixed mowers, boat engines, pretty much anything customers wanted to drop off and didn't care if they didn't get back for a month or so. Papi Bill was a clever enough mechanic but he was also a whiskey man,

30

Southern Comfort specifically. "Created right here in Louisiana," he often said when he poured a glass, and drinking it was always the first order of business. He'd start the day with a tumbler of SoCo and Coke, along with a couple of Tums. By mid-afternoon, he was skipping the mixer and the tumbler and could be found on a folding chair outside his workshop, drinking straight from the bottle, much of his unfinished work scattered in front of him like lawn decorations.

Michelle's parents were too overworked to care much about the public school she attended, where teachers considered anyone who showed up regularly and stayed out of trouble to be a standout student. Not only did she show up, but Michelle proved herself different right from the start. She turned in her assignments. She asked smart questions, often beyond the ken of her teachers: "That's an excellent question, Michelle. Why don't you look it up yourself, come back tomorrow, and share your answer with the class."

Most of all, Michelle was a voracious reader. In books, she could forget about her growling stomach, indifferent parents, and two older brothers who were drinking and stealing before they were teenagers. Michelle exhausted her elementary school's library by third grade and moved on to the town library, where she caught the interest of the librarian, a matron named Mrs. Truex whose dowdy clothing and cat glasses on a chain were right out of central casting. Bobbie Truex had a brother, Rex, who had emerged from the town's middling schools to become a successful car dealer in Baton Rouge. When he heard about the remarkable girl frequenting his sister's library, Rex became a patron of sorts for Michelle, first encouraging the girl on visits to his hometown, telling her she could do whatever she wanted, and then paying her expenses in college.

To say Michelle was the first member of her family to graduate from college was true but missed the point: She was the first Robidaux to *consider* college. To them, college was a place for rich kids. Sure, college kids may have book smarts, but the only book that counted for Michelle's family was the Good Book. As for medical school, becoming an astronaut would have seemed less alien to family and neighbors living across the flat, sun-scorched stretch of land wedged between the Gulf and I-10. There wasn't a single medical school graduate from her zip code. Michelle's story was a testament to

her resolve. Now, though, the young woman began to wonder if she had traveled beyond the limit of that innate drive and intelligence. Maybe her reach now exceeded her grasp. Maybe striving to become a brain surgeon was too much for her. She thought about her upbringing and a family tree known more for boozing, brawling, and petty crime than any kind of success. For the first time in her life, Michelle started to question herself.

Prior to her arrival at Chelsea General, Michelle never doubted she was as smart as her Ivy League colleagues. But twice now, she had failed her exams, and it seemed everyone had abandoned her. They had been so excited to accept her into the program, and reveled in the telling of her story: *See that young doctor, she was raised on a dirt-poor farm.* She was an oddity to them, yet they took great pride in her achievements. They patted themselves on the back for taking her in at their prestigious hospital. Now only Tina Ridgeway seemed to care. A John F. Kennedy quote Michelle had first learned in second grade came uninvited and hit her like a slap: "Success has a thousand fathers; failure is an orphan." She was fast becoming Chelsea's orphan.

Tears formed in the corners of Michelle's

eyes, and she wiped them away with the backs of her hands before they could begin an unprofessional path from her tear ducts, past the conjunctiva, and down her cheeks.

"All right, look, Michelle, I know you're tired. Let's pick this up tomorrow," Tina said.

"Thanks, Dr. Ridgeway," Michelle said.

"Tina," Ridgeway reminded, "call me Tina."

"Right, Tina."

A beeper went off, and both doctors reached for their sides.

"It's mine," Tina said. She was hoping it would be Ty. It said simply, *311. 6.* A cloud crossed her face.

"Are you all right, Dr. Ridgeway?" Michelle asked.

Ridgeway sat staring at her beeper, and answered without looking up.

"Again, Michelle, it's Tina, just call me Tina. And yes, I am fine," she answered, perhaps a little too harshly. Tina realized her worry about Ty must have been broadcast across her face, and she quickly composed herself. As hard as they worked to keep it a secret, the hallway whispers had started. *What's going on with Ty and Tina? Are they dating, sleeping together, and what about her husband?* It probably didn't help

34

they ate lunch together and often sat next to each other at conferences. If Tina had a question about a patient, she always took the case to Ty. Still, it would probably surprise other doctors at Chelsea General to know that Tina had spent four nights in the last two weeks at Ty's apartment.

Tina knew life had a few hinge moments, when your actions or inactions could dictate your remaining path. That first night with Ty was one for her. It was both an admission and an indulgence: an admission that her marriage was all but over, and an indulgence in something improper. Her husband just assumed she was on call and was busy at the hospital. Truth was, he had stopped caring a couple of years before.

Now everyone was saying Ty Wilson might get fired or even worse. Ty hadn't even told her what had really happened in the operating room that night. He hadn't told anyone. But he was going to have to divulge all the details in Room 311 at 6 AM tomorrow.

CHAPTER 3

Across town in Dr. Sung Park's house, dinner had just been cleared. His wife, Pat, had loaded the dishwasher, wiped the table down, and packed away the leftovers. There was not a speck of food to be seen, and the house was almost silent. This was especially odd considering there were three children under the age of six. Everything in the home smacked of bargain shopping, right down to the sensible dress Pat wore. It had been on sale for 70 percent off at a wholesale department store. Still, Sung had given her a disapproving look when she showed him the bill.

The children were reading to themselves, the only sound coming from the turning of pages. Even the two-year-old was flipping through a cardboard book of animals without uttering a sound. Pat Park admonished the five-year-old when she giggled at something she had read.

"Your father is working," she said. Sung sat in his study reviewing a detailed paper on conjoined twin surgery. He was making meticulous notes, and drawing the operation step by step in a notepad he carried with him everywhere. He also used the exact same kind of pen every time. It was a red uni-ball micro pen with a .38mm tip. They cost fifty cents apiece at the office supply store, but Park got them for free. He pocketed them from the various department secretaries' desks when they were away. Now he was using them to detail a picture of two infant heads pointing in opposite directions with a band of veins still connecting them. He made bullet points of how much blood-thinning medication would be given at this point of the operation, along with the desired blood pressure of each twin. Even though their names were written on the medical records, he called them simply twin A and twin B. *Bad luck to use real names,* he thought to himself.

The following day, he was going to try to edge his way into the operating room, where his chairman was scheduled to separate the conjoined twins. Every other neurosurgeon including the legendary Ben Carson had turned the family away, saying it was too risky.

Still, "the Boss," as everyone called the chairman of Neurosurgery, was going to operate. Sung had been trying to take over the case, and when the chairman didn't budge, Sung had even tried to undermine him. He'd gone to the CEO of the hospital to remind him that he had a lower complication rate than the Boss. Sung had done his research, and learned the CEO, like many heads of hospitals, really didn't know anything about medicine, let alone brain surgery. So Sung had collected data. He handed the CEO a folder of information, including not only his low complication rates, but also his operative times, which were second only to Ty Wilson. He also had carefully copied his drawings of the operation step by step, and placed that in the folder, which Pat had bound for him this morning. The CEO pored over the papers for a few minutes, took a couple of sips of coffee, and then started grinning. For several seconds he didn't say a word, he sat just grinning and impassively staring at Park. Park thought the man might be having atypical symptoms of a stroke. Just as Sung was about to say something, the CEO came around the desk and put his hand on Sung's shoulder, like a schoolteacher might with a fifth grader. "I am telling you, Hooten find himself between eight-ball and hard place," Sung said. He regretted it as soon as the words had come out of his mouth. He had mixed up his metaphors, something that was very embarrassing to him. The CEO smiled and walked back behind his desk. "No he won't, Sung. He may find himself behind the eight-ball . . . or he may even be between a *rock* and a hard place . . . but not between an eight-ball and a hard place." Sung turned bright red, and the CEO waved him out of the office. On his way out, the smug ass had told Sung he should sit in the corner during the operation and take notes. It was all Sung could do to keep from screaming. After all, he had completed not one, but two full neurosurgery training programs. After he became a full-fledged neurosurgeon in his homeland of Korea, he emigrated to the United States, only to be told his training would not be enough to become certified. He was asked to complete another seven years of training, working well over a hundred hours a week. It would've dropped most men to their knees. Not Sung. Even though he was a full decade older than his co-residents at the time, he outworked them and beat them every step of the way. At the same time, he had studied and practiced weekends and nights to master the English language, although he still spoke with a choppiness that seemed to worsen when he was angry or nervous. He knew he would never even have a chance at becoming chairman himself unless his English was better. Being a foreigner was one thing. Sounding like a foreigner was another. The teenager at the kiosk in the local mall had smirked when he purchased Rosetta Stone for English from her.

Now nearly fifty years old, Sung was just starting his neurosurgery career and wanted to make up for lost time. Suddenly, in the quiet house, came a shrill one-second beep, followed by another. Sung reached out his hand without looking, and his wife placed his beeper in his hand. Even at home, he ran the place like an operating room.

The page said, *311. 6.*

Sung allowed himself a rare smile. Ty Wilson, the bright star of Chelsea General whose skills had put Sung's own formidable talents in the shadows, was going to be publicly crucified. Sung made a note to wake up especially early, so he could get a seat in the front row. He wanted to see Wilson squirm.

Dr. Sydney Saxena took her pager wherever

she went. It was an annoying habit, but without it she felt naked, exposed, in danger of failing. She wore her pager in the bathroom, the movies, even to her grandmother's funeral. She checked it more often than most people check their watches. She carried it now, in her left hand, jogging past the elegant Barton Hills homes where a number of her colleagues lived. She could often be seen texting while running.

Anytime Sydney went somewhere without her pager, even for a minute, she feared it would buzz and she would not be there when she was needed or, worse still, miss an opportunity. When a professor had asked her, "What's the worst part of being on call every other night?" Sydney had immediately responded, "You miss half the good cases."

Sydney always wanted to be the first to respond, to be the most dependable among the neurosurgical staff. While many of her colleagues had distractions like husbands, wives, children, she was unencumbered. Most of the time, Sydney viewed this as strength. When the hospital chiefs were looking for someone utterly committed to the hospital when the Boss retired, she wanted her name to be at the top of the list. Even if they denied the opportunity this time, they would not be able to pass her over twice.

Sydney ran at a clip that would cause a casual jogger to wilt, usually right around seven minutes a mile. On one level, running went against her fierce work ethic. She wanted to outwork everyone at the hospital, and running took time away from that commitment, no matter how fast she was. But she also wanted to be sharp and have fresh ideas. She'd once learned in a college psychology class from an aging hippie named Professor Quattlebaum that some of our best insights come when our minds are not engaged. Mowing lawns. Showering. Jogging. It was one of those bits of counterintuitive knowledge Sydney believed and adopted as her own. Now if only Professor Quattlebaum had had the flash of insight telling him to replace the threadbare corduroys he wore to every class. She smiled at the recollection.

Sydney checked her watch. She had been running for exactly fifty-six minutes and fifteen seconds, her eighth mile of a ten-mile run and feeling good. The air was warm and fresh, thanks to a cleansing rain earlier in the day. She felt as though she could run all night. Three miles back, on Washtenaw Avenue, she had passed the 555 Building and noted that Ty's fourteenth-floor window was dark. Sydney ran the schedule in her head and realized Ty was on call.

Then she passed Tina Ridgeway's home, a large, two-story Cape Cod–style house with faded gray shingles and black shutters. The Ridgeway minivan was there, but Tina's car wasn't. Sydney figured her colleague was at the hospital. Sydney prided herself on knowing what was going on at the hospital. Her mind wandered, and she wondered if anything was going on between Ty and Tina. They were spending a lot of time together. Sydney had a sixth sense for these things, and she smelled a whiff of added intimacy between the two doctors.

The thought of work of course prompted Sydney to suddenly stop and check her pager. Nothing. It was no surprise that Sydney hadn't been able to actually get through dinner and a complete romantic date for the last two years. If the pager went off, she stopped whatever she was doing and rushed to check it. Ross, her last real boyfriend, had gone so far as to buy an engagement ring. He had it in his pocket the night they went to Gandy Dancer, the nicest restaurant in town. He picked an evening when she wasn't on call and should have had no reason to wear her pager. After she answered it for the seventh time, though, disappearing for thirty minutes, Ross decided the ring was better off in his pocket. Afterward, Sydney didn't know why their relationship had soured, only that the vision she had of "punching the marriage ticket" as her career powered ahead had vanished with the empty cups of decaf at the Gandy Dancer.

Sydney headed downhill, her legs churning, moving away from the million-dollar homes toward the ranches and teardowns in the next neighborhood over, Sung Park's neighborhood. Even though he was making a good salary now as a neurosurgeon, he still lived in the same house he bought when he was a resident. She had asked him once if he was planning on getting a bigger place now that he had three children and a better-paying job. He looked at her for a long second, and then said, "Why?"

Sydney's pager went off. Her pulse quickened. She checked it without breaking stride. It said, *311. 6. Poor Ty,* she immediately thought. *The bigger they are, the harder they fall.* Ty was the big man on campus in the hospital, and was naturally gifted, but no one escaped Monday Mornings.

In the operating room, Ty stood over the

twenty-five-year-old woman's exposed brain. He now knew her name was Sheila, she was a teacher, and she'd been driving home after a long bike ride on the Kensington Park trail. Her father had given Ty these details while her mother sat next to him sobbing. When Ty handed over the consent form for surgery, the reality of the situation hit both parents, and they broke down. Ty had gently put his hands on their shoulders and said simply, "Don't worry, when she's in there with me, I will treat her like a member of my own family." Sheila's mother wiped her eyes, stood up, and gave Ty a hug. Her father signed the form giving permission for Ty to open up his daughter's brain with a series of drills, saws, and scalpels.

The rest of her head was covered by a light blue drape, framing the gray tissue visible through a round hole in the side of her skull. It had taken Ty just twenty-five minutes to open the skull, delicately cut the outer layer of the brain, and split the natural fissure between the frontal and temporal lobes. This was arguably one of the most difficult operations a brain surgeon could perform, but no one in the operating room seemed anxious. When Ty Wilson walked into the room, everything seemed to fall into a state of order and calm. Now Ty was carefully peering into the microscope, the bright light reflecting the gray-red brain onto his blue eyes. He needed to clip the aneurysm that had almost killed her earlier that night and could kill her in the days or weeks ahead if he did not disarm it.

The operating room was cold, and Eddie Vedder played over the stereo system: "Just Breathe." The Northwest grunge music was the choice of the anesthesiologist, a petite doctor named Mickie Mason. She stood next to a bank of devices monitoring the woman's vital signs. Most surgeons held strong opinions about what music played in the OR when they operated. Truth was, Ty didn't even hear it when he was in the zone, so he let the gas passer — his affectionate moniker for anesthesiologists — pick. In addition to Mason, a nurse stood behind Ty and slightly to his right, next to a tray of instruments. A resident stood on the other side of the operating table, studying every move of a surgeon considered one of the greatest natural "athletes" ever at Chelsea General.

Ty had cut through the thick, fibrous outer layer of the brain, the dura, with his usual quip: "That's one tough mother." The name for this outer membrane of the brain came from the Old English *dura mater* or

46

"tough mother," a piece of medical arcana passed along by his chief resident during training. The chief resident, now a full professor of neurosurgery at UCSF, where they had both trained, also made this quip at the start of every operation. Ty had performed more than a thousand operations on the brain since training. Still, at the start of each, he'd say, "That's one tough mother." It was now part ritual, part homage to his mentor.

Looking through the microscope, Ty could see the optic nerve, a thick white filament stretching toward the back of the skull. Nearby was the carotid artery, one of the major vessels supplying blood to the brain. On the other side of the artery was another nerve, a threadlike strand, almost imperceptible, even with microscopic magnification. "Gotcha," Tyler whispered to himself. Between the two structures deep in the brain, Ty found what he was looking for, the ballooned side of a blood vessel or aneurysm that had bulged and then burst with such catastrophic results. It looked every bit like a blood blister. Just as Villanueva suspected, the aneurysm was big enough to put pressure on that small strand, the oculomotor nerve, as it exited the brain stem. That was why her pupil had been dilated.

The brain was such an elaborate organ, there were times Ty wondered how it managed to function without complications for as many people as it did. So many things could throw the brain's delicate mechanisms out of balance, with lifelong, disastrous effects. A vessel could blow and spray blood across the delicate, spongy matter, the command center that controlled everything from breathing to consciousness. A single cell could grow out of control, squeezing out sight or memory or life itself. Lead in the blood, courtesy of a few chips of old paint, could dampen a child's learning for the rest of his or her life. A shortage of serotonin could result in crippling depression. A blow to the head could cause a bruise to the soft loops and folds of the brain and affect balance, speech, or judgment. The inability to produce enough dopamine resulted in the tremors of Parkinson's. A severe vitamin B_{12} deficiency could cause dementia. The list was almost endless. Protected by a helmet of bone, the brain was an organ of mind-boggling complexity and ability.

During his training, Ty's chief resident had challenged Ty and the three others who had made the cut into one of the smallest and most challenging subsets of modern medicine. He asked them why they thought they were good enough to operate on "the most complicated structure in the known universe." That phrase, too, stuck with Ty: *the most complicated structure in the known universe.*

Why, indeed. Ty's thoughts returned to the page he had received earlier: Room 311. Six o'clock in the morning.

Quinn McDaniel's mother had not asked him why he felt qualified to operate on her son's brain. She saw a confident, handsome surgeon, the very picture of what a surgeon should look like. She saw an attending neurosurgeon at a large teaching hospital with an international reputation. She figured everything would be fine. Before walking into surgery, the boy's mother had called after him, "Doctor. Take good care of him. He's my . . . well, everything." She smiled when she said it, a look of pride on her face.

Ty studied the woman's aneurysm.

"Straight clip."

"Straight clip," the surgical nurse replied, handing Ty the small metal object.

The woman lying on the table in front of him was somebody's "everything." A daughter. A wife. A mother. Ty again flashed on Quinn McDaniel's mother, and in that moment experienced an alien sensation in the operating room: doubt. It was almost like another presence in the room, a shadow looking over his shoulder. He had a slight shudder. Ty had never doubted his surgical skills. He had never had a reason to do so. His extraordinary dexterity, his cool under pressure, and his ability to figure out the three-dimensional puzzle presented by the brain came naturally to him. He could visualize the brain the way some could solve a Rubik's cube. Ty was grateful he possessed these skills. He had always considered them permanent, immutable. Now he wondered whether he had been fooling himself and others. Maybe he didn't have these extraordinary talents after all. Just ask Allison McDaniel.

Ty's pause broke the rhythm of the surgery, and the nurse looked at him, concerned. The break was unusual, out of the ordinary, and anything that deviated from the expected was cause for concern in the operating room. The resident, who had been leaning over, peering intently through the microscope at the operating field, stood up straight. He, too, looked over at Ty, wondering what the maestro was up to.

"Nancy, I think I'll go with a fenestrated clip instead." Ty handed the nurse the straight clip. He then took the other one. He turned to the resident.

"What do you think, Jason, fenestrated?" The question caught the resident by surprise. It was as though the all-star quarterback had just asked the third-string signal caller what play to call with two minutes left and the outcome of the game hanging in the balance.

"Um, sure, Ty. Fenestrated." Ty paused, and then nodded. The nurse placed the instrument in his hand, and he let out a silent breath. He counted to ten in his mind as his right hand directed the clip onto the blistered aneurysm. Barely perceptible were millions of micro motions between his thumb and forefinger coordinated with his wrist, all happening at lightning speed. And the clip was placed perfectly.

The rest of the operation was uneventful. Ty left the OR more tired than he should have been by what was a straightforward procedure for him. Two things were picking at his consciousness: the doubt he had experienced back there, and the page he had received earlier. The doubt was troubling, but he tried to push it from his consciousness as a freak and ultimately irrelevant experience. A rogue wave. He had never experienced doubt before and probably never would again, he reasoned. The page was far more disturbing. He would be answering for Quinn McDaniel in the morning, and he needed to be ready. Most of all, he needed a good night's sleep, but he knew the fatigue he felt as he traded his scrubs for a lab coat would not help. A good night's sleep was impossible. Room 311. Six o'clock in the morning.

CHAPTER 4

Room 311 was dim except for a bank of overhead lights focused on the front of the small auditorium. Ty Wilson stood in the band of light. Dressed in blue scrubs and a crisp white lab coat, he clasped his hands behind his back, giving the impression he was relaxed. Just waiting to talk to some of his friends on a Monday morning. Above his left pocket was his full name and DE-PARTMENT OF NEUROLOGICAL SURGERY, written in neat cursive. There was nothing in any of his pockets.

Truth was, Ty was anything but calm. He was nauseated as the epinephrine coursed through his blood and constricted the blood flow to his stomach. He tried breathing deeply and slowly, exhaling through his mouth, but his respiration was faster than he wanted, and even before he spoke Ty had started to sweat, ever so slightly, and beads started to form on his upper brow. He was

experiencing a reflex that had been pre-
served throughout all evolution in every
single animal species, including humans.
Fight or flight.

Apocrine, Ty thought, marveling for a moment on how this word from medical school
had bubbled into his consciousness on this
of all mornings. As medical students
learned, there are two kinds of perspiration:
eccrine, the healthy, cooling sweat of exercise, and apocrine, the hormone-drenched
sweat of fear. Ty had little doubt his body
was excreting apocrine.

Dogs could smell fear and desperation.
Women could, too, as far as Ty was concerned, although he'd reached this conclusion primarily through observation. He'd
watched friends, college roommates, med
school classmates — intelligent, perfectly
reasonable-looking men — who gave off the
whiff of desperation, and women could
sense it even before his friends opened their
mouths. Ty was sure he now gave off the
whiff of fear, and his colleagues' olfactory
glands three rows up were getting doused
with apocrine. He was usually the cool
observer, not the doc on the hot seat.

Ty had the irrational urge to simply bolt
up the stairs and not look back. Turn right,
sprint past Radiology, down the stairs, take

a left, pass the pharmacy and the gift shop, through the marbled lobby, and out through the revolving doors, escaping the orbit of the sprawling twelve-story hospital the way a rocket breaks the earth's gravitational pull. He'd pass the valet stand, the smoking patients from the lung cancer ward with their IV poles and their oxygen, the waiting relatives, the lingering vagrants. He'd pass Stan the sleeping security guard, the small food carts and trailers circling the hospital like satellites and serving everything from doughnuts to Chinese food, and run into the garage, where his Aston waited. He'd peel out of the garage, turn left on Linden through town, past the lakes, get on the interstate heading south, and not look back. Surely a hospital somewhere in Mexico or Costa Rica or Chile would value his training and skills, if not his choppy Spanish. Ty could almost see himself practicing somewhere else. Almost. But the inchoate picture in his mind's eye never fully materialized. He didn't want to be playing in the minors.

Ty could feel his fists tensing and his muscles swelling with more blood flow. He began fidgeting, tapping his feet. No question, Ty wanted to take flight, but that was not an option. Monday Mornings at Chelsea were the main reason he'd picked the hospital. Ty looked around Room 311, filled with sixty doctors or so, all the surgeons in his department. No one was skipping this particular meeting. They were seated in an ascending arc around Ty. Many of them held large cups of coffee, but they didn't take their eyes off him. It was as though they couldn't believe what they were seeing: Ty Wilson standing where no surgeon wanted to be, waiting to explain his mistake. You couldn't get to that spot without something going horribly wrong.

Ty could see Tina, Sydney, and Park, all in the front row. Tina, he noticed, looked grim. She tried giving Ty a reassuring smile, but wound up looking terrified. Of course, Dr. Harding L. Hooten, chief of surgery, the Boss, was there, too, front and center, looking severe and pinched with his small bifocals and bow tie. Hooten called the meeting and did his best to pick a time that would inconvenience the most people, reminding them who was the boss: 6 AM. Of course, Hooten himself had been in much earlier going over the final preps for his conjoined twin separation surgery.

There wasn't much to be said for Room 311. Unlike the Neurosurgery offices, it wasn't lavishly decorated. On the contrary, the carpet was worn in spots, and some of the seats creaked and groaned from age and wear under the fatigue-heavy weight of the assembled surgeons. Yet it was this small room, largely unknown to the hospital community at large, that drew many of the most gifted surgeons to Chelsea. The draw much like what an orthopedics fellow with gilded credentials might feel toward Rochester, Minnesota, and the Mayo Clinic rather than more forgiving climates and more generous salaries.

Room 311 was the place the finest surgeons were held to the highest standards. Asking doctors why they wanted to endure the gloves-off version of the Morbidity and Mortality gathering was like asking a soldier why he chose Ranger School. Life was full of creature comforts and compromise. Fuzzy lines and soft edges. Why not find a place where you didn't get any slack? Where merely *good* wasn't good enough. That's why doctors chose Chelsea. It wasn't the facility. Chelsea didn't have all the latest bells and whistles, the latest scanners and lasers — the devices other hospitals advertised on billboards. Nor did Chelsea's location set it apart. What Chelsea had — for surgeons anyway — was Room 311.

Ty knew all this. He'd been courted by a number of top hospitals. UCLA even gave him front-row tickets to a Lakers game. Weill Cornell had flown him in to New York City on a Gulfstream. He took a pass and signed on at Chelsea. It was in Room 311 that doctors and scientists had the courage to criticize one another, point out mistakes that might otherwise go unnoticed, and in the process advance science leaps and bounds faster than any other medical center. It was not a secret that more publications and text chapters had resulted from Chelsea's Monday Mornings than any other conference in the world. They were the best doctors around, and they liked being thought of that way. Of course, it meant many sacrificial lambs were offered up in an intellectual, yet still barbaric ritual.

The discussion of mistakes, complications, and death is often unsettling, even for seasoned surgeons. For that reason, Room 311 had also become a showcase for the spectrum of surgical personalities, from forthright and blunt to evasive and tentative. Some were quick to blame anesthesia, or any other specialty but their own. Others entertained: surgical showmen wielding black humor. Often, the conference room turned into a battle zone as academic wars were waged, with surgeons picking sides as in a more dignified street fight — sometimes only slightly more dignified. The meeting was fascinating not only in the sensitive topics discussed, but also the human drama that could ensue.

No one exemplified the hospital's exacting standards more than Hooten. The Boss. He looked like a dandy with his array of bow ties and the shock of silver-gray hair, but if his staff were like a platoon of Rangers, he was their demanding drill instructor. He'd been known to stop in unannounced in the recovery room, even the OR, to make sure everything was being run to Chelsea's standards. He'd chew out nurses for leaving charts open, where they could be seen by a passerby, or for allowing themselves to be interrupted while dispensing meds, increasing the chance of errors. He'd dress down a doctor ordering Foley catheters too frequently, raising the chance of infection, and surgeons for allowing surgical techs to triage weekend call. He'd even berated a janitor once for halfheartedly mopping: "You look like you're trying to paint the floor. You're supposed to be cleaning. Hospitals need to be clean." With that, Hooten grabbed the mop and started swabbing until the embarrassed janitor reclaimed it.

"Everything we do here should be focused

on healing. Clean hospitals help people heal." Hooten had said this loud enough so the doctors and nurses who had stopped to watch the spectacle of the head of surgery wielding a mop could hear. They shuffled away, heads down, all of them holding up their own sometimes faltering standards against Hooten's and not liking the comparison.

Ty tried to hold the image of Hooten with the mop in his head, but he couldn't. His respiration continued to be rapid. His heart was pounding much faster than his usual fifty-two beats per minute. His thoughts were disjointed, panicked. Ty tried to focus on his breathing. He took in a slow, even breath. In through the nose, the maxillary, the ethmoid . . . *Just stop,* he said silently. Out through the mouth. He breathed out slowly.

Ty had skydived on a dare as a high school senior in San Juan Capistrano and scuba dived with sharks in the Bahamas during a break in medical school. Both experiences had given him a few moments of terror, followed by the thrill of avoiding an untimely death. "Nothing makes you feel more alive than — almost dying," a friend had once said to him. It happened to be his only friend. Tragically, and ironically, that same friend had killed himself a few years ago. Ty winced, and tried to push all these thoughts away. None of those experiences prepared him for this, his first time in the hot seat. Standing in front of his peers to answer for what he'd done caused him not fear but dread. How would his peers judge his actions? Candor was the rule in this secret meeting, egos be damned.

Ty took another deep breath, trying to regain his *wa,* and began slowly. "At approximately three-thirty in the afternoon on October twenty-third, I was called to the emergency room to evaluate an eleven-year-old boy."

He paused, and in his mind's eye he saw Quinn McDaniel. The boy appeared perfect in every way. His hair and skin represented the vitality that came only with youth. His smile was a little crooked, and the smattering of freckles suggesting a love for the outdoors. He was carrying a soccer ball in his arms, and his cleats echoed loudly on the hospital's linoleum floors. Ty thought that if he had a son, he'd want him to look just like this kid. The boy was animated and full of liveliness, making Ty wonder why he had just received an emergency call from the ER to come see the boy.

"The boy arrived at the ER after a head-to-head collision with another boy during a soccer game. He presented as the picture of health. BP, heart rate, respiration, all normal. He was exceptionally fit," Ty continued to the assembled surgeons. Ty remembered reading once that if you were able to maintain the vitality you possess at age eleven, you could live twelve hundred years. *Not this kid,* he thought.

Ty and the ER doctor who had paged him, Max Goldman, stepped away from the child and his mother. Goldman had ordered a CT scan, not because he expected the images to show anything wrong, but to cover his ass in the event of a lawsuit. He told Ty as much.

"I know he looks fine," Goldman said. He spoke in a soft voice meant to reach Ty and no farther. "But there is something you'd better see." With that, the ER doctor had taken Ty to a small room, dark except for an LED computer screen and a keyboard. Goldman typed on the computer and began showing Ty one image after another.

"I couldn't believe what I was seeing," Ty continued to his peers. "I checked the name twice and the ID number, just to make sure. This boy had a very large malignant-appearing tumor in the left temporal lobe of his brain." Ty paused and composed himself. "At that moment, I made the decision that if this boy didn't get an operation immediately, he was at risk of sudden death."

"Dr. Wilson, did you bother to order any more tests?" The question came from Hooten. His tone was caustic. In addition to *the Boss*, Hardy Hooten often lived up to another, less flattering nickname that reflected his icy demeanor at times like this: Hardly Human.

"No, sir," Ty answered.

Someone Ty couldn't see asked, "Did you consider showing the boy's films to any of your esteemed colleagues?" The questioner emphasized *esteemed* in a way that insinuated Ty didn't think much of his fellow neurosurgeons.

"No," Ty answered, looking in the direction of the questioner. From his position in the glare at the front of the room, it was hard for him to see who was talking if they weren't in front rows. That wasn't a problem when Hooten was talking. He was right in Ty's face.

"Why didn't you ask for any help, Dr. Wilson?" Hooten asked.

"Didn't think I needed it," Ty answered.

"Didn't think you needed it," Hooten repeated, letting the words hang in the air.

"Potentially life-threatening surgery and you don't bother talking to anyone else? Consulting any of your colleagues?"

"That was obviously a mistake," someone near the back muttered.

Ty would have guessed that a comment like that came from Sung Park, but Sung was sitting in the front row, legs crossed. Park looked uncomfortable, rubbing his temples. Ty expected the man to be beaming, a competitor who had just witnessed his rival, the favorite, stumble. Even without Park's involvement, Ty could feel the tide of the room was starting to turn against him.

"How about a simple history . . . did you bother doing that before you cut the boy's head open?" Hooten again. *The grand inquisitor,* Ty thought. "If you weren't going to get help from your colleagues, what about from the patient — or the patient's mother?"

"In retrospect, it was inadequate."

Ty knew Hooten had been aiming at this line of questioning all along, but he wanted others in the room to see the value in consulting one another before driving home the true nature of Ty's failure.

"No patient history," Hooten said and waved off the murmurs in the room. "Dr. Wilson, continue." If this was going to be a public execution, Hooten wanted to make

64

sure he gave Ty all the rope he needed to hang himself. *Maybe I was too cocky,* Ty thought. He had been told that he was technically the most gifted surgeon the hospital staff had ever seen. He never doubted them. Now he was starting to second-guess himself. Not his skills in the OR, but his judgment. What if he had waited to operate?

"I mapped out a left-sided craniotomy with awake speech mapping," Ty continued. "After placing immobilization pins in the right frontal area and the left occiput, I asked the anesthesiologists to go ahead and wake the boy back up." During the operation, nurses were going to periodically test his speech by having him identify objects on flash cards. Quinn was lying on his side, his left cheekbone facing up. He opened his eyes, looking a little frightened as he awoke. When he saw Ty, he smiled.

"Hey, did I tell you . . . I always wanted to be a brain surgeon when I grow up," he'd told Ty. The sedative gave the boy's speech a drowsy quality. Quinn McDaniel paused, then added, "Or maybe a fireman . . ." The recollection was almost unbearable for Ty. He coughed, so he could choke back a tear.

"I made an incision from his zygoma in front of his left ear, all the way to the mid-

65

line. The bone was removed without incident."

"How was the patient doing during this part of the operation?" the Boss challenged.

"No problems, sir. He was awake and talking to the anesthesiologist."

"He had absolutely no pain?"

"No, sir, he said he felt a little pressure as I drilled through his skull, but that was about it."

"How about bleeding from his scalp?"

Ty nodded. "There was bleeding, but I could control it easily with cautery and clips."

"Continue," Hooten said.

Ty mentally transported himself back to the middle of that operating room. He had looked up at the clock and noted the time: 11:34 PM. *Okay,* he'd thought. *Time to take out a tumor.* This was no run-of-the-mill tumor, though.

"As soon as I saw the tumor, I knew it was malignant," Ty told the room. "It had tentacles reaching into the normal-appearing brain, and it was an angry reddish color."

At the moment, Ty had been overcome with a sinking, black dread. He knew the boy would eventually die of this brain tumor. Medical science had not advanced far enough to be able to save him. All he could do was remove what he could see, buy a little time for the boy and his mother. Ty had already started thinking about the conversation he was going to have with the mother, Allison McDaniel. He would have to tell her that her precious little boy would only have a year, maybe two left, and then he would die an awful death — his mind robbed of its function and his body slowly wasting away.

"I started to remove the tumor" — Ty looked right at Sung — "and it started to bleed. There was much more bleeding than I expected." Ty's voice trailed off. The surgeons in the room were fixed on him. Tina Ridgeway looked like she was about to throw up.

Hooten broke the silence. His voice was quiet and measured and contained the sort of finality that a well-made door makes when it closes.

"Hindsight is twenty-twenty, Dr. Wilson. Tell us what you would have found if you had done a detailed history on the boy." The room was deathly quiet. Ty's knees felt weak. There was nothing left to say.

"The boy was healthy. The mother was healthy and had no chronic or heritable conditions."

"And the father."

"The boy doesn't live with his father. Never knew his father. I never thought —"

Hooten suddenly interjected: "You. Never. Thought." He made it sound like a dark oath. His words hung in the room, an accusation, a lesson to the rest of them.

"Thinking," Hooten nearly spat. "I don't care what any one of you think." He waved a hand toward the assembled surgeons. "I want you to know. We are healers but we are also clinicians, scientists, we follow time-honored reasoned analysis. We have methods. This is what happens if we follow whatever it is we happen to be thinking."

Hooten turned back toward Ty.

"Let me ask again . . . Dr. Wilson, what would you have learned if you had taken a detailed history before surgery, including the boy's biological father?" Ty wanted to hate Hooten at this moment, but he couldn't. He knew the old doctor was right. Ty knew he was wrong, and the costs of his mistake could not be calculated in any meaningful way. A boy had died sooner than he had to. "Dr. Wilson?"

"I would have learned the boy had a fifty-fifty chance of inheriting von Willebrand disease and had a risk for uncontrollable bleeding. I would have learned —"

The back doors to Room 311 flew open. Ty stopped. The assembled surgeons looked back: George Villanueva. He strode forward, gave Tina Ridgeway a little shoulder rub, and then looked up at the Boss.

"Hey, what did I miss? Did pretty boy explain how he killed the kid yet?"

Ty flinched noticeably, but then was transported back to the night he'd last seen Quinn. With the persistent bleeding, the anesthesiologist had long since dispensed with his newspaper reading and was peering frantically over the sterile drape that separated surgeons and sleepers. The music had been turned off some time ago. "Uh, Ty," he whispered so the boy wouldn't hear him, ". . . we have three blood transfusions going, and we can't keep up. His heart is starting to fail." Ty shot him a glance and then motioned to put the boy to sleep. Syringes were pushed and a tube was placed in the boy's mouth. Ty was back at work, aggressively trying to stop the bleeding in a boy whose blood would simply not clot. *What . . . is . . . happening . . . ?*

"Chest tray!" Ty shouted to the now-assembled group of a dozen nurses. He was going to attempt a last-ditch effort to save the boy. He would open up his chest and

69

begin an open-heart massage. He would pump the boy's heart until they could get enough blood in him.

Ty's hands were flailing wildly as he was describing everything to the surgeons in the secret meeting room. He had almost forgotten where he was, until a stern voice jarred him back to the present. Room 311, just after 6 AM.

"Did you really think that would work?" Hooten asked.

Ty looked momentarily confused and then met his inquisitor's eyes head-on. "No, sir, I didn't."

After the boy died, Dr. Tyler Wilson walked numbly into the locker room. It looked every bit like a room you would find in a gym. One of his favorite technicians was in there and cheerily asked how things had gone with the boy. Ty stared at him blankly and said nothing. "Oh . . . sorry. Well, you can't win them all," the technician said softly as Ty sat down and began to take off his clogs. He was soaked to the skin with young Quinn's blood. His feet were damp from the blood that had seeped through the small ventilation holes in his clogs. He removed all the bloody clothing, including his underwear, which were red-tinged, and threw everything in the hamper. In the small adjoining shower, he scrubbed his skin till it was raw, trying to cleanse himself of the blood and his despair. He changed into a shirt and tie. Most of all, he did not want Quinn McDaniel's mother to see any traces of her son's blood. By the time he walked out of the locker room and into the empty waiting room, it was nearly four in the morning. Only Allison McDaniel was sitting in there.

She looked into his eyes, and she knew. Her face collapsed.

The sight of her struck Ty like a blow. He wanted to turn around. He knew other surgeons who sent their residents out to let family members know a loved one had died. That would have been easy. He could have moved on to the next case with barely a glance back. But Ty had vowed years earlier — after what had happened when his own brother and later a sister died — that he would give the bad news himself, no matter what.

Ty remembered his mother's face in a hospital three thousand miles away and thirty years earlier when she got the news about his brother, Ted. A brain tumor had been diagnosed just a few months earlier, and he had fought like crazy. He had been young and healthy, and then he was suddenly dead. She didn't learn of his death from the surgeon but a hospital social worker. For some reason, this seemed to make the news both harder to comprehend and harder to take. In both cases, Quinn McDaniel's and Ted Wilson's, the searing grief had an almost physiological effect on the mothers — as though their features collapsed with their faith in the world. The cheeks and muscles around their mouths seemed to drop with the weight of the news. The color left their faces. Their bodies sagged.

Ty was with his mother at the time. He was eight. His father and two sisters had gone out to pick up some food. Watching his mother in her moment of grief was much more upsetting to Ty than the news of his brother's death, which he didn't understand at first.

"I'm sorry, ma'am, your son didn't make it through surgery" were the words the social worker had spoken that day three decades earlier. Ty didn't know what that meant. Was Ted back in the hospital room with the cool bed and the TV bolted to the wall? Ty hoped so. He never told his parents, but he had hoped his brother would get to stay in the hospital forever. Whenever he visited his brother, Ted would ask if he had an E Ticket. Ty would hand him a make-believe Disneyland ticket and climb up on the bed, and Ted would hit the buttons to make the sections of the bed rise and fall. Watching his mother, he knew something much, much worse had happened, though he wasn't sure what. He could not imagine life without his big brother. The notion of Ted dying was not even in the realm of the possible for young Ty, who idolized his older brother to the point of mimicking his pigeon-toed gait and squinty stare.

The tragedy devoured his parents' relationship. His father would disappear for long stretches. When he was home, he said little. He wandered around their small home as though he were lost. His mother dove into work. She was a realtor and spent most weekends driving clients around Southern California. She specialized in first-time home buyers even though the commissions were smaller and financing was often a problem. Ty wondered if she somehow liked being around the hope these young couples carried with them. His parents' marriage didn't last long after Ted's death. Maybe a year or two. Their bond eroded and then collapsed under the burden of the grief.

When Ty was a teenager, his mother and

father reunited briefly in another ER for another family tragedy. They were in their late forties but looked much older. Even though they were both remarried, they hugged for a long time when they saw each other. They shared a rare and horrible bond: a parent's grief multiplied now over two children. Ty's sister Christine was already in the OR undergoing emergency surgery when they arrived. Christine had been standing in line at a convenience store waiting to buy a Coke and some gum. All of her friends were outside waving to her when they had seen a man enter the store in a hurry.

"It seemed like just a moment had passed when we saw a few bright flashes of light and heard a loud noise," those friends of Christine had told Ty's parents. The gunman had never been found. He had left two people dead at the scene and Christine with a devastating bullet hole in the back of her brain. The prognosis was not good.

When the young neurosurgeon emerged, he informed Ty and his parents drily that Christine had lived but would be in a vegetative state for the rest of her life. His tone was so clinical, so cold, he could have been a service rep at the local car dealership telling them they needed new tires. In that moment, whatever flicker of life remained in his parents extinguished. They breathed, their hearts beat, but the spark of life was gone.

At the time, though, the news had the opposite effect on Ty. It transformed him, awakened his drive, gave his life purpose. His brother's death years earlier triggered in Ty an outrage at the callousness of the surgeon and a fury at the unfairness of the world, a rage that made Ty a volatile teenager. He was easy to anger and indifferent about school. His sister's state sparked in Ty something else entirely: a desire to be a neurosurgeon who could save patients and render them functional when others could not. From that moment on, Ty approached life with a single-minded purpose that made him a top student and eventually one of the best neurosurgeons in the country. Ty never forgot about the way his family had been treated, though. Doctors had ducked out when they should have been talking to Ty's mother. He never forgot how much a doctor's lack of compassion had added to his mother's pain. It was no surprise, then, that while Ty could be remarkably arrogant to his colleagues in medicine, with his patients and their families a remarkable humility and compassion emerged.

Standing in front of Allison McDaniel with the worst news he could give her, Ty's thoughts returned to those California hospitals: the news of his brother's death delivered casually by a hospital bureaucrat, his sister lying in a sterile long-term care facility, and his subsequent vow to be the surgeon who could save the impossible cases. Ty had become aware tears were burning a path down his cheeks. "Things didn't go so well in there, did they?" Allison asked softly. Ty cleared his throat. "No, ma'am," he replied softly. "I am afraid we lost your son tonight." Allison started to sob, and Ty took her hands into his own.

"I know you did all you could," Allison said. Ty was too choked up to answer. Allison McDaniel walked over to him and gave him a hug. Ty found the embrace comforting and somehow unnerving: Chelsea General's star surgeon needed comforting from the mother of the patient he had just killed. That was how he saw it. Allison slowly collected her belongings and started to walk out of the room. Just before leaving, she turned. She wiped away a tear while looking at Ty and said, "I know what happened in there must've been so hard for you."

Around the corner, nurse Monique Tran

had also been in tears. She was calling her boyfriend from a quiet corridor.

"I've decided to keep the baby." With that, she couldn't say any more. She hung up.

CHAPTER 5

Mitchell S. "Mitch" Tompkins checked the notes on a yellow legal pad and fingered a diamond-crusted gold band on his right hand. He gave a little tug on his Italian suit coat and turned a set of too-shiny white teeth toward Tina Ridgeway. Tina sat upright, legs crossed, her elegant hands folded in her lap in an effort not to show how uncomfortable the deposition was making her. She wore scrubs, sneakers, and her spotless white coat.

"Now, Dr. Ridgeway, before the surgery, did you tell Mary Cash exactly how you planned to destroy her sense of smell?"

Tina returned the stare, winced slightly, and took a deep breath.

"Of course not. We didn't plan anything of the sort."

"You did it anyway, though. Didn't you?" Tompkins pressured.

Tina paused, and tried to choose her words carefully. "No operation is without risks."

Tompkins paced the conference room on the twelfth floor of Chelsea General when he talked. Like the rest of the floor, the room was elegant, with a cherry-and-oak table and high-backed leather chairs all around. A few of Hooten's paintings hung on the wall, along with gold-plated light sconces. It was perhaps the worst place to hold a malpractice deposition, but Tompkins had insisted and the hospital lawyers had relented. Tina closed her eyes and tried to remain calm. If Mitchell S. "Mitch" Tompkins planned to rile her up, he was succeeding. She had seen the man's name before. It was on the back of every phone book, above a picture of him surrounded by concerned-looking patients. HAVE YOU BEEN WRONGED IN AN INJURY? HAVE YOU HAD A BAD MEDICAL OUTCOME? Tompkins didn't look as good as the picture. In the photograph, he gazed at the camera with a confident air and the hint of a smile. Somehow, the picture made him look tall. In person, he was medium height and build. His handsome features were a little puffy, his face pale, with dark circles under his eyes, but he had swagger, and he was using it right now.

He was perched under an expensive chandelier. "You say no surgery is without risks. So then of course, before the operation you told Mary Cash about the risks?"

"Yes."

"You, personally —"

"All our patients sign a consent —"

"Did you see her sign the consent? Did you personally see her sign the consent?"

Tina looked over at the hospital's lawyer, who was reading his BlackBerry. The stenographer looked at Tina, waiting for her answer.

"Usually, that's the responsibility of the resident, to go over the risks with the patient and have the patient sign the consent form."

"So for all you know, Mary Cash didn't even sign the consent."

"I'm sure she signed it."

"But you didn't see her sign it. How can you be sure that's her signature? It could be anyone's."

The hospital attorney looked up, interested the way he might find someone walking down the street with a black eye interesting, and then returned to his BlackBerry.

"Yes, but —"

"For the record," Tompkins said, looking at the stenographer. "You are telling me you have no idea what risks — if any — Mary Cash was told of before this surgery."

"We could ask —"

"Yes or no? Do you have direct personal knowledge of what risks Mary Cash was aware of before her surgery?"

Again, Tina looked to the hospital attorney. *A four-hundred-dollar-an-hour mute,* she thought. Shouldn't he object or something? Was she supposed to endure this meekly?

Tompkins leaned close to Tina. He was enjoying every minute of this. He folded his arms in a practiced way, like someone on Broadway who wanted to make sure the folks in the back row didn't miss the gesture.

"I have all day, Dr. Ridgeway. Yes or no."

"No," Tina said, deflated. "I did not personally hear what Mary Cash was told before her surgery."

Tina tried to imagine what her father, the renowned internist Thomas Ridgeway, or grandfather, Dr. Nathaniel Ridgeway, a crusty family practitioner in Vermont, would do with the plaintiff's attorney now in her face. She couldn't picture either of them sitting where she was at all. They would have gotten up and walked out without a second thought.

Her thoughts turned to Mass General.

One of her favorite memories of childhood was playing hide-and-seek with her father and older brother in the Ether Dome, a semicircular surgical amphitheater where anesthesia was demonstrated for the first time. Her father was always "It." They would scatter to different curved rows and crouch behind the white, wooden partitions, trying not to squeal or giggle as his footfalls approached. Afterward, when the vapor lights had come back on, her father would take them into his adjoining office in the Bulfinch Building, crouching to fit his six-foot, four-inch frame under the arched doors built when the average American was a good deal shorter and the hospital received patients by boat. There the eminent Dr. Thomas Ridgeway would reach into the large square freezer next to a lab bench and pull out paper-wrapped ice cream sandwiches for his children from among the tissue samples.

His co-workers would make a fuss of Tina and her brother. They'd always ask her brother, "Are you going to be an important doctor like your father?" Over time, she became increasingly annoyed that the lab techs and other doctors never asked her this question. Maybe her resolve to become a doctor began then. Even if it hadn't, the burden of continuing the family's legacy in medicine fell to her as soon as her brother dropped out of college. From that point on, her father and grandfather assumed Tina would be going to medical school and becoming the next Dr. Ridgeway in the family.

The deposition was now entering its second hour with no letup in sight. The facts were straightforward, but the lawyer appeared determined to wear down Tina, to get her to say something careless. Something he could have her read out loud at the trial, no doubt, Tina thought. She'd watched enough legal dramas on television to know how this would play out if she lost her cool and so, apparently, had Tompkins.

Mary Cash had arrived at Chelsea General with a meningioma, a benign tumor that could be removed surgically. One of the possible risks was damage to the olfactory nerve that ran near the cancerous growth. If that was nicked or cut, the patient would lose the sense of smell. The patients who heard about this potential side effect often dismissed it without a second thought. Compared with a tumor growing in their brain, smell was nothing, they reasoned. But smell was perhaps the least appreciated of the senses. For the unfortunate few who did lose it, the change could be dramatic. They'd lose the ability to smell the bloom of flowers or the smell of bread baking or fresh-cut grass. Possibly most upsetting, though, was the realization that when you could no longer smell your food, it never tasted as good. As a consequence, many would eat less, lose weight, and appreciate life less.

That's where Mitch Tompkins came in. He was suing Chelsea General, Dr. Tina Ridgeway, resident Michelle Robidaux, and every other doctor or nurse who had so much as looked at Mary Cash. If it weren't for the outrageous sum Tompkins was demanding, the hospital would have settled by now. Tompkins wanted twenty-two million dollars: one million for failure to adequately warn Mary Cash of the risks, one million for damaging the nerve, ten million for lost earnings, and ten million for loss of "hedonic pleasure." *Hedonic pleasure* was a catchall phrase referring to life's enjoyment. Plaintiff's lawyers used it if the outcome of their treatment left them unable to walk, see, play golf, have sex. You name it. There was even the case of a woman who had a small bone lodged in her throat that escaped the attention of the ER doc. She claimed the injury sustained resulted in her inability to perform fellatio, proving that any and all of life's pleasures could be included as Exhibit A in a malpractice suit.

Unless the hospital came close to his demand, Tompkins promised to take the case to trial and slather on the sympathy for Mary Cash like butter on corn bread. His ace in the hole: Mary Cash was a James Beard Award–winning chef. She needed her sense of smell to work. A chef who couldn't smell was like an artist who couldn't see. Cases this strong came along once a decade.

"When I get through with this hospital, people bleeding to death will drive an hour out of the way to avoid Chelsea General," Tompkins promised the hospital attorney after he filed suit at the Oakland County courthouse. "And forget about the bonuses for the hospital executives. That money's going to pay off the suit. Remember, the jury isn't limited to awarding twenty-two million." A third of twenty-two million dollars, of course, was seven million and change. That was Tompkins's cut. Like shooting fish in a barrel.

In the conference room, Tompkins paced, barely able to contain his glee. He ran his fingers over the expensive hand-screen-printed wallpaper.

"Now, Dr. Ridgeway, tell me how Mary

85

Cash's career was destroyed. Walk me through this. How do you go about cutting someone's olfactory nerve?"

When she was growing up, doctors were revered in the community. They were healers, civic leaders, wise men — and they were mostly men. They didn't make as much money as many specialists these days, but patients treated their word as the gospel. They didn't Google their symptoms and arrive at the doctor's only after the supplements or other pop remedies failed. And if something went wrong, it was God's will, fate, or simply bad luck. Tina couldn't remember her father facing a single malpractice suit in his forty-year career.

Tina narrated the operation step by step for the plaintiff's attorney. She had explained the procedure dozens of times for med students, so it was second nature. After the patient's head was immobilized, an incision was made on the scalp and the skull was exposed. Then a burr hole was perforated behind Mary Cash's right eye. The hole allowed a larger hole to be sawed in the young woman's skull, which gave the surgeon access to the brain. From there, it was a matter of gently cutting away the outer layers of the brain and then resecting the tumor. Because a meningioma can sit so close to the olfactory nerve, there is always the danger of nerve damage.

Tompkins was sitting during Tina's narration. Now that she had finished, he was standing again.

"Very interesting, Dr. Ridgeway. Fascinating, really. You described it so well, I almost feel as though I can do the surgery myself."

Tina said nothing.

"Now, when you say, 'A burr hole was made,' or 'The tumor was resected' — who was doing the cutting and resecting on Mary Cash? I'm assuming it was you. After all, you are an attending physician, the surgeon of record, and you wouldn't want to give this talented, James Beard Award–winning chef second-class treatment."

Tompkins paused and looked at the hospital attorney. The attorney tried to give Tompkins a *what-me-worried* look, but he did look a little worried. Tompkins turned back to Tina.

"So, you were performing this surgery, right?"

"No," Tina answered.

"No?" Tompkins feigned surprise. "All right then, who was operating on this young, talented, attractive chef with a whole career ahead of her, a rising star in the culinary world?"

"Dr. Robidaux."

"Dr. Robidaux?"

"Yes, Michelle Robidaux. A resident in the Department of Neurosurgery."

"You mean, you allowed a doctor in training, a student if you will, to operate on the brain of this young woman, lying defenseless on the table, as she was, her trust entirely with you?"

"This is a teaching hospital, Mr. Tompkins."

"So, what you're telling me is that Mary Cash was cannon fodder. Someone for Dr. Robidaux to practice on." Tompkins almost spat the name *Robidaux*. "My client was a guinea pig, if you will? Sort of like the Tuskegee syphilis experiments."

Tompkins was in full trial mode now, even though it was just the four of them in the room with him, the two lawyers, Tina, and the stenographer. His inflection wouldn't show up in the deposition transcript, but the plaintiff's attorney was giving the hospital's counsel a heaping taste of what his courtroom questioning of the esteemed Dr. Tina Ridgeway might sound like if the case went before a jury.

Again, Tina looked over at the hospital attorney. He was paying attention now. No more messaging on his BlackBerry. Still, he remained mute, making a few surreptitious notes on a legal pad. Tina wasn't sure which was worse, indifference or concern.

"Dr. Robidaux is a competent doctor."

"Competent," Tompkins repeated as though he were clearing bile from his throat. "Competent. When I go to get my brain operated on, I don't know about you, Dr. Ridgeway, but I want more than competent. I want an outstanding surgeon operating on my brain. Competent. Huh!"

Tina was flustered now.

"What I mean to say, Mr. Tompkins, is she is perfectly —"

"Did I ask a question, Dr. Ridgeway?" Tompkins interrupted. He turned to the stenographer. "Strike the doctor's previous *ex parte* commentary." He pivoted on his heels back toward Tina, looking a little like a game-show host with his thousand-dollar suit, expensive haircut, and extensive grooming.

"How was it that Dr. Robidaux was chosen to operate on my client?"

"That was my decision. I thought she was perfectly capable of handling a meningioma —"

"And she needed the practice?"

"No."

"Well, how many of these had she performed, before she cut on my client?"

"I'd have to check —"

"I think you know perfectly well. How many, Dr. Ridgeway?"

"None."

"None!" Tompkins looked as though he had just had the last bite of a delicious meal and was about to signal for the check. "None," he said again, shaking his head. "That's just rich." The lawyer's expression at that moment was the very epitome of smug.

Tina reddened. Her restraint fell away. Full-blooded anger replaced it.

"That's what a teaching hospital is, Mr. Tompkins. You know that as well as I do. We have the best doctors in the world because we have teaching hospitals. Residents learn at teaching hospitals. No one hatches from an egg as a polished surgeon."

Now the hospital attorney looked alarmed. He tried to interrupt. "Tina."

"One patient may suffer, but Dr. Robidaux is a better doctor, a better surgeon for the scores of others she'll treat in the years to come."

"Tina!"

Tina ended her diatribe. Tompkins turned to the stenographer.

"Did you get that?"

CHAPTER 6

Villanueva rolled up toward the massive suburban home. Looking at the enormous brick structure, with its white-columned portico, fountain, and circular drive, George was amazed he'd allowed his ex-wife to convince him they needed to buy such an ungodly monstrosity. What was he thinking?

He couldn't see any lights on in the house, but that was nothing new, either. The whole neighborhood looked as if it had been hit by a neutron bomb. Not a sign of human life anywhere among street after street of McMansions in Bloomfield Hills. If you have seven thousand square feet of living space, who needs to be outside playing or, God forbid, rubbing shoulders with the neighbors? Never mind that it was a perfect fall day, or that many of the lawns were so well groomed you could get out your clubs and practice your short game on them.

In Villanueva's hometown, Dexter, Michigan, you were lucky to have a small patch of grass in front of your house, and if you did you kept it behind a chain-link fence. Kids in Dexter generally played in the street or at the ragged park at the edge of town. They played until dinner or until dark and sometimes later. Football. Baseball. Basketball. Wrestling. It didn't matter. There were constant tests of athletic skills, of toughness. And there were dares, usually from the older kids. Run across the yard with the Doberman. Ding Dong ditch Ed Dobierski, who was known to have a shotgun by the door. Sprint down the train trestle as the locomotive approached. Young George thrived on these and other challenges and spent most of his waking hours roaming the streets or playing in the park.

Villanueva couldn't have gone home after school if he'd wanted to. His mother actually locked him out of the house until dinner. This prevented her rapidly growing son, whom she called Jorge until the day she died, from devouring all the food she was cooking. It also kept him from messing up her orderly house. Villanueva never imagined he'd live in the type of gargantuan home he and his now ex-wife purchased. Maybe that's why he'd gone along with her. It was beyond his imagination — even if it was god-awful.

Villanueva turned his Jeep into the drive and pulled up to the front door. A thin film of sweat covered his face, and his head pounded from the previous night's rum and Cokes at his favorite bar, O'Reilly's. He had left alone, much to his chagrin, and he made a mental note that he needed to drop a few pounds. It was definitely hurting his mojo at the Irish pub. Villanueva had found the bar as his marriage was falling apart. It was close to the hospital, for one thing. Even more important, O'Reilly's was small, dark, and unpretentious. There were no plants, and the decor consisted of plastic beer lights and other handouts from distributors, plus the odd knickknacks brought by customers. There were Michigan and Michigan State football helmets gathering dust on a shelf behind the bar. Assorted bumper stickers adorned the beer coolers below the bottles of hard alcohol. One read: YOUR PROCTOLOGIST CALLED, HE FOUND YOUR HEAD. And another: MY MIND IS LIKE A STEEL TRAP: RUSTY AND ILLEGAL IN 37 STATES. O'Reilly's was the way a bar should be, in George's view. It was the kind of place where the bartender didn't blink if someone ordered a boilermaker and didn't need to find a book to make a sidecar or some other cocktail from another era. Of course, George's drink was simple enough, rum and Coke. He loved the Havana Club dark Cuban rum the best. Villanueva saw it as the perfect synergy of caffeine and alcohol. A little too perfect.

Toward the end of his marriage, Villanueva had come home so drunk a couple of times, he wasn't sure which of the identical curving roads in the enormous, labyrinthine development was his own. They all had botanical names — Magnolia Lane, Azalea Circle, Ivy Trace — and he couldn't read the signs in the dark in his inebriated condition anyway. They were all bracketed by nearly identical, imposing brick homes that screamed for all to see that the owners had "made it." And they all ended in cul-de-sacs, with grassy round circles at the end for the children to play on if they ever got off the Nintendos or Xboxes or PlayStations and went outside. *Cul-de-sacs.* Even that got under Villanueva's skin. "When I was growing up, we called 'em dead ends," he would tell his ex when he wanted to get a rise out of her.

George rang the bell, hoping Nick was not on some computer game with the volume cranked. No answer. He rang again. No sign of Lisa. He guessed she was off shopping, making sure she spent every dime of the fifteen thousand in living expenses George paid each month. By arrangement of the court and the "his and hers" divorce attorneys Villanueva paid for, Sunday was George's day with his son this week. Still no answer. George balled up his fist into the size of small ham and rapped on the door. He could hear the sound of the knock dissipate in the chilled, dead air.

George rubbed his throbbing temples and bent over to look through the window. He was beginning to worry that Nick had given up on him. George was not always faithful about driving out to spend the day with his son. If he had too much to drink, or hooked up with a nurse or a barfly, George would blow it off. He'd call and tell Nick something had come up at the hospital. "No problem," Nick would say. George put his conscience at ease by telling himself the last thing an eighth grader wanted to do was hang out with his father, although he knew that was a lie.

George had almost never seen his own father, who worked in the local meatpacking plant. He'd moved up to the day shift by the time George was in grade school but would often pick up extra shifts at night and on weekends to help make ends meet. The work was so bone-wearying, George's father would arrive home from the plant, sit in the one nice chair in the house, and light a cigarette. With the cigarette burning between his lips, he would massage the knuckles on his right hand. Although George didn't know this until later, his father would grip the same heavy saw for hours as one dangling carcass after another reached him on what could only be described as an assembly line. The fingers on his hand would lock around the saw by the end of the shift, and he'd have to pry them loose with his other hand. Gato still thought of his father as he held a scalpel in the OR and peered down into the muscle he was incising. Maybe he and his father weren't that different after all.

Peering through the beveled glass, George could see his son in the living room, propped up on the enormous sectional couch playing some sort of handheld video game. Nick looked up, caught his father's eye, and then returned to the video game. *The little shit,* Villanueva thought as his respiration ratcheted up a notch.

"Nick," he said, and then, "C'mon."

George gave a sharp rap on the glass and gave Nick a palms-up *sorry-about-last-week-but-things-happen* gesture. George had missed their day the previous weekend. He had spent the night with a nurse who worked in the NICU. She was a big woman, but who was he to cast stones?

Nick didn't look up. The Big Cat could feel the blood rushing to his head.

"Nick!" Villanueva said. "Open the door. I'm sorry about last week. Hospital emergency. Nick, I said I'm sorry. C'mon."

Nothing.

"Nick! Open the damn door!"

Villanueva's nostrils flared. His face reddened. He ripped off his sunglasses and mopped the sweat from his face with a bare hand. He was considering the best way to apply his considerable force to the problem of getting into the house and pulling his son off the couch when Nick rose slowly from the overstuffed furniture and ambled toward the foyer. Nick opened the door, a rush of air-conditioning greeting Villanueva. Nick's eyes were blank as he looked at his father. George resisted the urge to throttle the kid.

"Hey, Nick. How ya doing?" Villanueva said with as much enthusiasm as he could muster.

"Hi, Dad," Nick said. His voice was flat. He was medium height and slight, in that awkward half-grown, fully self-conscious stage. George himself had skipped this phase, morphing from husky elementary school kid to man-child in a burst of hormone-fueled growth in sixth and seventh grades.

"Sorry about last week, Nick. Hey, I got Lions tickets for today."

Nick looked down at his feet.

"Great seats, Nick."

"I dunno."

When Villanueva was a kid, he would have killed to go to a Lions game with his father. There was no money, and his father always seemed so tired. The first Lions game his father saw was the first game of the season of the Big Cat's rookie year, and by then the smoking had already fried his lungs. He showed up at the game with his mother and an oxygen tank in tow.

Standing face-to-face with his own son, George pulled the cloth from the shoulder of his Hawaiian shirt and wiped his brow. Seemed awfully hot for an October day.

"All right, fuck it. Pardon my French. What should we do then?"

Nick remained focused on his black Converse low-tops. "I dunno," he said again.

"Cat got your tongue?" George gave his son a playful swat on the shoulder, knocking him sideways and nearly off his feet. He'd forgotten how slight his kid was. Nick

98

looked up, annoyed.

"Dad!"

"Sorry, Nick. Didn't mean to," George's voice trailed off.

"I sort of made plans today."

"Oh. Uh . . . okay. Just thought you might want to hang out with the old man. Catch a game. Got great seats." George paused.

"Football's not really my thing, either," Nick added.

"Okay." George was at a rare loss for words. He hadn't come with a Plan B. He tried to think what his son's *thing* was. As a boy, Nick had been obsessed with dinosaurs, extreme weather, asteroids, black holes. Either his nose was in a book, or he was watching a show on Discovery or Animal Planet or the History Channel. On the playground in preschool, while the other kids climbed the equipment or chased one another, Nick would sit off by himself, drawing in the sand or throwing it up in small handfuls and watching the wind carry it away.

George had signed him up for youth football, baseball, and basketball. Nick resisted every practice and played only the minimum required. He was awful. The kids on his team tormented him, their taunting and physical shots tempered only by the size of Nick's father, who sometimes came to practice and watched. In short, Nick's sports were torture for both father and son.

When Nick was ten, George's ex put a stop to it. Much to George's relief, she pulled Nick from all sports, signed the boy up for science camp and cello, and bought a family membership at the city's natural history museum. Still, it puzzled George how a male child with half his genetic code could be so different. Shouldn't Nick be twice as big as he was now? Where was the hunger for physical contact? Where was the desire to measure himself as a man?

Father and son passed an awkward moment of silence. "Well, have a good day, Nick. I'll see you next Saturday, for sure. Okay?"

"Okay," Nick said, his voice brighter. He was already walking back toward the couch.

As George returned to his Jeep, he found himself walking with a little more bounce in his step. He was relieved to be free of a day of awkward conversations and heavy silences. It was as though he and Nick spoke different languages. By Saturday or Sunday night, depending which weekend day Villanueva had with his son that week, George was usually spent.

Even before he reached the car, George's

palpable sense of relief was followed by a surge of guilt so strong he felt he could reach out and touch it. Shouldn't he want to spend the day with his son? Isn't that what fathers did? Good fathers, anyway. He sat down in the Jeep, gripped the steering wheel, and stared at the sunny sky. Then he put the key in the ignition, started the car, and backed out of the driveway.

CHAPTER 7

Park loved operating on Sunday morning. The hospital was quiet. There were no scheduling problems or fights for OR time. Even the emergency room was at an ebb following the Saturday-night high tide of gunshot wounds, stabbings, drug overdoses, broken bones, heart attacks, and lesser maladies. As he walked from the physicians' side of the garage through the general parking area, he didn't encounter the usual tide of wheelchairs, walkers, strollers, and clots of families clogging the elevator down to the lobby. Nor were there the visitors or patients — usually older and whiter — who would gawk at him and then his hospital name tag and back. Chelsea was more diverse than much of Michigan but somehow it still managed to surprise a certain percentage of the population that the lean, intense Korean man sharing the elevator with them was a full-fledged neurosurgeon.

They spoke to him as if he were a five-year-old, overly enunciating their words and amping up their volume. On Sunday morning, Park usually had the elevator to himself.

There was another thing Park liked about Sunday mornings. More often than not, he was the senior surgeon at the hospital. For a few quiet hours, he was king of Chelsea General. He knew this was a trivial thing. There was no real power in being the senior surgeon there, and Park realized the distinction was simply a statistical artifact, an error in perception, a product of his desire to work Sunday mornings while other attending physicians for religious or other reasons chose to take the day off. Technically, he could fire people if he wanted when he was the senior surgeon, and he had done it a few times. Of course, they always laughed it off because they would all be reinstated on Monday. Still, on Sundays Park walked the polished halls of Chelsea General with a magisterial stride.

This Sunday morning was better than most: Park had scheduled an elective deep brain stimulation. The patient's name was Ruth Hostetler. She came from a town Park had never heard of near the Michigan-Ohio state line. Getting her to agree to undergo the operation on a Sunday took a little doing, but her husband convinced her that God would be on their side on the Sabbath.

Ruth was thirty-five, and for the previous two and a half years she had suffered from an uncontrollable tremor. Her hands shook so violently that she could not write or drive a car. Eating was a challenge, and Ruth had dropped almost forty pounds. She was plump when the tremors started. She had shed many pounds since. She passed through her ideal weight and now looked gaunt, almost haunted.

Ruth wore cotton print dresses and had a well-scrubbed girlish look. She looked to Park like an actress on a soap commercial or playing the part of a pioneer woman of the American West. The couple had come to Park two weeks earlier on a referral from a Pakistani doctor who had trained under Park and was now working as a general practitioner on a J-1 visa in an underserved area in rural Ohio.

Seated across from Park in his office at the time, Levi had kept his hands folded in his lap; Ruth's flopped like bony fish pulled from some brackish backwater. The couple had asked Park if the tremors were a sign from God. Was Ruth being punished for something they had done? Park shook his head and dismissed the question with a wave of the hand. Park had once forbidden a family from praying in the waiting room. He had stormed in and said in loud, choppy English in front of a crowd, "If it is God you are looking for, He will be in Operating Room Three with your loved one, and right now He feels like He is being second-guessed."

"God has nothing to do with this. It's your brain that's punishing you," Park told the couple, smiling at his own joke. The Hostetlers did not return the smile.

"Doctor, we know God works in mysterious ways and has a purpose for all He does," Levi Hostetler said. "We believe we were sent to you for a reason. Maybe so you could hear the Word. Do you have a personal relationship with Jesus Christ, Doctor?"

Park didn't hesitate one second. He stood up and started ushering the couple to the door.

"This is a hospital, not a church," he muttered loudly in his choppy English. "I don't believe in God. I believe in science. I believe in data. Outcomes. Facts." He let the word linger, while giving the couple a hard stare. "When you want to talk about these things, you tell Dr. Khan and he can make another appointment."

Ruth stopped just outside Park's office. She did not want to leave.

"You want facts. I had a glass of wine the other day. My MeeMa told me to drink it. Said it would relieve the stress. I don't normally partake in alcohol. It's against the Word. But you know what? For the first time in a year, those tremors went away."

Park had been about to close the door on this annoying couple. Now he stopped. This case was interesting all of a sudden.

"You don't drink alcohol normally?"

"No, sir."

Park turned to the husband for verification.

"She doesn't."

"How about depression medicine? Lithium?" Park asked.

"No, sir," Ruth said.

Park was intrigued. He turned to Levi.

"Does she have tremors when sleeping?"

"Yes, Doctor. As a matter of fact she does."

Park now forgot he was showing the couple the door and walked back into his office. He waved for the Hostetlers to follow. He grabbed a pad, excited.

"Come. Sit. This may be true essential tremors," Park said. "Might be something we can do." Essential tremor had the somewhat unusual characteristic of getting better when someone drank alcohol, whereas most other tremors became worse.

The couple looked at each other, unclear on what the fast-talking Korean doctor was saying, but with his sudden optimism so strong, it made them smile. Levi leaned forward. He nodded toward the wedding ring on Park's left hand.

"You're a married man. If Ruth was your wife, what would you do?"

Park sat up straight, a wry smirk sneaking into the corners of his mouth.

"You didn't first ask me what I think about my wife."

Levi looked puzzled for a moment, then Park burst into a gale of laughter, the palm of his right hand coming down on his right quadriceps with a smack. The Hostetlers smiled wanly. Patients routinely asked Park what he would do if he were the patient, or his wife was the patient, or his daughter, and Park always responded with his joke. Park thought the question was utterly ridiculous: What would he do if this patient were his wife? Patients did not want to think for themselves. Why didn't they ask him what the chances were for a complication?

When his own laughter subsided, Park told the Hostetlers in all seriousness, "I will do what the best science tells me to do. That is all."

A week or so before the operation, Park had convened his cadre of foreign-born residents to discuss treatment options for Mrs. Hostetler: Wei Yoo, Hyun Kim, Mahendra Kumar, Aisha Ali, Rashmi Patel. These young doctors had, for the most part, defied incredible odds to distinguish themselves in their home countries and receive invitations to US medical schools; then they distinguished themselves once again in medical school to receive one of the coveted surgical residency spots at Chelsea General or an even more coveted neurosurgical fellowship at the hospital.

Rashmi Patel was the only one of the five Park acolytes who grew up in privilege, coming of age on the hills above Mumbai. Now she and the others — a Chinese, a Korean, another Indian, and a Pakistani — stood before their mentor for what Park called his post-graduate education. English — accented and sometimes fractured — was their common language. They also shared a competitive drive, a hunger for success in a world where the odds were stacked against them at each step, and a belief in Park's promise to make them better prepared than the Anglo colleagues who could rely on looks and connections to ease their way in the world. That promise included Park's withering office examinations.

"Traditional treatment for severe essential tremor?"

"Anti-seizure medication," Aisha Ali said.

"What else? That is not all. You need to know this, Aisha," Park said. The senior doctor gave off an air of omniscience, but he, too, had been studying up on essential tremors.

"Beta-blockers," Mahendra Kumar added.

"For everybody?"

"I suppose so," Kumar answered.

"No," Park said. "Beta-blockers can cause confusion in older patients. Beta-blockers for younger patients. Side effects?"

Kumar paused. He looked crestfallen.

"Fatigue. Shortness of breath."

"You're guessing, Mahendra. You're right, but you are guessing. You guess with patients, they will die."

"Side effects from beta-blockers include fatigue, shortness of breath, dizziness, and nausea," Rashmi Patel said in her clipped British accent. "More serious side effects for beta-blockers: hypotension, ataxia, difficulty attending."

"You forgot the other possible drugs for

essential tremor," Park told Patel. Never mind that he hadn't asked her. Whenever his charges rose up too far, Park knocked them down a peg. The nail that sticks up gets hammered down. To Park's way of thinking, this kept them hungry. "Wei?"

"Benzodiazepines."

"What else, Wei? You need to know this. You been sleeping late?" Wei did not sleep late. She barely slept at all. Between her thirty-hour shifts at the hospital and studying in a language that was sometimes so frustrating it brought tears to her eyes, Wei averaged between three and four hours a night. Her work habits were extreme, even among her equally driven foreign-born colleagues. From them, she earned the nickname *the Machine.* From them, it was a compliment.

"Anyone?" Park looked around. The younger doctors looked down and fidgeted. "Carbonic anhydrase inhibitors."

Park was pleased he knew something this group didn't, but he peered from one to the next, shaking his head with deep disappointment. "You're not ready for the big league. Maybe you should go back to medical school. Or find a program where you can guess. Maybe some other program that specializes in mediocrity." Park glared at

Mahendra Kumar.

"Now we turn to our patient and essential tremor. What is the difference between intention tremor and essential tremor?"

"Intention tremor is dyskinetic movement during voluntary movement," Hyun Kim said before someone else could contribute. Silence during these grillings was noted by Park and considered weak by the other acolytes. It was an unwritten rule they should all subject themselves to Park's abuse more or less equally.

"Etiology?"

"Cerebro-cerebellum."

"How is essential tremor treated?"

"Medication is the most common —"

Park cut him off. "My daughter could tell me that. Isoniazid. Also, odansetron. Propranolol. Primidone. Not very effective. Let us consider a surgical option for our patient." Park instinctively avoided her name, Ruth. Despite hundreds of hours of practice, a name with both an *r* and a *th* was asking for trouble. He had never mastered either sound, and he now conceded he never would.

"Deep brain stimulation?" Aisha Ali asked, unsure.

"Is this the way you will talk to your patients, as though you are hesitant? Some

111

uneducated foreigner asking where is the bathroom please?" Park asked.

"No, but I thought it was a last resort." Aisha Ali was the most outspoken of Park's Posse, as the group of foreign-born groupies was known around the hospital.

"It's been used for twenty years with good success."

Truth was, Park had decided he was going to use deep brain stimulation on Ruth Hostetler before he had gathered the small cadre of young doctors together.

So early that Sunday morning, the woman lay flat in an MRI wearing a large curved device on her head. The stereotactic frame looked like an oversize sextant, the navigational tool used by ship captains in the age of exploration to measure the angle of the sun and other celestial objects. Park was using the frame for much the same purpose: to help him navigate his probe to the exact coordinates in the brain to stop his patient's tremors. Along the curved line of the frame atop the patient's head like a metallic Mohawk were numbers that would tell Park the exact spot he needed to drill the hole in her head.

Inside the magnetic resonance imaging tube, the device beat out its rhythm, sending powerful magnetic wave pulses through her brain. The magnet in the machine pulled on the cells in her brain, then let them quickly return to their normal position. The little bit of energy that was given off during that process could be measured, and the machine would use that information to create an image of slice after slice of Ruth Hostetler's brain, until a three-dimensional picture emerged. Deep in her cerebrum, Park saw what he was looking for: a small gray area, called the ventral intermediate nucleus of the thalamus, near the middle of her brain. The stereotactic frame told Park the exact coordinates where he should enter the brain.

Ruth Hostetler was wheeled back to the operating room, her hands doing a silent but wild dance in her lap, where a small crowd of neurosurgical fellows and others waited — all young doctors training under Park for a year after their residency. No one worked their fellows or residents as hard as Park, and these MDs — again, most of them foreign born — took it as a badge of honor to be subordinates to the brusque, abrasive, and brilliant surgeon. In the OR, the patient's head was immobilized but her hands continued to flop and flutter.

Having a crowd in the OR to observe,

energized Park. He had never had a group this large observing his work. Then again, he had never before performed a deep brain stimulation for an essential tremor. The patient was still awake, under only a local anesthetic, as Park allowed Dr. Kin Chang to drill the hole. Most neurosurgeons would allow the patient to select some music to help drown out the noise of the drilling taking place on their head. Park never even considered that; it would be just one more distraction. When Kin Chang was barely finished, Park stepped up. He was wearing his surgical loupes, which resembled a pair of glasses with small jeweler's lenses attached to each eyepiece.

"Now we start deep brain stimulation," Park said. He threaded the probe along the angle dictated by the stereotactic brace until he had reached a depth indicated by the MRI. He nodded at the technician standing in the corner of the room. A set amount of current already chosen by Park had been dialed into the savvy piece of machinery, and the technician now pushed a button, which sent the current through the probe.

Within a split second, a look of pure terror filled Ruth Hostetler's face.

"Dear God, no. Please, Heavenly Father, no. No." With that, the patient let out a guttural scream that caused the doctors gathered around to recoil. Park didn't budge. He just paused, and looked fascinated.

Park removed the probe. Ruth Hostetler stopped her anguished cry. She was still breathing fast. She closed her eyes and opened them several times as though to wipe clean the memory of what she had just experienced. Park said nothing to his terrified patient, who only moments earlier had been in a hell of the doctor's making. Instead, he looked carefully at the probe, the way a tennis player who'd just whiffed a shot might look at his racket. He spoke to the assembled doctors.

"If there is such a thing as a *fear* center in the brain, I just found it." Park turned to the nearest acolyte. "Dr. Singh, you and I will write paper."

There was a smattering of laughter, muffled by the surgical masks.

Park checked his coordinates again and reinserted the electrical lead. A slight nod and the electricity was passed again. This time, the tremors suddenly stopped.

"Now, Miss Hostetler, please snap the fingers of your left hand." Ruth Hostetler snapped her fingers. She snapped repeatedly, grinning. The doctors in the operating room applauded. Tears of joy ran in straight lines down Ruth Hostetler's sunken cheeks.

A moment later her mood changed. She became flushed, and a strange look crossed her face. She opened her mouth as if to say something but stopped. Flushed himself from the success of the operation, Park did not notice the change.

"Dr. Singh, close please."

With that, he left the room and went up to his office, thinking he had just performed a textbook operation. *Maybe I really should write up something on the fear center,* Park thought.

Two hours later, Park entered Ruth Hostetler's room like a conquering king, a comet followed by a tail of fellows, residents, and medical students, in that order. The brace had been removed from the woman's head, and she was sitting upright in bed. She held one of her husband's hands in both of hers and gazed at him with an intensity Park could not place, though he thought there was something alluring about her. Levi Hostetler, on the other hand, did not look happy. Perhaps, Park thought, he was upset that science had cured what prayers could not. The man strode toward Park.

116

"Is this your idea of a sick joke?"

The question was so unexpected, for a moment Park didn't know what to say.

"I don't understand."

"My wife."

"Yes," Park said, trying to get the conversation back on track. "No more tremors. The procedure work beautifully."

"No more tremors but there's something else," Ruth Hostetler's husband said. He looked uncomfortably at the small platoon of doctors in the room, then leaned in close to Park. "May I have a word alone?"

"This is teaching hospital. It's okay."

The man took a deep breath. "All right then. My wife is having these desires. These urges. Sexual urges."

"That's good. You two are married, right?" Park's comment was met with a collective chuckle from his entourage.

"Dr. Park," Levi Hostetler said, getting angrier. "The ability to control our base impulses is what sets man apart from beasts. I can't have a wife who is in heat like some sort of dog. That is not godly at all. James, Chapter One, verses fourteen and fifteen: 'But each person is tempted when he is lured and enticed by his own desire. Then desire when it has conceived gives birth to sin, and sin when it is fully grown brings

117

forth death.' "

Park was again rendered speechless. But he was not going to let some Bible-quoting husband ruin his successful surgery. It was Park's turn to get angry, and he was flustered enough that when he spoke his English became more fractured and his accent stronger.

"Mr. Hostetler. Your wife's hand still. No tremor. She can eat. She can drive. She can work." He paused. "This other thing." Park glanced nervously at Ruth Hostetler, who looked as though she was ready to rip off her hospital gown at any moment. "Maybe you'll see it's a blessing."

Without waiting for an answer, Park walked from the room, followed by his phalanx of acolytes.

As they entered the hallway outside the room, one male med student at the tail end of the group turned to another. "He's complaining? The guy should pay extra. Prisoners with conjugal privileges get more than I do."

CHAPTER 8

Drs. George Villanueva and Ty Wilson carried hot dogs and beer to what turned out to be very good seats in the domed stadium, near midfield and up just high enough to gain a good perspective on the field. Light and sound were both muted inside the massive arena as the Lions and Chargers battled. Only Villanueva's booming voice seemed to pierce the still air, cutting through it like a scalpel through a pustule.

"So, this EMT gets called to a house in Ypsilanti. When they get there, they find the patient in perfect health but one small problem. He has a recently expired canary up his ass." George paused as he bit off and swallowed half a hot dog.

Ty didn't know where the story was heading, but smiled anyway. He was enjoying this outing with the Big Cat. The two of them didn't socialize much. For the most part, they met only at hospital functions, but Ty viewed this as Villanueva's peace offering after the M&M. Ty saw no reason to hold a grudge.

"The EMT examines the guy and, I'm not shittin' you here, looks him straight in the eye and says, 'Dude, you gotta do a better job chewing your food.' "

Villanueva let out a roar of laughter, sending shock waves through his massive gut that nearly launched the two and a half remaining hot dogs off his cardboard tray. Ty laughed. When George caught his breath, he looked over at a Ty, serious now.

"Fired his ass the next day," he said.

"No shit?"

"Hand to God," Villanueva said.

The two men turned their attention back to the field, where the players were warming up. The Big Cat could not attend a pro game, especially a Lions game, without a mix of emotions. Nostalgia, for one. Not so much for the game itself. That was hard work, a struggle. As a guard, Villanueva spent much of the game absorbing and deflecting the abuse brought upon him by defensive linemen, blitzing linebackers and the occasional defensive back. They would smack the side of Villanueva's helmet, send a forearm under his face mask. He'd even had players try to gouge his eyes. No,

George did not miss the game itself. It was the camaraderie he missed. The guys. They were part of a team, a unit. They won together and they lost together. They shared sacrifice and success. They hit the town together after the game, before the soreness had set like paint.

Villanueva once heard a commentator describe playing professional football as akin to being in a car accident every week, and he thought the comparison was as apt as any. Professional football was carried out on "any given Sunday," but had its own form of Monday Mornings. Simply getting out of bed was often a struggle. Still, the Big Cat had loved being part of an elite group of athletes. He'd loved playing in the National Football League with all its trappings, not least the young nubile women who seemed to know exactly which hotel the players were staying in and which ones were up for some action off the field.

When he went to a game as a spectator George also experienced something he imagined fathers of high school players did almost every Friday night across the country. He wasn't sure there was a word for it. The emotion was part panic, part wistful, the notion that time had passed and, in some ways, his own time had passed with it.

There were young men on the field doing what he'd done as a young man. By extension, that meant he was no longer a young man. *No shit,* George thought as most of the stadium stood for the opening kickoff.

Villanueva noticed Ty didn't stand till a few seconds later. Distracted no doubt about the kid. The Big Cat turned his attention to the field, following not the ball as it arced toward the Lions' return man but the line of blockers in front of him. As soon as he caught the ball, they moved upfield. As a rookie, George played on special teams. He was one of those guys. Special teams was a place where you could make a name for yourself for fearless play and big hits. In one game against the Packers he had decided to propel himself at the wedge buster, who'd in turn launched himself at the four blockers arrayed in front of the ball carrier. George was knocked out cold. The wedge buster, a kid named Stanton, was out for the season.

It was after this game that Villanueva's father decided to express his dissatisfaction about George's career choice. They were sitting in a booth at the back of a generic hotel restaurant. His mom had a worried look. His dad was harder to read. The smoking had damaged his body's ability to absorb oxygen, which meant he had a portable oxygen tank anytime he left the house. It also meant his face carried a perpetually pinched expression. George recalled his father's gray pallor and how thin he looked.

"Son, you are a smart boy. *Muy inteligente.*" His father paused to catch his breath. "When I was at the plant, I always imagined you'd have a job where you wore a tie to work." His father paused again. Breathed deeply and began again. "Yes, you are well paid. But what you do is not so different than what I did. Using your brawn, not your brains. I want more for you, Jorge."

Villanueva's father had peered at him intently, trying to get his message across with his receding black eyes because speaking was such an effort. Looking back, George still became a little choked up when he realized his father must have been planning a much longer speech but cut it short. His father died the next year and never saw how the Big Cat had remade himself when his playing days were done. He had used his brains after all. At the time, Villanueva was simply a twenty-one-year-old kid who considered himself stronger and badder than anyone out there.

"C'mon, *Papi.* We won. Time to celebrate."

Villanueva had hoisted his frosted mug of beer and downed it. His father hadn't budged. As he pictured his father sitting there, already one foot in the next world, George could see disappointment in his half-dead eyes, and the Big Cat wondered if father-son relationships were ever uncomplicated. Was anyone ever free of the burden of a father's expectations? Villanueva snorted at the notion that even now, when he was at the height of a career that was all about using his *inteligencia,* he didn't wear a tie, and he wondered whether his father would be disappointed. Then he thought of his own son, Nick, and wondered if his life would be marked by both a father and a son who were disappointed in him.

Villanueva took another gulp of beer and returned his gaze to the field where the Lions had just given up a big run. Most Lions fans were disappointed. George saw how the pulling guard had taken out both the defensive end and the pursuing line-backer and smiled. Couldn't have done it any better himself.

Two hours and three quarters of football later, Villanueva was hoarse from yelling and his enunciation was slurred from eight or nine beers. George had a unique way of watching football. He cheered for the offense no matter which team had possession. And just like in the ER, Gato always picked up things on the field everyone else missed.

"Great block, Witherspoon! Hey, Mitchell, how's it feel to get knocked on your ass?" Villanueva's voice was so loud Ty thought there was a fifty-fifty chance the players could actually hear him.

During a TV timeout, when players from both teams were standing around looking like quarterhorses before the next race, George turned to Ty.

"I had a kid once."

"Once? Don't you have a son?" Ty was confused.

"A kid. A kid I couldn't shake. A six-year-old. Hit by a drunk driver."

Ty shook his head in disgust. He tried to picture the scene. The normally unflappable EMTs racing into the emergency department with panicked looks, hoping they were wrong and the small unmoving body on the gurney was not going to die. Hoping the absence of vitals wouldn't matter. Nor would the fixed pupils. Nor would every other bit of data they were trained to collect. The hippocampus, the subjective part of their brains where they stored the memories of their own children, held on to the irrational hope that since the boy was so young, and since the doctors at Chelsea were among the best in the world, the boy might have a chance to survive. And the next day or the next week, his case would be the one they asked about, knowing the answer before they asked but needing to know.

"When he came in, he had no pulse," Villanueva said. "His head was bigger'n mine. His body was torn to shit. Could have pronounced him right there." Villanueva paused. "We started CPR. Steroids. Epi. You name it. Still, the poor kid never stood a chance. Hadn't thought about him for years until your case came up. You ask around. Everyone's got a kid." Ty felt a surge of bile in his throat.

George turned back toward the game. Ty waited for more, but Villanueva was back to cheering for the offense. The Lions this time.

"Helluva block, Smith. Helluva block."

"Hey, George," Ty said above the din, nodding toward the field. "You miss it?"

"Shit, I'm lucky I got out of the game before my knees were shot and I needed a couple of TKAs." Still watching the players, he added, "You know what Mickey Mantle said when someone asked him if he missed

baseball? He said, 'I miss the guys.' "
Villanueva nodded to himself at the truth of
this statement.

A beer vendor wended his way up the
aisle. Villanueva raised a hand almost the
size of a dinner plate.

"Yo, beer man. Two!"

Ty had been thinking a lot about "his kid"
lately. He'd been thinking even more about
Quinn McDaniel's mother, Allison, who'd
told him her son was her "everything." The
mention alone had seemed to light her up
from the inside. Ty felt he owed her something, though he couldn't say what. Also, he
wondered again how she was doing and
promised himself he'd find out, knowing
full well the hospital's attorney, colleagues,
and common sense all argued against it.

CHAPTER 9

Tina arrived at Harding Hooten's office on the top floor of the hospital at the appointed hour. Hooten and the hospital's attorney were waiting in a pair of chairs in a small sitting area in front of his desk. Not a good sign. Hooten was wearing his white lab coat and a striped bow tie. The attorney wore a generic but expensive suit. Neither one of them was smiling. The last time Tina had been to Hooten's office was when he hired her to be an attending. There were smiles all around then.

"Tina, sit." Hooten motioned to the couch. She sat. Hooten adjusted his bow tie and began. "I want to talk about Dr. Robidaux. I've been speaking with Todd about the lawsuit brought against the hospital as the result of her work. Of course, we are insured, but paying out a big judgment is never in the best interest of the hospital. I've had to call the CEO to let him know about this, and, as you can imagine, that was not a pleasant conversation."

"Dr. Hooten," Tina began. "I made the judgment that Dr. Robidaux was ready for the procedure."

"Tina, we get in trouble when we have residents perform surgeries like this one."

"We do it every day, Dr. Hooten. Isn't the old saw, 'See one, do one, teach one'?"

"You were the attending, you were clearly more qualified."

"The attending is always more qualified."

"But in this case —"

"This case is no different than hundreds of others at this hospital every day. If the attendings do all the cases, how are the residents going to learn?"

Hooten sighed. He was annoyed Tina had challenged him. He took a breath and started over. He adopted the voice you might use to talk a potential jumper from the ledge of building.

"Tina, you and I know patients expect the best here. And for the most part we give it to them. It's a testament to your skills and the skills of the other doctors at this facility. You know what they say, 'If you get shot or get in a wreck, just hope you're near Chelsea General.' That glib commentary carries with it more than a grain of clinical truth. We handle very challenging surgical cases with few complications."

Hooten paused again and sighed. His hands were clasped in front of him. Tina's jaw was set, and she sat with her weight perched on the edge of her seat, waiting to hear whether Hooten was going to throw Michelle Robidaux under the bus.

"Now, here's this young chef who can no longer smell —"

"That side effect is something even the most experienced surgeon encounters now and then," Tina interrupted. Her voice was more defensive, shriller, than she wanted.

"Damn it, Tina, let me finish."

The attorney, who had been sitting with his hands folded in his lap as he thumbed his BlackBerry, looked up and spoke for the first time during the meeting. "Michelle Robidaux was not the most experienced surgeon, though, was she?"

Tina scowled at the lawyer and then turned back to Hooten.

"Tina, I'm going to get to the crux of the matter. Todd here has recommended that we terminate our contract with Michelle Robidaux, effective immediately."

Tina flushed. She felt her stomach release a spurt of acid, and she was momentarily without words. She silently counted to ten

130

to calm herself down. "So, this is how we back our residents. This is a teaching hospital, Dr. Hooten. We teach. Residents learn. We don't throw them under the bus. You want to discipline someone, discipline me. I assigned her the case."

"Tina, I know how hard you've worked with this resident, but she may not be Chelsea material —"

"This is just wrong and you know it." Tina could think of nothing else to say. She stared at Hooten, her jaw set.

The attorney spoke up, looking at Hooten as he did. "The hospital is just too exposed on this one."

Tina ran through the cascade of events that would unfold for Michelle Robidaux. She would lose her job, her wages, her standing in the medical community. She would lose her legal representation and whatever shred of self-respect remained. She would probably return to Louisiana, where her family would no doubt let her know how foolish she'd been to think folks at big-name hospitals would accept their kind. Who knew what would happen after that? She felt her gut clench as she envisioned the next days and months for Michelle Robidaux, the first in her family to go to college.

"I can tell nothing I say is going to matter," Tina said. Without another word, she got up and walked from the office.

"Tina, don't turn your back on me," Hooten called after her. She didn't look back.

Park enjoyed the spotlight, even when he was presenting at M&M, even if it meant explaining Ruth Hostetler's post-operative sequelae of unbidden sexual desire. Park had toiled in obscurity for too long, first in Korea and then in the United States, not to savor his moments standing front and center. It was tough being on the bottom rung of the ladder, looking up, when you knew you were the smartest man in the room, and Park had little doubt he was the smartest man in the room most of the time.

He looked around at the doctors seated in front of him. He saw his fellow attending neurosurgeons Tina Ridgeway and Ty Wilson sitting next to each other. Tina Ridgeway was smart. Ty Wilson had magic hands, but he was no intellect. Neither one of them could match Park's command of data, research, knowledge. Harding Hooten might pose a legitimate challenge, Park thought, but he was nearing retirement and could not match the raw drive Park brought to his job.

"We all know the story of the famous Phineas Gage in 1848," Park began. "He was construction foreman for a railroad in Vermont, blasting rock, when a thirteen-pound tamping iron shot through his brain. The bar entered left cheek, traversed his frontal lobe, and exited here." Park pointed to a spot just above his forehead, directly above the bridge of his nose.

"Did he get choppered to Chelsea General?" Villanueva called out. There was a smattering of laughter.

"I gotta make rounds at seven, can we skip ahead to the twenty-first century," someone else called from the back of the room.

"Sounds like he was stuck between the eight-ball and a hard place," came a third voice. Sung scowled.

Everything was a joke to Americans, Park thought. Life was serious business, bound by laws of obligation, honor, and family, but Americans thought they were living in one of those comedies they watched on television, with the action punctuated by artificial laughter every ten or fifteen seconds. Perhaps the pleasure centers of their brains had been rewired at a young age. When Park was a child, he would return home from school and either study, practice violin, or help his parents in their small and failing general store.

This was one of the American traits that vexed him. There were many others. Americans were also always in a hurry. They ate fast, drove fast, rushed from one thing to the next. They flipped channels, read headlines or abstracts or executive summaries, and then moved on. Shouldn't you truly understand something before continuing to the next thing? This morning he was offering the assembled doctors a gift, a sculpture of ideas on the nature of brain injury, but they wanted him to rush through it. No one here wanted to savor the breadth of understanding the medical profession had gleaned in an eyeblink of history. Park was flustered. As a result, he spoke faster, with choppier English, and his grammar started falling apart.

"We all know Phineas live, but he is changed man. His personality surly. He swears a lot. His reasoning skills, diminished. His doctor offer him one thousand dollars for a pocketful of pebbles he collect, and Phineas refuse."

"Dr. Park," Hooten injected in a quiet voice. "This discourse is best suited for another time. Would you mind if we present

134

the case of Ruth Hostetler?"

Park sighed, irritated that his history lesson wasn't hitting the mark. He explained the facts of the odd woman in the print dress. He told his colleagues how he had placed a stereotactic frame on the patient, secured with screws that were placed through her skin and into the skull. He'd then made a precisely fourteen-millimeter incision over the right top of her head and used a perforating drill to expose her brain. A thin probe was then snaked directly into her brain, having been measured perfectly the night before. A slight charge was given, and the deep tissue stimulation had eliminated the patient's tremors but produced a strange side effect, an awakening of carnal desire in this deeply religious woman.

"Was this side effect, this carnal desire you describe, was it directed only at her husband or was it directed at others in the room? You, for example?" Villanueva asked to more guffaws.

"George may want her phone number," a male voice called from the back of the room.

"Gentlemen," Hooten said. "We are not in a locker room. We are in a time-honored forum established so that we may learn from our mistakes. So we can become better surgeons and make this a better hospital."

"Ruth Hostetler is like a modern Phineas Gage," Park said. "We learn a lot about the brain, but there are things that remain unknown to us at this time."

"Would you perform this procedure differently next time?" Hooten asked.

"Because etiology of side effect is not known, I say no. I do the same way," Park said. He thought about the question a little more. "Two choices for us: Do not do deep tissue stimulation. Try medicine to solve the problem. Or, do deep tissue stimulation and accept the fact we do not know everything that may happen. I do the same way."

"Very well, Dr. Park," Hooten said. "A cautionary tale," he added to the room at large.

Joining the doctors in the queue shuffling out of the room, Ty turned to Tina. "Did you see the study that found there are two hundred thirty-seven reasons people have sex?"

"Missed it," she said, laughing.

"There were the obvious ones: 'I was drunk.' 'For pleasure.' 'To reproduce.' There was also 'to feel better about myself.' 'To be closer to God.' 'For revenge.' 'For power.' Need to add number two thirty-eight. Deep brain stimulation."

"If the word gets out, the procedure could

challenge breast augs in popularity," Tina mused.

"No doubt."

The two reached the hallway outside Room 311. Tina turned right. Ty turned left.

"You're not heading this way?"

"Got something to do," Ty said.

Every time a doctor checks a patient's records, he or she leaves electronic fingerprints. The hospital software was written to prevent curious doctors checking out the blood alcohol level of the Wolverines wideout admitted to Chelsea General after a car accident or the rap star's lab results. Administrators take these breaches seriously. Doctors who weren't directly involved in a patient's care were warned to stay away from that patient's electronic record. Chelsea General went so far as to kick a senior resident out of the orthopedics program for his curiosity over whether the rap star was high on marijuana or cocaine. Both, it turned out.

Ty found a computer in one of the hospital's backwaters, a room in Pediatrics. He didn't think the hospital would raise an institutional eyebrow if he checked Quinn McDaniel's records. The boy had been his patient, after all. Wasn't it laudable to review the records of his most damning case as a neurosurgeon? The software and those who monitored it would have no idea Ty wasn't interested in when Quinn's oxygen sats went south or how many pints of blood the boy had received before Ty had pronounced him. Ty wrote down only one bit of information from the boy's records: Allison McDaniel's address and phone number.

Even though Ty had officially done nothing wrong, he looked around. It was as though he was checking to see if store security was watching after he stuffed the James Worthy shirt into his pants. Ty had been so angry after his brother died that he'd done quite a bit of shoplifting, almost daring someone to stop him. Once, he took a basketball out of a box at a sporting goods store, inflated it with a pump the store was selling, and wrote his name on it with a black Sharpie he had brought with him. He then dribbled it out of the store. He never got caught. Even then he had quick hands and nerves.

As he left the room, he almost bumped into Monique Tran, who was pushing an older Vietnamese woman in a wheelchair. Monique was the scrub nurse who had been working the night of Quinn McDaniel's death. She had watched the life drain out of

138

the boy. Ty looked at Monique as though he'd seen a ghost.

"Don't look so happy to see me, Dr. Wilson," Monique joked.

"Sorry," Ty said. "My mind was somewhere else." He forced a smile.

"I guess."

Ty almost hadn't recognized her in civilian clothes instead of the scrubs and faux-snakeskin clogs she wore in the OR.

"Hey, Dr. Wilson, this is my grandmother."

Wilson had assumed the woman in the wheelchair was a patient and hadn't looked closely. Now he noted the same elegant cheekbones as Monique Tran. The old woman was tiny, practically disappearing in the wheelchair. A lot of his patients barely squeezed into that sized chair.

"Nice to meet you," Ty said. The older woman bowed her head slightly.

"Doesn't speak much English. She's here to get evaluated for a new hip. Didn't want to come but she couldn't sleep it hurt so badly. She's old school. Thinks pain is weakness. Have you seen that T-shirt? PAIN IS THE BODY'S WAY OF LETTING WEAKNESS OUT? That's her."

"I guess I haven't," Ty replied. Besides the clothes, there was something different about

Nurse Tran. And it wasn't just the mile-a-minute chatter. In the OR, she was practically mute.

"Well, Dr. Wilson, time to get her inside. Can't wait to hear what she has to say when we get a little Versed on board. Maybe get a little wisdom from the old country." She laughed.

Ty leaned over and affectionately shook hands with the older woman in the wheelchair. "Who is doing her hip?" he asked.

"We were thinking about Dr. David Martin, I hear he is very good?" Monique said cautiously.

"Uh, sure. Look, I don't normally do this, but I would recommend Dr. Tom Spinelli. I would have him do mine, if I ever needed one," Ty offered.

Monique thanked Ty and winked at him as she pushed past. The old woman nodded again as they passed. Monique had been thinking a lot about family since she'd decided to keep her baby. Now all she had to do was convince the father it was a good idea and convince her family that getting knocked up by a white boy, one from the South, no less, was all for the best. And, heck — his Vietnamese was getting better. Surely that would impress her parents.

Monique didn't mention it to Ty but she'd

been named after the old woman she was wheeling through the hospital — sort of. Her grandmother's real name was Binh, which meant "peace," but the sisters at Ecole Saint-Paul in Saigon had given her the French name Monique. Through primary and secondary school Tran Binh spent much of her time as Monique, and she had grown to love her alter ego. The name reminded her of the ease of her childhood before the war had crept into their life like mold.

Monique's grandmother had left Vietnam at thirty-five, pregnant with her fourth child — Monique's aunt Anh — and the family was suddenly destitute after growing up amid privilege on a leafy street near Tan Son Nhut air base. Her father had been a well-connected businessman, and her husband, Tran Van Vuong, worked for him.

Binh almost never spoke of her old life. When Catholic Social Services sponsored the Trans, they had already endured six squalid and dangerous months in a tent city in Thailand. Days after arriving in the United States, she had gone to work at a box factory to help the family make ends meet. She'd left her children with an older Vietnamese woman who lived nearby or with Monique's mother, who was just twelve years old at the time.

Monique's mother had eventually married a fellow refugee, and they'd always stuck close to their own community. Monique sighed and pushed her grandmother into the pre-op area. She thought about telling her about the baby after the IV drip started. Her grandmother was the one person who would probably understand.

CHAPTER 10

Sydney Saxena woke with a start. A cold rain was lashing the windows of her town house, but it wasn't the gusting wind or sheets of rain across the windows that jolted her upright, fully conscious, at four in the morning. It was a patient, Joanna Whitman, a large, fifty-two-year-old African American woman who worked for the city of Ann Arbor. The woman was not even Sydney's patient. Sydney had heard her history on grand rounds, and the story irritated her like an itch. She kept scratching but found no relief.

Sydney did not like mysteries. She liked to know. She needed to know on an almost pathological level, and this patient's story was like a cipher no one at Chelsea had decoded. Of course, on some level, Sydney also wanted to solve this mystery because she wanted to be *the* doctor to crack the case. Sydney knew nothing about Joanna

Whitman. She didn't know if she was a mother or grandmother. She didn't even know what she looked like. For Sydney, this was a clinical puzzle, devoid of any emotion.

Joanna Whitman had arrived at the hospital three months earlier with a runny nose, a headache, and a persistent cough. She had returned days earlier from Aruba, where she had traveled with her husband, and wondered if the circulating air in the plane had blown someone's flu bug her way. The junior resident who did the H&P suspected a viral infection, and told her it would likely resolve on its own. It didn't, and the woman returned two weeks later with fevers that were worse at night, feeling slightly winded going up stairs, and still suffering from that cough. A different resident saw her this time and prescribed amoxicillin and also Bactrim, along with codeine for the cough. He gave her strict instructions to take the full course of antibiotics, telling her the infection could in fact worsen if she didn't. "Yes, yes, I know. Antibiotic-resistant bacteria," she said in between coughs. The doctor had nothing to worry about. Joanna Whitman did not appear to be the noncompliant type, nor did she seem like a hypochondriac. There was something almost regal about the woman. The resident who gave her the course of antibiotics told her to come back if she didn't feel better.

Joanna Whitman did just that. She returned to Chelsea General a third time a month later and was diagnosed with bronchitis. She left with another handful of scripts. The cough continued.

During a fourth visit, the woman was sent to get a chest X-ray, which turned out to be normal. There was something unusual, however. Her blood oxygen sats were only 84 percent, and she complained of mild chest pain whenever she took a breath. The senior resident who saw her this time decided she had bronchitis with an asthma component. She was given more medicine and an inhaler. She was collecting diagnoses and medicines, but she was not getting better. She was getting worse.

Joanna Whitman then went away for a couple of weeks; she had returned only the day before. It was her fifth visit in three months. This time, the large woman complained of shortness of breath and was admitted overnight. Her husband, a dark-skinned man in a shirt and tie, sat at her bedside holding her hand, an expression of deep worry on his face. The worry was well founded. The doctors who had seen her, including the freshly minted residents, the senior residents, and the attending physicians, were now reduced to making educated guesses at what might be wrong with the woman, or to giving her medicines and tests to rule out different possibilities. Her chart was getting bigger, and that was a sure sign doctors had no idea of the diagnosis. Joanna Whitman was looking sallow, sickly, forlorn. As the rounding doctors walked from Joanna Whitman's bedside, one resident had quipped out of earshot that they needed to write GOK in her chart: God Only Knows.

Sydney had been thinking about her case off and on in the twenty hours since she had heard the story described by the senior resident on rounds. Sydney was a cardiothoracic surgeon, not a general medicine internist, and yet this case still bothered her. Something wasn't quite right. The arsenal of medicines Joanna Whitman had received had done nothing, or at least that's the way it looked.

This woman did not smoke, but she was heavy, and heavy was never good. Sydney thought it would take at least two of her to make one Joanna Whitman. The obesity did not seem to slow the patient down, though, even if she had complained of foot pain and swelling in the past.

Sydney had wondered if she was exposed to airborne irritants or toxic chemicals in her daily life. Studies had shown that waste dumps and other environmental hazards were located more often in minority and low-income communities. Joanna was a midlevel bureaucrat in the city's planning department, though, and lived in a middle-class neighborhood not far from Sydney.

Not many surgeons went on medical rounds, but Sydney found them interesting and went whenever she had time. That meant enduring the ribbing from the medical attendings: "How does an internist stop an elevator door from closing? With his hands." Internists don't need their hands. "So how does a surgeon stop an elevator door from closing? With her head." Ba da boom. She thought too many doctors, once they had made the choice between surgery and internal medicine, never strayed across to the other side. Doctors who became internists stereotyped surgeons as scalpel-happy cowboys. Surgeons saw the other side as ineffectual practitioners who analyzed and diagnosed but couldn't fix problems. There was some element of truth in both stereotypes, of course, but only some.

Her father taught economics at Furman, a

small, liberal arts college in South Carolina, and her mother was a columnist at *The Greenville News.* When Sydney was in high school, her father had come upon Sydney reading an obscure history of the Algerian crisis and labeled her an autodidact. Sydney blushed, thinking he was referring what she had been up to in her bedroom when the lights were out and she thought her parents and sisters were asleep. She said nothing, but looked up the word as soon as she got a chance and realized her father was right. She really did like learning for the sake of learning.

In college, Sydney was a dual English–Biology major. She especially reveled in the mysteries that remained about the human experience. Why did we behave the way we did, and could it be predicted? How were genes connected to behaviors like compassion and morality?

She was fascinated by the basics of human development: How could the cells in the womb become differentiated and migrate where they needed to go as the fetus developed? She also relished arcane experiments that showed how people responded to the world around them: how those who took a dummy cancer drug in a clinical trial could lose all their hair (the nocebo effect);

how a child could regenerate a fingertip but an adult could not; how people became happier in anticipation of a happy event, or died of heart failure after the death of a longtime spouse.

Joanna Whitman presented a mystery, and Sydney felt an intense clinical curiosity. She suspected something was seriously wrong with the woman, but she could not put her finger on it. The doctors who had treated her had never strayed far from the initial diagnosis of bronchitis. Once a doctor read the chart, he was most likely to continue down the same path. It was a group-think mentality that occurred too often in hospitals. That was always dangerous, Sydney knew. They should have expanded the possible list of diagnoses, but what would those other possible diagnoses be? Whitman's heart rate was elevated but her lungs appeared clear. What was going on?

Now, at four in the morning, Sydney thought she knew. She stood by the window, the heavy rain beating an elaborate rhythm on the glass as she called the paging operator. She reached the junior resident on call at the hospital, a Dr. Tom Ottobrini.

"Dr. Ottobrini, this is Dr. Sydney Saxena. Mrs. Whitman needs a lung scan or a CT angio, and she needs it yesterday," she said breathlessly.

The junior resident was groggy. "Joanna Whitman? You mean the bronchitis?"

"No. Not 'the bronchitis.' Pulmonary embolism. Listen, we're damn lucky she hasn't thrown a large embolism already."

"Dr. Saxena. Aren't you a surgeon?"

Sydney continued, "Wake up your attending. Do what you need to do, but you need to do it now. We're lucky this poor lady hasn't boxed already."

"I don't know." The sleep-deprived resident now sounded suspicious, as though he were the target of some sort of prank. Residents never liked calling the attending — waking up their boss with questions that would show they were less than fully trained doctors able to handle whatever came their way. And they shared a special dread of waking up the senior doctor with a question or problem that was trivial or, worse, insipid.

"Listen, Tom, she's circling the drain. Who's your attending, Bobby Mitchell? Call him and blame it on me. We were in med school together at MGH."

"All right, Dr. Saxena, thanks for your call." The resident hung up. He sounded as though he was getting rid of a telemarketer.

Sydney was seething now. She skipped a shower, roughly brushed her hair, threw on pants, a blouse, and her white lab coat, and ran out of her town house. She forgot it was raining and didn't bring an umbrella as she half walked, half ran to the car. The cold drops hit her like a slap.

Twenty minutes later and still wet, she was on the fourth floor of Chelsea General. The place looked like it was in a state of hibernation. Most of the patients slept. Nurses were hunkered at their stations doing paperwork while they kept one eye on the monitors. A junior resident was walking the halls updating the prescriptions for the various patients.

Saxena walked up to a nurse.

"Joanna Whitman?"

The nurse checked the chart in front of her.

"Four-twelve."

"Thanks," she said. "Would you page Dr. Ottobrini and have him meet me there?"

"Yes —" The nurse squinted to read Sydney's name tag. "— Dr. Saxena?" She clearly didn't recognize the name.

Sydney walked down to the room. Joanna Whitman was sleeping, her breathing troubled. Sydney checked the chart. Her heart rate had been steadily rising over the last several hours.

She stepped into the hallway and almost bumped into Ottobrini, a rangy young doctor with puffy eyes, stubble, and an irritated look. Sydney was looking up at Ottobrini, but she took his irritated look and raised him a withering glare. No matter which side of the surgery-medicine divide she was on, Sydney was an attending, and he was a resident.

"Listen, Dr. Saxena, I called my senior resident and he said we shouldn't bother Dr. Mitchell with this. He said to hold off —"

Before Ottobrini could finish his sentence, a balding doctor with stooped shoulders joined them. Ottobrini was surprised to see him.

"Bill?"

"Tom." The senior resident turned to Sydney. "And you must be the intrusive Dr. Saxena." Despite his words, he didn't look or sound annoyed. A smile played at the edge of his mouth. He turned back to Ottobrini.

"Order a spiral CT for Mrs. Whitman." The junior resident's red eyes goggled. "Go on." Ottobrini went into the room and started writing on Joanna Whitman's chart.

The senior resident turned back to Sydney.

"Couldn't get back to sleep after he called." He held out his hand. "Bill Mc-

Manus."

"Sydney Saxena."

"I pictured you bigger. Maybe with a long crooked nose. A wart on your cheek."

"Give me a couple more years." Sydney laughed. With a start, she realized it was her thirty-fifth birthday.

"I hope you're right about this because up till now we haven't had a clue." Sydney felt a surge of admiration for this senior resident. Not many doctors were so willing to set aside their egos, even when the patient's best interest might be at stake. He looked at Sydney for a second, and then awkwardly put out his hand. She shook it, firmly. "Okay, well, thanks. We will let you know what the test shows," he said. She nodded confidently, and they separated, walking in opposite directions.

At noon, Sydney received a page to the fourth floor. "McManus," a voice answered. Her suspicions were correct, he went on to tell her: Joanna Whitman had a pulmonary embolism and was already on an around-the-clock infusion of heparin. She had been throwing small emboli to her lungs, which were impeding her breathing and causing symptoms similar to a lung infection. Bill McManus paused after describing the results of the scan and then out of the blue,

153

asked Sydney out on a date. Even though she was taken aback, she regained her composure quickly. And then, as she always did, she declined. She gave her pat answer and said she was committed. She didn't tell him that she was committed to the hospital. At least she was still getting asked, even at the "advanced" age of thirty-five, she thought to herself.

A few days later, McManus ran into Sydney at Joanna Whitman's bedside. Sydney wanted to finally meet the patient for herself. Whitman's husband now looked exhausted and relieved, instead of exhausted and worried. An IV bag dripped the blood thinner heparin into the patient's left arm. Sydney held her right hand.

"Well, look who's here," McManus said. Sydney couldn't help but appreciate the obvious joy he took in seeing her.

"Mrs. Whitman, I'm betting she hasn't told you this, and I'm embarrassed to admit this myself, but Dr. Saxena was the one who solved your medical mystery."

Joanna Whitman looked up at Sydney. She squeezed her hand between her own.

"Thank you, honey. I was beginning to think I was going crazy. Making up the symptoms out of the clear blue."

Sydney smiled.

"You take care, Mrs. Whitman."

As Sydney turned to go, Whitman's husband called after her. "Doctor."

Sydney stopped. He reached out his bony hand and shook hers.

"Thank you. Thank you."

That afternoon, Sydney did what she'd done every year on her birthday since she'd turned thirty. She drove to the playground not far from her town house. The rain had pushed east but the clouds remained and there was a chill breeze blowing, a harbinger of winter. Still, the hardier young mothers — or maybe those suffering from cabin fever — sat on benches while their bundled preschoolers chased one another, climbed the ladders, went feet-first down the slide, or simply sat in the damp wood chips, lost in their own world. The mothers chatted, always with one eye on their progeny.

"Be careful," they'd call out. Or, "Look at you!" to a little girl who went down a tornado slide. "Share!" to a boy who wouldn't give up the wagon he was pulling. "Carter, do not throw sand!" Words of praise, advice, and discipline in the years-long quest to produce happy, successful offspring.

One of the mothers jiggled an old-fashioned, dark blue stroller as she watched a child ramble around the brightly colored structure. Now and then, she peeked at the baby, reassuring herself that the infant was still sleeping.

Sydney picked an empty bench and watched the children and the mothers. This was her annual test to see if she harbored a desire to join them. Sydney knew deep in her biology she was programmed to want to reproduce. To pass on her genes. To continue the unbroken succession of parents and offspring from the primordial seas to this playground.

Sydney checked her watch and then began soaking up the scene. She wanted to see if she saw in the children's faces a hole in her own life. As she gazed at the mothers, she looked inward: Did she feel any pangs of jealousy? After twenty minutes, she decided she didn't. None at all. No tightening of her gut or tugging at her heart or tears in her eyes or other physiological signs that might signal a longing for motherhood.

Sydney could appreciate the mothers' tenderness, their devotion to their children, but watching them administer snacks, console hurt feelings, and tend bruised knees, she didn't feel an iota of envy. In fact she would be incredibly bored if she swapped places with any one of these women.

Sydney was pleased. She had expected to marry Ross, devote herself to him, be one of those female doctors who shared a practice so she could have time to raise a family. When Ross told her of his 180-degree change of heart, a tearful confession in the car after the fateful dinner, she was devastated. It was as though he had punched a hole in her heart, and her hopes for the future had flowed out through the hole. Aristotle had called hope a waking dream, and that is what she was living in her romance with Ross. When she thought about it now, though, she realized she hadn't really known Ross that well. It was the dream that attracted her.

After the breakup, Sydney stayed in bed for most of a week, getting up only to eat and go to the bathroom, and then it was over. She was done with him. More than that, she was done with the dream of sharing her life with another person, with the willingness to devote herself to pleasing a mate, or to make professional sacrifices for the sake of marriage. The weakness in her had been cauterized, she thought. She was now unencumbered, able to focus fully on being the best doctor she could be, and to one day be sitting in Hooten's chair.

When half an hour at the playground had passed, Sydney got up and walked back to her car, convinced that she was content with her place in life for at least another year. Then she headed to the second appointment she made for herself each birthday: a massage. After that, she'd go back to the hospital.

CHAPTER 11

Monday morning. Six am. The room smelled of freshly brewed coffee and shampooed hair. Most of the doctors in the room had on freshly pressed scrubs with a white coat, rubber clogs, and comfortable socks. They were easy to remove if you were sitting during a long operation, or were trying to catch a quick nap in the call room. It was as clean as you might ever see this group, save the few who had been on call the night before. They looked rumpled and tired, and were mostly huddled around their cell phones and computers, whispering orders to the ICU nurses. A few were trying to look relaxed and reading the newspaper, but the room was charged with anxiety.

Harding Hooten, Sydney Saxena, and Sung Park were in their usual spots in the front row. Hooten wore his trademark bow tie, and a heavily starched shirt. Villanueva sat in a middle row, looking like an Easter

Island boulder that had been dropped in the center of the room. He had his game face on, a nasty-looking scowl that would intimidate the toughest defensive lineman, let alone any member of the medical profession.

Fresh from his own appearance in the spotlight, Ty sat near the back of the amphitheater, by himself. People entering the room shot him a look of pity, and subconsciously felt a little bit better about themselves watching a man normally made of Teflon have this tragedy stuck to him. "It was about learning and getting better," these doctors had said to him when the topic had arisen. It was true. Ty's experience had already changed the protocol for surgical patients throughout the hospital. At Chelsea General, the laboratory profile for a patient going to the operating room would now include a test for various clotting disorders, and every doctor would be sure to ask about a family history that included any signs of bleeding problems. The mistake Ty Wilson had made would never happen again. It was the essence of Monday Mornings. One of the chief residents had already submitted a manuscript on the surgical complications in patients with von Willebrand disease.

■ ■ ■ ■

For Ty, though, the whole episode had
shaken his belief in himself. Sure, doctors
learn from their mistakes, even from their
patients' deaths, but as far as Ty was concerned that always happened to someone
else, not him. Other doctors tried reminding him that the boy's tumor would have
led to his death anyway. That was not an
excuse for Ty. He had killed a kid, and he
couldn't get beyond that simple fact. Explaining his role in Quinn McDaniel's death
gave him a new perspective on the proceedings. No doubt, death and complications
were the enemies of any doctor, but sometimes death happened. Sometimes, there
was no good explanation. Bad things happened to good people. Bad things happened
to good doctors. Sometimes. It was a mantra
he tried to chant. Bad things happened to
good doctors. Still, the vision of Quinn
McDaniel was entering his thoughts more
and more with each passing day. His smiling, freckled face looking at him, trusting
him. Ty wondered what a single mother did
when she was no longer a mother. At least
his own mother had his two sisters and him
when his brother died. She also had her

husband, Ty's dad — on paper anyway.

"Hi, Tina."

"Ready for Double-Oh-Seven?" Tina asked, as she slipped into the chair next to Ty. The surgeon on the hot seat was Dr. David Martin: his nickname, *007,* a license to kill. He was the same surgeon Ty had diplomatically warned Monique Tran and her grandmother about. Ty didn't have the heart to join the usual rancor, even though this would be the third time they had seen the infamous Dr. Martin up front at M&M in the past year. From what Ty had heard, today's case was the most egregious yet.

Martin entered disheveled, even though he'd had a full night of sleep. His brown hair looked as though he hadn't combed it in two or three days. He wore khaki pants, a rumpled shirt, and a sport coat that looked as if it had been sitting in the back of his trunk. No tie.

"Who's dressing him? You think he could have found a tie?" Tina said to no one in particular.

Orthopedist Dr. Tom Spinelli, a couple of seats over, leaned over toward Tina. "I heard his wife left him."

A doctor sitting behind them chimed in, "You can only call the fashion police so often before it's time to get out." The doc-

tors chuckled. Ty laughed despite himself.

At the front of the room, Hooten cleared his throat.

"Let's get on with this. We're here to talk about the death of Mary Michaelidis. Dr. Martin, I wish I could say it was good to see you again, but it is most definitely not good to see you again under these circumstances." Hooten stopped and glowered at Martin, who appeared lost. "Dr. Martin, you unfortunately are intimately acquainted with how this works. Go on then. Give us the gory details."

"Right, well. Mary Michaelidis. Thirty-nine. Schoolteacher. Mother of three. Avid runner. Thirty miles a week." Martin spoke low and fast, as though if he only went through the facts of the case quickly enough, he might escape from Room 311 unscathed. "She presented on August twelfth with soreness in her left hip. I thought it was from all the running she did. I prescribed a thousand milligrams of Extra Strength Tylenol daily until the pain subsided."

"An unusual choice, Dr. Martin. Regardless, did the pain subside?" Hooten asked. He sounded both weary and disgusted. He knew the answers, of course, and he, too, seemed to want to get it over with as quickly as possible.

"No. Well, I don't know. I didn't hear from her. The next time I saw her was last month. October seventeenth. No, the eighteenth. She was in the ER with a broken hip."

"The running, no doubt, Dr. Martin," Hooten said, caustic. Martin winced at Hooten's remark.

"No, sir. Imaging studies revealed stage four bone cancer."

Ty almost felt sorry for Martin. Ty had been on the other side now, and he held a new appreciation for what it was like to have your work held up to the harsh light of Room 311 and been found wanting. His sympathy for Martin didn't last long, though. Martin had been in front of the doctors for Morbidity and Mortality before, and his case histories never ended well. The doctor was a menace, Ty thought.

"And when you saw her that first time, did you do a full physical exam or even ask if she was limping? Did you order an X-ray? Any blood work?" Hooten paused a beat for effect and then continued. "I know you didn't, Dr. Martin." Hooten craned his neck to look at the younger doctors behind him. "I want the junior members of our surgical staff to see what can happen when we forget the little things. When we let a runner with a sore hip out the door without a second thought. When we do that, we let metastatic cancer run amok for another two months." Hooten paused.

"We all want to make headlines. To be pathfinders. Doctors at the top of our profession. We all want to separate the conjoined twins," Hooten continued, catching Park's gaze before twisting at the waist to look back toward the sixty or so surgeons behind him. "We all want to do the heart-lung transplant. Rebuild the shattered face. We can't do any of the big things, none of them, unless we do the little things perfectly."

It was times like this when Ty was proud to work at Chelsea General, to work under Harding Hooten. For all his brusqueness, here was a doctor in his fortieth year in medicine who didn't let things slide, who didn't suffer fools gladly, who didn't care what anyone thought.

Hooten turned back toward Martin.

"Tell us how our fairy tale ends, Dr. Martin."

"Mary Michaelidis was admitted to the Intensive Care Unit on October eighteenth. Aggressive cancer treatments began the next day. She never made it out of the hospital, and died yesterday."

"Three weeks from diagnosis."

"Yes, sir. Three weeks."

The case seemed to deflate everyone in the room. This wasn't a medical mystery from which they could learn. It was a lot closer to murder, although no one could say for sure what would have happened to Mary Michaelidis if her cancer had been diagnosed in August instead of October. Presenting this case at M&M was not intended to educate them in any way but to scare them. *This is what happens when doctors got sloppy.*

When he was doing his internal medicine year, Ty had done a rotation at an oncology unit. He remembered a patient there, a woman who had survived ovarian cancer for four years and had just learned the cancer was back. She said the cancer diagnosis four years earlier was the best thing that had ever happened to her. Before, she told Ty, she waited only for very special occasions to get out the good china. "Now," she said, "I know to bring out the good china every day."

Mary Michaelidis did not have a chance to use the good china. She didn't have a chance to say good-bye to her students, place a memento in her children's rooms, or share the bed with her husband one more night.

"Dr. Martin," Hooten said. "I am recommending to the board of this hospital and affiliated institutions that your medical privileges be pulled immediately. At that point, you will lose your admitting and operating privileges, and for all intents and purposes, you will be persona non grata here."

Hooten stopped. Martin looked around. He looked as though he was unsure if he was supposed to say something. A moment later Villanueva broke the silence. He was on his feet, his voice filling the room like a megaphone.

"That's it? That's it? This so-called doctor kills another patient and we tell him he is a *persona non grata.*" Villanueva pronounced the Latin as though he had rotten eggs in his mouth. George pointed to the front of the room. "This guy should be up on charges. In handcuffs. At the very least he should never get near another patient. Never."

"Dr. Villanueva," Hooten began calmly. "We have procedures and we must —"

Before he could get any further, Villanueva had pulled a rolled-up newspaper from his back pocket and was reading from the small type of the death notices.

" 'Mary Michaelidis. Thirty-nine. Beloved

167

wife of Stephen Michaelidis, who delighted in her laugh; beloved mother of David, ten, Darren, eight, and Danielle, six, who adored their mother's everyday kindnesses; beloved daughter of Francis X. and Martha Kelly, who wouldn't have dared to pray for a daughter as beautiful, kind, and loving as their Mary.' "

With that, George crumpled the paper and hurled it toward the front of the room. It fluttered and died just two or three rows short of Martin.

CHAPTER 12

After M&M, Ty began the day fusing a couple of spines and was cruising into the third case of the day, a Rathke's cleft cyst, when his self-doubt returned like the dark clouds of a storm front.

The patient was a thirty-year-old woman with the improbable name Sandy Shore. She had been experiencing sleeplessness, dizziness, diminished sex drive, and, most alarming, rapidly deteriorating vision. An MRI had revealed the fluid-filled sac growing near the pituitary gland at the base of the brain that characterized the rare Rathke's cleft cyst. More tests showed the tumor was growing fast, increasing the pressure on the optic nerve. If the operation wasn't performed in a matter of days or weeks, she would lose her vision.

To get to the tumor, Ty planned to access her brain through her nose and sinuses. From the patient's perspective, she would emerge from surgery with no scars and an almost immediate recovery. From Ty's point of view, the operation would result in less blood loss and a lower risk of infection. Ty had always enjoyed this relatively new route into the brain, called endoscopic transnasal brain surgery. The process seemed so much more clever than getting to the brain by brute force: peeling the skin from the face and cutting open the skull.

ETBS came with its own set of challenges, though. Ty needed to thread a narrow, lighted endoscope and attached miniature surgical tools into the soft tissue of the nasal opening. He wouldn't be looking directly at the tumor, but at a TV monitor, and using computer mapping to show him exactly where to find the tumor. He would then re-sect it bit by bit, pulling bits of harmful tumor out the nose, the same way the instruments had gone in.

But ETBS was not risk-free. Cerebro-spinal fluid could leak. It also required patience and thoroughness, bringing out the tumor little by little. The procedure de-manded a very light touch with tiny instru-ments. The surgery was certainly ingenious, but it was not foolproof.

Before he operated, Ty liked to take five minutes to find a quiet place in the hospital to visualize step by step what he hoped to accomplish. If it was his first operation of the day, he might sit in his car on the parking deck, close his eyes, and go through the procedure. He'd even move his hands as he went through his visualization. He'd heard that the Navy Blue Angels did this when they weren't flying, using phantom sticks, as a way to practice the incredible precision formations they managed when they were airborne. If it wasn't his first operation of the day, Ty would seek out the call room or the surgeons' changing room, often going into the small bathroom and turning off the light. Visualizing the procedure both calmed and focused Ty. Sometimes, he would repeat a word in his head, trying to access his inner chakras. You couldn't guess the word Ty used, if you tried. It was *gentle.* A brain surgeon's hands needed the soft touch of a velvet hammer.

Before Sandy Shore's operation, Ty didn't have time to visualize the entire procedure, and he had the feeling of being off balance from the moment he walked into the OR. The day's schedule started backing up from the get-go, when the anesthesiologist had trouble intubating the first patient, an obese man with a ruptured disk and a slipped vertebra. Getting an airway in the obese was difficult, Ty knew, because fat narrowed the space for the endotracheal tube. The surgery went without a hitch, but Ty was behind. The second operation was delayed when the scrub nurse was late. By the time he finished, Sandy Shore was already on the table and sedated.

Now, as he snaked the lighted scope and instrument through the woman's nose and sinus and checked the MRI again to see his target, he felt a chill of dread. ETBS was nothing new to Ty. He'd done the procedure two dozen times before. Even so, he couldn't shake the feeling that the surgery was going to end in disaster. He was almost waiting for a flash of bright red blood from a nick in the carotid artery to show up on the monitor. Ty paused. This sense of impending failure was new, and it frightened him to his core. He checked the MRI yet again. He closed his eyes for a moment and breathed out slowly, hoping to blow the fear out. It didn't work.

When he opened his eyes, he sensed the furtive glances of the circulatory nurse, the anesthesiologist, and the junior and senior residents. He had the feeling they knew the cold, dark doubt that had suffused his body like some sort of toxic IV.

In training, Ty would joke with his fellow

residents about who was suffering from the tightest sphincter. When they were trying a new procedure, first during general surgery internship and then in neurosurgery, everyone but Ty would suffer a case of nerves. His fellow residents in quieter moments or after a few drinks would admit waking up in the middle of the night in a cold sweat thinking about all the things that could go wrong at each step.

Ty's surgical skills became the stuff of hospital lore when he was a resident. He was called to a psych ward to examine a patient with ptosis. The man had been homeless and delusional, muttering about the CIA putting extra salt on his french fries to dehydrate him and how the Supreme Court had secretly killed Stevie Ray Vaughan. When he arrived, Ty walked past one man sweating and breathing hard as he hit a Ping-Pong ball and ran around the table to hit it back to himself. Others were zoned out and rocking. Ty's patient turned out to be James Brian Cooper, a man in his midforties looking intently out the window. Cooper did indeed have ptosis, a drooping eyelid.

Ty ordered an MRI. For some reason, no one had thought that Cooper's psychosis might have roots in his brain physiology until his left eyelid began to droop, but the scan showed a large bi-lobed meningioma on his frontal lobe. Ty attempted to talk to Cooper about the tumor in his brain, the surgery, and its risks, but informed consent in this case was more of a formality than a fact, much as it was in dealing with Alzheimer's and dementia patients. Cooper merely muttered something about Class 4/5 switching systems and the USS *Pomfret* before signing his name. To Ty's surprise, Cooper's signature was beautiful — neat loops and lines that could have come out of a penmanship textbook. The name he signed was a reminder that Cooper lived on the locked psych ward: *James Earl Carter.* Still, the handwriting made Ty wonder where this man had come from before his life on the streets. He did not show the liver function of a man who had spent his life hitting the bottle hard.

The operation was a stunning success. The tumor was removed from both hemispheres of his frontal lobe, responsible for judgment. The buzz at the hospital started almost immediately. In Post-Op, Cooper began asking about his wife. The nurses, thinking he was still waking up from anesthesia or delusional, ignored him. He finally grabbed one of them by the arm and started demanding answers. He told them he felt like he had just "awoken" and asked what year it was. When they skeptically told him, he began weeping. He asked for a piece of paper and began writing. He handed over an address and a phone number, again written in beautiful penmanship. Intrigued, a hospital social worker actually drove to the address when the phone number came back as disconnected. Bit by bit, Cooper's story emerged: The man had been a project manager at Pfizer until the tumor had started affecting his judgment. At first, he started making simple mistakes. He forgot to go to work on a Monday, but was showered and dressed at 6 AM on a Sunday. He had laughed it off at the time. On one occasion, he had spent an hour looking for his car keys when leaving the office, only to get a call from security. It turned out his keys were in the ignition, and the vehicle had been running all day long in the parking structure. From there, it had become much worse. His frontal lobes were slowly being consumed by the tumor. He began drinking, lost his job, his wife, and then his house. As the tumor further invaded the seat of "executive function," Cooper became homeless and paranoid, seemingly just another delusional man looking for a drink.

The hospital found his tearful ex-wife. She had remarried, but agreed to drive Cooper to his parents' home in Dahlonega, Georgia, where he began life anew after eleven lost years. It was the stuff of Hollywood, and the story of this medical awakening swept the hospital like kudzu spreading among the pines in Cooper's hometown. Soon doctors, residents, and house staff Ty didn't even know were congratulating him on the case. Ty's legend was born, and his subsequent skills and Zen in the OR only enhanced it. Other surgeons admired — even emulated — his cool, almost spiritual approach to the operating room, but they could not match his skill. And while Ty did not hesitate to perform even the most complicated operations, other surgeons dwelled on the knowledge that even operations that were considered routine, such as a total knee, were in reality complicated procedures. The old knee needed to be removed at just the right point, with the bone sawed at the proper angle. The artificial knee had to be set correctly. There were risks of infection, which could kill a patient; there were risks the knee would not be aligned perfectly, which would limit the knee's usefulness; there were risks of damaging the surrounding ligaments, which could cause an irregular gait; and then there was the risk of the unknown, especially with anesthesia.

Medicine was designed to bring the best results to the most patients, and surgery was no different. The buzz phrase was *evidence-based medicine.* Doctors and surgeons based their work on probabilities, but there were always statistical outliers: Patients who responded in unexpected and deadly ways to anesthesia. Or patients whose blood didn't clot the way it was supposed to, or who reacted to medicine in ways the journal articles never predicted. There were even patients whose body parts were not where they were supposed to be. Ty remembered one patient in general surgery who had been born with a single kidney but didn't know it until they told her; another who had an extra spur on her humerus bone near her elbow, a congenital defect common enough to have a name, supracondylar process; another who had abnormally long metacarpal bones on both ring fingers. Pulmonary veins were notorious for their anatomical abnormalities.

All this could give residents night sweats. Ty remembered a fidgety, nail-biting resident named Kowalski. The joke among fellow residents was that Kowalski's sphincter was so tight, if you stuck coal up his ass, you'd make diamonds. They had even stuck some laxatives in his coffee once, to loosen him up. He spent half the day in the bathroom, and came out more neurotic than ever. Kowalski tried amassing knowledge as a way to prepare himself for the strange and unpredictable. What do you do if you discover cirrhosis unexpectedly during surgery? What if you find a surprise lesion during cardiac surgery? If there was a single case in the medical literature of a bowel obstruction presenting as appendicitis, he wanted to know about it. Kowalski tried studying next to orange slices because the sense of smell is so closely linked to memory. He thought this would help burn this information into his brain. Not satisfied with mere eighteen-hour days, Kowalski started taking modafinil to read for longer stretches. If it worked for air force pilots flying halfway around the world and back, why not give it a shot? Kowalski lost weight. His skin took on a grayish pallor, and the dark circles under his eyes made him appear haunted. He became irritable and prone to wild mood swings. One day, Kowalski was operating when he discovered a left-sided gallbladder. Somehow, he'd failed to encounter this possibility in his dogged reading of the journals. The exhausted, stressed, overemotional resident asked the circulating nurse to call the attending and walked out of the OR. The next day, he left the surgical program. He decided living in fear of the next operation was no way to go through life. He became a successful dermatologist.

Ty was different. Even with brand-new procedures or patients with very poor chances of survival, Ty was always loose. Even when the patient died post-op — even when the patient died on the table — Ty knew he had executed the procedure as well as anyone. Had he been deluding himself all this time? Had all this success bloated his ego and clouded his judgment? Had his overconfidence allowed him to kill Quinn McDaniel?

Ty looked down at his patient and the tubes snaking out of her nose, which was the only part of her face visible. The rest of her body was hidden by blue surgical draping. Now it wasn't overarching confidence but dread that clouded his brain and froze his hands, which were the envy of the neurosurgical world. He had experienced this sweeping fear only two weeks before, clipping an aneurysm. Then, he had merely been undecided about which type of clip to use. This was far worse. This was paralyzing. Ty felt an anger welling inside him.

Ty turned to Mac Ryan, the senior resident.

"Mac, you ready to try ETBS?" Mac's eyes above his surgical mask showed surprise.

"Sure, Ty." This was an unexpected gift. Residents were always eager to do more. Usually, though, surgeons told residents ahead of time if they were going to be taking the lead in surgery, especially one as involved as this.

"I'll walk you through it."

Ty was sure Mac had read all the literature on the procedure. His senior resident was nothing if not thorough. Mac slid over next to Ty and took the instruments.

"Take a moment to get the feel of the endoscope."

Step by step, Ty talked Mac through the procedure, admiring — almost envying — the younger doctor's poise and patience.

When Sandy Shore was in recovery and long after Mac had showered and left, Ty sat in the locker room. He was furious at himself, at his lack of nerve and loss of self-assurance. He'd gone into medicine for two reasons: to be better than the doctors who allowed his brother to die, and to treat his patients' families better than he had been treated. Rushing Quinn McDaniel into surgery without checking the possibility of a bleeding problem was a rookie mistake. Worse than a rookie mistake. It was an omission that had cost a boy and his mother dearly.

Ty changed out of his scrubs and threw them into the hamper in the corner. He put on his clothes and slammed his locker. He slammed it so hard the metal door didn't latch shut. Ty grabbed the locker door and slammed it again. Then he walked out the door.

CHAPTER 13

At exactly 6:14 am, Ty found himself back in front of the M&M room. This time, though, he was unable to control his sweats and his shakes. He was drenched and shivering. He looked out into the audience, and everyone there was laughing and pointing at him. Park, Sydney, and even Tina. She mouthed, *I'm sorry,* and began laughing so hard she doubled over. "The prodigal son . . . yeah right," someone muttered. He looked over at Hooten, waiting for him to start. Strangely, every time Hooten opened his mouth to say a word, all that anyone could hear was a buzzing noise. It was as if there were a huge insect inside the man. Hooten tried again, and again made a buzzing noise. Again, the same thing. *Bzzz. Bzzzz. Bzzzz.* It was terrifying. Something seemed to have taken over the Boss.

Tina rushed forward. Ty was paralyzed. But

instead of running toward Hooten, she came running straight for Ty. She was moving quickly, and suddenly her hands were on him. She shook Ty by the shoulders. She looked him right in the face, and then she was making that same weird buzzing noise. Slowly, the buzz turned into words. Ty stared hard at her face to try to understand what she was saying. "Wap," she said. "Waup. Wake up!" she shouted. Ty rubbed his eyes in his own bed. Tina handed him the buzzing pager. It took him a full minute to acclimate himself. "Bad dream?" Tina asked with a sweet but worried look. She ran her fingers through his wet hair. "Yeah," Ty muttered as he looked at his pager. *Level 1 trauma. Epidural hematoma. ER 20 minutes. Medevac chopper,* it read. Ty checked his watch, gave Tina a quick kiss, and jumped out of bed. Just minutes later he was putting on his leather jacket and grabbing his helmet off the back of his Suzuki Hayabusa. Ty knew it was unusual to be riding a motorcycle, given his career choice taking care of head injuries. But the first time someone had explained that this particular bike might just be the fastest in the world, it was all but preordained that he would have one. Ty blasted down Washtenaw Avenue, a beautiful two-lane stretch of road with no traffic lights. He picked up speed, and looked up to see the trauma chopper flying just over him. His patient was on that helicopter. Ty pulled back on the throttle — the Hayabusa responded quickly. And for a few minutes down the nearly abandoned road, it was a man and his motorcycle keeping up with the chopper in the sky. Ty felt exhilarated as he flew by the Washtenaw County Medical Center, forgetting for at least a little while the angst that had crept into his core.

Inside the county medical center, Park sat with his hands folded in the radiologist's waiting room. He heard the loud motorcycle engine roar outside the window and silently cursed. *I will probably be operating on that guy later on, if he isn't brain-dead and donating his organs,* Park thought. He looked around the sterile waiting room. There was the usual collection of untouched preventive health pamphlets on quitting smoking and reducing your chances for a stroke, along with well-worn gossip and women's magazines with articles on celebrity scandals, becoming thinner, enjoying sex more, and simplifying your life. *So much mental energy wasted in the United States,* Park thought.

Park had undergone an MRI an hour and a half earlier and had been waiting ever since. He had told his loyal cadre of residents back at Chelsea General he was at his daughter's cello recital. Since he never took time off for anything, they were enthusiastic. The excuse was starting to wear thin, though. His daughter was surprisingly very good for her age, but she would have to play an entire concerto to take up as much time as he'd spent out of the hospital.

The doctor had poked his head out a few minutes earlier.

"Mr. Song." Park didn't look up. "Mr. Song," the doctor said again, this time louder. Park remembered that he had signed up using his wife's maiden name. He looked up. "I've looked at your MRI. I'll be ready to talk to you in just a minute."

Park didn't want word getting back to Chelsea General about the MRI. He never wanted to show weakness. After all, it was most likely nothing but stress causing the intermittent headaches that had started six weeks earlier and seemed to be increasing in frequency. At first, he tried ignoring them. He was a firm believer in mind over matter. Hadn't he endured residency's years of thirty-six-hour days not once, but twice? When he could not will away his headaches,

Park began taking Tylenol. By the time he made his appointment at Washtenaw County, he was popping Tylenol like candy.

After the doctor, Milner or Miller, whatever it was, had said he'd be right out, he'd disappeared again. Park checked his watch. Fifteen minutes, and counting. The front desk, too, was abandoned, leaving Park and an elderly man and his wife there to languish in the waiting room. The overhead fluorescent lights were starting to bother him. Were they flickering? He bowed his head and picked up one of the pamphlets: *Your Guide to Smoking Cessation.* Park knew what *cessation* meant, thanks to the English-language and vocabulary-building cassette lessons he kept in his car. He'd played them in his ancient Honda until each cassette's title was worn to nothing. He knew the tapes by heart, but he still played them every time he got in the car. They calmed him. *"Cessation: a ceasing. An end; Chimera: a fire-breathing female monster with a lion's head, a goat's body, and a serpent's tail; or, a thing that is hoped or wished for but in fact is illusory; Cognizant: having knowledge or being aware of."*

Park put down the pamphlet and began pacing around the room. He was fidgety, and he couldn't sit still. For Park, doing nothing violated some basic rule. He was hardwired that way. He was a doer. If you weren't doing something, you weren't going to accomplish anything. Doing nothing was wasted opportunity. Doing nothing was something that obese diabetic Americans did between doctor's appointments.

After so many years, he still found much about American culture difficult to understand. Here was a hospital spending money on a pamphlet suggesting people give up smoking one of the most addictive substances on the planet — when stern warning labels, common sense, family member pleadings, the sight of emphysemics with portable oxygen delivered through their nasal canula, and the near certainty of a miserable death had all failed. A pamphlet? That was going to work?

Much seemed backward about his adoptive homeland. American parents deferred to children, shaping their lives to meet the extracurricular whims and social engagements of their offspring. They kept a calendar for their children as though the youngsters were royals and the elders social secretaries, organizing their work schedules so all the carpools to the various sports and lessons would be covered. The parents even placed stickers on the back windows of their minivans showing silhouettes of gymnasts or football helmets or soccer balls. The icons were labeled BRITNEY or KELSEY or BRANDON. The message was clear: The parents were there to promote and boast of their athletic accomplishments. What trivial pursuits!

Pet owners were perhaps the most baffling to Park. They obediently walked their dogs, even in the most inclement weather, carefully scooping up their turds and carrying them home in plastic bags as though they were some sort of prize. They even gave the dogs the same surname as the owner. It seemed so disrespectful and uncivilized.

Bored with pacing in the waiting room, Park walked up to the front desk and peered over the counter, looking for the doctor, a nurse, the receptionist, anyone he could pester. The office looked deserted. Probably a drug rep serving everyone lunch. It was a beautiful woman, no doubt, showing too much cleavage and persuading the doctors to prescribe her product. He remembered one of them had even tried to give him a book once. It was the story of a Viagra salesman, and the title was *Hard Sell.* Unacceptable, Park thought.

Park opened the door that read NO UNAC-COMPANIED PATIENTS BEYOND THIS

POINT and headed down the corridor. Framed children's art decorated the hallway between examination rooms. When he neared the end, he saw an MRI on a light box. It was an axial cut of the brain, Park instinctively thought. The image had contrast, and there was some motion artifact around the border. Probably a lazy technician, Park mused, but he had to admit it was a pretty clear image. He moved closer. The picture showed a bright mass in the right hemisphere. It wasn't a solid mass, but rather somewhat blurry and uneven with rough borders and scalloped edges. *No doubt,* Park said silently, *a classic glioblastoma multiforme.* Probably the most malignant tumor known not just in the brain, but in the entire human body. No cure, and no proven effective treatments. Whoever this poor bastard was would need an operating room immediately. Park shook his head. Even he would have trouble handling that one. He guessed the patient had six months to a year to live. He wanted to tell Milner or Miller, that slow doctor, that he should refer the patient who had this scan over to his clinic. Park looked at the scan again and the patient's name in the lower corner of the image caught his eye: SONG. Park did a double take. His wife's maiden name.

Strange. Then he remembered. Song. His alias. He nearly threw up.

It had been just ten minutes since Ty arrived at the hospital, parking his motorcycle outside the ER entrance seconds before the helicopter landed. He ran up to the helipad. "Gimme the bullet," he shouted over the whir of the helicopter blades as he helped wheel the patient toward the open glass doors to the hospital.

"Three-passenger MVA," the medic shouted. "Father was driving, and was killed at the scene. This is the ten-year-old son, with likely epidural hematoma, and mother is about five minutes out with an intracerebral blood clot in the right frontal lobe . . . she doesn't look good, and is going to need an operation quickly as well."

Ty looked at the chart. "Ahmad," he read. *Oh yeah, the dad was Dr. Ahmad, the pediatrician.* "Oh my God," Ty said, "I knew him really well."

The medic looked hard at him. "Well, then maybe you knew about his drug habit?" The medic paused. "Yeah, everyone's favorite pediatrician was high as a kite when he rolled the family minivan."

Just then the next chopper could be heard approaching the helipad with Mrs. Ahmad.

"We need another neurosurgeon stat — who is on backup call?" Ty shouted. The nurse looked down. "Park," she said. Sung Park.

Ten miles away at the county medical center, Park tried to collect himself as he stood staring at the scan. He was trying to find some explanation for what he was seeing. There was no mistaking it. He had gone from denial to anger to acceptance in the last five minutes and now his knees buckled. He reached out to one of the walls for support, knocking a six-year-old's framed rendition of a butterfly to the floor. The shattering glass brought the doctor and a nurse.

Sung Park drove his Honda down the road back to Chelsea General with his MRI film in an oversize manila envelope. His eyes were red, and he subconsciously wiped away the moisture from his eyes. His pager was going off next to him, but he could not hear it. *Rhapsody in Blue* played on his car radio. He turned it up. It was one of the first American songs he'd heard in his homeland of Korea, and it was then he'd first dreamed of moving to the United States. There was something about that classical music infused with jazz that appealed to Park. It represented a sort of musical kaleidoscope of

America, its melting pot, and its metropolitan madness. It had a steely rhythm and just enough rattle bang — Park used to play it over and over again in his tiny dorm room outside Seoul. His hands were perfectly placed at the 10 and 2 positions on the steering wheel, and he drove the speed limit. He ignored the person honking behind him, trying to pester him to drive faster. All he could think about was the number of patients he had seen over the years with glioblastoma. Some had lived as long as a few years, but most didn't make it past 14 months — 14.6 months to be precise. Ted Kennedy had lived about that long, and ironically so did George Gershwin, the composer of the music in Park's car, a now morbid soundtrack to his life.

He made a single call after telling Milner — Miller, whatever his name was — that he was an idiot when he tried to console Park and tell him the tumor might be benign. He told Harding Hooten's executive assistant, Ann Holland, when she answered, that he needed to see Dr. Hooten right away. At first, she was a little reluctant to schedule a meeting.

"It's an emergency," Park said.

He then fumbled with his jacket, scooped up his films, and walked out.

■ ■ ■ ■

Park took the elevator up to the twelfth floor, walked down the hall and into Hooten's office. He stared hard at the Rothko and then regained his composure. Since the time when he was a very young man, Park had relied on his determination and scientific mind, and he was going to use them now to improve his odds as much as he could. He had not gone through medical training twice to lose it all to cancer, he thought.

Hooten was waiting for him. "Sung," he said by way of greeting.

Park slid the MRI out of its sleeve and passed it to Hooten. The chief of surgery pushed up his reading glasses and held it up to the light.

"Nasty-looking tumor. You are going to have your hands full with this one." Hooten checked the name along the bottom of the MRI. "I would tell Mr. Song not to buy the family-size jar of mayonnaise." Hooten shook his head.

"I am Song," Park said evenly. "That is my film."

"My God," Hooten said. He appeared stunned.

"I want you to operate as soon as possible. Tomorrow. The day after tomorrow." Park passed a list to Hooten. "Here is the name of the anesthesiologist, the nurses, and the others I want assisting with the surgery."

"Sung, you should wait a week. Give you time to get your affairs in order?"

"Any delay will hurt my chances."

"Yes, but I wouldn't rush into this."

"It's not rushing. It's the logical decision."

Hooten looked at the film again for a long time and then up at Park. "You sure about this, Sung?"

Park felt a pang of doubt, but stared ahead with determination.

"All right, see you in pre-op at six."

Park reached out and shook Hooten's hand.

CHAPTER 14

Villanueva sat on his stool in the emergency room, combination air traffic controller, conductor, and ringmaster. He didn't need a radar screen, baton, or whip. The Big Cat waved his massive arms and called out like a carnival barker. He was in his element. He sent the fractured hip one way, a dehydrated child another, a baby with a high fever a third.

Paramedics brought in a drunk stinking of urine, his hair greasy and matted, his clothes filthy.

"Thanks for the gift, guys," Villanueva said. "But I feel bad, I didn't get you anything." The paramedics smiled and rolled their eyes. They'd heard the Big Cat's patter before.

"Catch us next time," one of the paramedics joked back.

"Next time, you'll be taking a case like this to county, right, boys?"

Another gurney arrived a moment later, refocusing Villanueva. This one carried a white-haired man knocked unconscious by his common-law wife. El Gato pointed to Trauma Bay 3.

The common-law wife walked in complaining of back pain, and Villanueva steered her to the opposite side of the OR, trying to prevent more fireworks between the two. She was moaning, saying "the bastard" had pushed her over a coffee table. *This must be what it's like to be a Hollywood maître d'. Keep the rival agents away from each other,* Villanueva thought.

The cases were not always so benign. Chelsea General had the occasional gunshot victims from turf wars among gangs. Sometimes members of both gangs would arrive by ambulance, and Villanueva had to make sure there was plenty of room — and at least a couple of real cops — between the two sides. The hospital had its own police force but they were no match for the young gangsters. They kept people from parking illegally out front and wandered the halls giving directions to patients and family members lost in Chelsea General's labyrinth. Villanueva called the ER's regular cop on duty Barney Fife. He was a frail narcoleptic who spent much of his shift sleeping.

"Who's got the back?" Villanueva called out, waving toward the woman who said she'd been pushed over the coffee table. "Smythe. That's you."

"Certainly, Dr. V," Smythe answered. Smythe was originally from London and retained his *Masterpiece Theatre* accent despite living in North Carolina from age twelve on.

"Hey, Smythe," Villanueva called out with an atrocious imitation of the junior doctor's upper-crust accent. "Why is it I'm twice as smart as you and you sound twice as smart as I am?"

The nurses sitting behind Villanueva laughed. "You got that right, Dr. Villanueva," one said. "He sounds smart with a capital *S*," she added with an exaggerated English accent.

Another piped up, "I'd much rather have the gent with the accent take care o' me."

"You're going to get the Big Cat angry!" a third nurse chided playfully.

A nervous-looking resident walked back studying a chart, trying to avoid Villanueva's detection.

"Not so fast, Dr. Um-So," Villanueva called out to him. The doctor's real name was Kauffman, but everyone called him Dr. Um-So, though Villanueva was the only one who did it to his face. Um-So stopped.

Villanueva grabbed the chart the younger doctor carried. "You avoiding me?"

"No, Dr. Villanueva. I got this case."

"What case is so important you can't talk to the Big Cat?"

"Man complaining of bloody stools."

"You're choosing bloody stools over me."

The nurses laughed.

"No, Doctor, um."

"You're saying bloody stools are more important than a little quality time with me. That's what I'm hearing."

Um-So was clearly flustered. He stammered but said nothing intelligible.

"Why are you wasting time with the case?" Villanueva asked. "It sounds like a job for Dick the Butt Doctor." Villanueva never tired of this joke. Richard Lincoln was the chief of Proctology. He was an outstanding physician but that didn't prevent him from being known as Dick the Butt Doctor. Villanueva returned his attention to Kauffman.

"You read all the journals. Tell me something I don't know."

Kauffman thought about it for a minute.

"Um so," Kauffman began. His verbal tic appeared to be hardwired. Half a dozen doctors and nurses within earshot had to turn away so he wouldn't see them laughing. "Noninvasive motion ventilation in COPD patients can be implemented —"

Villanueva interrupted again. "Saw that. Severe neurological dysfunction and pH less than 7.25 do not constitute absolute contraindications blah, blah, blah. Tell me something I don't know."

Kauffman thought for a moment. The hint of a smile on his face.

"Um so, laparoscopic surgeons who excel at video games make 47 percent fewer errors —"

"— and work 37 percent faster than their peers," Villanueva finished for him. "*Archives of Surgery.* You can do better!"

Kauffman held up his chart by way of an excuse, but Villanueva shook his head.

"I'm counting on you."

"Um so, did you know the word *bedlam* comes from the Bethlehem Hospital for the Criminally Insane, in London."

"No shit?" Villanueva clapped Kauffman on the back. "Now, that's interesting."

Their banter was interrupted by the husband in Trauma Bay 3. Like a sedated lion whose tranquilizer had just run out, he sat up with a roar, startling everyone in the room.

"What'd she hit me with?" he demanded.

"Relax, Mr. Merriweather." Johnson, the neurologist, gently pushed the man's shoulders back down onto the examination table. "Looks like a large blunt object. Now let's see how your eyes are working."

Hearing the question, the common-law Mrs. Merriweather stopped her dissertation on back pain and her good-for-nothing, common-law husband and called across the room.

"It was the goddamn lamp."

Villanueva scanned the room and located Barney Fife snoozing with a *People* magazine over his eyes. The Big Cat slid off his stool and sidled toward the midpoint between the feuding couple. Villanueva was once again ready to revive his offensive lineman skills and block a mad rush. When it became apparent the man simply wanted to know what had laid him low, Villanueva returned to his stool, directing traffic and conducting the ER symphony. On his way, he grabbed a doughnut from a three-day-old box sitting on the nurses' desk. He took a bite just as he perched himself up on the stool, smiling. Two seconds later the stool simply collapsed. First there was a crack in one of the steel-reinforced wooden legs. As Villanueva started to look down, the other legs broke right in the middle, landing the seat of the stool and Villanueva smack on the floor. It was quite a sight, a 350-pound Hispanic man in barely fitting scrubs rolling around on the ground trying to right himself. More embarrassed than hurt, Villanueva eventually got his footing. Now that he was clearly all right, mild giggles started to break out in the crowd that had gathered.

Seeing the entire ER looking his way but pretending not to, he adjusted his scrubs and gave a small bow, inadvertently mooning anyone behind him. A couple of the nurses clapped.

Villanueva started to examine the remnants of the stool, half expecting to find an obvious defect. Then he looked around. "One question," he boomed. "Was this stool already broken before I got here?" The giggles turned into uproarious laughter. Villanueva tried his best to look angry, but eventually joining the laughter while stuffing the rest of the doughnut in his mouth.

CHAPTER 15

Sydney left the OR to answer a page. She wasn't worried. The operation, a CABG, was almost done. She thought everyone knew the acronym until one day she received a call from the billing office where a new staff member wondered why Sydney had billed twelve thousand dollars for cabbage. Sydney had patiently explained it was coronary artery bypass grafting. "No, CABG was an acronym, not an abbreviation," she had patiently explained. There was a response on the other end of the line, to which Sydney replied, "Actually, I am not the only one in the country to use that acronym," with a little less patience.

The chest was still open, but senior resident Sanford Williams appeared to have everything well in hand when she stepped out into the scrub area. Williams had come a long way and was now one of the best young surgeons at the hospital. Sydney had a great deal of pride in her residents, and spent a lot of time training them in the operating room as well as in the animal labs. She had started with Williams seven years ago showing him how to attach skin grafts on the backs of rats. Now he was methodically sewing blood vessels together on top of a beating heart with suture too small to be seen by the human eye. Sydney was returning a call to the paging operator when she heard shouting from the OR.

She hung up her cell and hurried back into the OR. She saw Williams and nurse Monique Tran nose-to-nose — or they would have been nose-to-nose if Tran wasn't a foot shorter than the surgeon. A tall Southern man, Williams wore clothes that would best be described as preppy when he wasn't in the operating room. Even now, he wore a surgical scrub cap that had an argyle pattern. Tran, on the other hand, was a diminutive Vietnamese woman who wore Birkenstocks and baggy shirts. They were about as opposite as they came. Right now they both wore masks, but their narrowed eyes and their tone — even muffled — made their anger and frustration clear with most of their features covered.

Next to the doctor and nurse, bloody detritus was spread across the floor beside an overturned track bin fitted with a red bag for medical waste. Packaging, syringes, tubing, tissue, blue surgical draping stained dark, gloves, a couple of once-white towels, now crimson with splotches of blood. Above the mess on the floor, a rack held little bits of blood gauze, each in its own compartment.

Behind Monique and Williams, a junior resident stood frozen over the patient's split sternum holding the large curved suture needle loaded with a wire.

"I don't care," Tran said.

"You don't care?"

"I don't care. The patient can lie there all friggin' night for all I care." Monique crossed her arms, a gesture of defiance and resolve in case he didn't catch the meaning of her words. "No one is closing this patient until we find that four-by-four."

"I did not leave a four-by-four in the patient," Williams said, almost shouting. "That is not something I do." Neither he nor Tran had seen Sydney come back into the OR. "You are so — *Gây phiền nhiễu.*"

"*Chao?* . . . Are you calling me annoying? Don't try your god-awful Vietnamese on me. Look, maybe even the great Sanford Williams left a four-by-four in the patient . . ." Tran gesticulated.

Williams now crossed his arms and tilted his head back, appraising. Calmer now.

"Since when have you become so emotional?"

"Twenty-two went in. Only twenty-one came out. Either do an X-ray or help me find the missing four-by-four in the red bags. No one is leaving until we find it."

"Like hell." Williams turned to the junior resident. "Close him."

"You want emotional?" Tran asked, poking Williams in the chest. "How's that for emotional."

"Jesus, Monique."

The resident remained frozen over the empty chest cavity, needle and suture in hand. He was like an obedient child waiting to be told by a parent to start eating.

Sydney, too, watched and said nothing. She was trying to decipher what she was seeing. She knew the cause of the outburst must have been more than a missing 4×4, but she couldn't figure out what. And since she couldn't figure it out, she couldn't decide what she — as the senior doctor there — should be doing. And when the heck did Sanford learn Vietnamese? She waited and watched. She thought the answer to what was happening here might suddenly become clear. That was the nature of a puzzle. Look long enough, and maybe you will notice something you missed, just like Joanna Whitman. Yes, there was more than just a missing gauze at stake here, but what?

There was something else, though. There was a rawness and passion between these two, and suddenly Sydney felt the awkward thrill of the voyeur. She was watching something, for lack of a better word, "real." And for that reason, too, she was loath to interrupt. So often the nurses and the residents acted around her the way they were supposed to act: obedient and eager.

Monique Tran glowered at Williams. The Red Hot Chili Peppers played loudly through the ceiling speakers, *Southern girl with a scarlet drawl* . . .

Sydney had playlists for the various parts of the operation. She liked Bryan Ferry or some other soothing vocals for pre-op and the initial incision. During the operation itself Sydney liked U2, which she always found uplifting. When it was closing time, the beat was hard and fast.

Without a word, Tran bent down on the floor and began sorting through bloody pieces of flesh, sterilization kits — everything that had been tossed in the medical waste bag during the two hours they had been operating. She was muttering as she did, a rapid-fire Vietnamese invective.

"You think I tossed it in here. Mr. Smart-Ass. I mean, Dr. Smart-Ass. We'll see. You think you know friggin' everything. You don't even know how to say pho," Monique said, not pronouncing the Vietnamese dish *faux* but more like *fuh.*

It was only now that Williams noticed Sydney taking it all in. The sight startled him.

"Dr. Saxena."

Monique Tran looked up, and she, too, was startled to see Sydney Saxena standing in the OR.

"Dr. Williams. May I have a moment?"

Sydney did not like to countermand Williams, who was the surgeon in charge inside the OR in her absence. But she was the surgeon of record should anything go wrong. More than that, there was a right and a wrong, and in this case Williams was wrong. Sydney and Williams pushed through the double doors. She looked at the young surgeon.

"Monique is such an obstructionist —" He stopped, blushed, then awaited word from his attending.

"She's right. Look, every year, more than a thousand patients have something left in their body during surgery. In fact, it is closer to fifteen hundred. It is not a sign of weakness to forget something — but if you never bothered to check, well, that is unforgivable. Not to mention, my name is going on the operative record. I don't want to be coming back here tomorrow to dig out your gauze. I don't want to get sued, and I sure as hell don't want to be in front of the rabid spectators in the coliseum next Monday morning." The last comment got Williams's attention.

"Either you order an X-ray or I do. Or you can join Monique on the floor with the red bag waste." Sydney was trying hard to act the way Hooten might in a situation like this. It was no secret to anyone that she was angling for his job one day. "You can't close up the patient without knowing."

Williams pursed his lips and sucked air through his nostrils. He turned and pushed his way back into the OR.

"Okay. We're doing an X-ray." Twenty minutes later the missing 4×4 rectangle of gauze was located in the patient's chest cavity.

CHAPTER 16

The operation on the Ahmad boy was straightforward and had gone well. The boy was awake now, and was starting to ask questions. Ty shined a bright light into both his eyes and asked him to lift both his arms in the air. He looked at the curvilinear incision he'd made on the boy's scalp. Ty silently dictated into a small recording device that would produce an electronic record for the boy's chart. "Pupils are equal, round, and reactive," Ty said. "He has full power in all four limbs, and he is oriented to person, place, and time," he finished. He wanted to add, *The boy still doesn't know his father is dead or that the kindly pediatrician had smoked a joint prior to buckling his son into the car.* He thought better of it. Hooten had emerged from his twelfth-floor sanctuary to help operate on Mrs. Ahmad. Surprisingly, he wasn't at all upset that Sung Park couldn't be located. Mrs. Ahmad was still sedated, but she would wake up soon to start reassembling her family's shattered lives.

Sandy Shore's Rathke's cleft cyst had also been completed without incident. Mac was a quick learner with good hands and an unshakable confidence Ty now envied. Ty mused that he was now on the outside, looking in. No matter how many ways he surgically dissected the situation in his mind, he kept coming back to the same conclusion. He had all but put a gun to Quinn McDaniel's head and pulled the trigger. It was an assassination. Isn't that what you would call a reckless mistake like the one he'd made? He felt a little spill of gastric acid in his stomach. The boy's death had shaken his mojo, his *wa,* the kind of fusion of thought and action that the philosopher Mihaly Csikszentmihalyi called *flow.* Whatever Ty once had, he now realized he had lost it. The pressing question was: How could he get it back? He tried not to think about what he'd do if he couldn't.

Changing out of his scrubs, Ty thought about how quickly his confidence had fled. He had done the two spines without a thought, and then seized up when he needed his skills most. He had started thinking, and that was it. The doubts flooded in. He made a mental note not to think too much and almost nervously laughed out loud. The quickest way to obsess on something was to try not to think about it. Just ask any baseball player in a batting slump, or basketball player at the free-throw line.

Ty had been a standout athlete in high school. He pitched and played outfield for San Luis Obispo High, and was shooting guard for the Tigers basketball team. Ty remembered teammates with mental blocks that crippled their abilities to perform in games. Don Blankenship, the first baseman on his baseball team, would choke when he had to make even the shortest throw. His arm would move forward and the ball would travel almost straight down into the ground. Fortunately for the Tigers, first basemen did not need to throw often. This strange mental block was not limited to obscure high school players. The New York Yankees' Chuck Knoblauch had suffered a similar curse. And there were well-documented cases of major-league pitchers whose careers were ruined when they suddenly lost their pinpoint control.

Then there was Ty's teammate on the high school basketball team, a sinewy power forward named Trent Brown. He missed a foul shot in the district finals one year and from that point on made only about a third of his free throws, an abysmal percentage. Ty thought Trent's horrific foul shooting cost him a Division I scholarship — all because he could not overcome the belief he could not perform the simple act of shooting a ball into the hoop from the free-throw line fourteen feet away.

Golfers called these jitters "the yips," and sports psychologists made good money helping athletes overcome these mental hang-ups. Of course, sports were not the only arena where you could choke. *I'm proof of that,* Ty thought. Remembering his days as a standout athlete gave him an idea. He was supposed to prepare a lecture on the use of the hormone progesterone for traumatic brain injuries. It was an idea he'd developed with one of his colleagues in the ER. They noticed women often did better than men after similar head injuries. They thought it might be the female hormone progesterone that was somehow protecting the brain. Turned out they were right, and Ty wrote his fifteenth publication for the *New England Journal of Medicine.* Instead of working on his talk, he left the hospital on his Hayabusa, went home to his condo, and changed into shorts, a T-shirt, and high-tops. He took a quick peek in the mirror and pushed away a couple of gray hairs that had started to creep in along his sideburns. His cobalt-blue eyes looked right back at him, challenging him. Then he drove down Oak Street to a local elementary school playground where high school players and a few adults gathered in the afternoons to play basketball on the asphalt court. Ty left his pager behind.

When they chose up sides, Ty was picked last, but he stayed with the run-and-gun high schoolers, to the younger players' surprise. Ty's game was typically smooth. He moved fluidly, cut quickly, and found an open space to take a pass, square up to the basket, and let loose with his textbook jump shot. He was also a smart player. He anticipated where the ball was going to be. He put his body in position to get the offensive rebound, set a pick or dodge one, box out the opposing player on defense, kick out for a fast break. He quickly gauged his most useful role on a pickup team and filled it, whether it was shooting, rebounding, or ball handling. As a result his teams usually won. These were all products of his restless childhood days in California, playing hours upon hours of pickup basketball, playing at every opportunity until his focus shifted from petty crime and sports to doing whatever it took to be the best surgeon he could be.

But as they moved up and down the court now, Ty did not find his rhythm. The first time he got the ball on the wing, he hurried his shot and missed the basket entirely. The next time, he drove to the basket but had the ball stripped from his hands by an opposing player half his age. The player raced downcourt and laid the ball into the hoop.

After that, Ty knew he wouldn't get another pass, so he did his best hustling up and down the court looking for loose balls and rebounds. But his knack for finding his space on the court and his role on the team eluded him. He was bumping into his own teammates, and they were becoming aggravated with the "old man" they'd been stuck with. Instead of finding a spot under the basket and holding it, he'd tried to bully his way past the opposing teammates.

Ty usually found the hard-charging up and down of a pickup game tiring in an exhilarating way. But as he ran the length of the court chasing another layup by the other team, Ty found himself enjoying his exhaustion only as a form of self-punishment. Breathing hard, he grabbed an offensive rebound and went up hard against a rail-thin high school student. The teenager fell back, holding his nose.

"Damn, man," someone said behind him as the defender sat on the hardtop and dabbed his nose with a T-shirt.

Ty breathed a big sigh.

"Sorry about that," Ty said. He reached out his hand as a gesture of conciliation. The high schooler swatted it away.

Ty turned and walked off the court with a wave. As he made his way to his motorcycle, he felt none of the normal pleasure of exercising his body to exhaustion. He felt irritable, and then it occurred to him that he had been playing in anger, not with joy. He'd had the idea that the release of hoops, the physicality, would somehow cleanse him of the mental demon that was stalking him. It didn't. As he drove home, the fear remained that he would choke during his next operation — or worse, that he would perform the operation with catastrophic results. Ty noticed his breathing was elevated, and it wasn't from the basketball. He needed to do something. He needed to shake this doubt that gripped him — that had infected him like a retrovirus. Ty had an idea. More accurately, he returned to an idea he'd had a week earlier.

Ty showered, changed, and then checked his wallet to see if he still had the scrap of paper he had placed there. He did. He checked the address on Google Maps, got his car, and drove to an apartment building a few miles from his own, behind a Kroger grocery store. Ty took a deep breath, got out of the car, and walked to the building.

Confronting his fears head-on had been Ty's credo since his brother's death.

Ty rang the buzzer under the name A. MCDANIEL — 5H.

"Yes?"

"Allison, this is Ty Wilson." There was a pause. "Dr. Wilson. From Chelsea General. I wondered if you had a moment."

There was another pause, followed by a buzz. Ty pulled the door open and took the elevator up to the fifth floor. The carpet in the hallway was worn, and the lighting was dim. Ty knocked on the door. Allison opened it a moment later, looking a little suspicious. When he had seen her before, her hair was pulled back and she was dressed in a gray pantsuit. Now her shoulder-length hair hung loose; she was wearing blue jeans and a simple V-neck white T-shirt. She was barefoot. She looked younger than she had at the hospital but also very tired.

"Hi, Ms. McDaniel. Allison," Ty began. He realized he had not thought about what he was going to say when she opened the door. He had another reflexive thought: that she was a beautiful woman. "I was wondering if we could talk. I've been thinking about your son."

Two small children ran around behind Allison. Ty looked at the children, who looked so little they could be Quinn's younger siblings. Allison saw his confusion.

"That's my niece and nephew. Since I lost my job, I'm watching them for my sister." Ty didn't know what to say. He saw the woman swallow hard. "Listen, it's hard to talk when I'm watching the kids. You want to get a cup of coffee sometime, call me. There's a Starbucks just down the street."

She held up a finger for him to wait and disappeared for a moment. When she returned, she handed him a piece of paper with a phone number on it.

"There's my cell phone number." Her voice was calm, flat, and noncommittal.

"Okay. Thanks." Ty took the paper as Allison shut the door. He lingered for a moment outside the door. As he walked away, Ty wondered what he was thinking by showing up at her apartment unannounced. What could she give him? She had lost everything. He knew he should feel selfish for what he had just done, but for the first time in a while, he felt a slight sense of relief.

CHAPTER 17

Tina sat at the large farm table in the kitchen sipping a glass of expensive Chardonnay. Her husband, Mark, stood by the six-burner Wolf stove holding a spatula as he pan-fried sole. A covered casserole dish with green beans amandine rested on the counter. Their six-year-old daughter Ashley sat between them in a wheelchair specially designed for children with cerebral palsy, with a tray like a high chair. The girl's head lolled to one side. The sounds of two older girls singing a pop song in another room drifted into the kitchen.

"You're not listening," Tina said.

"I am listening," Mark said. Between him and his wife, an air of tension. This palpable, almost visible wall had been growing for months now, adding a sharp and clipped edge to their words, making their conversations strained. But they were still married; they were still roommates. They needed at the very least to relay information about the children and their own schedules.

Mark's schedule had become a lot less complicated. He'd lost his job as an architect when the Michigan economy cratered. He was now home full-time, and his initial flurry of job hunting had waned to nothing. Few job seekers were as unattractive in the market as an architect. Builder maybe. So Mark had shifted his energies to their three daughters. He helped the older girls get ready for middle school and then took Ashley to day care in the morning. In the afternoon, Mark was home with Ashley until the older girls returned home on the school bus. His plan had been to get in shape during his free time in the morning, but as often as not he returned to bed and slept the morning away. He didn't have the energy. Just listening to Tina seemed to require more energy than he had.

"Michelle Robidaux has a single bad outcome — something that could have happened to any of us — and they're going to ruin her career."

"Shit happens," Mark said. "Wasn't that what you told me when Richter and Griffin sent me packing?"

"Mark!" Tina motioned toward Ashley, who banged on her tray.

"Sorry. Didn't you say she was having trouble anyway?" Mark asked.

"That's not the point, Mark," Tina said in a tone that was both cold and condescending. "The hospital is supposed to stand by its people."

They had been married for fifteen years, and he seemed to Tina to be willfully ignorant of the way medicine worked. He had his head in the sand. No wonder he'd had no clue he was going to get canned when his firm needed to tighten the belt.

"I really don't think you listen to me. You hear what I'm telling you, obviously, but are you really listening? We're talking about a young doctor here. I think you're in your own world. Hospitals are supposed to protect their people, not toss them when there are problems," Tina said, with emphasis as though that might help her get through to her husband.

Tina's husband turned to the stove for a moment to flip the fish. His mouth was closed and his gaze was fixed on the pan. She could see the masseter muscle flexing on his jaw. He paused a second and then turned back to Tina and pointed the spatula at her, his voice now erupting with anger.

"Wives and mothers are supposed to stand by their people, too."

"Excuse me?"

"How well have you stood by your husband? Or your children? It has been an incredibly difficult year. We've had our troubles. We're having trouble, and where are you?"

"Mark, what are you talking about?"

"You're never here. I can't even reach you when I need to."

Ashley banged on her tray again and made a keening noise. Tina looked at her daughter, then Mark, but said nothing.

"Any nurse or resident or physician can reach you all hours of the day, any day of the week, but I couldn't get hold of you at the hospital most days if my life depended on it."

"Where is this coming from?" Tina asked.

Ashley knocked one of the toys off her tray, and Mark reached down to pick it up. He had tears of frustration in his eyes when he stood up.

"Where did it come from? Right here. It comes from me," he said.

Again, Mark went back to the stove. He turned the burner off and walked to the doorway.

"Madison. Mackenzie. Dinner," he called.

Tina looked at him, her lips pursed, with

an expression suggesting indifference.

Mark grabbed a stack of plates and quickly set them around the table, not looking at Tina as he slammed a plate down in her spot. Mark grabbed paper napkins, forks, and knives and put them around the table. He then went to the stove and placed the fish on a serving platter.

Tina and Mark were glowering at each other when the two teenage girls burst into the room. The moment they entered the kitchen they saw the tension between their parents.

"What's for dinner?" Mackenzie asked. Madison walked over to the stove and peered into the frying pan.

"Gross. Fish? Again," Madison added.

"That's rude, Madison," Tina said. Her voice was calm. "Apologize to your father."

"Sorry, Dad. But it is gross."

"That's it — go to your room," Tina said. "Go to your room, now."

"Mom!"

"It's all right," Mark said, looking at his wife. "All things considered, it's a relatively small slight." Tina glowered.

The older girls looked from their father to their mother and sat down to dinner. Their eyes downcast, they began eating in silence. With tears streaming down her smooth cheeks, Mackenzie stopped eating and looked up.

"It tastes good, Dad," Mackenzie said.

"Thanks," Mark said. His voice was flat.

"Is everything going to be okay?" Mackenzie asked, her voice now breaking with sobs. The question caused Madison to start crying. Ashley banged on her tray. The question hung in the air for a moment. Mark said nothing. He turned to Tina as though he, too, wanted an answer.

Tina turned to the girls.

"Don't be ridiculous, Mackenzie," Tina said in a voice as soothing as she could make it. "You'll see someday. Marriage is . . ." She paused. "Marriage is not always easy, but your father and I love each other." Tina spoke almost as though she was trying to convince herself. "Come here. You, too, Madison."

The girls walked over to their mother. She turned in her chair and opened her arms. The girls folded their lanky bodies into Tina's embrace. Mark watched, lips pursed, as their two daughters bent and nuzzled with their mother.

CHAPTER 18

Paramedics rushed through the swinging doors of the ER. They had the distinctive look of panic on their faces. Lying on the stretcher was an elderly woman, her blood-soaked blouse ripped open. A small white sweater had been sheared from her body, and now lay tattered at the end of the gurney. Her polyester brown pants were covered with splotches of blood. Patches of adhesive gauze, serving as a chest seal, did little to close the gaping wound across her chest. There was a distinctive sucking sound coming from her right rib cage. Blood speckled her white hair and face and pooled on the gurney next to her frail, limp body. One of the paramedics squeezed the bag end of a breathing tube protruding from the elderly woman's mouth while desperately trying to hold pressure on the chest gauze.

"Sweet Jesus," Villanueva muttered from his stool. "Eight!" he called to the EMTs, and they rushed toward the back of the emergency room where the Code Team was waiting. His eyes were quickly scanning, and he didn't like what he saw. A flail chest, pale limbs, and no obvious movements from her arms or legs.

"Eighty-two," he muttered to himself. The elderly woman's heart was still beating, but the rhythm was weak and irregular.

Villanueva rocketed off the stool and met the paramedics at the trauma bay. He grabbed a penlight from a nurse walking by, flipped back the elderly woman's eyelids, and started looking at her pupils.

"Hang in there," he said.

The chief resident started calling orders almost as fast as the words could come out of his mouth. "Eighty-two-year-old with a shotgun blast to the right chest. Hemodynamically unstable with a flail chest and near complete exsanguination at the scene. Two bags of LR hanging. We are out of time people, let's go!" he shouted. Two residents, nurses, techs working fast: running a central line, starting a blood transfusion, getting the blood gases, getting the epinephrine and atropine just in case she went from V-fib to asystole — flat line.

Villanueva stepped back, shaken. He grabbed the sleeve of one of the EMTs.

"What'd you bring me?"

"Shotgun, close range," the EMT said. "It was her grandson that pulled the trigger."

"Sweet Jesus," Villanueva said again. "And I didn't get you anything." It was a standard Villanueva retort, but this time it wasn't delivered with the usual verve.

The EMT pointed across the ER. "He's right over there. He did Grandma then shot himself with a thirty-eight."

Villanueva looked at the wiry young man in the trauma bay. His skin was ashen. His upper lip was split on either side of his mouth in what forensic pathologists called "devil's horns," caused by the intense gases from the muzzle blast pushing out through the mouth. Villanueva also noticed a teardrop inked below his remaining, left eye.

"Piece of shit," Villanueva said, his anger spiking as he looked from the old woman to the young man. He started rushing toward the man, his nostrils flaring, picking up speed. "I am going to strangle that piece of shit."

He nearly ran over a nurse who jumped back the way you might jump back from a rampaging bull. As he reached the huddle of doctors and nurses around the young man, a petite resident stepped in his path

226

and held her hands up, cringing with the impact she expected any moment.

"Dr. Villanueva, he's dead. No EEG activity." Villanueva stopped, processing the information. "The organ harvest team has already been notified."

Protocol called for observing the patient for twelve hours before his organs could be removed. Villanueva looked again at the man. From his new vantage point, closer and lower to the man, he could see the exit wound, hidden beneath his long, greasy hair just above his right temporal lobe. A large chunk of his skull had been shot away. He noticed something else: A swastika tattoo adorned his right shoulder.

"Get him out of here," Villanueva said. His anger was returning in force.

The neurologist had arrived in the ER, Dr. Susan Nguyen, and she ambled up to the man.

"Dr. Villanueva, a moment with the patient, if I may."

"He's not a patient. He's a piece of shit." Villanueva stood his ground.

"George. I need to take a look," she said more forcefully.

He moved fast, and was up in her face in a split second. She covered her face and head, worried she was going to get hit, and several people braced and gasped. He stopped himself, squinted hard at her, and then turned away. "No. He's brain-dead, and I don't need a friggin' neurologist to tell me that.

"Just get him out of here and out of my sight," he yelled for good measure. Then, to himself, he added, "Find a nice dark hole he can wait in until the transplant people can get to him, and he can maybe do some good."

Villanueva watched as a pair of orderlies wheeled the man out of the ER into a hallway that led to the main hospital building. Dr. Nguyen was still standing in the ER. "You have no idea if he is a candidate for organ donation, Jorge! For crying out loud, we don't even know if he really is brain-dead."

But Villanueva was already walking back into the middle of the ER. When he turned back to Trauma Bay 8, it was clear the old woman had died, her skin already gray. Nurses gently removed the various tubes and monitors that had invaded her body. Villanueva took off his glasses and rubbed his eyes hard. He walked and stumbled back to his stool, looking back over his shoulder a few times at the elderly woman, now being transported to the morgue.

Sitting on the stool, staring into the distance, Villanueva was suddenly transported to the small town where he grew up. He could almost see the looks of fear, or disgust, or pure hate his family got sometimes as they ambled down the town's main street. Just for being there. His father's one luxury was to take the family to The Family Diner on Main Street after Mass on Sundays, when he wasn't working. Even as a boy five or six years old, George could see the narrowed eyes, the looks of disapproval, as his mother and father walked with him and his two sisters from church. For what? Because their skin was darker than folks whose grandparents had grown up in Dexter, whose ancestors had traveled west from Germany or Denmark or England to settle in this small town in a state they, too, probably couldn't pronounce when they arrived. Even fellow Catholics who turned to George's family in church and shook their hands with a smile and a "peace be with you" seemed to have a change of attitude outside the dark, brick church with its dusty smell and muted light.

Villanueva's own grandfather was a Mexican from the state of Durango. His father, George's great-grandfather, had been a miner in El Palmito and died in his forties when he was kicked by a horse. George never met his grandfather. He dropped dead in his fifties, when George was just a baby, and Villanueva had no idea how he decided to settle in southeastern Michigan. He worked as a blacksmith in the few years that remained before repairing wagon wheels and shoeing horses became irrelevant. Then he worked as a laborer, finally landing a job as a janitor at the local high school.

At the diner, George would order the Big Breakfast Special, and his *Papi* would joke with the waitress about his son's appetite. "Soon, the chickens will have to work overtime to keep up with this boy," or "You sure you got enough food back there?" He would make these comments proudly. He was the provider, and his son was quickly becoming a big, strong kid.

When George was a teenager, and some freakish combination of genes and chance turned him into a hulking figure, things changed for the Villanuevas. Sports was a big deal in Dexter, and being a football star conferred status on the entire family. His father would be greeted by those who had previously ignored him: "How's the team looking?" "How's George feeling?" "Tell him to eat his Wheaties for Friday night's game! I hear Pius is strong this year."

George himself had transformed from the colossal kid of an immigrant slaughterhouse worker to someone the town, including the local police, wanted to look out for and take care of. When he and his football buddies would throw a post-game beer party that got out of control, a local cop named Pederson would arrive and tell them to keep it down and that they'd all be spending the night right there.

"Call your parents. I know everyone here is drunk. I'm going to be waiting just down the road. Anyone tries to leave is getting arrested."

It didn't hurt that Pederson was a big football fan and wanted to make sure George was always healthy for the upcoming games. Nowadays Villanueva spent a lot of time taking care of drunk teenagers who wrecked their own cars, but didn't have a Pederson looking out for them. Ultimately, George graduated from high school and made the town proud by starring at Michigan and then playing in the NFL. Even to this day, ESPN would show highlight clips from a few of his days in the big leagues. If one of those clips aired on the TV in the ER waiting room, nurses and doctors would gather around. They would cheer as George lumbered in front of the running back on a sweep or defended the quarterback from rushing defenders. Gato, never a stranger to attention, could often be found in the middle of the crowd gesticulating wildly and loudly narrating exactly what had happened during that particular game.

Still, the Big Cat never completely got over the slurs and slights he heard and felt as a child: When the white children didn't invite him to their birthday parties or play with him on the playground. When they didn't want to eat food he had touched or come over to his house.

There was one incident that burned into George's memory. When he was six, the meatpacking plant held a special day for its workers. There were pony rides and carnival games. The company also sent its Hot Dog Hot Rod from the headquarters in Madison, Wisconsin. It was a bun-colored sports car decked out with a giant red hot dog above its Space Age cockpit. A driver in a special uniform was taking the children of plant workers for a spin around town. Young George waited for almost an hour for his turn. As he was about to get in the car, a boy in George's grade named Steve ran up and tried to cut the line.

"I'm next," George protested.

"He's been waiting," the driver said,

shrugging.

"I didn't know they let wetbacks in the Hot Dog Hot Rod," Steve said.

George didn't find out until later what a wetback was, but he knew he was being insulted and he knew it had something to do with his heritage. Worse than the comment itself was the driver's reaction. He laughed and gave another shrug as though he couldn't agree more, but what was he going to do. The ride was ruined for George, and his radar for ethnic slights was fine-tuned from that day on.

Seeing the white supremacist arrive in Chelsea General Emergency Department, his Emergency Department, was like someone pulling off the scab on those childhood insults and rejections. He was relieved to see the man wheeled away. Even in that moment, Villanueva was self-aware enough to realize that he had acted out of passion and not reason, and he hoped it wouldn't come back to bite him on the ass.

CHAPTER 19

Sung Park's wife, Pat, and his two daughters flanked the gurney as the anesthesiologist pushed Park down the hallway. The wheels squeaked on the freshly waxed linoleum. The IV bag of Lactated Ringer's hanging from a pole swayed with the tall anesthesiologist's steps. Park was the first elective surgery of the day.

Pat Park rested a hand on her husband's left shoulder and said nothing. Each daughter held one of Park's hands, which were pinned to his sides by the gurney's railings. His five-year-old daughter Emily's eyes were red from crying but she tried to put on a brave face, her lower lip quivering with the effort.

Park's two-year-old son Peter was home with a neighbor's teenage daughter, who would take him to a church preschool, happily unaware of his father's tenuous condition.

Sedated but awake, Sung Park lay on his back in his hospital gown, looking up at the fluorescent lights. Under the effects of the anxiolytic Versed, Park wasn't focused on the operation. He was thinking that the lights passing overhead looked like stripes on the highway. He also wondered if the hospital should consider painting the ceiling a more soothing color, as it was the only thing a patient, lying flat on his back, could see. Might make for an interesting controlled study, he thought to himself. He, too, said nothing.

Pushing the gurney, Dr. Reginald Culbreath broke the silence. Culbreath's name was on the list of doctors Park had presented to Hooten the day before, along with the neurosurgical resident Aisha Ali, circulating nurse Melinda Brown, and scrub nurse La-Tanya Scott. Culbreath was a tall, pear-shaped, African American doctor with a taste for jazz and bad jokes.

"All right, Sung," he said. "Time to see how the other half lives." He patted the shoulder not taken by Pat Park's small hand. Park had never been admitted to the hospital, never broken a bone, never been to the emergency room. He had never even called in sick. He truly had no idea how the other half lived, and lying on the gurney was giving him a new perspective. Park himself hardly ever entered the operating room until the patient was already under general anesthesia. He wondered to himself if that might change, after this experience. Before he was sedated, he bridled at the sensation of not being in control, of relying on others. Now, flat on his back, high on the anti-anxiety med Versed, he didn't care much one way or the other.

As Culbreath turned the final corner toward the OR, Park still said nothing. Park had done plenty of glioblastomas. He knew firsthand what a daunting surgical challenge he posed for Harding Hooten. For one thing, the extent of the malignant gliomas often extended beyond what showed up on MRIs. They were nasty invasive cancers whose rubbery tentacles often invaded the surrounding tissue. They were like the vine that overwhelmed the trees and fences along Northern highways, he thought. He made a mental note to remember this analogy the next time he spoke about glioblastomas, but he knew the sedative made it unlikely he would. At some other level, he knew he might never teach again. He knew this would devastate him, but in the narcotic cloud he didn't care.

Lying awake in his bed at home a couple

of hours earlier, Park had felt a spike of fear as he pondered his prognosis. As if the presence of a fast-moving cancer in his brain were not enough, malignant glioblastomas attacked a person's very nature: potentially affecting personality, speech, learning, memory, cognitive ability. Park had briefly considered suicide as a logical response to his diagnosis. A glioblastoma was like a checkmate, Park had thought. You're trapped. Nowhere to go. Game over. But Park was not a quitter. Resolve seemed to be part of his fabric, what he was made of, so he would fight this cancer.

Park knew the median survival rate for a tumor like his was 73.4 weeks. He hadn't given his wife the statistics, but she had been married to a brain surgeon long enough to know that his diagnosis almost certainly meant their life together would be measured in months, maybe years, but not decades. He was grateful Pat handled the family finances already. There would not be much for her to learn when he was gone. He had reviewed the paperwork in a folder at the back of his filing cabinet. He remembered when he and his wife had sat down with a lawyer during the third trimester of Pat's pregnancy. They had methodically filled out the papers creating a will. At one point, the lawyer had asked Park, "What do you want to happen if you are in a terminal condition?" Park had stared hard at the lawyer and said, "Sir, we are all in a terminal condition." He thought he was being a tough guy who could stare death in the face and never blink. Truth was, he had been brave because he never imagined being in the scenario the lawyer had been trying to describe. He felt a tear well up, but didn't want to take his hands away from his daughters. He casually turned his head and wiped the tear away with the pillow edge.

The gurney reached the end of the hallway. A large sign on the double doors read: SURGICAL PERSONNEL ONLY BEYOND THIS POINT. Culbreath turned to Park's wife and children.

"End of the line. You're going to have to stop here, Pat." Most family members didn't get to escort their loved one down the hallway between Pre-Op and the operating room, but Culbreath had called them back and let them walk with Sung to the OR.

"Thanks, Reggie," Pat said.

Park's wife bent over and kissed her husband on the forehead, then turned away from the gurney so her husband and children could not see her cry.

"We love you, Daddy," Natalie, the younger of his daughters, called as the gurney went through the double doors where Harding Hooten was already scrubbing in, with his surgical loupes and headlamp clamped around his head.

Sung tipped his head back to answer, but he was already through the doors.

As Sung Park was heading into the operating room, Tina Ridgeway was standing in an examination room at The Free Clinic, a mile and a half away on a map but a world away in every other sense. Chelsea General stood as the town's most venerable landmark, its original six-story brick building proudly facing the street and now ringed on three sides by an ever-expanding constellation of enormous additions and parking decks in styles and materials reflecting the tastes of their day. Altogether, the campus — as administrators liked to call it — covered more than six blocks and a hundred acres, and the buildings and decks were connected by a web of tunnels and elevated walkways. The Free Clinic, on the other hand, was a low, squat concrete building, a former print shop between a fast-food chicken restaurant and a discount store. Inside, the carpet was frayed, and makeshift exam rooms were stocked with volunteer doctors and donated supplies. She hadn't told Hooten yet — heck, she hadn't even told Ty — but she wanted to leave her job at the most preeminent medical institution in the country and use her skills here. Sure, she was a neurosurgeon, but she could provide many of the medical services so dramatically needed, yet woefully unavailable.

Tina checked the blood sugar reading on her patient, a Darryl Leggett. It was off the charts.

"Your blood sugar's pretty high, Mr. Leggett. Right around three hundred. What's going on?"

"Couldn't afford test strips." He looked down at his feet, a little embarrassed. "Been rolling the dice the last couple days, I guess."

"What about your medicine?" Tina asked as she unlocked a cabinet and pulled out a vial of insulin and a syringe.

"C'mon, Doc. How can I afford that if I can't even get the strips?"

"Why'd you come in today?"

"My eyes started getting a little blurry."

Tina handed her patient a glass of water as she gave him an injection. Tina disposed of the spent syringe and turned to him.

"We've got insulin. We've got test strips.

You run out, Mr. Leggett, you come here."

"All right, Doc, and thank you. So much."

She smiled at Darryl. *Thank you* — it wasn't something she was used to hearing.

At The Free Clinic, Tina came alive. There was hardly any paperwork, no departmental politics, no bureaucracy; there were no lawyers, little protocol. It was simply her knowledge and skill as a doctor pitted against an incredible array of medical problems that walked or hobbled or wheeled through the door, most of them festering for too long — because the patient either couldn't afford to take care of them or couldn't afford to miss work or couldn't get a ride or didn't know where to go. Sometimes, Tina suspected, her patients at The Free Clinic delayed their visit because they had internalized the belief that they and — by extension — their health problems simply didn't matter in the greater scheme of things.

Patients she saw put off being treated for almost everything. After Mr. Leggett left, a fifty-year-old woman named Patty Steinkuhler arrived with five teeth rotten to the gumline. From Tina's experience at The Free Clinic, teeth were dead last when it came to health priorities. Tina called an oral surgeon who had agreed to take a couple of cases a month from the clinic.

A Salvadoran infant with a high fever was next. *Bring it on,* Tina thought. *I can do this, and I can make a difference.* For some reason, this made her think of home. With Mark, Tina wasn't sure anything would make a difference anymore. The older girls, too, seemed increasingly remote. They went to Mark with their issues. The sad thing was, Tina was gone so much she wasn't exactly sure what their issues were. Tina made a mental note to spend some one-on-one time with them. Her thought was interrupted by what she saw through the clinic's plate-glass window: an old man clutching his chest.

"Come on," Tina said to DeShawn, who managed the clinic. The two of them ran out the door. Tina was exhilarated.

CHAPTER 20

The transplant team arrived in Earl Jasper's room in the Neuro Intensive Care Unit exactly eleven hours and fifty-nine minutes after he had left Chelsea General's emergency room on Dr. George Villanueva's orders.

Jasper, the white supremacist who had killed his grandmother, remained motionless in the large mechanized bed. He was attached to monitors that showed his heartbeat and blood oxygen levels. A hose from Jasper's mouth led to a large ventilator on the other side of his bed. The machine exhaled with a loud whoosh every few seconds, causing Jasper's torso to rise. A monitor registered a tone each time the ventilator breathed for Jasper. The goal was fourteen breaths a minute, with a tidal volume of seven hundred. Other than the machine, there was none of the usual activity that surrounded a patient in an ICU.

A police officer dozed on a chair in the corner of the room. Until Jasper was pronounced dead, he was officially wanted for first-degree murder. The officer was not supposed to leave Jasper's side, but deeming him a low flight risk, he had spent much of his time, when he wasn't sleeping, at the nurses' station and the cafeteria. The peach cobbler, he found, was excellent.

Nurses on the ward had greeted Jasper's arrival early that morning with a mixture of chagrin and disbelief. It was as though someone had keyed their car, or someone's dog had taken a crap on their lawn. Many of the nurses were African American, and having a neo-Nazi in their midst posed an ethical challenge. As the morning shift arrived, they huddled in the nurses' station with the overnight crew. They wondered aloud about whether they were somehow condoning his worldviews if they treated him decently, or treated him at all. They also considered the consequences of denying Jasper care. Was that the right thing to do? Would that force him to be transferred to a different hospital? Or would they simply get fired?

As they were hashing out these issues, the hospital's chief of nursing Nancy Woldridge arrived unannounced, interrupting their nascent plotting. Woldridge was a tall, rail-thin white woman with coiffed white hair. She walked with a pronounced limp from a childhood bicycle accident. The nurses gathered around Woldridge at the semicircular nursing station, arms crossed, lips pursed, expressions sullen. They did not like management coming down to tell them what they had to do, especially when it involved a racist cracker like Earl Jasper.

"I'm not going to require anyone here to care for that man in there," Woldridge began, her voice carrying just the hint of a Southern accent. The nurses looked at one another, surprised.

"He's going to be lonely," one of the nurses quipped. They all laughed, even Woldridge. When the laughing died down, Woldridge continued, looking at each nurse as she spoke.

"You nurses are among the best we have here at Chelsea General. You deal with very complicated patients and you do it very, very well. You're also professionals with a capital *P*." Woldridge paused for a moment.

"I'm not going to force any of you to care for the patient in there," Woldridge said again. "But I'm hoping I can count on your professionalism. I'm hoping I can count on the pride you take in how well you do the hundreds of little things that make you such outstanding nurses. I am not going to force anyone here to take care of that man, but I'm hoping I can get volunteers. I'm not asking you to like him, or to understand him, or even respect him." Woldridge paused. "I'm hoping you are willing to care for him."

Woldridge's thin face turned from one nurse to another. "But let me see a show of hands on who is willing to not only care for him, but give him the best care you are capable of. The kind of care you'd give to a member of your own family. Anyone who does, I think, will be showing how much better you are than he is."

Woldridge looked around for a show of hands. The nurses looked at one another. Finally, the head nurse, Nicki Hampton, raised her hand. Then a second nurse, and a third. Finally all the nurses raised their hands.

"Thank you. You make me proud," Woldridge said. She shook each of their hands, thanking them by name, and then she limped down the hall toward the elevator.

As a result of Woldridge's speech, when chief transplant surgeon Dr. John Magee approached Jasper's bedside, he found a patient with a head wound that had been immaculately dressed and wrapped. Looking at him, you wouldn't know Jasper was loathed by everyone in the ward.

Even with the neatly wrapped bandages, though, it was obvious that part of the right side of Jasper's head was missing. Bandages also covered his missing right eye, and a silastic catheter drained blood-tinged fluid from his brain.

"Is he ready to go?" Magee asked. He was short and stocky, with an annoyed look. He was already dressed in scrubs with a book of transplant protocols under his arm. On his walk over to the ICU, he had called the operating room to make sure his instruments and team were at the ready.

"I think so," said Nicki Hampton. "Let me just ask our resident, Dr. Robidaux." The final exam to confirm that he was brain-dead needed to be done. Hampton walked away as Magee did nothing to hide his impatience.

Michelle Robidaux approached the patient the way a zookeeper might approach a hissing cobra. It was obvious she had never done this before. Magee stood with his arms folded, drumming the fingers of his right hand on his left forearm.

"Take your time," the transplant surgeon said. "You don't want to startle him with any sudden movements." Hampton covered a laugh with her hand. Others in the room weren't as polite.

"Mr. Jasper. I'm Dr. Robidaux, can you open your eye?" she said as though she were calling to someone behind a closed door. Magee threw his hands up. Other doctors on the team shook their heads.

"Look, can you speed this up. We have six patients around the country waiting for these organs."

Looking unnerved, Michelle leaned over Jasper and opened his left eyelid. She shined a penlight into the eye from an inch away.

"Left pupil fixed and dilated." She then lifted the man's limp arm and pinched the base of his fingernail. Jasper made no attempt to pull his hand away.

"No response to pain stimulus."

Magee rolled his eyes and snickered. A flustered Michelle approached Jasper and shouted in his ear.

"Mr. Jasper, if you can hear me, hold up two fingers."

"Oh come on," Magee drawled to more laughter from the assembled group.

Jasper's right arm went up, two fingers extended. The laughter died. The police officer in the corner sat bolt-upright.

"Whoa," Michelle said. She was so startled

she had jumped back away from Jasper as though she had raised the dead herself. For a split second — before logic regained control of her consciousness — she wondered if she had invoked some sort of Louisiana voodoo.

Jasper had the scratchy blue ink of a prison tattoo on the fingers of each hand. The left hand spelled love, one letter on each finger: L-O-V-E. The right hand spelled hate: H-A-T-E. Robidaux noticed the blue ink on the two fingers Jasper extended — the index and middle fingers — spelled H-A.

Michelle let her breathing return to normal and then leaned close to Jasper once again. "All right, Mr. Jasper. How about three fingers?"

His arm still aloft, the patient lowered his index finger until only his middle finger was raised. He was flipping the bird at the assembled medical team.

Magee's face reddened. Without a word, he turned and left the room.

"Next time you want the transplant team, make sure your fucking patient is dead," he said.

Michelle had recovered from her shock and was now almost giddy.

"We almost removed this man's heart, his kidneys, his liver, his left cornea — and he is actually still alive," she said. She paused for a moment. "Who declared him brain-dead in the first place?"

"Well, El Gato sent him up here," said Hampton, the nurse. "Don't know what neurologist saw him."

CHAPTER 21

Tina Ridgeway was standing in the lobby of
Chelsea General answering a resident's
question about surgical versus nonsurgical
approaches for Parkinson's disease when
Buck Tierney, the chief of cardiothoracic
surgery, strutted through the main entrance
with the hospital CEO, Morgan Smith.
Tierney always strutted rather than walked,
chest out, chin up, like some sort of rooster,
but now he was grinning from ear to ear,
slapping Smith on the back like they were
fraternity brothers at Michigan on the way
to the big game.

Tina looked around for some sort of
explanation for this ebullience. She didn't
trust Tierney and his outsized ego. If he was
showboating with the CEO, something was
up. Out of the corner of her eye, Tina saw
the chief of medicine, Dr. Nicholas Brenkovski, heading for the elevator.

"Excuse me," she said to the resident and

half walked, half ran to catch up with him. Tina was friends with Brenkovski and his wife. They each had a house near South Beach in Edgartown, on Martha's Vineyard, and would sometimes have each over for cocktails and boiled lobster. Tina caught him just before he got on the elevator.

"Nick, could I have a word?"

The two doctors stepped out of the stream of traffic heading to and from the elevator.

"Tina, how are you?" Even though he had been in the United States for more than twenty years, Nick retained a trace of his Russian accent.

"Nick, I just saw Buck Tierney and Morgan Smith walk in the hospital looking like a couple of lovebirds. You seem to know everything that happens around here. What's going on?"

"Tina, you haven't heard? Our friend Buck has convinced Morgan to build a new, forty-million-dollar cardiac care wing. He will run it by the board, but it looks like a done deal. We will be *the* cardiac hospital of the state, maybe the region."

"But how did he pull that off?"

By all accounts, Whitfield Bradford Tierney III lived a charmed life. Chelsea General's chief of cardiothoracic surgery was a square-shouldered, square-jawed former football star known to all as Buck, the nickname he'd received when he bagged a five-point buck a few weeks before his sixth birthday. Buck Tierney had been named Michigan's outstanding high school athlete in 1970 and had gone on to play quarterback for the University of Michigan. From Michigan and a Rose Bowl win, he had gone on to Wayne State University Medical School, married a former Miss Ann Arbor, and had three picture-perfect children as he built a reputation as a top-notch surgeon. Buck had also remained in good shape, something he shrugged off when people mentioned it, but which he worked hard at in his fully equipped basement gym.

Even in his fifties, Buck looked like he could strap on the helmet and hold his own on the football field. When he wasn't performing heart surgery, Tierney had applied his considerable athletic prowess to golf. As a result, he was a scratch golfer, or pretty close to it.

Buck Tierney honed his golfing skills at the old Lake Club, which was less well known than Augusta but at least as exclusive. The joke was if you didn't know which lake — and there were plenty in the area — you couldn't join. Tierney was one of the club's 150 members. The roster was a who's who of Michigan's old money elite. The CEOs of Ford and GM were known to be members, prizing the club's exclusivity and the course laid out around gorgeous Cavanaugh Lake. That Tierney, who came from an old Chelsea family, received an invitation to join when he was a young surgeon just getting his practice going was a testament to how effortlessly he moved in society's rarefied circles. A benefactor who was a big college football fan covered his dues for the first five years, and the dues could be substantial. It all depended on what sort of maintenance and upkeep were required at the club. Some years, members were assessed eight thousand dollars. Other years, they were assessed eighty thousand. The bill was simply the club's expenses divided by 150. As the saying went, if you had to ask . . .

Another of the club's members was Morgan Smith, the hospital CEO and the club's first African American member. Before signing on to run the hospital, Smith had made a fortune with a politically connected investment firm that catered to Detroit's African American elite. His move to the hospital was viewed as the first step in a political career. Smith also loved golf, but he was a rotund man without Tierney's physical gifts. Smith had spent his college days in the library, sweating out accounting, business administration, marketing, and the like when he wasn't waiting tables. Smith was lucky if his golf score broke ninety, and that was with a couple of mulligans.

The two men would run into each other Saturday mornings in the clubhouse, and the chiseled Tierney would always invite the corpulent Smith to join him for a round. Smith would accept, and they would play a pleasant eighteen on what *Golf Digest* called "The Best Unknown Golf Course in America."

Before a recent Saturday outing, Tierney had taken the unusual step of calling Smith on a Wednesday to arrange a golf date. Smith was surprised, curious, maybe even a little suspicious, but he jumped at any opportunity to spend eighteen holes with Tierney. He always enjoyed a chance to absorb some of the legendary Buck Tierney's skills. So when the cardiac surgeon paused on the fourth tee, a 480-yard monster with a dogleg left, Smith was not surprised.

"You know, Morgan, I'm not getting any younger." Tierney teed up his ball and launched a three-hundred-yard rocket down the fairway.

"Could have fooled me," Smith said, laughing.

"Well, a man gets to be my age, he starts thinking about his legacy."

"Don't we all," Smith said.

Smith teed his ball up, swung hard, and sent a ground ball skittering past a magnificent pine tree and into some thick underbrush.

"Take another one, Morgan. Try pausing at the top of your backswing."

Smith put down another ball, followed Tierney's direction and launched a high, straight drive down the fairway.

"Will you look at that," Smith said.

"Not bad," Tierney said, chuckling. They climbed in the cart. "As I was saying, I've been thinking about what will survive me, not only with my kids, but at the hospital."

"Okay," Smith said neutrally.

"Been talkin' to some folks." Tierney stopped the cart before they'd reached Smith's drive. "I'll put my cards on the table, Morgan. I think I can raise twenty million for a new cardiac wing. Do you think you can get the board to match that? Make Chelsea General the premier heart hospital in the Midwest."

Smith took off his Lake Club cap and

wiped his brow with his forearm. He was smiling.

"I don't see why not."

"Course, if you could see it in your heart to make it the Whitfield Bradford Tierney the Third Center for Cardiac Care, I would be grateful."

"That's a mouthful."

"Has kind of a nice ring to it, don't you think?"

"Hell, no one will know that's you."

"What are you suggesting?"

"How about the Buck Tierney Center for Cardiac Care?"

"Now you're talkin', Morgan." Tierney chuckled, pushed down on the gas, and the cart moved down the fairway.

Back at the hospital the following week, Smith had scheduled a meeting of the board. Tierney and Smith were returning from an off-site meeting with the heads of marketing and public relations when Tina saw them and then rushed to catch up with Brenkovski. The news had hit her like a slap.

"Tina, you do not look happy about this," Brenkovski said.

"I know cardiac care is a profitable service line, Nick, but don't you think this will suck the air out of the room? If we're solely a cardiac hospital, what does that mean for the rest of our patients, especially the ones who aren't as well off? We're not going to be investing much in anything else," Tina said.

Brenkovski shrugged. Tina realized a tirade would be misplaced. So much seemed to be going in the wrong direction these days. There was the lawsuit facing the resident Michelle Robidaux, and Mark's outburst at home; even her friend Ty Wilson seemed distant these days.

"It's just one more thing," she added. A cloud had crossed her usually implacable facade.

"My dear Tina. Do not fret." He grabbed her by the shoulders. "Relax. Maybe take a weekend with Mark somewhere. Life is good."

"Thanks," Tina said and walked away, unconvinced.

Later that day, Tina stood at The Free Clinic holding the stethoscope to the muscled, stooped back of a patient who told her simply to call him "Rise — like the sun." He was her final patient of the day. Tina had not taken Brenkovski's advice and escaped with Mark. She didn't need a weekend away with him. The Free Clinic was all the escape she needed, and she found herself spending more and more time there.

After learning about the new cardiac wing, she called DeShawn, the clinic manager, to see how it was going. He told her the place was swamped. A young resident was covering for the first time, and things had gotten backed up. It was also Friday rush — folks who didn't want to spend the weekend sick. Tina had hurried over.

"All right, Rise. Take a deep breath," Tina said. The man took in a lungful of air through his nose. "Now exhale." Rise continued to hold his breath. "Exhale, Mr., ah, Rise." Rise looked up, confused. "Let out your air." He breathed out.

Tina enjoyed doing her part in offering preventive medicine for many who considered the emergency room their first stop when they got sick. And she liked helping the junior doctor who looked so grateful when she arrived.

However, unlike the stories politicians liked to tell about people showing up in the emergency room with the sniffles, Tina's experience was that these folks waited way too long to get medical care — from the ER or anywhere else. They held the kinds of jobs that didn't pay them if they called in sick. Tina recalled one man in his early forties who had walked in with his infant daughter, and a bulging fibrous growth on the side of his head that had swollen one eye shut.

"Why'd you decide to come in today?" the chief resident had asked as casually as possible.

"I can't see out my eye no more," the man said matter-of-factly.

There was another man who arrived with his testicles swollen to the size of volleyballs as the result of a long-untreated hernia. The chief resident had asked him the same question.

"Couldn't find any jeans that fit."

These were the most blatant cases, but there were others who arrived with stage 4 colon cancer, ignoring the bloody stools they'd experienced for more than a year and only coming in when abdominal cramps started doubling them up with pain. There were others who let teeth become so abscessed, the infection reached their brains.

Cases like these were an open challenge to Tina. She took them to heart. So, while other doctors played golf on Fridays or left early for their homes on Lake Michigan or the Upper Peninsula, she did her part. She realized her efforts were statistically insignificant, but they made her feel better and they did make a difference to the individuals she was able to help. The way Tina saw it, she couldn't *not* help these people.

Tina moved the stethoscope on Rise's back.

"Another deep breath." Her concentration was broken by her pager. It said simply, *311. 6.*

CHAPTER 22

Villanueva was dressed in a slightly rumpled white dress shirt. His thin, 1980s-throwback tie only came to halfway down his torso, and he was wearing an old tweed jacket, the only one he owned that fit him. His thinning hair was slicked back across his head, and he was sweating, even though he was walking at a slow pace to dinner with his son. His pager was going off, but the sound was muffled by the considerable abdominal bulge covering the device when he was upright. The numbers had been flashing *311. 6.* for quite some time. He wasn't on call, and he hadn't been paying attention in the movie theater, where he and Nick had seen the five o'clock show of a horror movie about a man with a brain infection that caused him to commit all sorts of bloody murders. Maybe all the screaming had distracted Villanueva. His son had picked out the movie, just as he had picked out the restaurant, a place that served vegetarian pitas.

Parking was always a problem in this neighborhood, which prided itself in its grungy hipness, so they needed to walk a couple of blocks in the brisk fall air past the organic food store that smelled like an incense factory, and the henna stand that specialized in applying the dye to the protuberant abdomens of young, pregnant women. Villanueva had never heard of the restaurant, but Nick had informed him over the phone that he was now a vegetarian.

"Eating meat, it's bad for the environment. You know how many pounds of grain it takes to make each pound of meat, Dad?" he asked. "And that doesn't even count greenhouse gases cows burp up and fart. They damage the ozone."

Villanueva thought there was something odd about picking a movie where people were getting hacked to death every few minutes and then insisting on a vegetarian restaurant, but he bit his tongue. This night was going to be about Nick.

"Whatever you want, Nick," George said. But he couldn't resist adding, "You think I put a hole in the ozone after that time we ate at Taco Tony's?"

Before picking up his son, Villanueva

made sure he had a foot-long cheesesteak for lunch so he wouldn't be in red meat withdrawal for dinner and a movie. Now, as they walked past a white teenager with dreadlocks, the Big Cat finally looked down at his pager and read the numbers.

"Crap," he said.

"What is it?

"Your dad is going to get his ass handed to him on a silver platter first thing Monday morning."

"You? How come?" Villanueva looked down at his son. To his surprise, he saw that Nick was interested. More than that, his son seemed concerned about what happened to him. George was surprised, touched by the worried look on his son's face. He explained the case of Earl Jasper.

"I let my hatred of this guy cloud my judgment," Villanueva said. "I should have let the neurologist see him and given him the best care possible. And then, I should've strangled him."

Nick looked up, uneasily.

"I'm kidding, Nick," Villanueva added, giving a pat that nearly sent Nick sprawling on the sidewalk.

"Yeah," Nick said, forcing a laugh and tenderly rubbing his shoulder.

They turned the corner into a small

square where white rastas, Dead Heads, and teenage beggars hung out with aging hippies banging on various percussion instruments. Villanueva thought he could smell the dope mixed in with the patchouli oil. *People must be selling drugs by the trunk load down here.*

"What a friggin' circus," Villanueva said.

"It's always like this," Nick said.

"You come down here a lot? Why do you come down here?" Villanueva tried to sound casual but couldn't keep the prosecutorial tone out of his voice.

"Sometimes," Nick answered. As soon as the answer was out of his mouth he amended it: "Not much."

Villanueva was thoughtful for a moment. He realized how much there was about his son he didn't know. His moment of introspection was interrupted by a woman's loud voice.

"Let me be. Get your damn hands offa me."

A small crowd had gathered in their path. An African American woman in her early twenties was trying to pull herself loose from what appeared to be her boyfriend. He was a hard-looking man, also in his early twenties, wearing a green military jacket. Every time she jerked away from him, he'd grabbed her sleeve or her wrist. Each time she tried to free herself from his grasp, he got a little bit rougher.

"Please, K.C. Let me be."

"You're not going anywhere." As he tussled with her, his fist struck her across the cheekbone. She stopped struggling.

Villanueva and his son slowed to take in the scene. For some reason, the man caught Nick staring at him.

"What you looking at?" he asked Nick. His voice was menacing. "I asked you a question." Nick was speechless.

Villanueva walked through the circle of onlookers until he was standing in front of the man. When Nick realized what his father was doing, he regained his voice and called after him.

"Dad." Too late.

The woman and man both looked surprised when they saw Villanueva appear at their sides. Her cheek was red and swelling.

"Who the fuck you think you are, fat man?" the man asked Villanueva.

"She wants to go. Let her go." Villanueva said. He sounded as though he was explaining the most reasonable thing in the world.

"I get it, you think you're Dr. Phil and shit. I have been itching to kick some ass."

The woman looked panicked. She turned

to Villanueva, "You best bugger out. He whacked."

"You want to go," Villanueva said to her. "Go." With that, he stepped between the stunned couple, looking the man in the eye. His girlfriend, if that's who she was, stared for a second and then turned and started walking away fast. After she'd passed the onlookers, she broke into a run. She didn't look back.

The man glared at Villanueva. His jaw muscles bunched.

"You want to get all in my business, mother-fucker," he said. "I should cap your ass right here."

With that, he swept back his fatigue jacket and put his hand on the barrel of a pistol.

"Dad, come on," Nick pleaded from the periphery. He was so scared he had tears in his eyes.

There was a *whoop, whoop* from a police car, and the flashing lights of the cruiser started dancing across the scene. The man removed his hand from his gun and punched Villanueva hard in the chest. Villanueva had braced himself for the blow, which was a lot like a defensive lineman trying to bust through the line. He didn't budge. The man looked at Villanueva, incredulous, doing his malevolent best to look threatening but clearly unnerved. Villanueva stared back.

"All right, let's break it up."

As the patrolman approached, the man broke off his stare and stalked off. Villanueva watched him for a moment and then found Nick in the dispersing crowd.

"Dad, you're crazy."

"I grew up with punks like him."

"I mean it."

Villanueva rubbed his chest. "He packed more of a punch than I thought."

"You could have gotten shot or something."

"And miss a vegetarian dinner with you, Nick?"

"Dad, I'm serious."

They turned the corner and found the small restaurant.

CHAPTER 23

From surgery, they wheeled Park to the Neuro Intensive Care Unit, where an ethnic melting pot of loyal residents hovered around their mentor. Next to the coffeepot and microwave at the nurses' station, one of them had left a box of assorted teas. Earl Grey for the Pakistanis and Indians, green tea for the Koreans, rooibos for the African residents. The residents poured tea, fidgeted, and waited to see how their mentor, the hard straight arrow pointed their way in their adopted country, was faring. They clustered there, talking quietly in their variously accented English, going over all the possible complications and post-operative scenarios for Park. "At least it was well away from Brodmann's area forty-four and forty-six," one resident said professorially. "Yes, but what about the fine motor movements he requires?" said another with a clipped British accent. Still another resident, with choppy English similar to Park's, said, "It all depends on how aggressive Dr. Hooten was. Did he go after all the tumor or did he try to preserve some of Dr. Park's function?" Finally, the nurses shooed them all away.

After nearly twelve hours in the OR, Hooten left the hospital, got in his Volvo, and headed for home. He was completely spent but satisfied he had done everything he could to remove as much of Park's glioblastoma as possible. In the past, he would have left the operating room and returned to his office to finish up some paperwork, but he was bone-tired. He tried to convince himself the added stress of operating on a friend and co-worker had wrung him out, but he knew that wasn't true. There was a point during every surgery — when the lights were on, the blue draping framed the tumor, and his eyes were looking into the large microscope suspended over the patient — that Hooten forgot he was looking at a fellow human. In that small rectangle of flesh, he saw a medical problem, a tumor to be resected, an aneurysm to be clipped. The truth about his fatigue was more elemental. He was simply getting older. He couldn't pull the hours he had when he'd first become chief of surgery at Chelsea General.

Still, he could be proud of his work. Looking through a microscope positioned over a small hole cut in Park's head, Hooten had carefully reached Park's tumor after cutting through the dura and splitting the sylvian fissure. He exposed the middle fossa of the skull and lifted the temporal lobe. Once he had exposed the tumor and separated it from the normal surrounding brain using a combination of bipolar cautery, suction, and small cottonoids, he had used an ultrasonic tissue aspirator to remove bit after tiny bit of his colleague's tumor. To guide him, Hooten used a stereotactic probe that looked like a meat thermometer. The probe had two round reflective balls that a pair of electronic eyes picked up and compared with the three-dimensional MRI image on a screen near the foot of the operating table. By seeing where the probe was relative to the pre-op image of the tumor, Hooten knew where he was. It was like a GPS inside the brain. The tumor also looked different from the tissue around it. It was slightly grayer and more purplish in color. When his eyes and the probe told him he had removed all the tumor possible, Hooten gently handed the instruments back to the nurse. "Head Games" is what the residents called this 3-D navigation system. At first, Hooten

271

had dismissed the new technology as just that — another video game disguised as an intraoperative tool. Over the years, however, he had become quite facile with the device. *For an old dog, I can still learn many new tricks,* he thought to himself. For five minutes, he said nothing, instead just staring through the microscope lens and trickling in very small amounts of irrigation fluid through a small catheter. He was carefully evaluating for any remnant tumor that the imaging technology may have missed, but his experienced eyes could catch. He also searched for any errant drops of red that could be a harbinger of more significant future bleeding in Park's brain. During this five-minute period, no one in the OR made a sound. After he was convinced, he let the chief resident close.

Hooten knew there was more to the glioblastoma than he could see, though. GBMs did not have a defined edge the way some other brain tumors did, and malignant cells lurked beyond what was visible to Hooten as he looked down into the wrinkles and folds of tissue that held the obstinate, determined person the chief of surgery had come to admire. As he drove home listening to the news on CNN, Hooten knew with the dread he always felt after a GBM resection that even if he'd done his best work, he had not gotten all of Park's tumor. Sometimes the small remnants could suddenly swell angrily in response to the insult they had just endured. Some of those remnants could simply remain, hidden for a time, only to suddenly start growing and replicating with a fury.

A story came on from Afghanistan with the latest news on the war on terror, and Hooten reflected that the glioblastoma cells he couldn't see were little different from an al-Qaeda sleeper cell. They lurked unseen in the brain before a violent resurgence. Even with traditional radiation and chemotherapy, the chance of a glioblastoma recurring was 100 percent. The question was not *if* but *when*. Unfortunately for far too many patients, the tumor came back — usually not far from the original spot in the brain — within a matter of months. Patients were lucky if they went a year without a recurrence. The chance of surviving a year with a GBM was a little less than a third. The five-year survival rate was 2 percent, and Hooten suspected those cases had been misdiagnosed.

But doctors had not thrown in the towel against glioblastomas. A new chemo drug seemed to buy patients a little time, and

Hooten had immediately enrolled Park in a clinical trial that might buy him still more. It was a vaccine trial. The tissue from Park's tumor was collected and bagged. Chelsea General would send it off to a lab to make a custom, personalized vaccine. The vaccine would enlist his own immune system to fight his tumor. It was like a red flag to the white blood cells that detected foreign cells. Park would get his first dose in three months.

The vaccine was a weapon also designed to counter another malevolent aspect of GBMs — their ability to turn off the body's natural defenses against tumors and allow them to grow unchecked.

When he was telling medical students about this aspect of glioblastomas, Hooten, the inveterate birder, always likened this sort of perversion to the cuckoo. Female cuckoos lay their eggs in the nest of another bird and leave them for that bird to hatch. Aiding the ruse, cuckoo eggs look like those of the unwitting host bird. The cuckoo eggs then hatch earlier and the chicks grow faster, receiving their food all the while from the other species. This allows for the final insult: The cuckoo chicks, which resemble the species whose nest they have infiltrated, push out the host's eggs or smaller chicks, claiming the nest for themselves.

By shutting off the host body's white blood defenders, GBMs were no less ruthless than the cuckoo. Unlike the cuckoo, though, this wasn't Darwinism taken to the extreme. This was simply a human body being conned into allowing rapidly dividing cells to run amok in the worst possible place, the brain.

When he operated on glioblastoma patients, Hooten was always tempted to take out a larger area of the brain than the MRI and the probe indicated. He might get a few more cancerous cells this way. But Hooten knew this was a fool's errand. Excising more of the brain might reduce the number of tumor cells remaining, but it would increase the chances that Park would not be *Park* when he emerged from the anesthetic fog. Somewhere in the tissue lived an impossibly complicated web of neurons that made up the memory, the personality, the abilities that were the essence of Sung Park. Being overly aggressive also would not lessen the chance of the GBM coming back.

Hooten hoped that given the surgery, then radiation, chemo, and the customized vaccine, Park would have a chance. Maybe this vaccine would be a quantum step forward in GBM treatment. Perhaps Park would be on the side of the divide, one of the lucky ones there when medicine advanced a step in its fight against premature death.

Pat Park arrived after lunch and sat in the waiting area, knitting a gray scarf as she waited for her husband to emerge from surgery. She left at four to pick up her daughters at their after-school music program and then returned to continue her vigil.

When Sung Park was wheeled into Post-Op, the residents cycled through his room, checking his vitals and his chart closely and returning to the family waiting area to tell Pat everything was okay. She was touched, and a bit surprised that so many people cared about her husband. She was crying softly to herself when Hooten walked into the room.

Before leaving the hospital, Hooten had decided to stop by and speak to Pat Park. When he saw her crying, he walked over and gave her a hug. He realized he barely knew the woman. The Parks never attended the holiday party, as Sung had usually offered to take call on those days. Even then, he knew Park had been trying to impress him with his work skills, even at the expense of Pat and the kids. Hooten felt a pang of regret. Truth was, he didn't have much to say, other than the operation had gone as well as could be expected. Hooten was careful not to paint too rosy a picture, although he suspected Park himself had given his wife a clear-eyed view of the operation and his grim prognosis.

Hooten explained that his colleague was lucky — the tumor was in a nondominant area of the brain, meaning Park's chance of losing his speech or ability to understand was slim. The operation had gone seamlessly, and Hooten thought the chances of Park retaining his ability to move and speak were good.

"If you need anything at all, call me," Hooten said. He wrote his home and cell phone numbers on the back of his business card and handed it to Pat. He finally walked out, feeling more exhausted than he could ever remember.

Chapter 24

Park awoke to find his wife and two daughters standing by his bedside. His vision was blurry and his thinking fuzzy, but Park was relieved to find them there. He took in their smiling faces and then took a deep breath. He enjoyed a strange sense of contentment. A rare sense of peace.

"Gahm-sah-hahm-ni-da," Park croaked in Korean. Thank you. His throat was dry and his voice barely audible, but the words came out clearly. Park wasn't sure why he thanked his wife and daughters; nor was he sure why he was speaking Korean. He spoke English at home, unless he and his wife were alone or he wanted to speak privately to her in front of the kids. It just came out: Thank you. The words weren't exactly what he intended, but pretty close. He meant to say *thankful.*

Park's voice was weak and rough. Weak, no doubt from the strain of surgery. Raspy from the intubation, he thought. Still, Park realized he was able to form thoughts, to enunciate, to express himself. Park's own father had suffered a stroke in his eighties and could not speak the names of places. The frustration brought tears to his eyes. Park's operation had not seemed to damage his brain or alter his consciousness. That was always a risk in brain surgery. The brain, after all, was complicated. *There is hope,* Park thought.

"Daddy!" five-year-old Emily said. "You're finally awake." She jumped up and down. "Hi Daddy!" Natalie said.

Park's wife took his hand. She had tears in her eyes.

"Sung," she said as if his name itself were a thing of wonder. "Sung," she repeated.

"What day is it?" Park added in English, his voice still a dry whisper, like sandpaper.

"Saturday," she said.

Park offered the hint of a smile, closed his eyes, and fell back asleep.

In a small Asian neighborhood home in Ann Arbor, Monique Tran sat next to Sanford Williams. Sanford wore jeans and a freshly pressed white buttondown shirt. Monique wore clogs, jeans, a flowered blouse, and a loose gray hoodie. Her hands were jammed in the hoodie's pockets. They sat squeezed between her parents, who were dressed as though they were heading to church. Her younger sisters, grandparents, aunts, uncles, cousins — eighteen people in all — filled the small room in an arc, all looking intently at Sanford. The young doctor's unlined face had the pinched look of someone experiencing severe intestinal distress. Monique gave him a pat on the knee.

"You okay, honey? You look like you're going to lose your lunch." Monique turned to the assembled family members. "People, it's not polite to stare, okay?"

Monique's family looked down momentarily and then resumed their unwavering gaze.

"Are we all here? Mom, you sure you don't want to invite even more people, maybe the Nguyens, to come over?" Monique's mother, sitting next to Sanford, started to get up. "Kidding, Mom." She returned to the couch. "Okay, people. This is Sanford. We work together at Chelsea General. And . . . we are engaged."

Monique pulled her left hand from her hoodie and held it out. On her ring finger she wore a large diamond ring on a simple band. She moved her hand from side to side as though she were a model on a home shopping channel.

"Nice, isn't it?"

Among the assembled family members, there was a buzz of murmurs commenting on the news, a mix of admiration for the ring and shock at the announcement. Mostly shock. Sanford looked at Monique's father, whose expression was unchanged, a grim mask, and then around the room expecting a handshake or two, a congratulatory pat on the back, maybe. Only Monique's grandmother sat smiling nearby in a wheelchair, still recovering from her hip replacement. He strained to hear what the Trans were saying, but they were speaking in Vietnamese.

"What are they saying?" he whispered to Monique.

"Don't worry your pretty little head about it," she said, giving his knee another pat. Sanford's gut tightened another notch.

"Mom and Dad," Monique said, looking first at her mother and then her father. The assembled family members quieted. "You may have noticed he is not Vietnamese. But like us, he does come from another country . . . Alabama." Confused looks. "That's a joke. I know your heart was set on a nice Vietnamese boy," Monique continued, looking first at one parent, then the other. "Sanford is a doctor, though. Aren't you, honey? And what can I say? The heart sometimes has a mind of its own." Monique paused and then laughed. "That makes no sense! Anyway, I've been teaching him some Vietnamese. Introduce yourself, Sanford."

Sanford cleared his throat. His face, usually pale from the long hours in the hospital, was paler than normal.

"Chào. Tôi tên là Sanford Williams," Sanford said. Hi, my name is Sanford Williams. He spoke this simple phrase with all the earnestness he could muster — as though he had these few words alone to convey his intentions toward Monique.

A couple of the younger cousins laughed.

"Pretty good, huh?" Monique said.

"Now tell them what you call me."

"Bạn gái." Girlfriend.

There were a few nods of approbation and appreciative smiles. Sanford looked around the room. Maybe the tide was turning.

"Now tell them what I call you?"

Sanford looked around the room, alarmed. "Here?"

"Tell them my nickname for you."

"But that wouldn't be appropriate."

"They like hearing you speak Vietnamese. It's cute." Monique turned from her fiancée to her relatives. "Don't you, Tran family?"

Monique didn't wait for a response. She turned back to Sanford. "Go on."

"Are you sure?"

"Sure."

" 'Cause it just doesn't seem right."

She pinched Sanford's cheek. He flushed.

"We just love hearing the white boy speaking our language."

"Okay." Sanford shrugged. "If you say so." He cleared his throat. *"Bu yunghu con ngua."* Monique's eyes widened in distress. Color rose on her cheeks. An aunt gasped. Children gaped. The assembled Trans recoiled as though a tear gas canister had dropped in their midst. Sanford looked around, alarmed.

Monique's father stood and grasped Sanford behind the arm, on his triceps, and pulled him from the couch.

"Time to go," he said. They were the first words he'd uttered since they arrived.

Monique and Sanford hustled from the small, tidy house, across the porch and down the stairs to Sanford's car.

"Are you crazy?" Monique asked.

"You said."

"I didn't mean *that* nickname."

"But —"

"You're a doctor. You're supposed to be smart."

"I said I didn't think it was a good idea."

Sanford used his key remote to unlock the Honda. The Trans had assembled on the porch and were glowering at Sanford. The young doctor looked nervously at the porch as Monique got in the car. All that was missing were the pitchforks and torches. He walked around the car and got behind the wheel.

"I didn't mean *Bu yunghu con ngua*," Monique said.

"But —" Sanford sputtered again. He started the car, not looking back. He pulled away the way he might flee a forest fire or a bank robbery. A block from the house, Monique started up again.

"Dumb ass. What sort of person says 'hung like a horse' in front of his fiancée's parents?" Monique smiled and then she started laughing. "Is that the way y'all do it in Alabama?"

Sanford tried to smile along, but the trauma seemed to have paralyzed his zygomatic major.

"Well, what did you mean when you said nickname?"

"*Gầu trắng.* White bear."

"But you never call me that."

"I do, too."

They drove another block or two in silence.

"Dumb ass!" Monique said, laughing again and punching Sanford in the shoulder. This time Sanford laughed. "That's your nickname from now on. Dumb ass."

CHAPTER 25

Dr. Ty Wilson waved to Allison McDaniel when she entered Angelo's restaurant, a small breakfast dive known for its blueberry French waffles and raisin toast. Over the phone Allison had said she needed diversions on Sunday mornings because she didn't watch her sister's children that day. Still, as he waited for her, Wilson had wondered what he was doing. All rational thought argued against this meeting. He was sure Harding Hooten, the hospital attorney, and everyone else at the hospital would argue against it. Yet somehow, he felt compelled. Was he punishing himself? Or was this something else? A quest for his own personal redemption?

Ty had experienced something like an out-of-body experience watching his fingers punch Allison McDaniel's number on his cell phone. To his surprise, she had agreed to the meeting.

"Good morning, Ms. McDaniel."

"Allison, please," she said, sliding into the booth across from Ty.

A waitress walked up.

"Coffee?" he said to Allison.

"Sure."

Ty was drinking decaffeinated tea. He had never developed his colleagues' taste for coffee, the stronger the better. Even without caffeine, though, he'd felt jittery since he arrived, like a high school freshman before a date. *Some date,* Ty thought.

Allison took a sip of black coffee and looked up at Ty. "So, why'd you want to meet with me?" she asked as casually as possible.

"Honestly, I'm not quite sure." He hesitated. "Can I ask, why did you agree to come?"

"You were the last person to see my son alive. You're a connection to Quinn," Allison replied. "Also, I'm curious. My son couldn't have been the first person who ever died during surgery." She paused. "Honestly, I'm not sure why a big-shot surgeon at Chelsea General needs to see me." She pushed her hair behind her ears and looked down at her clothing. "I'm a mess." With a sigh she took a sip of her coffee.

"You know, I probably shouldn't tell you

this but in the days after Quinn — after I lost my son, I would convince myself I was dreaming. That the whole thing was a dream, and I was simply asleep in the middle of it all. That I just needed to force myself to wake up. And I'd tell myself that there would surely be a sign in the next sixty seconds proving that to be the case. A horrible dream."

As Allison spoke, her voice started getting thick with emotion.

"I'd start counting. One Mississippi. Two Mississippi. Three Mississippi. And before I'd hit ten, a dog would bark. Or someone would honk their horn. Or I'd hear a car radio somewhere."

Allison's voice caught like a baseball card in the spoke of a boy's bicycle, and she closed her eyes. A pair of silent tears traced parallel lines down her slightly freckled cheeks.

"I knew it wasn't a dream, but for those few seconds, I was free." Allison laughed but it was more a snort of self-derision than anything mirthful. She wiped her tears quickly with both hands. "Like I said, I'm a mess. I haven't been sleeping. I lost my job. I lost the one bright light in my life."

Allison took a deep breath. She looked closely at Ty. Stared at him. "What do you want from me, Dr. Wilson? Are you worried about a lawsuit?"

"Allison, please. It's not that," Ty said.

"Okay . . . I mean, what could I possibly tell you that you don't know already? So, I'm wondering if there is something else you want to tell me. Why am I here, Dr. Wilson?"

Ty had been thinking about that question since he'd sat down in the booth. When he spoke, he struggled to find the right words. "No one has affected me the way your son Quinn has. After he died, I've questioned every one of the decisions I made that night. And I've also questioned just about every decision I've made since."

Allison sipped her coffee. She watched Ty the way you might watch a stray dog.

"I am sorry, Ty . . . But what do you want from me?"

"I don't know. I don't know," Ty said. All of a sudden, calling Quinn McDaniel's mother seemed like a terrible idea. "Maybe I just want to say I'm sorry."

"I know you're sorry. I never doubted that you were sorry."

Ty couldn't help but wonder whether the hospital attorney was at that moment squeezing his temples like Obi-Wan Kenobi, sensing a strong disturbance in the Force. Could he tell that a doctor somewhere was straying? Doctors at Chelsea General were not supposed to apologize to their patients, certainly not to the mother of a deceased child. Chelsea General's attorneys did not want any tacit admission of guilt, regardless of how justified or well meaning it might be. In their view, it wasn't only love that meant never having to say you're sorry. Medicine, too. Apologizing simply was not done at Chelsea General, at least not anywhere outside Room 311, at six o'clock on a Monday morning.

Other hospitals had evolved their policies on the apology and now encouraged doctors under the right circumstances to come clean and express their regret over a bad outcome. They'd come to believe that saying sorry was not only the right thing to do, but actually lowered litigation costs. While other hospitals had joined what became known as the "Sorry Works" campaign, Chelsea General's attorney — and the outside firm the hospital hired when it went to court — remained firmly planted in the field of thought that concluded only a judge's order should prompt an apology. They viewed "Sorry Works" as some sort of New Age pabulum, an unwarranted dropping of the guard.

The food arrived. Allison had waffles with strawberries. Ty was eating a spinach egg-white omelet. They took a few bites in silence. It started raining. "Lucky it isn't snow," Ty quipped, trying to break the awkward silence.

"What do you normally do on Sundays?" Allison asked.

Ty took this as an opportunity to ramble on about his love for his motorcycle, pickup basketball games, and his recent meditation classes. They both laughed at that. "I guess . . . on Sundays, we spend much of the day planning for Mondays, Monday Mornings," he concluded. He knew she couldn't possibly know the deeper meaning of that.

Allison smiled. "I have a question for you."

"Sure."

"If you didn't operate, the tumor would have killed Quinn, wouldn't it?" She looked pained as she asked it, and incredibly vulnerable.

"Yes," Ty answered gently. "You probably would have had six or eight months with your son, but the tumor would have been fatal if we'd done nothing."

That was the difference between surgery and internal medicine. If Ty had decided the brain tumor was inoperable, Quinn would have died of a brain tumor. With internal medicine, various diseases became compounded and collectively were responsible for the patient's downfall. A patient died of heart disease and diabetes, perhaps worsened by obesity. Internists treated a disease, hoping to stop the progression. If they were lucky, they managed it, reduced the frequency or severity of the symptoms. Rarely did they cure anyone. Life was different for surgeons. They were making a bet each time they operated. They were wagering their skills against the symptoms, whether it was a tumor, a leaky heart valve, or a bum knee. If the operation was not successful, if the tumor spread or the heart failed or the knee continued to hurt, the surgeon had failed. No one said the patient died of heart disease or cancer. The patient died in surgery, or despite it. The dynamic was completely different.

"Look, I have lost people in my life, Allison. And . . . I have never forgiven . . ." He let the words trail off.

"Are you looking for forgiveness, Dr. Wilson?"

Ty just stared at his plate, unsure how to respond.

Ty and Allison finished their breakfast

with few words beyond pleasantries about the food. On the way out the door, Ty thanked Allison for meeting him. She made a motion to hug him, but decided to put out her hand instead. "Thank you. The waffles were delicious." Still holding his hand, she said, "I am not sure what *it* is, but I hope you find *it*." As they parted ways, Ty was left with a sinking feeling of unfinished business. He watched her go and wanted to call her name. First, though, he knew he would need to figure out what he needed from this woman. "Allison," he said, too softly for her to hear.

CHAPTER 26

Harding Hooten grabbed the keys out from the foyer table and headed for the door. The grandfather clock by the enormous wood door showed the time: twelve thirty.

"Back soon, Mar," he said.

"You're going back?" Martha asked, incredulous.

Hooten had come home for lunch, a salad, and taken a half-hour nap. He and Martha played a game of cribbage. When Hooten rose after taking a drubbing, the usual outcome, his wife had assumed he was going to grab a book or the newspaper and put his feet up on the sunporch. It was Sunday afternoon, and she assumed — hoped, anyway — her husband was taking the rest of the day off. There were doctors fresh from training who took Sunday afternoons off.

Hooten had turned sixty-seven the previous July, and Martha had been trying to get him to slow down for at least that long. She'd given up on trying to get him to retire. She had stopped asking after the husband of a friend, the gregarious CEO of a small company, had retired on his sixty-fifth birthday, languished at home for a month of utter boredom, and then dropped dead of a heart attack.

What Martha knew, but Hooten's colleagues didn't, was that the chief of surgery didn't have to work at all. He had inherited one-quarter of an immense family fortune. His colleagues may have guessed that there was more to Hooten than met the eye — at least in terms of personal wealth — if they'd taken the time to examine the Audubon prints in his office and realized they were genuine, not reproductions. Of course, Hooten would probably have given any doctors lolling in his anteroom a tongue lashing for shirking their duties long before they studied the looping signature *J. J. Audubon,* the line across the *A* sweeping across his last name like the tail feather of a quetzal.

His own father, Mayhew, was a doctor who had seen the rise of lawsuits and hung up his white lab coat for a pin-striped suit and started selling malpractice insurance. He made a killing, amassing a fortune in the years after World War II. Hooten had three bothers, and they now shared the family summer estate on Mackinac Island, an enormous white clapboard affair on the water, with a wraparound porch and gabled windows on the third floor.

Martha met her future husband while he was still in residency in New York in the late 1960s. At some point, he had invited her to spend a long weekend at the family estate. The weekend marked a rare respite from the grind of residency and the first time Martha had met Hooten's parents.

Hooten purchased the airline tickets, and they had flown Pan Am from Kennedy International Airport, which had been renamed recently enough that some people still called it Idlewild. They landed in Detroit, and a car was waiting for them. When Hardy didn't raise an eyebrow, Martha realized there was more to this earnest, diligent, honorable man she had fallen for than his bow ties and the tender way he touched her cheek when they kissed.

Rolling up to the sprawling family mansion, Martha realized that what drove Hooten had nothing to do with money. As the country convulsed around them after the Martin Luther King assassination and riots, Robert Kennedy's assassination, the Vietnam War protests, Chicago's violent

Democratic convention, Hooten remained focused on his training. His only diversions were Martha and his growing expertise in birding. He almost never slept.

Martha learned quickly that Hardy's work ethic was undiminished by family money and unmoved by the pot-and-protest-stoked ethos around the Columbia University campus not far from his apartment. That he maintained this feverish schedule into his fifties and sixties was a testament to his drive and his love of medicine.

Four decades after they'd met, Martha knew the hospital was still the center of Hardy's life. She feared he would die of boredom if he retired, like his friend. Having him only part of the day beat that alternative, she reminded herself when she was home alone.

"I've got a piece of unpleasant business to attend to," he said at the threshold as his wife straightened his bow tie.

At the hospital, he had the paging operator send a message to Michelle Robidaux, asking her to come to the twelfth floor. She arrived, still ebullient from her recent back-from-the-dead experience. Michelle wondered if a journal would be interested in Earl Jasper as a case study. She'd seen case studies in the *New England Journal of Medi-*

cine. The thought of her byline in the *New England Journal* made her almost giddy. She'd already started thinking of a title: "Failure of Glasgow Metrics to Ascertain Minimum Brain Consciousness — A Case Study." The title needed work, for sure, but she saw career-advancing possibilities in the racist killer. He might just be the break she needed.

Hooten's admin waved Michelle through, and moments later she was standing in front of the great man himself. She had only formally met him once, at orientation, *And now he knows my name,* Michelle thought. *I am the resident who kept a conscious man from being cut up like a catfish.* The thought of noodlers grabbing for organs made her smirk despite herself.

"Dr. Robidaux, thanks for coming up," Hooten said.

"Sure," Michelle said. She bounced on the balls of her feet, almost giddy with anticipation. She hadn't yet realized that his grave expression and grim tone were not in line with her vision of the meeting. This was not the look of a man congratulating a junior colleague. Michelle had no idea what was coming.

"I'm not sure if you're aware of the reason I called you up here."

"I think so, sir. Earl Jasper?"

Hooten looked perplexed for a moment. "No, I asked you to see me because of the meningioma resection you performed on a patient named Mary Cash."

It was Michelle's turn to look perplexed. The name was such a departure from what she expected, the young doctor was lost for a moment. "You may recall," Hooten continued, "Ms. Cash had a serious complication. Lost her olfaction. As a chef, this was a life-altering event for her."

Michelle's elation evaporated. The embarrassment of remembering the case caused a tightening of her stomach muscles and the blood vessels below the surface of her skin to dilate and become suffused with blood. Michelle's cheeks reddened.

"Yes, yes, I do remember the case. Yes, sir." Now Michelle realized she had not been called to the legendary Harding Hooten's office to be congratulated for saving the hospital the horrible embarrassment of killing a conscious man. She had been summoned about an operation that had gone badly. Her operation. Michelle felt as though someone had squeezed the air out of her.

"As you know, the young woman is suing the hospital. That in and of itself is not unusual. In this case, however, we are going to have to respond aggressively, and as the hospital legal counsel sees fit." Hooten paused. This was a distasteful business. "It is with regret that I am terminating your employment at this hospital, effective immediately."

Again, the words did not sink in right away. Michelle felt as though she were at the bottom of a pool, and the words were reaching her one at a time.

"Terminate?"

Before Hooten could answer the question, a harried woman in a pantsuit entered his office carrying a legal pad and a sheaf of papers. She looked from the stunned Michelle Robidaux to Hooten. The woman's eyes widened in surprise and then her cheeks flushed with anger.

"Dr. Hooten? I thought we agreed that you would wait for me."

"You said two o'clock. It is now two ten."

The woman took a deep breath and quietly muttered, "On a Sunday? Really, Dr. Hooten?" She turned her attention to Michelle.

"Michelle Robidaux. My name is Nancy Lowenstein. I work in human resources here at the hospital. I'm here to make your transition as smooth as possible."

"Transition?" Michelle asked. "That's what you call it?"

Michelle was now gulping for air, trying to hold back the sobs, trying not to think of what she would tell her parents, Mrs. Truex the librarian, and her brother, Michelle's benefactor.

Hooten stood up.

"Ms. Lowenstein. I will leave you to it."

With that, he stood up, grabbing his white lab coat on the way out the door.

CHAPTER 27

At precisely 6 am, Dr. Harding Hooten stood before the assemblage of bleary-eyed surgeons in Room 311.

"Before we get to the business of the day, I want to let you know that our colleague Dr. Sung Park is doing as well as can be expected. He's moved from neurological intensive care to a private room here in the hospital. I know you share my wishes that his recovery be swift and lasting."

Hooten paused and then nodded to Villanueva, who sat in the front row like an oversize schoolboy at the principal's office.

"And now my colleague George Villanueva will present the case of Earl Jasper."

Hooten returned to his seat next to Sydney, among the few who looked wide awake. Truth be told, Sydney had already run eight miles that morning. She was on call and knew she wouldn't get another chance to exercise that day.

Villanueva stood up and walked to the front of the room. His plan was to come clean, admit wrongdoing, and move on. That was the way things worked in Monday Mornings. Spell out your shortcomings in painful detail, submit to the questioning of the assembled surgeons, and put the episode behind you. You might even learn something through this Socratic *mea culpa*. This Earl Jasper case just rubbed Villanueva the wrong way. He could see nothing redeeming about this racist SOB at all. Like a mosquito, Earl Jasper had done nothing to justify his place in the world.

A couple of decades earlier, Villanueva had raised his right hand in Hill Auditorium, looking up at the beautiful, arched, art deco stage, and taken an oath. Swelled with pride — and the doughnuts that fueled his late nights — the Big Cat had sworn he would "prescribe regimens for the good of my patients according to my ability and my judgment and never do harm to anyone." Clearly, not allowing the neurologist to see Jasper in the Emergency Department was not the correct regimen for this patient. Yet the scumbag had made it. No harm, no foul.

Easy, Villanueva told himself. Submit to the proceedings. Take his lumps. It was no different from Mondays in the NFL. If you missed a blocking assignment, the coach was going to rewind and play and rewind the film of that mistake over and over and over. Fire out of the stance, miss the block, jump back to the three-point stance, fire out again, and so on. Missed assignments could be dangerous. The quarterback or running back could take a serious hit. But no one died from a missed blocking assignment. Not yet, anyway.

Monday Mornings were sacred. They were there to save lives. To learn from mistakes. To allow the participants to rededicate themselves to practicing the best medicine humanly possible. Villanueva knew this. Still, he couldn't put the vision of Jasper's grandmother out of his head. An old woman torn up by a shotgun blast at close range. Why couldn't she have been the one to survive? He'd read in the newspaper that Jasper's grandmother had raised him, and that he'd gone into a rage and shot her when she wouldn't give him twenty bucks.

"Dr. Villanueva, we're ready for your presentation," Hooten said.

Grandma never stood a chance, Villanueva thought, and then began.

"Let me give it to you in a nutshell. This neo-Nazi dirtbag who had just killed his grandmother showed up in my ER."

Hooten interrupted, "Dr. Villanueva, Morbidity and Mortality is a time-honored medical proceeding. I expect the appropriate decorum."

Ty Wilson nudged Tina Ridgeway, who sat next to him. "That's the Gato we know and love," he said.

"That's the Hooten we know and love," Tina answered.

Chastened, Villanueva continued, his voice not quite as combative.

"Mr. Earl Jasper presented in the ER with a single gunshot wound to the head, with the wound penetrating his hard palate, inferior turbinate, middle turbinate, superior turbinate, ethmoid bone, entering his frontal lobe and exiting through the skull above his right eye. By all appearances, this dirtbag — excuse me, Mr. Jasper — had died of lead poisoning —"

"Dr. Villanueva," Hooten cautioned. His tone was now cold and biting. He was losing his patience.

"How did you know that? How did you know he died?" a surgeon called from the back of the room.

Villanueva took another deep breath. When he was pushed, Villanueva liked to push back — hard. When he was challenged, he liked to destroy the challenger. If someone gave him a cheap shot on the football field, he did his best to take that person's head off the next chance he got. Villanueva fought the impulse to say something about the large hole in Jasper's skull, but he knew he was wrong, and he decided to come clean. He held his hands up in submission.

"All right, you win."

"It's not about winning," Hooten scolded. Villanueva paid no attention to him and plowed ahead, looking at his shoes and feeling every bit like a chastened schoolboy.

"I let my emotions cloud my judgment. I was too busy looking at that damn swastika to pay attention to the patient."

"Since when do we need to judge people worthy before we treat them?" called one surgeon from the back of the room.

"Tell me about it," an ER doctor added. "All the noncompliant, abusive alcoholics I see."

"I admit it, I was wrong," Villanueva said. "I. Was. Wrong." The room was completely silent. This was a monumental moment, even given the history of Monday Mornings. Villanueva hung his head, and was about to continue when he heard a noise.

A smattering of applause started in the back of the room and began building. Confused, Villanueva looked up. He'd never heard his fellow surgeons applauding an admission like his. He saw the doctors standing now, cheering. He was bewildered for a moment, and even started to raise his hands in acknowledgment. Then he realized they weren't applauding his public admission. They were looking toward the back of the room. Villanueva followed their gaze. There, his arm intertwined with his wife's, was Dr. Sung Park taking a seat. His head was bandaged, and he looked weak and pale, but he was smiling.

Villanueva began clapping along with his colleagues.

Hooten now stood and turned to find the source of the commotion. When he saw Park, he raised his fists as a boxer might.

"Bravo, Sung!" Hooten called. "Bravo."

Doctors were now leaving their seats to crowd around Park, shake his hand. Park looked almost shy, surrounded by his peers. Next to him, Pat Park beamed, tears streaming down her cheeks.

After M&M, Park's wife took him back to his room at the hospital. Ty and a number of other surgeons went to the cafeteria in search of a few calories before their days began. The cafeteria was an enormous rectangular room that had undergone a makeover in recent years designed to give the illusion that it wasn't an enormous rectangular room.

Stations for omelets, cold cereal, and coffee sprouted away from the long, stainless-steel line serving up eggs, grits, pancakes, hash browns, bacon, and other foods most cardiologists forbid their patients from eating. There were also the calorie-laden cinnamon pastries and doughnuts that led to many of the medical problems being treated in the hospital. Cloth banners hung from the ceiling at the midpoint of the room, near the cashiers, to divide the space and muffle the noise. Still, the overall impression was something between a Picadilly Cafeteria and a medium-security prison.

Ty sat down in a far corner of the room with a bowl of cereal and a cup of green tea. Park's entrance had given him a charge. He hadn't expected it; nor would he have guessed that his groggy and cynical colleagues would give the oddball neurosurgeon such a rousing welcome. The scene left him feeling somehow lighter than he'd felt in a while. On a whim, he'd bought the single-serving bowl of Froot Loops, a cereal he hadn't eaten since grade school.

Tina sat down across from Ty with a cup

of coffee. She did a double take at his Froot
Loops.

"They say you are what you eat. Where
does that leave you?" She smiled wryly.

Ty laughed and failed to think of a snappy
rejoinder. "Oh yeah?"

"Yeah."

He picked a neon green Froot Loop from
his bowl and tossed it into Tina's coffee.
The sugar-coated sphere floated in the
center of the cup, a circle within a circle.

Villanueva sat down at the table with a
jumbo coffee and a plate stacked with eggs,
bacon, and hash browns. Ty turned to him.

"I thought you were in detention."

"How much did you pay Park to interrupt
M and M?" Tina asked Villanueva.

"I never expected you of all people to be
such a cynic, Dr. Ridgeway," Villanueva said.

"You obviously don't know Dr. Ridgeway," Ty said, without thinking. He looked
at Tina, and they both blushed and looked
away.

Villanueva took a big bite out of a Danish
and eyed the two neurosurgeons. There was
a spark between the two, for sure. He
wondered if they had acted on this attrac-
tion. Anything was possible, but he doubted
it. A guy like Ty could have any woman he
wanted. Villanueva envied the younger

doctor's athletic physique and California cool. Tina Ridgeway was a very attractive woman, but she had kids, and was married. Not that being married was a showstopper. Just ask his wife's divorce lawyer, who had gathered a full dossier of Villanueva's moral turpitude, complete with lurid black-and-white photos of his extracurricular rendez-vous.

Sydney arrived with an egg-white omelet with tomato and peppers. "Mind if I join you?"

"Please."

"So, George, Park saved you," Sydney said.

"Saved by Park's glioblastoma," Villanueva said.

"Park's Glioblastoma, sounds like the name of a band," Ty said.

"More bands should take advantage of our rich nomenclature," Villanueva said. "Like 'Palpable Mass.' A band with a name like that could be big."

"Nice," Ty said. "How about 'the Myoclonic Jerks.' "

"I like it," Sydney said.

" 'The Suppurating Sores,' " Villanueva added.

"Glad I'm not eating," Tina said.

" 'The Constipated Stools,' " Ty added.

"Now you guys are just getting gross," Sydney said, laughing.

CHAPTER 28

Ten minutes later, Sydney arrived on the clinical patient care floor. The senior resident Melody McHenry, blinking back fatigue, greeted her in the hallway next to the nursing station. She ran through the relative state of recovery of patients who had undergone operations in the previous forty-eight hours.

Almost as an afterthought, she added, "We had a surgical consult from pediatrics. A five-year-old with a minor hit to her head and a history of surgical repair of a volvulus arrived in the ED yesterday afternoon. Vomiting. Constipation. Lethargy. Latham did a consult last night. X-rays and KUB film showed dilated loops of bowel, possible early partial bowel obstruction. He gave the girl two 250cc boluses of normal saline, plus five percent dextrose in half normal saline at 40cc per hour. Inserted a nasogastric tube and admitted. He asked me to take a look a few hours ago, but I got kind of busy with these other patients."

Sydney listened, her expression becoming one of concern.

"So, no one has seen her overnight? Where is she?"

"She's on Five-A."

"Let's go."

McHenry and Sydney walked back the way Sydney had come, McHenry scurrying to keep up.

"I was told by the nurses that she looked stable. Abdomen nondistended. No sign of peritonitis."

"Did you do another KUB?"

"Um, no," McHenry said. "I asked for an infectious disease consult. Also, I'm getting our pediatric surgical fellow to take a look."

"What's happening to the blood count?"

McHenry didn't answer. She didn't know.

Sydney began walking faster still, moving ahead of McHenry. She pushed through a doorway outside, cut across a patient drop-off bay and into another double door.

"What room is she in?"

Before McHenry could answer a nurse intercepted them in the hallway. Her grave expression matched Sydney's.

"The girl in room two forty-five doesn't look right."

"Two forty-five. That's her."

"What's going on?" Sydney asked.

"Real lethargic. Didn't respond to a needle stick." As most pediatric nurses know, it is an awful sound when a child cries while getting an IV. Silence, however, is far worse.

Sydney and McHenry went into the room, the nurse a step behind. Sydney picked up the chart at the end of the bed and took out her stethoscope. The girl was thin, with brown skin that appeared somehow chalky. She looked tiny in the big bed. Sydney held the stethoscope to the girl's chest, checking her watch as she did.

"One ninety-two." She flipped through the chart. "The blood count had a shift to the left." Sydney gave an accusing look at the senior resident but said nothing. "We need an OR. Now." McHenry rushed from the room.

Sydney turned to the nurse. "Have somebody find this girl's parents, someone to give us consent, and have them meet me at Inman Seven. Start antibiotic therapy and get her to Pre-Op."

Sydney walked fast down the corridor, through a tunnel, and then up one flight to the reach the ORs.

Within the hour, the girl was intubated

and lying unconscious with her gut opened. Sydney scrubbed in with the pediatric surgeons and located a foot-long section of dead bowel. When they heard the girl had lost consciousness as she was being moved from the bed to a gurney, the doctors were sure they had the right diagnosis. Sydney placed clamps on either side. Before she could start removing the foot-long section, the drone of a flat-lining EKG interrupted her. The anesthesiologist dropped her book and jumped up. She checked the leads on the EKG, saw that they were still connected, then reached onto the cart and grabbed a small vial.

"Point one m-l epinephrine bolus."

She took a syringe, drew the drug from the vial, and squeezed the clear liquid into the IV port.

Sydney began chest compressions, and the anesthesiologist started trying to put in a central line.

"Let's defib," Sydney said.

The circulating nurse picked up the defibrillator, removed the blue drape from the girl's chest, and placed the paddles against her skin.

"Clear."

The shock jolted the small body, but the EKG continued its steady beep.

Sydney and the anesthesiologist took a half step back. The anesthesiologist grabbed another syringe and drew liquid from another vial.

"Adding point five milligrams atropine."

Sydney and the anesthesiologist continued with the CPR, with Sydney doing the compressions and the anesthesiologist pushing the medications. The pediatric surgeons placed damp sterile towels over the young girl's abdomen.

The nurse rubbed the paddles together as the device recharged.

"Clear."

She returned the paddles to the girl's chest and hit the button. Again the small body jolted upward.

This time, the EKG began beeping a regular beat. Sydney let out a long, slow breath. She waited to see if the girl's heart was back.

The rest of the operation went without complications. Sydney left the OR and without changing her scrubs, went up to Hooten's office. She walked past Hooten's startled receptionist into the chief of surgery's office.

Hooten was on the phone.

"Morgan, I need to call you back. There's something I need to attend to. Dr. Saxena?"

"Harding, I'm worried about complacency at this hospital. I just had a little girl who almost died because of a casual attitude toward diagnosing what turned out to be an emergent situation."

"You're the attending, Dr. Saxena. I suggest you put the fear of God in whatever residents or interns are responsible."

"This isn't the first time. And it's not just my service. Ordering tests and asking for consults are easy at a hospital like this. We need our young doctors to take responsibility. We need them to behave more like country doctors."

"Very well. We'll have a mandatory seminar this coming Saturday for our junior staff. You will give the talk. I trust you will be sufficiently blunt."

"You bet I will." Sydney turned to go. "Thank you, Harding." As she started to leave, Hooten called after her.

"Remember, between the idea and the reality. Between the motion and the act, falls the shadow."

Sydney laughed. "T. S. Eliot."

She walked out. She and Hooten shared an intense desire for perfection, and they had both been dual English–Biology majors.

Hooten picked up the phone and punched a number from memory.

"Sorry for the interruption, Morgan. You were asking me whom I'd recommend as my replacement when I retire. I think I know the perfect doctor. I'll tell you about her the next time we meet for lunch."

Tina was back at The Free Clinic. She'd reached the point where she looked forward to her time treating the indigent so much, she resisted returning to the hospital. She'd come to think of the *Free* in *Free Clinic* as her own freedom rather than the cost of the care she provided. Tina rationalized her time away from her paying job as the hospital underwriting care for the underserved who lived nearby. Weren't hospitals supposed to do that anyway?

Tina wasn't shirking at Chelsea General. She still taught medical students, went to clinic, and performed surgery, but she didn't do anything extra. She was fulfilling her obligations . . . barely. And at Chelsea General, that was the exception, not the rule. Chelsea General was the place where doctors ran cutting-edge clinical trials or instituted groundbreaking reforms to guard against things like hospital-acquired infections. Chelsea General was the Everest most doctors dreamed of climbing. Not for Tina. Not anymore.

Somehow, the frequent furloughs she granted herself from the hospital to work at The Free Clinic made Tina's beauty more radiant. They seemed to relax the muscles in her face imperceptibly. The double takes she got from men and women alike during the normal course of moving through the world increased, along with her happiness. Not that she was looking for the attention. Even in the threadbare surroundings of the clinic, Tina looked glamorous in her white lab coat and heels. Standing in the small examination room, she looked more like a model on a photo shoot playing a doctor than an actual doctor peering down the throat of a child with a phlegmatic cough, which she was at that moment.

"Say ahh," Tina instructed. Tina was just noticing the blisters along the inside of the cheeks when she heard the chime of the clinic's front door. The child had the Coxsackie virus, better known as hand, foot, and mouth disease.

"Let me see your hands," Tina said to the little girl, gently holding her wrists and turning them palms-up.

"Can I help you?" she heard her assistant DeShawn ask.

"I need to see a doctor."

"Have a seat."

"I said, I need a doctor."

Tina stopped her examination and listened.

"Sir, could you please take a seat," DeShawn said. "We have a first-come, first-served policy here. She'll be out as soon as she can."

"She. Who is this bitch? This doctor bitch."

"Sir, please."

The Free Clinic was small, and Tina, her young patient, and the patient's mother could hear every word. Tina's first thought was *hostile attribution bias* — the mind-set that when things didn't go your way, it was because people were out to get you. Classic paranoia. But then Tina noticed her patient with her mouth open. She was looking at her mother, fear in her eyes. The mother didn't know what to say. She looked at Tina. Tina flushed.

"One moment."

Tina stepped out of the examination room to see a man about thirty-five years old standing with his arms crossed giving DeShawn the evil eye. His short brown hair looked as though he used his fingers as a comb, and he wore an old green fatigue jacket. Some sort of serpentine tattoo sprouted from beneath the neckline of a faded white T-shirt.

"Sir, can I ask you to please watch your offensive language."

"Offensive language," the man parroted.

"I'm a big girl. I can take it, but there are children here."

"A big girl." The man eyed Tina up and down. He looked like a starving man sizing up a porterhouse steak. "You are, aren't you? I bet you can take it."

DeShawn stood.

"Sir, I'm going to have to ask you to leave."

The man locked in on DeShawn. He was much smaller than DeShawn but he was wiry, his jaw was set, and he looked like he wouldn't mind taking a punch or two to get in a few of his own. DeShawn had been a bouncer at a local club, and usually that was enough to command order at The Free Clinic.

Tina stepped forward.

"I'm Dr. Ridgeway," she said extending her hand. Her gesture seemed to catch the man off guard.

"K. C.," the man said, almost reluctantly. He was enjoying the confrontation. He shook Tina's hand.

"K. C., we're going to get to you as soon as we can."

"Forget it. I gotta go." The man took a couple of steps toward the door. "I'll come back when your boyfriend's not here."

"K. C., DeShawn is not my boyfriend. He works here."

"You gotta boyfriend? I bet you need a boyfriend." He sized Tina up again. "I could make you happy."

"Mr. — K. C. — I'm a doctor here. If you're interested in free treatment, come back."

"I'll come back. Count on it."

K. C. opened the door and left.

CHAPTER 29

Ty sautéed tofu with blueberries, red peppers, pineapple, and ginger, and looked out the window of his penthouse apartment. Rain was hitting the window in sheets, blurring the lights of the buildings nearby. Ty had always enjoyed being alone. It was one reason he'd never wanted to maintain a relationship for more than a couple of months. No matter how beautiful or witty or thoughtful his companion, sooner or later, usually sooner, he began to feel suffocated. He would escape to the hospital, where he could immerse himself in his work and avoid the woman who was at that point plotting how to reform his incorrigible bachelor ways.

Ty stirred a little soy sauce into his mix, dumped it into a shallow bowl, and sat down at the glass-and-steel table by the window. As he began eating with chopsticks — Ty believed this was healthier because it prompted him to eat slower — he looked out the rain-streaked window but felt none of the sense of peace that usually accompanied these quiet dinners alone. While most people needed to turn the television on to keep themselves company, Ty liked silence. He reveled in it.

Tonight was different. Ty was on edge. He was beginning a four-day weekend to mull things over, but he had a sense of being frayed, jumpy. He walked across the room, found his remote, turned on the television, and flipped until he found a basketball game. It was a desultory early-season game pitting the Pistons against the Mavericks. He watched for a few minutes as he ate. The game was in the second quarter, and the players seemed to be going through the motions, waiting for the fourth quarter when the game mattered. He pondered a job where you could do less than your best and no one died. Most jobs were like that.

Ty got up, walked across the room, and turned off the television. His sense of peace did not return with the announcers' patter gone, and he realized in a flash why he was edgy. Ty wasn't really alone. His constant companion these days was his accuser, the voice in his head telling him that he was not competent, that he had been fooling himself, that he had been fooling others. That he was nothing but an imposter. The by-product of this poisonous self-judge was doubt. Ty was racked by uncertainty. How could one case trigger such a strong reaction when he had sailed through his career so far? It seemed absurd, but he had tried laughing it off, sweating it off, and waiting it out, and the doubt remained. Ty had done some research, and he found a study show-ing that unconsciously attempting to avoid errors actually resulted in more errors. How could you possibly eliminate unconscious thoughts? It was like being told not to think about the pink elephant. It was like a nega-tive feedback loop. The more he tried to squelch his feelings of doubt, they more they took center stage in his thoughts.

There was another reason Ty was edgy. It had been fifteen days since he had punted on the ETBS. He hadn't performed an operation since. He'd been to clinic and to M&M, but he had avoided the OR with a deep fear that was a new and powerful force in his life. More than two weeks. It was the longest Ty had gone without performing surgery since he'd finished his training. The residents loved the extra experience in the OR, but every day Ty stayed in town and didn't operate, he was succumbing to his cowardice. He hated the feeling. He hadn't gone into medicine or surgery to walk away from the tough decisions. Just the opposite.

Ty looked out the window again. The rain had subsided. The storm was heading east. He could now see the moon, flickering between fast-moving clouds scudding across the night sky. Ty had an idea. He walked over to his laptop, typed in Delta.com, and then checked his watch. He rinsed his plate and put it in the dishwasher. Then he went to his room, threw a few things in an overnight bag, and walked out the door.

Park scheduled his radiation at night. He did not like to enter the hospital during the day as a patient. In this way, he did his best to keep these two identities separate. Sung Park, the doctor. Sung Park, the patient. He knew this thinking wasn't entirely logical. He was both doctor and patient. He knew that. Even so, each night, one of his residents would pick him up at his house and drive him to Chelsea General; because of the risk of a seizure, his insurance company didn't want him driving. His wife offered to take him, but she was needed to run the household, get the children to bed. It was simpler this way.

In a large room dominated by a hulking

radiation machine, he would lie down on the gurney, which the radiation therapist called "the couch." She fitted Park's custom-made plastic mesh mask over his face and clipped it down. He'd overheard a younger cancer patient refer to this as his "Jason" mask, though he didn't know why.

The top of the so-called couch then slid out, placing him under the oculus of the machine. It looked like an eye peering down on him, but the orb wasn't "seeing" Park. This was the source of the high-intensity X-rays. The eyes of the machine were panels that the radiation therapist called arms, which made Park think of his word-power cassettes. *"Anthropomorphism: Giving human attributes to animals or nonliving things."*

With the lights dimmed, the machine pivoted around Park, whose head was pinned looking straight up. The arms recorded where the small marks on the ears, neck, and forehead of the mask were located so the radiation would be aimed precisely. Once it started, Park heard a buzzing but felt nothing. Park had, of course, prescribed post-operative radiation therapy for his patients, but he'd never given it much thought. It was simply the standard of care.

As a patient, the process was full of wonderment for Park, a literal-minded individual who made a point of believing what he could see. As the machine arced around his head, he knew cells inside his brain were receiving a three-dimensional bombardment of X-ray energy. He knew photons were damaging the DNA of cancer cells that remained after his surgery — and some healthy cells. That way they wouldn't be able to divide. But how did he know, really? The radiation was invisible.

Immobilized on the flat gurney, Park was uncharacteristically still for a man of movement, of action and accomplishment. Stuck under the formfitting mask, his mind was liberated, free to wander, to muse. There were always things to do. Musing was something Park had considered a waste of time.

Now he wondered about perception and reality. As he considered the invisible beams doing damage at a cellular level inside his head at that very moment, he thought of other aspects of his life that were invisible yet vital to his well-being. Love, for example. Surely, he knew his wife loved him, and he loved her. If Pat were gone, his life would be diminished. She was vital to his well-being. His children, too. His mother had died the previous year of a stroke, and he had experienced a profound sense of loss even though he talked to his mother only a few times a year. There was a love and bond between them, now forever severed.

With the lights dimmed night after night, Park's mind wandered as Mozart's "Violin Concerto no. 5 in A Major" played. He'd requested the song in part because it roused him at some spiritual level. He thought the music might trigger the release of dopamine and might help with his healing. Also, the song had played a profound role in his life. He was scheduled to play this piece at his tryout for Korea's most prestigious music academy. His inability to master it had ended the violin career his parents dreamed he'd pursue and turned Park to science.

Park had always been a linear thinker. Input and outcome were directly correlated. If you applied more effort, you got more results. Life could be broken down into a series of simple algebraic equations. If x yielded y, then $2x$ would equal $2y$. In this way, you could produce the results you wanted. Park's dogged work ethic was the product of this belief, and he had used it in Korea, rising above his humble upbringing to receive admission into medical school and then being accepted into its most challenging field, neurosurgery. He had done it again in the United States by going through a second neurosurgical residency.

Lying on his back, the invisible beams striking his brain, Park was beginning to rethink this linear mind-set. His life had not followed a logical path. His inability to master a piece of music written for violin 250 years earlier in Germany had shunted his life from one track to another. His cancer, too, was the result of no direct input. His diet was good. He was fit from walking. He had not been exposed to high doses of any known carcinogen. One day he was living one life. The next day he was living a different one. He had undergone a profound change, and not as the result of any simple formula.

As a doctor, he'd heard other glioblastoma patients talk about how their lives were transformed the instant the cancer revealed itself. One minute, they were driving in a familiar neighborhood, and the next they didn't know the way home. One minute, they were cleaning the garage. The next, the left side of their body ceased functioning. One minute, they were holding a conversation and the next, they found it difficult to speak.

Park had studied quantum mechanics as part of his undergraduate education at the University of Seoul, but he had been skeptical. How could one thing become something completely different under certain circumstances? Now he was beginning to view himself under this light. Maybe life wasn't as much levers and pulleys that could be manipulated as it was a series of switches that turned on and off.

When Park rose from the gurney each night after the radiation machine stopped humming, there had barely been enough time to hear a single movement of the concerto. Still, he had spent the brief time pondering questions he had never even considered thus far in his life, and he left the hospital feeling oddly refreshed.

CHAPTER 30

Sydney stood next to the makeshift stage and jumped up and down to ward off the cold. She was wearing shorts and her CHELSEA GENERAL 10K T-shirt, even though the temperature was only in the high forties. ABBA's "Mamma Mia" pulsed from large, overmodulated speakers set up on either side of the windblown stage, and a woman stood in front of a group of runners, leading them in pre-race stretching. The song ended, and the DJ flipped on his microphone.

"Mamma Mia, it's cold out here. Everyone keep moving! Before you head to the starting line, I want to hand the mike over to Morgan Smith, he's the big cheese, *le grand fromage,* at Chelsea General, the sponsor that's made this race possible. Put those frozen mitts together for Morgan Smith."

Smith took the microphone to a smattering of applause.

"Thanks. My name is Morgan Smith. I'm the CEO at Chelsea General. Just want to welcome all of you here. Chelsea General is proud to sponsor the race. This is the eighth year of the Chelsea General 10K. Even though it's cold, you all need to stay hydrated. There will be water stops along the course. Chelsea General will be with you every step of the way. And that's the kind of hospital we are, too. From the best neonatal unit in the Midwest to outstanding geriatric care."

Smith looked over toward Sydney, who gave him a wave as she hopped up and down on one foot, then the other.

"We've got a young doctor here —" Smith put a hand over his microphone and leaned toward Sydney with a look that made it clear he had forgotten her name.

"Sydney Saxena," she called.

"We've got Dr. Sydney Saxena here. She's going to tell you a little bit about saving lives."

He turned and handed the microphone to Sydney. She blew on her hands, stiff and red with cold, and took the mike.

"Good morning. I'm Dr. Sydney Saxena. We're all excited to run and get the blood moving. Just want to tell you, if you ever find a loved one, a friend, a stranger who's not breathing or whose heart has stopped, you can help. Anyone can help. And it's simple. Don't worry about mouth-to-mouth. That's good news, right? Chest compressions alone will keep the blood moving to the brain and heart until help arrives."

Sydney remembered training as a lifeguard in high school, the dreaded fear of having to perform mouth-to-mouth resuscitation on something other than the rubber dummy, really only a head and chest. That was bad enough, its creepy pupil-less eyes staring straight ahead, its skin-colored lips tasting like the Listerine used to clean the "mouth" between would-be lifeguards.

Sydney looked out at the large pack of runners, jumping up and down to stay warm, stretching, talking. It was hard to know if anyone was listening. As she scanned the small group in front of her, she saw him. Bill McManus. He smiled and nodded at her. He still looked exhausted, but he looked more athletic in shorts and a long-sleeved T-shirt than he had in a wrinkled lab coat.

"So if you come upon someone who has stopped breathing, first, you or someone else needs to call nine-one-one. Then you need to see if there is a defibrillator nearby. If not, all you have to do is chest compressions. That will keep the blood flowing to the heart and brain. Find a spot between the nipples and push, arms straight, one hand on top of the other." Sydney put her hands on top of each other, and straightened her arms to demonstrate. "And don't be shy about the compressions. You want to push hard. Break a sweat. Keep going until medical help arrives. Any questions?"

Sydney looked around. McManus had his hand up. Sydney ignored the fellow doctor and tried not to laugh.

"Okay then. You're all heroes in waiting. Good luck with the run today!"

There was a smattering of applause.

Sydney looked around for someone to take the microphone. She found the DJ bent under his table of electronics, wolfing down a powdered doughnut. He brushed the confectioner's sugar from his hands. As she handed off the mike, she heard a voice behind her.

"You didn't call on me," McManus said. "I had a question."

"I can only imagine what your question is, Dr. McManus," Sydney said, emphasizing the word *doctor.* The hint of a smile played at the corner of her mouth.

"I was going to ask if you could do mouth-to-mouth if you wanted to."

He grinned slyly, a fan of wrinkles framing his light blue eyes. Sydney shook her head, bemused, although she had an image of kissing this wiseass doc standing in front of her. To her surprise, she found the thought attractive. Kissing this Dr. McManus might just be enjoyable.

"You know," McManus said. "When I was a lifeguard I dreamed of saving a beautiful girl in need of mouth-to-mouth. Someone like you."

"I guess that makes you an optimist. When I was a lifeguard, I feared halitosis grandpa after a massive MI."

McManus laughed. "I guess that makes you a realist."

Grinning, the two doctors stood fidgeting in the cold for a moment. Something about this doctor sparked something deep inside Sydney. It was a feeling she had walled off after Ross had dropped her cold after their near-engagement dinner. Sydney knew if she waited a minute, she would be mad at Dr. Bill McManus for evoking this feeling in her. She viewed men who distracted her, who tempted her to expose her feelings, as duplicitous — malevolent plotters out to derail her professional life. She did not want to invest emotions in a relationship that was doomed to fail.

McManus leaned closer. He was squinting with an inquisitive look on his face.

"If I was a neurologist maybe I could guess what's going on in there." He pointed to her head.

"Dark thoughts, Dr. McManus, dark, dark thoughts," she confessed.

"What could be so dark?" McManus asked. Sydney shrugged. "You're young. You're smart. You're beautiful, you're in great shape."

"And you're full of shit."

"Not at all! If you need a dummy for your demonstration, I'm your guy," McManus said, seemingly emboldened by his own words.

"A dummy? I doubt that."

"But just to be clear, I'd be disappointed if you don't include mouth-to-mouth."

Sydney shook her head.

"Dr. McManus!" she said, pretending to be shocked. It had been a while since a man flirted with her this way. To be fair, she had put up a force field of professionalism to ward off any untoward thoughts. Now, though, she could almost see her defenses dropping. There was something attractive about this gangly, puffy-eyed doctor. What, exactly, she had no idea. He looked like he hadn't slept more than four hours a night in a very long time. His skin was pale from far too many hours under fluorescent lights. His body was all oddball angles, and his hair apparently hadn't seen a comb in days. She couldn't explain what it was with Dr. Bill McManus, but she felt very safe with him. The feeling made her far bolder than she had been since she couldn't remember when. Up to a point.

"Tell you what," Sydney said. "You beat me today and you can be my dummy."

"Really?" McManus had another idea. "If you win, will you make sure I haven't collapsed on the course trying to beat you?" He paused for a moment. "And if you find me prone on the pavement, in respiratory distress . . ." Sydney saw where this was going and smiled despite herself. "Will you resuscitate me — you know — using mouth-to-mouth?"

She laughed. "You're bad."

The PA system interrupted them: "Runners, please make your way to the starting line."

"Good luck," Sydney said as they joined one of several streams of participants flowing together in front of a large starting banner.

"Hey, thanks."

"Let me rephrase that. Moderate luck."

McManus laughed.

Across town, Tina Ridgeway punched the gas on the family minivan as it strained uphill. Mark sat fuming in the passenger's seat. He wore a sport coat and tie. The girls and Ashley were in the back, dressed in their Sunday best. Tina always thought of them that way: the girls and Ashley, as though cerebral palsy put her youngest daughter in a category by herself.

"Does going to church have to be a crisis?" Mark asked.

"I cannot leave the house a mess."

"Wouldn't you rather be on time?"

"It's not either-or, Mark. How many children do I have? Jesus."

"Nice talk on a Sunday."

"Don't be an ass."

"Mom! Dad!" Madison called from the back.

"I'm glad you could find the time to read the paper while the house is a disaster," Tina said.

Mackenzie started crying. Mark reached back and touched his daughter's cheek.

Tina turned into the church's driveway. She shook her head and said nothing. She pulled into a spot and slammed the car into park.

Mark hopped out and opened the sliding door as Tina opened the hatch to get Ashley's chair. Madison and Mackenzie started walking toward the large brick church without them. Mark helped Ashley into her chair and strapped her in.

Mark began singing through gritted teeth: "I've got joy, joy, joy, joy down in my heart. Where? Down in my heart." Hearing a melody, Ashley started happily banging her tray.

"You're a real prick sometimes," Tina said quietly and walked ahead to catch up to Madison and Mackenzie. She didn't look back. If she wasn't so mad, she might have started crying herself, something she hadn't done in a very long time.

CHAPTER 31

Ty sat by the pool of the Delano Hotel, reading a paperback thriller, with a half-emptied bottle of SPF-30 sunscreen sitting next to him. The fate of the free world depended on a gruff loner who had been expelled from the CIA for insubordination. It was always the outsider who was the hero in the airport newsstand thrillers. The Miami sun and salt air had put Ty into a blissful, half-dazed soporific state.

He looked up from the book and enjoyed the undulating, curved lines of the pool's edge, the geometric tile work on the deck, the flickering pattern beneath the water's surface. The Delano was known for its whimsical art deco styling, including a round pool house with portholes, and Ty found the throwback design somehow soothing. Around him couples fringed the pool, their chairs arranged in pairs like dominoes. Younger couples reclined around the water, soaking up the sun facedown, arms across the other's back, or partially reclined reading or drinking *mojitos,* another signature, brought out by mocha-skinned waiters in long white pants and white guayabera shirts. Older couples opted for tables shaded by umbrellas the blue-green of 1950s kitchen linoleum.

Some of the women were topless, and Ty marveled how he could fly to a place so foreign and exotic without ever leaving the United States. Seeing the nearly naked women and the intertwined couples made him long for companionship, a woman close by his side, sleek and available. His thoughts turned to Tina Ridgeway. She was married, of course, but Ty always felt a singular connection with her. And of course, there was no denying the stunning brunette possessed a classical beauty undiminished by age. Right now, Ty imagined he and Tina swimming in the pool, or the ocean beyond, and then heading up to the room for a shower before getting in bed, light streaming through the sheer curtains across the two of them in the small, sparsely furnished room.

The fantasy engaged Ty's mind briefly, but then a wave of fatigue washed over him as the rays of the South Florida sun drained his nervous energy. Ty reclined his chair all the way. He put the book down on the pool deck, closed his eyes beneath his sunglasses, and began drifting off. For some reason, Monique Tran suddenly entered into his mind. She'd looked different somehow when he had seen her in the parking deck with her grandmother. A rosiness to her cheeks, and a slight fullness in her face. *Hmm . . . is she pregnant?* he thought as he finally fell completely asleep.

Dr. Sanford Williams stood at the front of the courtroom next to Monique Tran. He wore a suit. She wore a satin evening gown, even though it was eleven in the morning. The courtroom was empty except for the judge and their two witnesses.

Of course, Monique and Sanford didn't have to dress up. There was no dress requirement for a courthouse wedding, but they still wanted the occasion to be festive.

"I don't want to be the knocked-up chick in the T-shirt and the tattoo, getting married at the courthouse," Monique had said a couple of weeks earlier.

" 'Cause you already have the tattoo," Sanford said, teasing. It was true. Monique had a small peace frog on her shoulder. She and her BFF from high school had gotten matching tattoos the summer after graduation. At the time, the peace frog somehow seemed the embodiment of what they were all about.

Sanford adjusted his navy-blue suit coat and took Monique's small hands in his. He hadn't worn the suit since the day he finished medical school. He was relieved it still fit, though barely. As a resident, he ate when he could, which sometimes meant Pop-Tarts from the vending machine. He also ate knowing he couldn't predict when he might eat again, which meant he'd get the shortbread cookies to go with the Pop-Tarts, just in case. He'd gobble them down before his stomach knew what hit it. It was ironic that even Chelsea General offered fat-laden, high-sodium food in the cafeteria, which he and his cardiac patients often purchased. That his suit pants were only moderately snug was a break.

Monique's sheer gown, the color of eggplant, strained at the midsection. Now in her second trimester, she had started showing in everything but scrubs.

Coming from a good Baptist family, this evidence of premarital intercourse embarrassed Sanford even though the modern courtroom was empty except for his bride-to-be; her cousin, a goth college student who called herself Marilyn and served as

344

their photographer; his roommate and fellow doctor Carter Lawton, their second witness; and the judge.

Washtenaw County judge Ann Mattson, in her black robes and tennis shoes, stood between the couple. She was squeezing the wedding ceremony between a landlord-tenant dispute and a theft-by-kiting case.

The decision to get married at the courthouse in Ann Arbor took both Monique and Sanford some time to reach. Both were used to large family weddings presided over by a man of the cloth. Sanford, in Baptist churches. Monique, in the Catholic Church. But given the distinct possibilities that their families would approve neither of the union, nor of the pregnancy, the couple had weighed their options. The first option was to end the pregnancy and then worry about their future. Monique had considered this as a way to save face with her strict Vietnamese family. Sanford, though, had never been enthusiastic about that option. "How could *you* be?" he had asked Monique. But for a time, they didn't know what else to do. Even though both were raised in households where abortion was morally wrong, they viewed the pregnancy as a mistake that needed to be addressed.

Adoption was an option, but Monique did

not want to endure forty weeks of pregnancy only to hand over the baby to a stranger. She didn't want to go through pregnancy, period. She was twenty-two, single, and working hard — on odd and always-changing shifts. She had never imagined spending her twenties saddled with a child. She simply never thought of herself as the young, single mother lugging a kid everywhere she went. Monique had always felt sorry for those twenty-something mothers.

All that changed when she watched the McDaniel boy die during surgery, the life draining out of him despite Ty Wilson's frantic efforts. She was struck by the preciousness and fragility of existence. She almost felt obliged to have her baby. Monique had in some way participated in the death. She had worked alongside Dr. Wilson, assisting him as he did what he could to save the boy. And when he couldn't, Monique began to think of the child in her belly as some sort of karmic balance. When she saw the McDaniel boy die during surgery, the picture of what she should do resolved itself in her mind. She would keep the baby. Her age, her schedule, the disapproval of her parents and extended family be damned. And if her child was a boy, she would name him Quinn. She knew it would sound corny and illogical if she tried to explain this reasoning to anyone — even Sanford — so she kept that part to herself.

As Ty was finally drifting off to sleep down in Miami, thinking of Monique, she was thinking of him. She had hardly ever spoken to him, except for the advice he had given her in the parking garage. She laughed to herself at the quirk of fate that had allowed Ty to have such an impact on her life. Sanford gave her a look and mouthed a *shush*.

"Monique Tran, Sanford Williams, under the law of the state of Michigan, I am authorized to solemnize the vows between you."

Marilyn danced around them, clicking pictures with her large SLR camera.

Once Monique told Sanford she planned to keep the baby, something seemed to change in him, Monique thought. He took her more seriously. He was more solicitous of her needs as she endured morning sickness and started getting strange cravings. She'd never even liked cottage cheese before. Now she was eating it for breakfast.

Sanford had proposed on the roof of the hospital. He'd waited around for her to get off her graveyard shift and said he wanted to show her something. The ring was modest, less than a carat. Monique didn't fault him. Sanford owed more than a hundred thousand dollars after medical school, and on his resident's salary he was only able to make the minimum loan payments.

Once they'd decided to marry, they chose to make it official as soon as possible — without the headache of their families. The process was surprisingly easy. They'd paid a twenty-dollar fee to the county, observed the three-day waiting period to get their license, and then scheduled a time with the judge. The court got another ten bucks.

Now Sanford held her two hands in his. He looked in her eyes, and she looked in his. She had loved his blue-green eyes in the OR, shining brightly above his mask, before they even knew each other.

"Do you, Sanford, take Monique to be your lawfully wedded wife?"

"I do."

"And do you, Monique, take Sanford to be your lawfully wedded husband?"

"Heck yeah."

Sanford laughed and shook his head and then something surprising happened. He was suddenly choked up. He loved Monique, but if he was being completely honest with himself, he never would have proposed if she wasn't pregnant. It was the right thing to do, and he approached the nuptials with his fingers crossed. Now, for the first time, he could see himself spending the rest of his life with this woman, could see his love for her growing, could see their lives together as an adventure. He looked at her out of the corner of his eye, and saw the steady stream of tears flowing down her cheek. He leaned over powerfully, and kissed the bride.

On Sunday evening, Ty was sitting at an outdoor restaurant on South Beach eating fish with black beans and rice when his pager went off. *311. 6.* Ty turned off the pager. He held a ticket for a flight later that night scheduled to get him back to Michigan around midnight. He wasn't going to take it. They didn't know it yet at Chelsea General, but Ty had other plans.

CHAPTER 32

Villanueva was on a toilet in the hospital when his cell phone rang. He didn't hesitate for a second and answered. He always enjoyed multitasking, and for some reason got an extra kick out of talking on the phone when he was sitting on the toilet. He considered it a practical joke, of sorts. *If they could see me now,* he'd tell himself, *they'd be the ones shitting.* In this case, he saw the caller ID and knew instantly it wasn't going to be a pleasant call.

"Hello, Lisa. You're up early."

"Are you on the toilet?"

"Uh . . ."

"George, what were you thinking?"

"You're not going to say, *Hello, how are you? Thanks for sending the checks, so I can keep my five-thousand-square-foot monstrosity toasty warm and my Range Rover filled with gas and my toes painted a glossy hue of harlot?*"

"You've always got a joke. George. This is not a joke."

"Okay, I'll bite. What's got your designer thongs in a wad?"

"You could have gotten yourself killed. In front of your son! This is your idea of parenting?"

"What?" As soon as Villanueva asked the question, he remembered the confrontation. "Oh, that."

"Yes, that. What were you thinking?"

"You know me, Lisa. I'm all about peace and love. Just had to straighten out some jag-off."

"Jesus, George. Why you? That's why we have police. Nick was terrified."

"Terrified?"

"Yes, George."

Villanueva checked his watch. The thought of enduring another ten minutes or so of this harangue was not something he welcomed. It was 5:55 AM. Saved by the bell.

"Lisa, I'd love to chat. I've got M and M."

"Well, that's just wonderful. Listen, if you want to commit suicide, do it on your own time and not in front of your highly impressionable son!"

"Roger that. Suicide. Own time." His ex hung up before he had finished.

By the time Villanueva reached Room

311, Buck Tierney was standing at the front of the room before the assembled surgeons. Tierney stood ramrod-straight at parade rest, his hands behind his back and legs spread shoulder width. Even though he had never gone beyond ROTC as an undergrad, Tierney liked to give off a military bearing. He gave the impression he was a general readying his troops for a great battle. From his perspective, that wasn't too far off. Life was about winning other people over to your point of view.

"Good to see all of you this morning. Wish I could serve you up some eggs and home fries." The assembled surgeons were used to Buck's down-home shtick and didn't respond. Tierney rocked on his heels and continued. "I wanted to answer something Dr. Saxena proposed the last time we were here. You may recall she suggested we not let instrument reps in the OR. Now, first of all, let me be clear, this conversation isn't about Dr. Saxena, whom I have no doubt is an outstanding doctor."

Sitting next to Hooten, Sydney Saxena bristled.

"And don't get me wrong, I'm all for maintaining the sanctity of our decision-making abilities as doctors, but facts are facts. And whether or not Dr. Saxena likes to admit it, the truth of the matter is a rep may know more about the stent or graft or hip than many surgeons do. He might know more about the latest heart valve than even you do, Dr. Saxena."

Sydney stood and held up her hands as though he were an errant motorist about to run a stop sign. "Dr. Tierney —"

Buck barreled ahead. "The reps — they've been around 'em more. They've seen more operations using 'em. If they want to spend a couple hours in the OR while we use their device, I say more power to 'em. More power to us, really."

"Dr. Tierney, if I may," Saxena said as politely as possible. "As medical professionals, we are the ultimate arbiters of what care our patients receive."

"No one says we have to listen to 'em."

"Buck, whether or not you want to admit it, those reps are influencing sacred medical decisions, and they are doing it to benefit their own pocketbook. Look, we had a case in here a year or so ago where the rep during a TKA said one of our surgeons needed to shave a little more bone off the tibia, so his own prosthetic would fit. Now, that advice happened to be wrong, but our surgeon listened to him. The outcome was less than desirable."

There were a few murmurs of assent among the surgeons. The orthopedist who had performed the surgery, Dr. Joseph Polanski, stared straight ahead and said nothing.

"I do remember that case. The woman was left with a limp," a doctor a few rows behind him called out.

Buck held up his hands.

"Dr. Saxena, you're just cherry-pickin' examples here. I could give you ten other examples where the rep gave advice that was not only medically sound, but prevented a bad outcome."

There were murmurs of assent to Tierney's argument. One surgeon called from the back, "Some of those guys are good, no question. You know Troy Richardson, with Bravo Devices? I had an improper alignment of the calcaneus for the screw, and he pointed it out."

Tierney looked at Saxena and held a hand out toward the surgeon, as though he were presenting evidence in court. Saxena ignored him and turned to the large cadre of doctors surrounding her.

"I know we're all busy," she said. "But do we want to be relying on ex-football-players and sorority presidents to be telling us what we should or should not be doing in the OR?"

"They know their stuff," Tierney said.

"They know *their* stuff. They're going to spend that hour or two in the OR convincing you that *their* stuff is the only way to go. What if you want to use some other company's stuff?"

"I don't know about you, Dr. Saxena, but I am not going to let one of these reps push me around," Tierney said. His tone was clear: The only reason Sydney wanted to ban the reps was that she was a patsy.

"Would you let a detailer in the examination room while you considered what drug might be appropriate for your patient?" Saxena asked.

"Now you're talking about Medicine. We all know those worms in Medicine are pushovers and need all the protection they can get."

A wave of laughter went through the room.

"We," Tierney said with gusto. "We are surgeons!" The mostly male crowd roared their approval.

"Now you're talking!" one surgeon called.

Sydney shook her head. She could see she had been badly beaten by Tierney's demagoguery. The experience was deflating.

Villanueva, his enormous mass immobile

for most of the debate, stood up. Sydney's hopes rose.

"Buck. I don't suppose your argument is any way colored by Bravo Devices' ten-million-dollar pledge for a 'Bravo Ambulatory Care' center for your new heart wing, is it?"

Tierney reddened.

"Dr. Villanueva, I resent the insinuation. You are impugning my honor, and I will not stand here and allow you or anyone else to impugn my honor."

"What are you, the prince of England? Who talks like that?"

Buck took a step toward Villanueva. Hooten stood.

"Gentlemen, enough!"

Hooten turned toward Chelsea General's surgical staff. "By a show of hands, let me know how many of you are in favor of barring representatives of medical device companies from the OR?"

The hands of half a dozen doctors went up, Sydney, Tina, and Villanueva among them.

"How many are opposed and would like to keep the status quo?"

The remaining forty or so hands went up.

"All right then. It is settled," Hooten said authoritatively.

■ ■ ■ ■

Early that afternoon, Park's wife came to pick him up at his office. Park didn't mind relinquishing the driving to her. He looked forward to Pat's arrival each afternoon.

Sung had worried the surgery and radiation would affect what he prized most of all — his hard-won knowledge. So far, he felt sharp as ever. He'd be starting a monthly course of chemo pills soon, though, and that could also scramble his brain.

"One step at a time," Pat told him. Or, "One day at a time."

He'd tried to take her advice. He hadn't reviewed the latest medical literature on his scheduled chemo or calibrated his life expectancy based on the latest data and the success of his treatment thus far.

Something else: Park appreciated each day at the teaching hospital. Instead of sizing up his own abilities against his colleagues', he'd begun to value their talents. Instead of viewing patients as abstract medical problems, he started seeing them as people.

Park noticed how fellow staffers at Chelsea General now treated him differently. No longer did they deal with him as an unpleasant necessity in their lives. They approached

357

him with kindness. They took the time to quiz him about his family. They asked if there was anything they could do for him. Each night, the radiation oncologist, a Dr. Eduardo Hernandez, clasped Park's hands in his own and wished him well before stepping out of the room so the radiation machine could perform its task. With his life on the line, he was finally welcomed into Chelsea General. Always an outsider, Park the patient had somehow become one of them. Park treasured it, and also noted this as yet another example of the odd behavior of Americans.

Pat put an arm around his waist, a public gesture of affection that was new since his diagnosis. Before, he had made it clear that she should stay away from the hospital, and he would have scolded her for showing affection there — or anywhere in public, for that matter. Now he was enjoying having Pat at his side. Her slim arm around his soft midsection was comforting.

"Let's get you home for a nap."

"Yes."

They began making their way to the parking garage.

"And then maybe we can go out for dinner," Sung said. "The two of us."

"A date?" They had not gone on a date in

years. Park saw that he had surprised her and he saw that she was smiling. It was the expression of a little girl. Park said nothing, but he experienced a deep joy seeing her so happy.

They took a few more steps. "Do we know any babysitters?" Park asked. They had never left their children with anyone who was not family. Park's father was in Korea and Pat's family — a mother, father, and brother — lived in New Jersey and rarely visited. So the kids went everywhere with them. Even when they appeared at colleagues' parties, they would arrive early with the children in tow. If it was a formal event or a hospital function, Sung Park would go alone.

"I think there are some older girls in the neighborhood."

"Good," Park said.

"Tonight may be difficult."

"I see." Doubt entered Park's voice.

"But we will go on a date as soon as we can find a babysitter. Soon. Okay?" Still with her arm around his waist, she pulled her husband tight.

"A date!" Park said.

CHAPTER 33

Instead of boarding the flight that would bring him home in time for Monday Morning and Room 311, Ty booked a flight the following morning from Miami to Houston and on to Phoenix. Once he landed at Sky Harbor International, he rented a car and headed north on 87 until he reached the turnoff for Fountain Hills.

He had never missed a Monday Morning meeting during his time at the hospital. Part of that was chance. They weren't held every week, and when he'd vacationed in Italy three years earlier and Southern California the previous year, he'd planned it around a break in the M&M schedule. When he rented a cabin on the Upper Peninsula for a couple of weeks one summer, Ty had come back for M&M and then resumed his vacation. Once, he'd driven his motorcycle all night to return from a college friend's wedding in Philadelphia. Another time, he had walked in after operating all night on a patient whose skull fractured when she was launched through a windshield.

Ty turned into a condominium development set into a hillside and pulled up in front of an adobe-colored, stucco home with a living room window made of glass bricks and a small deck over a two-door garage. The deck offered up a view of rooftops stretching across the valley and low mountains in the distance. Even though it was late autumn, the temperature was pushing ninety. He didn't see his sister's car, but he assumed it was in the garage. He'd heard stories about cars getting so hot people used potholders on the steering wheel. He was pretty sure that was an urban legend, but you never knew.

Ty parked his rental and knocked on the door. His sister Kate answered so quickly, Ty was left knocking in thin air. Brother and sister spent a moment just looking at each other, and then exchanged an affectionate hug.

Everything was in order. The house was so meticulously maintained you'd never guess she had two preschool-aged children — unless you noticed the foam corners neatly affixed to the coffee table or the childproof outlet covers. Kate watched Ty as he walked to the couch and sat down. She wore a look of concern. It was as though she was trying to determine if this visitor was really her older brother. Kate pulled up a chair and sat facing him.

"Ty, what's going on?"

"I wouldn't have asked if you could see me if it wasn't important."

"Of course. I can take a day off for big brother. So what's happening? I'm worried about you."

"I gave you the gist of it in my text. Just having a hard time shaking this," Ty said. He found it difficult to continue. Kate took his hand. The move seemed to flip a switch. This was the one person in the world who really knew him, who could understand him, who loved him always without hesitation.

Ty began sobbing. The grief welled up from deep inside. It was as though her touch had released whatever was holding it back. Kate leaned forward and put her hands on Ty's shoulder. Ty's sobs came in waves: grief not only for Quinn McDaniel and Allison McDaniel, but his brother, Ted, and his sister Christine. Whatever stopper had held those feelings in check was released. It was as though he was vomiting grief.

"Ty, it's okay. Whatever it is, it's okay.

You're a good doctor. A great doctor."

"But this wasn't supposed to happen," Ty said through his tears. "It wasn't supposed to happen." He looked down at her Navajo-patterned rug as he spoke.

"It's okay, Ty."

"After Ted died. And Christine was shot. I told myself I was going to be the one, *the* doctor. The doctor who could save people like Ted, like Christine, when no one else could. And then this kid. Quinn McDaniel. Kate, I was supposed to be the one who could save him. I was created . . . evolved, somehow designed to do . . . *this*." He paused. "Ridiculous, right?" Ty let out a long sigh.

"You know what?" Kate said. "You're right." Ty looked up at her. "It *is* ridiculous," she continued.

Kate gazed at her big brother as he wiped his eyes. One of Ty's best friends, maybe his only friend, a pediatric heart transplant surgeon, had killed himself on Christmas Eve, a few years ago. He had left a note: *I can't bear the thought of not being able to save another child.* Despite the thousands of kids who were alive because of him, the surgeon was incapable of remembering anything other than the children who hadn't made it. Kate remembered this story warily.

"Women always say they want a man who cries. That's until they actually see him crying," Ty said. Kate gave him a sympathetic smile. He shook his head and wiped his eyes again. "I'm in a terrible place, and I can't figure out how to fix it."

"Now you're just being silly." Kate stood up and walked toward the kitchen. "You want a cup of green tea?"

Ty joined Kate in the small kitchen. She put water in the kettle and turned on the gas burner.

"You don't think we'd lose two siblings and emerge without any scars, do you?" she said. She spoke quietly. "I think that's partly why I got into the insurance business. I wanted to know risks, and to better understand them."

"I guess," Ty said. He was still spent from his crying jag.

"I can tell you, professionally speaking, we as a society do a crappy job weighing risks."

"Yeah?"

"We feel safer at the wheel of the car than we do flying in a plane. We're at much greater risk. We're more afraid of risks produced by people, like radiation from cell phones, than natural radiation from the sun, but the sun is much more dangerous. We're more afraid when the uncertainty is high. More afraid of risks we're aware of. More afraid of new risks."

"I know you're going somewhere with this, but I'm not following."

"We're hardwired to weigh risks a certain way. We can't help it."

Steam whistled through the spout of the kettle, and Kate poured them both tea. She returned to the table with the steaming mugs.

"Drink some of this. You always loved green tea, even when everyone else thought it was earthy, crunchy, New Agey." Kate smiled.

"Thanks, sis, lots of antioxidants. And I am kind of earthy crunchy . . . I even meditate nowadays." Ty sipped his tea. "Now, weren't you telling me something about risk?"

"Yes. What happened with that boy."

"Quinn McDaniel."

"Yes, Quinn McDaniel. Well, he threw your own actuarial tables out the window. All of a sudden, a seemingly healthy boy can have a much higher risk for dying — even with one of the best surgeons in the world operating on him. You're driving the car but you're not in total control, even if you think you are."

"Not sure I'm tracking."

Kate took a sip. Ty watched his sister. He could practically see the gears turning in her head.

"Bad things happen to good people. With your training and your skill, you've done everything you could to tip the odds against that. But *bad* things still happen to *good* people. Even with the wonderful Ty Wilson performing their surgery. Look, big brother, it's not about finding redemption, or somehow tipping the scales of bad toward the good side of things. That will never work."

"So what *am* I supposed to do?"

"Ty." She sat next to him on the ottoman. "Learn from your mistakes and then move on. It's the most important thing you can do."

Ty rode with Kate to the preschool to pick up her two young daughters, Lydia and Liza. Together they gave their uncle Ty an enthusiastic embrace. Kate peeled an orange and gave the girls slices.

"Do you need to spend the night?"

"No." Ty hadn't given much thought to his plans. He felt much lighter than he had when he'd arrived.

"It wouldn't be a problem. The girls would love to have a sleepover with Uncle

Ty. And you can see Henry. His flight gets in later."

"No. I should —" Ty paused. Should what? He assumed he'd head back to Michigan and Chelsea General after this stop in Phoenix, but should he?

"So what are you going to do now?" Kate asked as though she were reading his thoughts. "Are you going home? Are you going to go back to the hospital?"

"I don't know. I haven't decided."

Ty hugged his sister and nieces good-bye and went back to his car.

"Tell Henry I am sorry I missed him, and I will see him soon."

"No you won't." Kate smiled. "But he loves you anyway."

He drove out of the subdivision and turned toward Phoenix and the airport. He saw a gas station ahead and pulled into it. He just needed time to think.

CHAPTER 34

When his son coughed, breathed his last breath, and rolled over, dead, everyone around gasped. Villanueva, though, was thrilled. Nick was on stage. Performing. This was the same catatonic couch potato whose vocabulary consisted of a succession of barely audible grunts. Here he was, in makeup. Acting. Villanueva couldn't have been more proud if Nick had just caught the winning touchdown in the final minutes of the championship game. He knew first-hand the thrill of a crowd, and he was ecstatic he and his son now shared this experience.

The big man was not worried a whit that Nick's stage debut consisted of a very small part in a student-written and -directed high school production. He was seeing a new side to the scrawny, almost mute boy who'd seemed incapable of much of anything but watching television and playing video games for a couple of years now. Until an hour or so earlier, he had worried that his son was an ineffable loser, a nice boy lost in his co-cooned PlayStation world, his hand permanently attached to a video game controller. Could this be the same boy who had spent most of his adolescence staring at his feet and mumbling when George spoke to him?

Seeing his son on stage, El Gato was busting at his very large seams. He had to resist the very strong urge to clap the shoulder of the stooped parent next to him and proclaim on the spot: *That's my boy that just died up there!*

More than pride, Villanueva experienced a surge of parental relief. It dawned on him how worried he'd been about his son making his way in the world. Seeing the boy in public like this allayed those fears. Most of them, anyway. Maybe things wouldn't turn out so badly for the kid. Maybe he'd graduate from college. Maybe he'd hold down a job somewhere. Maybe — and George had to take this one on faith — just maybe his son might find some companion to date, a love to marry. Nick acting was like a thread, the first one Villanueva had seen with any hope of becoming the fabric of a happy and — George hated to think this way — normal life.

So what if he was becoming one of those theater kids and not a jock. Villanueva didn't care. Every kid needed a place. Maybe Nick wouldn't be one of those kids living in the basement into their twenties and beyond, looking for handouts and home-cooked meals.

Villanueva's expectations for Nick had lowered considerably since his days coaching the boy in youth football. At this point, George didn't care if the boy had no interest in sports or looked like a strong breeze could uproot him. If he could take part in a play, perhaps there were other talents that lay beneath the boy's taciturn adolescent surface.

Half an hour after Nick's dying scene, even before the velvet curtain hit the stage at North High auditorium, Villanueva was on his feet, clapping. Other parents joined him in the standing ovation. *They're cheering my son,* Villanueva thought, only conceding to himself a moment later they might also be cheering their own sons and daughters. Villanueva didn't care. He put two sausage-size index fingers in his mouth and whistled.

The cast took turns taking bows, in ascending order of their roles. Nick was in one of the first small groups to move to the front of the raised stage, hold hands, and bow. Villanueva yelled "Bravo" and whistled again, this time catching Nick's eye. The boy looked away, but he was smiling.

Villanueva vaguely remembered Nick asking if he should try out for the part. He had encouraged his son, assuming he wouldn't get a part but thinking he should get his ass off the couch, at least for however long it took to audition. Villanueva had no idea what that entailed but it couldn't be worse than his default, which was doing nothing — or at least nothing that required human interaction.

Nick had never told him that he'd tried out, nor that he'd made it. His ex had called and clued him in only because she couldn't make the performance. She didn't say why, and Villanueva didn't ask. Even though the thought of spending an evening with the ex was akin to a day of periodontal surgery, the thought of her with another man was still one he tried to avoid.

Nick met his father in the auditorium lobby. They stood amid the eddies and swirls of other actors, parents, friends. Nick was doing his best to hold back a smile, to be cool. *Who knows?* Villanueva thought, *maybe the boy will get his ass laid.* Nick had wiped most of the makeup off his face, but missed the spots around his ears and temples. Villanueva wrapped his son in a bear hug.

"Dad!" Nick said. On one level, he sounded alarmed. On another, pleased.

"Strong work, Nick. You and me. We gotta celebrate."

"Okay." Nick sounded guarded.

"You were great!"

"Thanks, Dad."

They navigated their way through the clots of parents and children and pushed through the double doors leading outside. As they walked down the steps from the auditorium to the high school's massive parking lot, Villanueva stopped.

"Nick, I gotta ask, could you feel the audience? Could you feel the energy?"

Nick looked surprised, as though his father was in on a secret. "Yeah, Dad, I could."

"Pretty cool, isn't it."

"Yeah."

They started walking again, and Nick glanced sidelong at his father. He wore a smirk that he could not suppress. When Villanueva put his arm around his son's shoulder, the teenager didn't even shrug it off as a public embarrassment. They made their way down the long row of SUVs and minivans until they reached Villanueva's convertible roadster. Villanueva sensed his son was not telling him something.

"What is it, Nick? You got something else going on?"

"There's sort of a cast party. Do you think you could take me there?"

Squint.

"We'll celebrate another time."

"Sure, Dad."

"That a promise?"

"Sure." Nick sounded enthusiastic.

"You were great."

"It was a pretty small part."

"You were great," George said again, squeezing his son on the shoulder.

"Thanks."

Villanueva folded his enormous bulk into the coupe, looking more than a little like Fred Flintstone. His son got in next to him.

"Where to, son?"

Chapter 35

Ty undid the buttons of her silk blouse, one by one, taking his time, savoring the moment, his excitement growing. He was not entirely sure how he had arrived at this place, by the picture window in his darkened penthouse apartment. She had suggested the rendezvous when she called Ty as he sat at the gas station in Phoenix. When he saw the call was from Tina, he knew he'd go back to Michigan. Whatever amorphous thoughts he'd had about doing anything else vanished.

When he'd opened the door, she had leaned over without a word and kissed him on the mouth, a hand on his hip. There was a hunger in her kiss that surprised Ty and threw him off guard, at least for a moment. He hadn't expected this. Not from her. But when he recovered from his surprise, he had pulled her against him. Now she was pulling the T-shirt over his head, and no thought of right or wrong entered Ty's mind.

Ty removed her bra, and pulled her on top of him on the long couch in his living room. After the anguish of the previous weeks, he allowed himself to be swallowed in the moment, the sum total of his universe consisting of the face in front of his, the body pressing against him.

As they kissed, Ty had one thought: Tina Ridgeway's beauty took his breath away. He knew this was a cliché but it was true. He was dazzled by her beauty, blinded by it. That she was married, that she was a co-worker and a friend, those thoughts would come later, he knew. For now, he ran his hand along the small of her back and allowed himself to become lost in the moment.

Tina left Ty's apartment before dawn. Ty was still sleeping, and she managed to dress and walk out the door without waking him. As she drove home, the passion of the night faded and was replaced by not only fatigue but also a sinking feeling of regret.

Tina had always prided herself on doing the right thing, even when it was unpopular. She had argued in favor of the resident Michelle Robidaux, not so much because she thought the young woman would turn out to be an outstanding surgeon as because teaching hospitals were supposed to teach, not castigate struggling young doctors.

As a resident herself, she had run afoul of one of her attendings, the imperious Gerald Esposito, who had written her up for telling a patient about an alternative treatment to the one he was recommending. Tina received word to be in the office of the chief of the residency program the next day at one o'clock. Literally quivering with fear, sure that her medical career was over, Tina had arrived at Dr. Daniel Barrow's office at the appointed hour. When she sat down, Barrow had held up the report detailing her transgressions.

"You know what I think of this?" Barrow leaned over and ripped the report in two, dropping it in the trash can next to his desk.

Tina looked from the ripped report back to Barrow. He raised his eyebrows at her, as she absorbed the institutional insolence she had just witnessed.

"I'm not worried in the least about you. You're going to be a fine doctor. Now get back to work."

Tina didn't know what to say, so she said nothing. Walking down the narrow paths between old brick buildings that led back to the hospital, Tina had first laughed and then cried at her good fortune.

What would Dr. Barrow think of her now? She had let Michelle Robidaux down. She had allowed Chelsea General to toss out Michelle Robidaux when the young doctor had become legally inconvenient. And she had let herself down, selfishly betraying her marriage vows, her sense of self, and her friendship with Ty.

Mark was asleep when she arrived home but lifted his head and looked over at her as she slid between the sheets. He looked at her vacantly, his eyes flat.

"Sorry," Tina said. "I had a case." Mark didn't respond. He looked at her for a moment more, his mask-like expression unnerving her. The spark in the marriage had fizzled sometime earlier, maybe a year, maybe more. They both knew it, though neither mentioned how their relationship had devolved from intimacy into a series of bloodless interactions, flat discussions of who would pick up one of the girls at ballet or go to the store or call the plumber. Neither acknowledged out loud that their marriage was dying. Saying it aloud would somehow make it real, and they would have to do something about it. Up until that point, neither had the inclination or energy to do that.

Now, as Tina looked at Mark's expressionless face, his almost dead eyes, a frisson of fear caused her to shiver. She worried he would raise the issue now, when she was tired and feeling guilty. When she *was* guilty. Mark rolled over and went back to sleep, his breathing slow and rhythmic.

Tina remained wide awake, despite fatigue so deep her limbs felt like alien appendages. She replayed Mark's look. Was that suspicion? Could he see she was suffused with the afterglow of sex? It had been a while since Mark had seen her like that. If Tina had to guess, she would say it was before their second child was born. The conception of child number three was a fluke, the product of too much wine at, ironically enough, a hospital party.

As Tina repositioned herself on the pillow as softly as possibly, as though she might literally make waves with any hasty or clumsy motion, she thought about that article Ty had mentioned detailing the more than two hundred reasons people had sex. Most involved permutations of power and self-esteem. She wondered if that was also the category her night with Ty would fit into. True, she had always connected with him. Lately, however, when she saw Ty at the hospital, there was something unusual in his expression, a vulnerability.

The hours with Ty had been like a dream, and she had craved the intimacy. Now, as the predawn thrum of traffic became audible from the highway a mile or so away, Tina wondered what she had been thinking. What was she hoping to accomplish? Also, she experienced shame. She had broken her vows again. Even though she considered them largely empty, Ridgeways did not break their vows. They did not go against their word. The betrayal gave her a sick feeling in her gut.

As a teenager, before she had gone on a date, her father would always call after her, "Remember who you are." She took this seriously. She stayed clear when her summer friends in Edgartown met some prep cook in a walk-in refrigerator to buy pot, or when they used fake IDs to buy six-packs, vodka, tequila, and more from the package store. She wasn't a total nerd. She went to the parties on South Beach, but she left before hormones and alcohol-fueled thinking made skinny-dipping, tipping lifeguard stands, and unprotected sex seem like good ideas. Her father's admonition was in her head when she grabbed her boyfriend's wrist as he tried to slide a hand down her pants in the cramped backseat of his parents' BMW. Another of her father's sayings: "Don't do anything you wouldn't want printed in the newspaper."

Tina rolled over and faced away from her husband, but despite her fatigue she could not find sleep. She thought about the headline from that night's transgression: "Respected Doctor Guilty of Adultery." Or, "Married Mother of Three Seduces Doctor." She lay there for a few more minutes stewing in her thoughts. Finally unwilling to lie there another minute longer, she got out of bed, went to the kitchen, and started the coffee machine. A hint of purple was visible behind the trees at the far end of their small backyard.

As the coffee gurgled, Tina thought of the time when she was five or six. She, her brother, and her parents had gone to the Dukes County Agricultural Fair, the highlight of the summer on Martha's Vineyard. Wandering among the quilts and pies and artwork inside the old Grange Hall, she had become separated from her family. She went outside, thinking maybe they were ahead of her. In growing panic, she walked aimlessly among the dirt and straw and the fast-moving swirl of the crowd, a churning maelstrom of legs and feet from her vantage point. Day was giving way to night, and

Tina watched a girl her own age getting lemonade squeezed from lemons and shaken with sugar and water. She walked some more, her panic growing. She walked down a corridor of carnival games and food and was distracted by the blinking lights around a booth in which you threw darts and tried to pop balloons to win stuffed animals. Darts were arranged in threes on the counter in front of the game, and enormous stuffed animals were tacked to the wall on either side of the bright balloons. The carnie running the game had leaned over the counter, his weathered, tanned face close, blocking her path. "Are you lost?" he leered.

Tina had backed away from the cigarette breath, her heart pounding, and bumped into a teenage boy.

"Watch it."

She spun around. It was now dark, the lights from the Tilt-A-Whirl spinning around in front of her. Kids screaming. The fairgoers were silhouettes among the brightly lighted rides and games. At that moment, she was certain she would never see her family again. Tears came to her eyes. She was terrified. She stopped moving and stood as people walked past.

That's when she heard her father's distinc-

tive whistle, an up-and-down, almost whimsical sound he used at the beach when he
wanted them to come. She found him and
wrapped her arms around his legs.

"Daddy!"

"Heya, monkey."

Tina could always count on her father to
rescue her when she was lost. Tina adored
her father. She picked up the phone and
called. He answered on the first ring.

"Hi, Dad."

"Hi, Tina. Kind of early for you academic
docs, isn't it?" Tina's father liked to chide
her about her life in a teaching hospital,
though his ribbing was filled with pride. He
acted as though he himself had not spent
most of his career in academic medicine
before taking over his father's practice in
Vermont in his sixties.

"Just wanted to see how it's going up
there."

"Got our first big snow. You know what
that means. Big business. Broken ribs. Heart
attacks. Sprained knees. But it is beautiful.
What are you doing calling so early?"

"Just wanted to see how you're doing."

"Anytime you want to help out the old
man, we'll stick your name on the shingle.
Ridgeway and Ridgeway, Practitioners of
the Ancient Healing Arts."

"Sounds good."

"I'm serious, monkey. Anytime."

"Thanks, Dad."

Tina said good-bye and imagined herself for a moment in rural Vermont, bringing patients into the world and seeing them out. Serving as ob-gyn, family practitioner, urologist, oncologist, and every other stripe of medicine. The image seemed attractive. For all the professional prestige that came with working at a large teaching hospital, Tina admired the country doctors who often had only themselves and their medical knowledge to rely on in an emergency.

She wondered for a moment what her father would think about her scrapping her career at Chelsea General. She was angry with herself for even raising the question. Her father had always been a towering figure. She admired him, but at the same time she was growing to realize just how much control he had exerted on her path through life. Once her brother had strayed from the expectation he would become a doctor, it had been a foregone conclusion that Tina would become an MD and go into academic medicine. No doubt, she chose her own specialty, but the rest was preordained. Tina was thinking about this when she heard the rest of the family begin to stir.

CHAPTER 36

At that moment, Harding Hooten stood on his back deck and listened. Nothing thrilled him like the dawn chorus. He heard cardinals, a mourning dove, the rapid-fire knocking of a woodpecker. Was that a bluebird he heard? Hooten enjoyed a deep satisfaction from birding, though he had little time for it. This quiet moment before dawn was about all he could count on, and that meant listening, not watching.

Hooten's fascination with birds began as a medical student, when a fellow first-year at Columbia had approached him and asked if he was "a birder." Hooten paused for a moment trying to grasp the man's name from his memory. The fellow had looked somewhat like a stork himself. What was his damn name? Hooten dug hard. He was doing this more often lately, trying to remember a name, an address, a fact from his life. He had taken to stopping what he was doing until he found the neuronal pathway that gave him his answer, but it was getting harder.

Hooten pictured his former classmate, six-foot-six, spindly, bushy eyebrows. He even remembered what he was wearing that morning: blue work pants and a denim shirt. Same thing he wore every day they went out. Hooten saw him leaning close to patients, listening with his head cocked to the side, not missing a word as he took histories. His expressive eyes always seemed damp, as though from tears or glee. He was empathy personified. Amazing bedside manner. The switch flipped for Hooten.

Scott. That was his name: Clinton Scott. Hooten breathed a sigh of relief. Maybe he wasn't senile just yet. They called him Great Scott because patients would confess all sorts of dark secrets — drinking problems, domestic violence, even sexual troubles decades before erectile dysfunction became an acronym tossed around by athletic men on television commercials. Hooten breathed a sigh of relief. Clinton Scott. He dreaded the continuing march of age-related memory loss.

That fall morning in Upper Manhattan almost fifty years earlier, Scott had asked him if he was a birder.

"You mean a bird-watcher?" Hooten replied. Growing up in Camden, Maine, he had never given birds a second thought, other than to note that seagulls would eat almost anything they could choke down their gullets. A friend of his had worked at a doughnut shop and would lob unsold crullers at the birds, which would catch them and swallow them in stages like a sword swallower at a traveling carnival.

"I'll take that as a no," Scott said and handed him a pair of binoculars. "Let's go."

"But this is New York."

"Central Park is a wonderful place, but we want to be there when the sun comes up."

Hooten was tired. He had been up memorizing the bones of the hand, but Scott's enthusiasm was infectious. From that morning on, Hooten was a birder. On mornings he wasn't at the hospital, he went out with Scott. The outings were a reminder there was a world outside the hospital. Hooten found the serenity of watching and listening relaxing, even amid the long, long hours of residency.

Scott had gone on to become an endocrinologist and eventually head the Universidad de Ciencias Médicas in Costa Rica, no doubt attracted to the job because of the incredible diversity of bird life in that small Central American country. There were more species there than in all of the United States. At the last reunion, he'd heard Scott, one of his only true friends, had been killed in a car accident.

Hooten closed his eyes, listening, separating the cacophony of birdsongs into the different species. Even in the dark, the birds could communicate. It was a natural marvel, but on this morning, the ornithological orchestra did not soothe him. The peace he usually felt from the birdsongs did not last long. He was thinking of the upcoming M&M. An appalling lack of communication had almost resulted in the death of a child, and Hooten had decided he was not going to let this sort of benign neglect pass without making a few of his junior colleagues sweat. A patient who dies in the OR despite a surgeon's best efforts was one thing, but passing the buck while a child's condition deteriorated was something he was not going to tolerate as long he was chief of surgery.

There was something else troubling Hooten this morning. He knew Martha wanted him to retire, to spend more time with her, with the children and grandchildren, to spend time at the place on

Mackinac Island. But at the end of the day, what was his legacy? How could his stamp on Chelsea General be made lasting? The hospital might commission a portrait and hang his likeness in some corridor, or name a teaching service after him, but day to day how could his time at Chelsea General be measured?

Hooten had worked hard during his thirty-odd years at Chelsea General. As chief of surgery, he had routinely put in fourteen- or sixteen-hour days. He had done his best to make sure Chelsea General adopted the latest surgical techniques, that every surgeon under him paid attention to details, and that residents received the best training possible. Maybe most important, he ran M&M in a way designed to make every surgeon 100 percent accountable, and as a result had transformed the very way surgeons learned and benefited from one another's mistakes. Hooten had added a level of transparency to surgery rarely seen anywhere in the world. Still, his eyes clouded. The girl's case showed that despite the best practices, medicine fell to individuals, who too often were inclined to push their work on to the next physician or the next shift as a result of laziness, or fatigue, or lack of confidence, or dinner plans. Even on his watch, the patient sometimes got short-changed. The doctors, nurses, lab techs, pharmacists, therapists, social workers, orderlies inside the hospital who turned the institution from a large hodgepodge of buildings to a living, breathing organism were too often prone to the second law of thermodynamics: entropy — the tendency of disorder to increase over time. *Between the motion and the act falls the shadow.* Hooten's job was to prevent the shadow, to reverse the natural trend toward disorder, slothfulness, fuzzy thinking, shortcuts, and sloppy assumptions. He did not want his tenure at Chelsea General to end with a whimper. How was it possible to have his exacting standards last longer at the hospital than he did?

In the early glow of the day, Hooten watched a female cardinal perched on a branch, its coloring just starting to show tan-green. If Chelsea General was the sum total of the individuals, Hooten thought, then the only way the hospital maintained its high standards was to make sure the individual who took his place held the same standards he did. His replacement couldn't worry about being popular and had to be equally immune to flattery and intimidation.

For years, Hooten had thought Buck

Tierney might be right for the job. He was well connected, and that could only help the hospital as it competed for the big-dollar treatment centers. Also, Tierney's ego was so big he didn't seem to worry much about what others thought of him. But Hooten was rethinking his reasoning. He had seen in Sydney Saxena a tenacity and the kind of unyielding standards that could make her the perfect person. She was young, not even forty. Hooten had been almost fifty when he took the job, replacing the legendary Julian Hoff. But Saxena had the right mindset. She was driven to do the right thing and demanded excellence from everyone around her. She would not stand for shoddy medicine. Put her in place now, and she could keep the Department of Surgery in line for years. Now all he had to do was figure out how to overcome the resistance of folks like the CEO, Morgan Smith, who was vocally supportive of Tierney, and others on the board. Hooten was not naive. He knew the fact that Saxena was both young and a woman might hurt her chances among some of the old guard. Still, he knew she was the right person for the job.

CHAPTER 37

Ty walked through Chelsea General feeling
as though he suffered from a sort of hang-
over. He hadn't been drinking, but his
synapses seemed to be producing the same
sort of disjointed, unfocused thoughts. He
was unable to concentrate on anything for
more than a minute or two. This, from a
surgeon who was accustomed to performing intricate operations lasting eight hours
or more.

Weighing on Ty's consciousness, first and
foremost, was the death of Quinn
McDaniel. Unless Ty was fully engaged on
something else, the dead boy seemed to
intrude on his thoughts hourly. Ty tried to
make light of this, thinking of these thoughts
as the boy's ghost. It didn't help. He could
see Quinn looking up at him as he operated. He could see the trust in the boy's
eyes.

Then there was Quinn McDaniel's

mother. Ty's meeting with her at the diner had been unfulfilling. He wasn't sure what he wanted from the first meeting, but he itched to see her again. Ty reasoned that he needed to know why before he ventured down that path a second time. Wasn't his presence *salt in the wound* for this grieving mother?

Finally, there was Tina Ridgeway. She was a friend and confidante. Her support in the previous weeks had kept him from becoming more unmoored than he already felt. And then there were the rendezvous. Their after-hours meetings offered the kind of distraction that banished Quinn McDaniel for the hours they shared.

Beneath her opalescent beauty, though, Ty sensed a longing not unlike his own. A desire to escape, at least for a little while. And this, too, was unsettling for Ty. She was a married woman, which held the potential for emotional carnage beyond the two of them. She had a husband and children.

As his brain seemed to shuttle between these topics, none of them resolved or even fully scrutinized, Ty wound clockwise up the concrete fire stairs toward his small office in Neurosurgery. He hardly ever took an elevator. His brain was so scattered, he had to stop to check what floor he was on.

He was three floors short.

Ty continued up. He didn't hear a fire door above closing and almost bumped into Tina coming down the stairs.

"Ty! Good morning," she said.

"Tina?"

"Are you all right?" She stood a step above him, on the landing next to a fire door. Her voice held genuine concern.

"Just surprised. Didn't expect to see you."

"Are you avoiding me?"

"No. No. That's not it at all," Ty said. "Just thought I was the only one who took the stairs."

"I only take them down," Tina confessed.

They stood in silence for a moment. Ty saw something in Tina in that moment. A hard look behind the classic beauty.

"Ty, last night was my idea, and I thoroughly enjoyed it," Tina said quietly. Her soft voice resonated in the stairwell.

"I did, too, but —"

Tina held up a hand.

"Let me finish. You don't have to feel guilty about it. I've enjoyed our —" Tina paused. "I've enjoyed our, uh — special times together. But it's not going to happen again."

"You're right. I was being selfish. You're married. That's bad karma."

Tina waved off this line of thinking.

"I don't worry about karma anymore. I used to. I used to think growing up privileged as I did, karma was stacked against me. I tiptoed through life, waiting for the karma to even out. Then Ashley was born. And I realized things are going to happen in our lives, and it's egotistical to think we're responsible." Tina spoke as though the words were spilling out. "Daughters have cerebral palsy. Marriages go sour. But to think a divine being is up there with a score-card." Tina scoffed. "Bad things happen —"

"— to good people," Ty finished.

"Yes. Right. Anyway," Tina continued. "I'm not worrying about anyone's expectations anymore. I've been living the life others have expected of me. That's over. I'm going to live a life I can be proud of. I am going to be true to myself."

Ty found the look of determination on Tina's face slightly unsettling. She looked as though she had made some sort of major decision.

"Is there anything I can do?" Ty asked.

"You've done enough." She leaned over and kissed him on the forehead. She turned to go and stopped.

"Ty, I know you've been . . ." Tina paused searching for the right word. "Deeply troubled by the boy who died on the table. You've got to forgive yourself and move on. This hospital needs your skills."

Park stood at the bedside of Jordan Malchus, an arc of doctors around the bed. Park had ignored Hooten's advice to take time off, although he was now working about four hours a day instead of the fourteen that had been typical prior to his operation. The pull of medicine remained too strong for him to simply do nothing, which was how he considered staying home. And the chance to present at grand rounds was too good to pass up. Park loved the thrill of medical mysteries, and this man's case certainly qualified as one. Put simply, weak or not, Jordan Malchus's case was too interesting to ignore.

As Park spoke to the group, the man in the bed ignored them, and doodled on a small pad of paper as though someone was timing him. Those standing closest to him could see small shapes emerging on the white paper, one after another: ears. Each one beautifully rendered, anatomically perfect, yet each somehow conveying a different feeling. Sydney Saxena and Bill McManus stood next to each other a little farther back. Sydney couldn't make out what the shapes were. She figured the patient was nervous at being the center of attention and was scribbling random doodles on the pad.

"Mr. Malchus is a fifty-six-year-old with no prior relevant history who suffered a pair of aneurysms. The bleeds were clipped surgically. Subsequent angiogram was clear."

Park couldn't help but think for a moment about the ominous cloud on his own MRI and his dark prognosis, despite how well everything had gone so far. He took a deep breath and continued.

"From a neurosurgical perspective, Mr. Malchus is asymptomatic. From a psychological perspective, it is a different story.

"Prior to surgery, Mr. Malchus worked as a welder in a machine shop, fabricating large mufflers for buildings, cruise ships, and so on. I have talked to his wife, and she says he never expressed any interest whatsoever in art."

"I thought they were a bunch of pansies," Malchus interjected. Park ignored him.

"Mr. Malchus has emerged from surgery with a monomania for drawing. More specifically, Mr. Malchus draws ears. He has drawn them on the walls of his apartment. On canvas. He draws them now."

"We need to hear the voices. We all need to listen," the man said matter-of-factly, still not looking up. The assembled doctors edged forward. Those who hadn't recognized the shapes before now smiled and nodded to one another.

"Mr. Malchus sleeps very little. There are times he forgets his meals."

"You sound like my wife," the patient added, now with an edge in his voice. A couple of the junior doctors smiled until they realized Malchus was not joking.

"Mr. Malchus's wife has moved out," Park added.

"Good riddance," Malchus said.

"I add this personal fact because it reflects on —"

Without looking up, Malchus interrupted. "She doesn't understand the voices."

"The reason I include this in Mr. Malchus's history is that his wife has suggested her husband be prescribed a neurotropic medicine to mediate these symptoms," Park said. "I consulted with Dr. Johnson from Neurology, and he agreed."

Park placed a hand on the bedrail to steady himself and paused to catch his breath. He tired so easily.

"Why isn't he already taking something?" Sydney asked.

"Wouldn't that end his neurosis?" asked another.

"As I said, I have consulted with Dr. Johnson, and Mr. Malchus was offered this treatment option. He has declined any medication," Park said.

"We all need to listen to the voices," Malchus said again. "Can't you see? I need to help us hear them."

"Those ears are beautiful," McManus said, nodding toward the page now filled with ears. For the first time, Malchus looked up at the doctors who were gawking at him. He stared at McManus, their eyes meeting, his gaze unwavering. He looked at him with such a searing intensity that McManus involuntarily took half a step backward, as though he might get singed.

"Mr. Malchus is what is called an acquired savant. There are other cases in the literature. Men and women who had no interest in painting or poetry or music who suffered a traumatic brain injury that resulted in a new skill and singular focus," Park said. He paused again. He was out of breath.

"Apparently the art world has taken notice. He has a one-man show, *Stroke of Genius,* at the Marks Gallery next week."

"Isn't that the place that had an exhibit of cow fetuses in formaldehyde?" a small, bald doctor asked.

"My brother's an artist. He'd kill for a show at the Marks," a resident said, almost to herself.

"That's not our concern, is it?" Sydney asked. "Aren't we supposed to be worried about the well-being of the patient?"

"Isn't that part of Mr. Malchus's well-being?" McManus asked. His challenge was friendly. He was smiling and looking at Sydney when he asked the question.

"You tell her, my friend," Malchus growled. When Dr. Park asked him to come in for another MRI, overnight observation, the presentation of his case at grand rounds, Malchus had said that as long as they kept him supplied with writing materials, he didn't mind. He had thanked Park for working with the voices to give him this gift.

"So it's okay that he ignores his dietary needs?" Sydney asked McManus. "It's okay to ignore his wife?"

"She needed to get her fat ass out of there. The bitch tried to take my art supplies until I ate something."

Sydney glared at the patient for a moment and then turned back to McManus.

"This is what you would call healthy behavior?"

McManus shrugged. "Isn't a one-man

show at a gallery a sign of functioning in society?"

"And the rest doesn't matter? Skipping meals? The anti-social behavior?" Sydney asked. Her voice sounded strident. *I sound like a shrew,* she thought, appreciating the irony of her taking a stand against a single-minded work ethic. Every time she crossed paths with McManus, she seemed to act in strange and uncontrollable ways. Sydney felt her face go flush — another recurring theme in her encounters with McManus.

"If anti-social behavior and a propensity to work through meals were symptoms requiring psychotropic drugs, half the doctors on staff would have scripts for Haldol," McManus said with a wry grin. The physicians laughed.

"Well, Dr. McManus, I will mark you down in favor of improper and inadequate treatment of your patients," Sydney said suddenly. McManus looked confused.

Inside, Sydney was kicking herself. How did she become such a bitch? She heard echoes of herself in third grade, trying to put down any classmate who dared infringe on her role as the smartest kid in the class by answering one of Mrs. Fitzpatrick's brain teasers. Sydney guarded her role as star student zealously. Now she couldn't help but hear the childish tone in her voice. This, with a man she found attractive. She was mortified.

McManus, too, was speechless. After a moment of silence, he turned back to Park.

"Sorry for the interruption, Dr. Park."

Park, exhausted by the effort, finished as quickly as he could, and the doctors filed out of the room in the order they had come in, with Park leading the way, followed by the other attendings, chief residents, senior residents, junior residents, and med students. Sydney and McManus left the room and turned in opposite directions without another word between them.

Park's wife was waiting when he reached his office, and she drove him home.

CHAPTER 38

Villanueva was seated on his stool. Veteran nurse Roxanne Blake stood next to him. The ER was as quiet as it ever got for a Friday night. Even the normally blaring television in the waiting area was off.

"Is it cold out?" Villanueva asked.

"Nope."

"Big game on?"

"Not that I know of."

"American Idol?"

"No."

"What gives?"

"You got me, Dr. V."

"Where's the Magnet?"

"Off," the nurse answered. The Magnet was a tiny female resident. She'd earned the nickname because she was a vomit magnet. Every night she worked, the whole character of the ER changed with the prevalent theme being vomit, and lots of it. Drunks. Influenza. Food poisoning. It didn't matter.

"Too bad. She's got a streak going," Villanueva said. "Is Dr. Um-So working tonight? Torturing him is always good in a pinch."

"No such luck. He's off, too."

Villanueva surveyed his silent domain. When it was this slow, Villanueva got antsy. He was sure there would be a bus crash, or a fire, or, more likely, multiple shootings. Not that the possibilities worried him. There was an unwritten rule in hospitals. If things were quiet, no one was to point it out, or risk somehow jinxing it. That was not a rule Villanueva cared for. He enjoyed the rush of multiple traumas bursting through the door of the Emergency Department. He liked it better when they were already a little busy, though. It was like when he was waiting tables in high school at a little Mexican place called Guadalajara. He was a much better waiter when he was busy. When the restaurant was slow, he lost his timing. He arrived at tables late or early. The ED was no different.

"Not even a turkey symptom." Some patients came in complaining of vague pains, usually in the neck or back, simply in the hope of getting to a room and receiving a friendly meal — a sandwich, chips, juice, and a piece of fruit. At Chelsea General, it was a turkey sandwich. There was a well-known, almost mythical tale at Chelsea General, of two walk-ins who arrived a few minutes apart, each claiming ailments that were going to get them an X-ray and a sandwich. Through some mix-up, only one received the plastic meal tray. The man with the sandwich was about to take a bite when his fellow patient snatched it and stuffed it in his mouth. In response, Patient Number One threw a right cross that sent the sandwich and a tooth flying. He then picked up his sandwich off the ER floor and put it in his mouth.

Villanueva and Roxanne looked out over the library-still emergency room.

"You bored? We got a thripple in five," she said. The nurse knew Villanueva loved the oddities of the human condition: extra fingers or toes, quadruplets, glass eyes depicting flags or, Villanueva's favorite, the Marine Corps emblem. He also liked strange or ironic tattoos, like the man with the blue block letters on his calf spelling out the word TATTOO, and odd self-inflicted injuries like the man with his urethra painfully blocked with a peanut who confessed that he and a friend were playing "feed the elephant."

The Big Cat slid off his stool.

"A triple nipple. Why didn't you tell me?" Villanueva said. A thripple was officially known as an accessory nipple or supernumerary nipple and was surprisingly common. In medical school, Villanueva recalled, Professor Mort Rubenstein mentioned accessory nipples in passing and had asked the anatomy class, "Who here has an accessory nipple?" To Villanueva's surprise, Frank Braun had shot out of his chair in the lecture hall and hoisted his shirt.

"Got two," Braun said proudly. Below each of his regular nipples were very small supernumerary nipples.

Villanueva meandered over to Trauma Bay 5.

"How we doing over here, Dr. Wills?" Dr. Deanna Wills knew exactly what Villanueva was up to. She rolled her eyes but played along.

"Mr. Swanson, here, bruised a couple of ribs falling off his bike."

"I see," Villanueva said, as he conducted a seemingly authentic exam of the man's chest.

"A car turned right in front of me. The jerk didn't even stop." Having seen what he wanted to see, Gato was already walking out.

"Keep up the good work, Dr. Wills."

Villanueva wandered back to his stool, a small diversion in an otherwise dull night.

"This keeps up, I'm going to have to order pizza," he told Roxanne, the nurse.

"Don't jinx us, George." She was one of the few people at the hospital who called Villanueva by his first name.

The shift ended, still strangely quiet, and Villanueva walked into the cool night feeling unfulfilled. He got in his roadster and drove over to O'Reilly's. The bar didn't serve *mojitos* or frozen drinks, and the only thing that ended in *-tini* was a martini. No appletini or other cute specialty drinks and nothing that involved ginger or pomegranate juice. The Big Cat found his usual spot at the bar, noticing an attractive woman in her late thirties sitting two stools down. She was well proportioned and slim but not in a gaunt, obsessive way like his ex. The bartender placed a rum and Coke in front of Villanueva.

"What's the word, Soup?" Villanueva demanded, while still looking over at the woman. The bartender's name was Tom Campbell, but he went by the nickname Soupy.

"Hi, Doc. How they treating you at the hospital."

"You know me, Soup, just livin' the

dream," he said a little louder while turning his bar stool in the woman's direction.

The woman glanced over.

Soupy got the message.

"Dr. George Villanueva, I'd like you to meet this lovely creature of God, Megan."

George reached an enormous hand over.

"Nice to meet you," Villanueva said. He was picturing Megan naked.

"I couldn't help but overhear. Are you a doctor? The reason I ask is because I just saw something on TV and I've been dying to ask if it's true."

"Shoot."

"It's a little awkward."

"My middle name, little lady."

"All right, is it really true that human beings can smell emotions like desire?" The question alone seemed to crank up Villanueva's hormones. *Easy, Gato,* he said to himself. Villanueva tried to adopt a scholarly tone to mask the almost adolescent desire flooding his endocrine system.

"When people are sexually aroused, they produce specific hormones. Your own Love Potion Number Nine. All vertebrates have a vomeronasal organ to pick up signals like this. I suppose if your nose were good enough, you might be able to smell desire." Here George abandoned his academic air.

"Give me a heads-up if I need to start sniffing!"

Villanueva let loose with an enormous laugh that didn't give Megan a chance to be offended. When the eruption of mirth died down, the Big Cat leaned forward.

"Tell me about you," he said. Before she could answer, his cell phone buzzed. He did his best to ignore it but the buzz sounded again. Without taking his eyes off the woman next to him for more than a second, he pulled the phone from his pocket and checked the number. The caller ID said NICK.

"Do you need to get that?"

"It's nothing."

The phone buzzed again. After a fourth round, it fell silent.

"You sure you don't need to get that?"

"No. It's all right. I want to know more about Megan. For starters, how did such a beautiful woman wind up two stools down from me at O'Reilly's on a Friday night."

"What's a nice woman like me doing at a place like this? Really? That's your line?" Megan tipped her head back and laughed. George was smitten by the spontaneous outburst and her perfect teeth.

"Something like that."

"Soupy and I go way back."

"I met this lovely creature of God when I was tending bar at a place called the Oasis on St. Pete Beach."

"I guess that makes me a groupie. A Soupy groupie." Again, she tipped her head back and laughed.

"One of the pitfalls of the job," Campbell said and winked.

"You've got great taste in bartenders," Villanueva said to Megan and then turned to Campbell. "And you've got great taste in groupies."

As Villanueva continued the verbal dance that he hoped in Megan's mind would justify a trip back to his small home nearby for an alcohol-fueled romp, he had two thoughts. One: He needed to make a trip to the bathroom to pop a little blue pill he kept on hand for just such an occasion. Two: What did Nick want?

He was surprised to find himself giving his son's call a second thought. He would have ignored it completely only a month or so earlier. Nick almost never called, and when he did it was either to ask for money or to get a sympathetic ear about some perceived injustice his mother had committed — banning him from computer games for a week because he had gotten a C in history, for example. He wouldn't even bother calling back the next day. The next time he went out to see Nick, he'd say there was an emergency at the hospital, or he wouldn't even mention it. Not that Nick would bring it up. He'd just study his father with his downcast, sullen gaze.

Now Villanueva was having trouble getting the call out of his mind. If he didn't hurry up, he risked losing his mojo, not to mention the effects of the pill. Full-blooded lust pulsed through his arteries. The hormones made his vision more acute — offsetting the second rum and Coke now resting on the stained-wood bar in front of him — and his sense of touch more sensitive.

Still, what was up with Nick? He felt connected to his son in a way he hadn't in a long, long time, and the call weighed on him. For years, his relationship with his son had been guided by doing the minimum necessary to keep his guilt at being a horrible father down to an acceptable level. He was like the diabetic who reined in his diet just enough to avoid slumping into some sort of hyperglycemic state. There was more to it than guilt right now, though. Villanueva was worried something might be wrong. He was worried in a way he hadn't been since the boy had spiked a 104-degree fever when he was five. Nick might be with a girl himself and need a little fatherly advice. Maybe he was drunk at a party and needed a ride, too embarrassed to call his mom. He might have gotten his ass kicked or been in a car accident. Villanueva tried to put all these worries out of his mind. He had survived his teenage years. Nick would be fine.

Villanueva downed the second rum and Coke, and Soupy placed a third in front of him.

It had been a while since he'd taken a woman back to his house, and he did not want to miss this opportunity. What could he say? Villanueva loved women. His lust was equal opportunity: twenties, forties, blond hair, black hair, short, tall, Asian, Latin, African American, Anglo, he didn't care. He enjoyed women in all their remarkable variety. And Villanueva was already picturing himself undressing Megan slowly with some sexy Brazilian music playing on his ceiling-mounted speakers. Nothing like some sultry samba queen singing in Portuguese to set the mood.

Tomorrow, his son would still be his son, but the opportunity to hook up with Megan might have evaporated. Villanueva knew he had charisma, which compensated for other negatives: He was forty-eight, overweight, and overworked. Even with the "it" factor working in his favor, he also knew his chances of luring this pretty woman back to his house were directly correlated to her blood alcohol level. His own blood alcohol level was rising fast.

He and Soupy had a tacit arrangement. No matter how much Villanueva drank, his tab was twenty dollars, and he would toss Soupy another twenty as a tip.

"Last call, my friends," Campbell said.

Villanueva tossed forty bucks on the counter and turned to Megan.

"I live right around the corner if you want keep this party going. I've got this amazing tequila."

"Sure, why not?" Megan said. She laughed.

As they left the bar, Villanueva slipped a hand around her waist to steady her. And then it happened. His phone sounded again. Villanueva wasn't angry at the electronic buzz kill. He was worried. He took his right hand off the small of Megan's back and pulled his phone out of his pocket.

"Nick, what is it?" Villanueva asked.

"Dad, sorry to bother you." Nick sounded strange. There was a quiet desperation in his voice.

"No problem, kiddo, what's going on?"

"Dad, I am not doing well. I've been do-ing a lot of thinking lately." He paused. "And it keeps coming back to this feeling that nothing matters. Nothing I do or say. *I* don't seem to matter."

Megan took a step back and crossed her arms. Villanueva put a finger up to signal that he'd just be a minute.

"Listen to me, Nick, I'm not sure what got into you, but of course you matter. You mean everything to me." Villanueva didn't think about the words before he said them. What really surprised him was that they were true. This strange, scrawny boy did mean everything to him.

"What's the point, Dad? I mean, like, what's the point?" Nick's voice caught. He was trying not to cry.

"What the hell's gotten into you, Nick?"

"I don't know," Nick answered, and he began to cry.

Villanueva looked Megan up and down. A cool breeze had come up, and Megan's flimsy skirt blew across her legs. She had closed her eyes and tipped her head back. Villanueva sighed. What could he do? He'd probably think about this opportunity lost on his deathbed.

"Nick, I'm not sure where all this came from, but here's what I want you to do. Call

a cab right now and take it to my house."
At this Megan opened her eyes and made
an exaggerating pouting expression. "This
doesn't sound like something we can solve
on the phone. You got that. A cab."

"Okay."

"Do you know the number of a cab company?"

"No." Villanueva gave Nick the number
he always used when he was too shitfaced
to drive home.

"Are you at your mother's house?"

"Yeah."

"Where's your mother? Never mind. You
know what, I'll call you a cab. Hang in
there, all right?"

"Thanks, Dad," Nick said. He sounded
miserable.

"Yeah."

Villanueva called for a cab for his son.
Then he found Megan a cab and said goodbye. She kissed him on the cheek. They'd
traded phone numbers, and she promised
to call, but Villanueva wasn't going to hold
his breath. The Big Cat knew he probably
wouldn't bother calling her for a date,
either. If things didn't happen in the moment, they lost their appeal.

Sung and Pat Park sat across from each

other at a dark Italian restaurant. Pat had chosen Palio's on the recommendation of their next-door neighbor, the mother of their babysitter. It had taken a little while to find a sitter who was available. Pat had no idea how busy they were. She simply assumed other parents took their children with them when they went out.

Now the Parks sat across a red-checked tablecloth from each other. A small candle rested between them. Opera music played from mounted speakers. The dining area was tiny, more like a modest-size living room, which in fact it had once been. The neighborhood had been residential before hotels and businesses began crowding in.

The Parks had not been out alone since their younger daughter was born. That was four years earlier. The sensation was strange. Park felt almost untethered, giddy. When he was courting his wife, they had gone out to dinner in Seoul. Those dates were formal affairs, almost grave. Park had wanted to show Pat he was a man of learning, a man of substance, a man who could provide for his family. He spent much of their time together talking about himself as he might at a job interview. Pat had listened dutifully, perhaps showing that despite her degree in chemistry she was able to put herself second

416

and support him wholeheartedly.

The waiter arrived. He was a man about Park's age. "*Buona sera.* Welcome to Palio's." He held a small pencil and a pad, and spoke with a thick Italian accent.

"*Buona sera,*" Park said. It sounded more like *bone sare.* Park had never spoken a word of Italian in his life. To attempt it now was so out of character he surprised even himself. He had never before engaged in such whimsy.

"Very good, *signore.*"

"*Buona sera,*" Pat said. Her accent was better than Sung's. The waiter raised his eyebrows, jutted his lower lip, and nodded to show just how impressed he was.

"*Multi bene. E Italiana?*" he asked.

"Am I Italian?" Pat asked, giggling.

"*Si.*"

Pat laughed harder. At the sight of his wife, hand over her mouth, almost doubled over in laughter, Sung couldn't help himself. He began laughing at the ridiculousness of it all.

The waiter asked if they wanted something from the bar. As soon as Pat composed herself enough to speak, she began laughing again until tears gathered at the corners of her eyes. Again, Park laughed along with her. He couldn't think of the last time they had laughed like this.

CHAPTER 39

Monday morning. Room 311. Sydney Saxena stood at the front of the room of Chelsea's surgeons, a collection of some of the finest orthopods, chest cutters, vascular specialists, skull crackers, and others who donned scrubs and used well-intentioned violence to treat people for any number of deadly or chronic problems. These were men and women able to combine the physical talents of cutting, sewing, excising, replacing, repairing, attaching, reattaching, and thousands of other tasks big and small with the three-dimensional geometry of the body — the bones, muscles, ligaments, tendons, veins, arteries, nerves, lymph nodes, organs. They were able to match what they saw in the moment of surgery with their theoretical knowledge of what they should see given the diagnosis and patient history and what they'd seen before. And then they could adjust their plan accordingly. In the operating room, sports analogies are common, but quarterbacks calling an audible to counter a shifting defense or running from the pocket to avoid a blitzing cornerback had nothing on the brain surgeon scrambling to repair a ruptured aneurysm or the heart surgeon whose patient's vitals were failing.

Sydney Saxena was not standing in the front of Chelsea's surgeons to tell them how to do their jobs, or even to highlight an error in judgment or in execution. This morning was not the public flogging of the usual Monday Morning. It wasn't the Somebody Effed Up Conference Villanueva liked to call it.

"Thanks for coming, everyone," Sydney said. Hooten sat in his usual spot at the front of the room. Tina and Ty sat next to each other a couple of rows back. Villanueva sat on the aisle seat looking tired.

"I'm here this morning to talk about *Trypanosoma cruzi.*"

"Sydney, this is surgical M and M, not infectious diseases," came a call from the back of the room. "You sure you're in the right place?"

"I appreciate your concern," Sydney said with a wry smile. "But I am in the right place, and so are all of you.

420

"I implanted a pacemaker this past week on a Mr. R, who had severe cardiomyopathy as the result of *Trypanosoma cruzi,* which many of you no doubt know as Chagas disease."

With no doctor standing up front for a public flogging, the mood of the M&M was decidedly lighter than normal.

"Sydney, were you moonlighting in San Juan General?" orthopedic surgeon Stanley Gottlieb called from the back of the room.

Sydney smiled.

"Thank you, Stanley, you've just given me the segue I need. You see, I've been talking to the various departments here at Chelsea General. It seems that we are beginning to see diseases once reserved for the Third World and for tropical climates. It appears America's poor and America's immigrants are both more mobile and more vulnerable than we've seen — at least in our professional lifetimes.

"Let me give you an idea of some of the cases that have walked through our doors right here at Chelsea General." Sydney looked down at some typed notes. "Helminth infections, toxocariasis, cysticercosis, cytomegalovirus, toxoplasmosis, leishmaniasis, and, last but not least, leptospirosis. Untreated, these are chronic and debilitating. Most of them will not require surgical intervention, but we need to be mindful that these cases are in the realm of the possible — even in the United States, even in Michigan."

Ty tried to listen but he was distracted not only by the demons of Quinn McDaniel but by the now awkward feeling of sitting so close to Tina Ridgeway. Tina, too, seemed to be having trouble focusing.

"I almost forgot," Sydney added. "At Henry Ford, they had a case of Weil's disease. That is a hemorrhagic complication from a bacterial infection transmitted by rat urine. Are there any questions?"

Sydney looked around the room. She checked her watch.

"I've left you time for breakfast." A collective groan went up. *"Bon appétit."*

Tina entered the Maelstrom of orderlies pushing patients from their rooms to X-ray or the ER. There were doctors coming and going, and nurses beginning or ending their shifts, laughing and sharing stories. She saw relatives heading to the gift shop or the pharmacy or to see loved ones. It was the daily swirl that amid the chaos was somehow still a remarkable testament to order.

Tina had always believed the modern

teaching hospital represented the pinnacle of learning and culture, knowledge acquired generation by generation until medical doctors were able to defeat diseases such as smallpox and polio and treat deadly scourges like HIV and cancer. When her father was at Mass General at her age, there was no less compassion and doctors were no less smart, but the cumulative knowledge was primitive compared with that of Tina and her colleagues, just as his generation was light-years ahead of her grandfather's practice in rural Fairbury, Vermont. Tina had always felt immense pride in Chelsea General as an institution, an entity that combined great understanding and compassion, and in her own small role as a teacher and healer.

On this morning, as Tina walked among the men and women who worked there, and the patients with their friends and relatives, the whole place seemed somehow tarnished. She noticed grime by the baseboard in the corridor from the parking garage. She saw dust on the framed landscape that had decorated the wall as long as she had worked there. An orderly wheeled a patient toward her, and Tina noticed a crust of dried mucus on the old man's cheek that had not been cleaned.

The hospital that was always the source of such immense pride for her seemed like just another institution, filled with its own collective weaknesses, political motivations, profit incentives. Tina had not been naive. All institutions, even hospitals, were run by people, and the natural state of the individual was of selfishness. After her latest night with Ty, Tina knew this firsthand. But Chelsea General as an institution seemed to reflect a crassness Tina never thought she'd see in a teaching hospital. Only recently, it had been lobbying state legislatures not to grant a competing hospital a certificate of need to use gamma radiation treatment, even though lives would certainly be saved by it. Quite simply, Chelsea General didn't want business going elsewhere. And then there was Michelle's firing. To Tina, the resident's summary dismissal represented a level of cold calculation she never thought she'd see.

Michelle had come to her office before she'd left for Louisiana to figure out what to do next. Tina had received instructions from the hospital attorney not to discuss the case in any way. He said he was sure the young woman had lawyered up and was now intending to sue the hospital for breach of contract.

"I just wanted to say thank you" was all Michelle could get out before she started crying, jagged, oxygen-sucking sobs. Tina closed the door to her office and hugged the young doctor, patting a shoulder as she might have consoled one of her daughters, feeling like a betrayer. There was nothing Tina could say to make it right. She wrote her home and cell numbers on a piece of hospital stationery and told Michelle to call her anytime and to use her as a reference. The hospital attorney had instructed Tina to cease all communication with the fired doctor, but she refused to comply. She would not abandon Michelle completely. Now Tina realized she had in fact abandoned Michelle when the young MD needed her most. She had meekly allowed the hospital to throw this struggling doctor under the bus. When she was a resident, Dr. Daniel Barrow had stepped in on her behalf, tossing the report critical of her performance. She had done nothing more than protest halfheartedly to save Michelle. She had not raised any sort of formal protest. She hadn't written a letter to the CEO — or anyone else for that matter.

As a senior physician on the staff, she was a part of the hospital. The institution paid her checks and defined her professionally.

How could she remain on the staff if she no longer believed in its principles? The experience left her feeling dirty. But how could she leave? She was the family's sole breadwinner.

Worse still, Tina felt sullied by her latest tryst with Ty. She enjoyed their night together, not only for the pleasure she received, but for the obvious pleasure she was able to give him. She had sought it out, convincing herself she had every right to the companionship and sexual fulfillment she was not getting at home. Now, as she strode under the hospital's artificial lights, she could see clearly that it was a mistake. It was faulty logic fueled by self-pity. She had let herself down.

CHAPTER 40

Villanueva was on his perch wiping the pizza sauce from his mouth when a bus arrived with a man whose ears had been cut off. He was bawling curses and threats. A blood-soaked bandage was wrapped around his head. He was held down with restraints.

"Let me go, you fuckers. I need to go put the ears back where they can hear the voices. You shouldn't have brought them. The voices. They won't be able to hear the voices." One of the EMTs carried a small cooler. Villanueva figured the ears were in there.

Villanueva grabbed another piece of pizza from the box behind him and bit half of it with a single bite.

"Seven. Take him to seven," he called out, his mouth still full of pizza. The ED was a magnet for drunks, manics, delusionals, all of them seemingly with bloody head wounds spouting nonsense and needing staples, anti-psychotics, and more. As a resident, Villanueva once had a drunk with a gash in his head threaten to kill him if he tried to stitch him up. Villanueva had the lidocaine ready, planning to numb the wound before stitching him up with thread, but after the threat he traded the sutures for a stapler and called over a couple of male nurses to hold the man. Villanueva closed the wound with three quick, if inelegant, staples as the drunk howled with pain. The patient left without another word.

This earless individual with the bloody gauze around his head was obviously suffering from some sort of mania, but beyond that Villanueva could not figure out what he was talking about. Take the ears back? If he didn't want the ears back on his head, where exactly did he want them?

A med student approached warily. The EMTs said they didn't know his name, but the person who called 911 from a gallery said it was a Mr. Malchus, a famous artist.

"Can I get your name, sir?"

"Fuck off. What's *your* name so I can add you to my lawsuit?" Malchus could still hear, despite the loss of his outer ears and the gauze bandage wrapped around his head.

"The name is Villanueva." The Big Cat

had slid off his stool and now stood over the patient. "That's V-I-L-L-A-N-U-E-V-A. You want to pick on someone, try me on for size."

"Villanueva, get me out of here!" The man tugged at the restraints binding his wrists and ankles to the gurney.

One of the EMTs touched his nose, which took a sudden turn to the right. Dried blood was caked below his nostril.

"Fist?" Villanueva asked.

"Elbow."

Villanueva gave him a consoling pat on the shoulder. "Why don't you head over to X-ray?"

Smythe joined the group. "I recognize this man," he said in his clipped British accent.

"You picked a strange time to come out of the closet," Villanueva said.

"No —"

"One of your Oxford buddies?"

"No —"

"How about —"

"For Chrissakes, Villanueva, this man was the subject of grand rounds. An acquired savant. The toast of the art community for his remarkable renditions of ears."

"I guess he took that a little too far . . . All right, Mr. Malchus, what's it going to be?"

"Fuck off, fat man. You cannot hold me against my will."

"Either we hold you or the county holds you in the lockup. You assaulted the EMT, and you are a risk to yourself and others."

"You got that right." He struggled again to get his arms and legs loose, but could not. He allowed his bloody head to fall back on the gurney, breathing hard.

An ashen-faced woman arrived at the trauma bay. She was about thirty, pretty and stylishly dressed.

"Is Mr. Malchus going to be all right?"

"He'll be fine. Are you his daughter?"

"No, I rep— I represent Mr. Malchus's work."

"Well, you're going to have to talk some sense into him if he wants his ears back."

The mention of the ears caused the woman to shudder.

"He's lucky, ears are mostly cartilage so they're pretty resilient. Very slow metabolism. And they're in a cold saline bath. Even better. Even a severed finger can last twelve hours. In Anchorage, Alaska, some guy's girlfriend cut off his penis and flushed it down the toilet on a Saturday night. A municipal worker retrieved it Sunday morning, and the man was whole again that night. I was going to say *back in action* but I think that might have been an overstatement."

The woman forced a smile. Her pallor was turning a very pale gray-green. It was a shade you were unlikely to find in any of the city's finer art galleries.

Within an hour or two, Malchus's story — like all good stories — was all over the hospital. It spread from person to person, moving from the ER in concentric waves like a virulent infection: "Did you hear about the artist obsessed with ears?"

Within two hours of Malchus's boisterous arrival at the hospital, Ty heard the story in clinic, talking to a man whose dizziness had been identified as a benign glioma, which was pressing against valuable real estate in his brain.

Bill McManus heard it within minutes of arriving at the hospital, from one of his residents. He groaned, remembering his impassioned defense to Sydney of this man's right to remain artistic and unmedicated. Then he pulled out his cell phone and called the paging operator.

"Would you page Dr. Sydney Saxena for me?"

CHAPTER 41

So far, Park's recovery from surgery was
flawless. He had no infection, and his
subsequent MRI looked good. His platelets
and white blood counts were both good,
and Hooten had not missed any of the
tumor. Nothing you could see, anyway.
Sung knew better than to rejoice in being
NED — no evidence of disease — or to
consider the clean MRI as the basis of a
positive prognosis. A glioblastoma multiforme was the nastiest of nasty malignant
tumors. Park of all people knew how a
GBM could come roaring back without
warning and kill him in a matter of weeks.

Since he'd started his radiation treatment,
Park had gotten into the habit of taking his
older daughter to the bus stop in the morning. Somehow, beating his colleagues to the
hospital no longer seemed as important.

"Daddy, are you going to be bald?" Emily
asked him suddenly. Park was surprised by

the question.

"Why do you ask, Emily?"

"My friend Kaylee. She says when you have cancer you get bald."

Park wondered for a moment how this friend had acquired such cancer literacy.

"Is that so?"

"Well, are you?"

Park still had almost all his hair despite the operation. Hooten liked to perform a "shaveless" surgery. Hooten first washed Park's hair for six minutes with a Hibiclens scrub. He then used a comb to part the hair away from the incision site and then sterilized the area with betadine solution. Before Park's operation, the surgical tech had shaved a thin arc along the line of the incision. Unless you looked closely, you couldn't tell Park had undergone surgery. The hair around the wound camouflaged the scar. Hooten, and now many others, believed that patients who retained their hair recovered more quickly, because they didn't *look* sick. Aside from his somewhat gaunt appearance, you would never guess Park had undergone major brain surgery.

Standing at the bus stop, Park looked at his daughter. She awaited his answer. Her expression was both excited and concerned.

"Hair does not matter," Park said. "It's

what's under the hair that matters."

"Oh, Daddy," Emily said. "Does it hurt when you get bald? I don't want them to hurt you." She hugged her father. Park wrapped his arms around his daughter. He worried that she'd be too distracted by his cancer to learn anything at school.

"Do not worry about me, Emily," he said, adding, "It doesn't hurt to have your hair fall out. Just ask your uncle Lee."

Emily put her hands on her hips and cocked her head. Park laughed. Emily now saw that her father was joking and she laughed, too. Uncle Lee was Pat's sister's husband, a giant of a man with a monk-like fringe of hair.

Park had two more weeks of radiation. Then he would start taking a chemotherapy pill for the first four days of the month, which seemed a little more civilized than the traditional IV drip. Truth was, this regimen would do a lot more than leave him hairless as a newborn. The chemicals would certainly kill healthy cells as well as the cancerous ones, sickening and weakening him in the process. And he was concerned about what the powerful chemicals might do to his thinking and memory.

One of the chemotherapy's documented side effects was impairing cognitive abilities.

In fact, Park was at least as worried about problems with his thinking and memory as he was about the chemotherapy's success or failure. Park's mind was his greatest asset. He didn't have looks, or charisma, or even much wit, he thought. Most of the time he was too literal-minded to even understand the jokes his colleagues or daughters told him. His greatest assets were a vast depth of medical knowledge and dogged determination. The determination might help, Park thought. The medical knowledge only informed him of the slim odds he possessed for beating this cancer for long. If Park could choose between the chemo succeeding and leaving him fuzzy-thinking and the chemo failing and leaving his mind sharp for his remaining months, he would opt for the failure. Of course, that wasn't the choice. His choice was chemo or no chemo, and Park would go ahead with chemotherapy. Choosing otherwise was suicidal.

Park had a patient once who was worried about the chemotherapy damaging his short-term memory, so the man had started studying memorizing techniques and then memorizing anything and everything, from names in the phone book to cards in a deck. You could shuffle all fifty-two cards, show them to him once, and he would recite them back in order. He emerged from chemo-therapy with a stronger memory, thanks to his mnemonic techniques.

In many ways, modern medicine seemed a puzzling mix of harming and helping patients. Patients needed to be cut open to operate. Patients needed to be poisoned to go after the cancer cells. With radiation, Park was choosing to have colleagues aim potentially deadly beams of energy at his body. Not just any part of his body, but his brain. Someday in the future, Park was certain, radiation, chemotherapy, even brain surgery, would be looked upon as some sort of barbarism. Fifty years from now, or maybe a hundred, doctors would look back on modern medicine the way he looked back on bleeding patients as a way to release bad humors, a common practice in the eighteenth century.

Even treatments that weren't so old were crude and wrongheaded. One of his brain cancer patients had been subjected weekly to high doses of X-rays as an infant in the 1940s in an attempt to restore hearing to her left ear. As a result, she was left com-pletely deaf and blind. Almost weekly, it seemed, large studies and new research would raise doubts about long-held beliefs and common medical practices. The efficacy of angioplasty, radical mastectomy, arthroscopic knee surgery, prostate PSA tests and surgery . . . the list went on and on. Medicine seemed to lurch two steps back for every three it moved forward. Even with the scientific method, Park realized that what doctors knew — really knew — was small, and the limits to medical knowledge were vast. Sometimes, Park had to admit, the best thing doctors could do was get out of the way and allow the body's own natural healing abilities to take over.

As a patient with a brain tumor, of course, that was out of the question. Park would seek out every weapon in modern medicine's arsenal, including chemotherapy.

As a student of medical history, Park knew that the first chemotherapy agent employed against cancer had been mustard gas, in the 1940s. Doctors tried it against advanced lymphomas after discovering during World War I that mustard gas victims had low white blood cell counts. Even today, Park knew, doctors counted nitrogen mustards — related to the lethal chemical from the War to End All Wars — among their weapons against Hodgkin's disease and lymphatic cancers.

Three weeks or so into his chemo, Park would lose his hair, as his daughter Emily predicted. As he stood now at the bus stop, he wondered how his three children would react. Would they think him funny looking? Terrifying? Would they call him an alien? Would they see him any differently at all when he was balder than his brother-in-law? Outwardly, he'd be transformed. But inside, what would he look like? When the MRI reconstructed a three-dimensional picture of his brain, what would it show? That was what counted.

The bus arrived. Emily stepped high to get on the bus, pulling her small body up. She turned and gave him a quick wave and a smile before finding a seat next to another girl.

As Park walked back toward his house, his mind drifted to his vocabulary tape: *"Mnemonics: the process or technique of improving or developing the memory. Morose: gloomy or ill-humored. Morph: to transform."*

Park walked into the house, unhurried. Pat had been watching him through the window, and greeted him expectantly. "I am sorry," Sung suddenly said to his wife. "In case I don't get a chance to tell you later, I am sorry for leaving you."

CHAPTER 42

Ty awoke remembering little of the dream. All he remembered was his brother and sister standing next to him. Smiling at him. He couldn't remember where they were, or if they were anywhere in particular. Their smiles, though, exuded love. Ty woke with an incredible sense of relief and calm. It was as though he had emerged from a fever. It was the quiet after the storm. He knew the moment he awoke that Ty Wilson the surgeon was back. Ty felt a joy surging in him. He was back.

Ty was not one to believe in the interpretation of dreams. He knew there were dozens of books that translated dream imagery. He'd even heard of people who kept diaries of their dreams, so they could better act on them in their waking hours. Ty didn't buy it. Still, there was no denying that this morning he felt free from the paralyzing doubt. This emotional dream had somehow liberated him from his demons, and he didn't want to talk himself out of the sense of freedom he felt at that moment.

Ty rose and made a fresh fruit smoothie thinking about the dream. His brother and sister were the reasons he'd become a neurosurgeon. He wanted to develop the skills to vanquish death where others could not. Their deaths had pushed him, propelled him to become a top neurosurgeon, but he was only human. He was fallible. The pure love flowing from his brother and sister in his dream told him he had not violated his silent vows to them. All he could do was his best, and that was better than most. Ty laughed at the ridiculousness of it all. A dream had set him free. He was back.

Ty couldn't wait to get back to the OR. This was his calling, his purpose. The Okinawans called this sense of purpose *ikigai*. Before he went back to the hospital, though, Ty had one stop to make.

Ty knocked on the door of Allison McDaniel's apartment an hour later. She answered right away. She was wearing a stylish red coat and holding a cup of coffee. She was surprised to see him.

"Dr. Wilson. You look different."

"Ty, please. Call me Ty. Are you heading out?"

"Yeah, job interview."

"May I walk with you?"

"Sure." They started down the stairs.

"Allison, I'm not sure how to say this, so I'll just go ahead. I get the sense that you're a remarkable person. A generous and warm-hearted person. I'd like to take you to dinner. To get to know you better."

They reached the landing. Allison stopped. She looked hard at Ty as though she was trying to divine his motive.

"This isn't about Quinn?"

"No. It's about you."

Allison thought for a moment. She took a deep breath.

"Okay. Why not?" she said finally. She smiled. Ty didn't return the smile. There was something else he wanted to say. Something else he needed to say.

"Allison, I can't undo what happened. I wish I could. But I realize now I've got to move forward. It's all I can do. If I don't I sink. All I can do is be the best doctor I can be — and the best person I can be."

They reached Allison's car. She retrieved the key from her purse.

"I understand." She unlocked the car and then stopped. "You didn't say when." Ty looked confused. He thought she was asking when he planned to be the best doctor, the best person he could be. "When you want to have dinner?" Allison added.

"Oh, how about Friday night? Seven o'clock?"

"All right."

"Great. I'll see you then."

Allison got in her car and backed up. Ty watched her go. She gave him a little wave and then pulled away. If it was redemption Ty Wilson had been looking for, he hadn't found it. Now, though, he realized that it wasn't the point. Redemption only worked, he thought, if you believed in a perfect world, where good and evil were always in a state of perfect balance. It was naive, and he had finally realized it. In his dream, his brother and sister had figured it out, and they were trying to tell him. Sometimes bad things just happen to good people. "How the good people react," Ty said out loud, "that is what really counts."

McManus sat across from Sydney at a small Japanese restaurant. Their pagers rested between them. They had a deal: Whoever's went off first paid for dinner. Getting Sydney to agree to dinner was no easy task. McManus had found her after a lecture at the med school.

"I don't waste my time on wiseass, know-it-all doctors," Sydney said. She was still smarting from McManus questioning her judgment in the case of the ear-loving artist Malchus.

"Ouch" was all McManus could answer, and the genuine hurt in his voice made Sydney reconsider. Maybe she was being a little too harsh. A little.

"All right," she added. "I'll go out to dinner with you if you repeat after me: Crazy people need medication."

"Crazy people need medication."

"I should never have doubted Dr. Sydney Saxena, and I will never doubt her judgment again," Sydney added.

"Now you're going too far!" he exclaimed, but he said it with a smile on his face. "How about this? I realize that doubting the judgment of Dr. Sydney Saxena comes with potentially grave mental and physical consequences."

"Extremely grave consequences!" Sydney laughed.

And with that, she had relented. He had picked the restaurant, a small place in Chelsea that served yakitori — Japanese-style meat and vegetable skewers.

They ordered and then McManus excused

himself for a moment. When he returned, Sydney's pager was buzzing.

"I guess I know who's buying dinner!" McManus said. Sydney looked at the number on the pager. She frowned. It was unfamiliar. She pulled out her cell phone.

"If it's an emergency, I'm sure they'll page again," McManus said. Sydney ignored him and punched the number into her phone. A jaunty Latin beat emanated from McManus's pocket.

"I should have known!"

"Must be some sort of coincidence," McManus said, barely suppressing a grin.

"Now I know what sort of pathology I'm dealing with here."

McManus looked at his pager and saw the same unfamiliar number.

Driving to clinic, Ty felt the elation of someone healthy after a long illness. He was energized. He couldn't wait to see new patients. Pulling into the physicians' parking area he spotted a nurse getting out of her car. It was Monique Tran. He was immediately transported back to Room 14 on October 23. She had been there on the day Quinn McDaniel died. He took in a deep breath, and waited for all the feelings to come flooding back. But nothing happened.

Thinking of the boy did not cause a relapse of doubt.

Instead, Ty thought it strange Monique was parking there because nurses had their own parking three levels up in the garage. Then he saw a resident emerge from the car, Dr. Sanford Williams. The young doctor placed an arm around the shorter nurse. Ty now noticed the bulge in her pink scrub shirt. She was pregnant. It all clicked into place in his mind. Ty continued up the ramp to the next level. He thought about the awe and excitement that must come from bringing new life into the world. Right then, Ty's pager went off. He looked at it, and pure panic crossed his face.

CHAPTER 43

Inside the hospital, Marjorie Gonsalves was lying in a bed for observation. Her husband brought her around midnight, confused and near collapse. She had seen her doctor the day before complaining of abdominal pain and was now reporting the addition of pain in her chest. Also, she said she felt dizzy when she stood up. The resident considered gastritis, aortitis, and cirrhosis of the liver. But none seemed a good fit.

The forty-year-old woman said she didn't drink and used nonsteroidal anti-inflammatories only sparingly. Alcohol and prolonged use of NSAIDs were two common ways people could end up with inflammation in their stomach lining. Nor had she had surgery or a severe infection or an auto-immune disorder or chronic bile reflux, which were other possible causes of gastritis. The resident decided to hold off for the time being on an upper gastrointestinal endoscopy.

As for aortitis, an inflammation of the aorta, her chest pain and confusion when she arrived at Chelsea General certainly fit the bill of Phase III aortitis. Her history did not. She had not suffered from a trauma or infection. The woman had been happily married for twenty years and bristled when the medical student taking her history asked about gonorrhea, syphilis, or herpes. Nor did she have any history of TB or hepatitis. Also, the resident took the blood pressure on each arm. A difference would point to vascular obstruction. There was none.

Gonsalves had a lifelong history of allergies and asthma, but neither of these seemed to be a likely source of her troubles.

Stumped by the case and swamped by other admissions, the resident turned his attention elsewhere.

Marjorie Gonsalves's temperature had been normal when she was admitted at midnight, but it began to spike. At eight the following morning, it was 101. By afternoon, it was over 103.

Worse still, Gonsalves's list of symptoms began growing. The pain spread, and she began itching. Her eyes became puffy.

The resident finishing his shift thought it must be something to do with the patient's allergies. The resident who arrived that evening, Dr. Eduardo Torres, decided to order a differential. When this blood test came back an hour later, it showed Gonsalves's white blood cell count spiking along with her temperature, primarily because of eosinophils. These white blood cells, which stained orange-red, were possibly a sign of a viral infection. But what virus? Herpes and hepatitis had been ruled out.

Villanueva was leaving the cafeteria when Torres stopped him to see if he had any thoughts about what could be ailing Mrs. Gonsalves. Villanueva, for once, was stumped. He was experiencing some stomach pain himself and made a mental note to lighten up on the hot sauce with his grits. He told Torres to seek out Dr. Um-So.

"Guy's a friggin' encyclopedia," Villanueva said.

When Um-So, aka Kauffman, arrived at Mrs. Gonsalves's bedside, her voice was down to a barely audible croak. Outside her room, Torres explained why he had ruled out Cushing's disease and a host of other possibilities. He asked if Kauffman had ever seen an allergic reaction present these types of symptoms. Um-So said nothing. He looked through the door at Gonsalves. She stared up at the ceiling, arms crossed on her chest like a corpse. Kauffman stared for a long time, then he approached the bed and knelt close to her ear.

"Um so, Mrs. Gonsalves, do you like to cook?" Kauffman asked. Torres looked at him as though he'd lost his mind.

"Yes," Gonsalves croaked.

"You make linguica, chorizo?"

Here, Gonsalves offered an approximation of a smile. "Yes," she said again.

"Thanks."

Kauffman left the room. A bewildered Torres followed.

"Trichinosis," Um-So said. "See the cut on her finger. My mother used to cut herself like that all the time cooking. Um so, she must have tasted the seasoning on the raw pork when she was cooking." Worms from the raw meat had infected her body. Villanueva stood outside the room and smiled as Kauffman and Torres walked. He raised his eyebrows, as if to say *See, I told you he would figure it out.* Suddenly three shrills went off in rapid sequence. All three doctors reached for their pagers, and they all saw an unfamiliar number on the screen.

It was almost dark when Tina closed the front door of The Free Clinic and locked the deadbolt. She was alone. Usually, she and DeShawn walked out together, but he had left early because his twelve-year-old daughter was sick in bed with a fever. His wife worked a night shift at an Ann Arbor hotel as a front desk clerk, and the girl, Alisha, spent an hour alone most days between the time her mother left for work and her father got home. On this night, Tina insisted DeShawn be with his sick daughter.

Tina was putting the keys in her purse when the punch hit her left eye. She didn't know it was a punch. She felt as though something inside her head exploded. She turned and saw a familiar-looking man wearing a green fatigue jacket. "Told you I would be back, bitch," she heard. She blacked out before she hit the sidewalk. She didn't feel the second blow or the third or any of the other punches and kicks that followed. She didn't feel the baseball bat hitting her in the head or the chest or the abdomen.

Michelle had packed her bags and loaded her car to the ceiling with her belongings. Anything that didn't fit — the ficus tree, the coatrack — she simply gave away. She planned to drive straight through, from Michigan to Louisiana. Mapquest said the trip would take eighteen and a half hours.

She was hoping to cut some time off that. Still, she thought her resident training would come in handy. She was accustomed to staying up all night on caffeine and adrenaline. Caffeine was no problem. She had a large thermos of chicory coffee made for the trip. The adrenaline might be in short supply. She expected a long, boring drive through the night as she headed south toward Fort Wayne, Indiana, then west toward St. Louis before pointing the car south and passing through Missouri, Arkansas, Tennessee, Mississippi, and finally entering Louisiana. She prepared for the mind-numbing twelve-hundred-mile trip by lining up her favorite Cajun CDs on the visor on her old Civic. She planned to sing along at the top of her lungs as much as possible. Anything but think about what had happened at Chelsea General and what would happen in the weeks and months ahead.

Michelle had almost reached the on-ramp to I-94 when she was nagged by a piece of unfinished business and turned the car around.

Ten minutes later, she slowed outside The Free Clinic. *Too late,* she thought when she saw the lights out in the picture window. She was about to leave when she noticed the body lying in front of the clinic. It looked as though a homeless person had simply passed out by the front door. Michelle was about to pull away when an alarm in her brain went off. Something about the picture wasn't right, but she couldn't immediately figure it out. She scanned again, and figured it was just somebody sleeping off a bender waiting for the clinic to open in the morning. Then her breath caught in her throat. High-heeled shoes. She recognized them. She had, in fact, coveted them from afar, for their elegance and the regal bearing of their wearer.

Michelle pulled over and stopped the car. She ran to the unmoving form without closing the driver's door.

"Sweet Jesus," Michelle said out loud.

If she hadn't known who it was, Michelle would not have recognized her mentor, her lone supporter at Chelsea General when her residency hit the rocks. Tina's face was battered beyond recognition. Her eyes were swollen shut. Her lips were cracked and bleeding. Her nose had been broken. That was simply what Michelle could see. She checked for vitals. Tina's chest wasn't rising, and Michelle could tell several ribs were broken. A check for a pulse revealed nothing. Michelle pulled out her cell phone and called 911, put it on speaker, and immediately started chest compressions.

The paramedics arrived in the Emergency Department with Michelle walking behind the gurney. The entire staff seemed to be waiting in the trauma bay. Some were crying, and there was an audible gasp as people caught their first glimpse of a lifeless Tina Ridgeway. Villanueva marched into the foreground. The sight of his friend and colleague hit him like a punch. He hesitated momentarily, then went to work. He removed the trauma blankets covering Tina and hollered "Seven!" The gurney was quickly rolled in. Sanford and Tran came running in, followed in hot pursuit by Ty. "Tina . . . is that really Tina?" Ty asked no one in particular. He began to weep. McManus and Saxena ran into the ER, still dressed from their romantic dinner. "What happened?" Saxena shouted. Soon, everyone was jockeying for position, with all of Chelsea's finest working shoulder-to-shoulder trying to save one of their own. Hooten received a call at home and immediately returned to the hospital. He was the one to take Tina's husband, Mark, and their daughters into a private room to tell them what happened. Mark's sobs could be heard throughout the waiting room.

"The good news," Hooten told them, "is Tina is alive." Other than that, the news was grim. She had lost a lot of blood and had terrible injuries to her head. She had lost several of her teeth. Her jaw was broken. The orbit beneath one of her eyes was broken, as were several of her ribs. Her kidney was bruised. The worst news of all was that she had a severe brain injury. The trauma from the fall or possibly a kick in the head was causing her brain to swell. Villanueva and Ty had decided to induce a coma to slow the swelling and give poor Tina's brain a chance to recover. Villanueva sedated her and placed her under a special blanket to begin cooling her body. Ty collected himself, prepped the operating room, and was standing by ready for action, but everyone recognized that this type of brain injury wouldn't benefit from surgery. She could only heal on her own. It would be days before they'd know if Tina would survive and whether she had sustained any permanent brain damage in the attack.

CHAPTER 44

Maybe Harding Hooten should have taken a page out of Ty Wilson's playbook and done some deep breathing and meditation before he headed into the OR, but the case was an emergency. Maybe he shouldn't have scheduled the meeting in his office while he was covering the OR, but truth be told the get-together went far beyond its allotted time and the chance of a neurosurgical emergency requiring his presence was slim. Maybe he should have let a resident take the case. Maybe he should have checked the film one more time. Maybe he should have realized how much Tina's case was affecting him. Or how much stress he felt by firing Michelle Robidaux.

Eaton Lake was a friend, or, more accurately, their wives were. The women served together on a number of boards: the zoo board, the opera, the Alzheimer's association. Harding and Eaton had shared more than a few nights together at black-tie fund-raisers their wives had helped organize. Now Eaton wanted to make a real name for himself in Michigan's philanthropic community, and he went to see Hooten first. This was a huge opportunity for the hospital. When the doctor heard how much wealth Eaton had accumulated handling mergers and acquisitions, he was stunned. Eaton said he had $150 million — "give or take" — to give to the hospital. Maybe the knowledge that this man was so much wealthier than Hooten had ever imagined threw the doctor's internal compass off its usual meticulous setting.

Eaton's mother, like his wife's mother, had died of complications from Alzheimer's. Now he and his wife wanted to give money to the hospital to set up a center for Alzheimer's research and name it after their mothers: Susan Lake and Delores Costello. Hooten was telling Eaton his money could do more. They could broaden it to include Parkinson's and other degenerative brain diseases striking the elderly. Maybe Hooten should have simply congratulated Eaton on his generosity and put him in touch with the hospital's fund-raising folks, the smooth-talking, suit-wearing cadre who talked about "charitable remainder trusts" and other philanthropic incantations. He didn't.

Harding and Eaton were talking about their respective legacies the way they had talked about the relative merits of Glenlivet and Glenfiddich at one of the fund-raisers when the doctor's pager went off. Hooten did not have hundreds of millions of dollars, far from it, but he, too, was concerned about his legacy. At the end of the day, what did you have to show for a career? A brand-new building honoring your mother was something solid, concrete and glass, with ongoing research that could make its mark on medicine. Hooten had helped train hundreds of surgeons. They were his legacy, a sort of professional progeny far more amorphous than a building. That and his good name, synonymous with an exacting attention to detail and a commitment to the best surgical practices. Maybe he should have remembered that before he rushed from his office for the OR. He didn't. He was thinking he was too old and too senior to be hopping to every time someone in the OR got antsy.

An illegal immigrant had come to the emergency room from one of the glitzier suburbs, brought by a woman still in her high-end tennis outfit. To save a few bucks, she had picked him up after practice from

457

among the milling day laborers outside the big-box home improvement store. He was standing on her ladder, scooping leaves out her gutter, when he leaned too far and fell. His feet had apparently hit the boxwoods, flipping him backward. His head hit the patio flagstones, knocking him unconscious. The woman had driven the man to Chelsea General. Henry Ford was closer, but she apparently thought all indigent cases went to Chelsea General. Also, she thought St. Joseph's was too close to home. That's where she went. Day laborers went to Chelsea General.

A scan in the OR revealed a large blood collection on one side of the man's head. Hooten couldn't believe it. Here he was talking to a man about a gift that could transform Chelsea General and, with some luck, make a major breakthrough in some of the most heartbreaking neurological diseases — and he was called out to serve as the surgical equivalent of a glorified can opener. Hooten excused himself and spent ten minutes without success trying to find another neurosurgeon to do the operation.

"Eaton, I'd really like to continue our conversation. Can I talk you into relaxing up here for about twenty minutes. I've got a quick case."

"Sure thing, Harding. If I can convince your secretary to find me a cup of coffee. Can't go an hour without a caffeine fix. Terrible."

Hooten stepped into the large bathroom connected to his office and changed into his scrubs. He walked fast to the OR, still irked that he had to leave Eaton Lake hanging in his office while he had to handle this mindless case.

When he arrived at the OR, the anesthesiologists had already inserted a breathing tube and were patiently giving anesthesia. Hooten took a quick look at the scan, grabbed a razor, and began shaving the left side of John Doe's head, or, as the circulating nurse called him, Juan Doe. No time for a shaveless operation this time, he thought. Satisfied, Hooten told the nurse to prep the head. He stepped out of the OR to wash his hands.

A pair of vascular surgeons were walking by.

"Hooten, what a surprise."

"Didn't think you could find the OR without a guide."

"I can't believe you're not wearing a tie with those scrubs."

"I didn't realize it was comedy hour at Chelsea General," Hooten said as calmly as possible. He didn't want to let on that their gibes got under his skin this time, although he knew full well that the OR was its own universe. The normal protocol and pecking orders were set aside. It was the great equalizer. Status didn't matter. What counted were hard work and good technical skills.

Hooten worked quickly, cutting the skin and removing the bone. As soon as the bone came off, Hooten knew something was terribly wrong. The brain looked perfectly fine. No blood. No swelling. Nothing. Hooten began to panic. He ran over to the light box.

"These scans. They're up backward!"

"Most doctors check the scan themselves," the circulating nurse said.

Hooten was breathing rapidly, almost hyperventilating. He felt as though he might go vasovagal any second and keel over. This could not be happening. The chief of surgery had just committed a cardinal sin. *The* cardinal sin. He had operated on the wrong side of the head.

Hooten rushed back to the patient and started putting the bone back. He was shaking. He needed to flip the man as quickly as possible and remove the blood, but he had lost precious time, time that would cost the man dearly.

Chapter 45

The Karmann Ghia had seemed like a good idea when Villanueva handed over a cashier's check for fifty-five hundred dollars. He figured the vintage roadster would be a chick magnet for Nick. *The kid needs to get laid,* Villanueva thought. Standing behind the car, getting ready to give it another push, the big man was having second thoughts.

"When I say go, you pop the clutch and give it some gas."

"Okay, Dad," Nick said.

Villanueva had come up with the idea for the car in a flash and found an advertisement in the *Detroit Free Press* classifieds: *1971 Karmann Ghia. Mint Condition. Low Miles.* A friend growing up, Eric Ramirez, had a Karmann Ghia, a red one, and he got more ass than a toilet seat. Villanueva borrowed it once, but he just looked like Magilla Gorilla squeezed into the low-slung roadster.

Villanueva was smitten with the little car the moment he laid eyes on it. It was a shade of green no company would dare paint a car anymore. The man selling the car called it "Willow Green" as he ran a loving hand along the roofline. Looked more like the color of the kitchen linoleum in the apartment he grew up in. Also, the car had wood paneling on the inside.

Even after Villanueva said he'd buy the car, the seller needed to spend another twenty minutes talking about how the upholstery was original and how much work it took to get the original paint color restored with rubbing compound, polishing compound, and wax. The man lived in a small ranch house west of Detroit. Villanueva didn't even know where the town was until he Mapquested it. Then he called a cab to take him there, so he could drive the car home.

The seller was in his late fifties. He wore jeans and a flannel shirt and had a twitch in his left eye behind a thick set of glasses. He looked as though he had shaved for Villanueva's visit but missed a spot just below his jawline, leaving a small line of gray whiskers alongside the raw skin. Also, the man couldn't take his hands off the car. He stroked it like a beloved pet. Villanueva almost asked the guy why he was selling the car if he loved it so much, but he figured that would be inviting at least a thirty-minute sob story, and the last thing in the world he wanted was to see this man cry. He wanted to buy the car and be gone. Villanueva couldn't wait to see the look in Nick's eyes when he handed his son the keys. When Villanueva gave him the cashier's check for the asking price, the man took the check almost reluctantly.

Nick's reaction had been everything Villanueva had hoped for. The soon-to-be-sixteen-year-old lit up at the sight of the car even before learning that it was his. Of course, he only had a learner's permit and would have to wait several months before he could drive it legally without an adult along. Now, though, less than an hour after George gave Nick his first lesson on driving a stick, the engine was no longer turning over. George knew if he could just get the car moving, he could have Nick release the clutch, and the car would start. "We're going to give you a lesson on how to pop the clutch," George told his son cheerfully.

The big cat didn't give a second thought to

who should be pushing and who should be sitting in the driver's seat. The first couple of times, Villanueva had leaned his enormous bulk onto the low trunk of the Karmann Ghia to get it moving, Nick had popped the clutch but forgotten to give the car any gas. It had chugged once or twice and died.

Now Villanueva churned his legs again, picking up speed. He enjoyed the sensation of the little car giving way to his force. He felt as though he were twenty years old again and pushing a blocking sled at Michigan, his fellow linemen at his side, the offensive line coach riding the sled and exhorting them to work harder. Villanueva's enormous legs moved faster and faster over the asphalt, and Nick popped the clutch and hit the gas. The roadster coughed and jerked forward.

Even as he saw the car sputter away in a cloud of exhaust, Villanueva started to feel pressure in his left arm and his chest. The crushing pain of the heart attack came on so suddenly his brain was tricked into thinking Nick must have put the car in reverse and hit him. It was worse than any forearm shiver. Worse than lying at the bottom of a goal-line pileup. As Nick drove off, oblivious to the catastrophe unfolding behind him, the big man stumbled and fell, face-down, his right fist balled up. Villanueva did not hear his son return, or his frantic exhortations for him to wake up, or the hysterical call to 911, or the arrival of the paramedics, who tried to jump-start him the way he and his son had attempted to jumpstart the car. He did not hear the wail of the ambulance as his massive, prone form sped toward Chelsea General, nor did he hear the wail of his son in the emergency room when he was pronounced.

CHAPTER 46

Hooten skipped the bird-watching and headed straight for the hospital at 5 AM. He didn't want to make a big deal about vacating his office, nor did he want some sort of funereal procession of colleagues coming by to wish him well, none of them daring to mention the horrible mistake that had precipitated his sudden departure. The silence would hang over the room like a suffocating gas.

Hooten wished someone would have the nerve to bring it up, to rebuke him, accuse him of hypocrisy for all the times he'd made junior surgeons squirm for less egregious lapses. Hooten wished he could stand in front of his colleagues and own up to his mistake at M&M instead of slinking out under the cover of darkness.

The hospital's lawyer said he did not want Hooten to linger, a lame duck and a legal liability. Hooten threatened to stay, to ride it out, but he knew he needed to step down. Somehow, the case had made it into the *Free Press* and was picked up by the Associated Press, illustrating the desperation of the undocumented, dying for five dollars an hour. The story ran in papers across the country, a black eye for the hospital that Hooten had worked so hard to better.

As a final act to show he retained a shred of control, Hooten threatened an age-discrimination lawsuit until the hospital granted his one wish. Smith and the board reluctantly agreed, and for that Hooten was grateful. The hospital would be a better place as a result.

"Maybe it's for the best," Martha had said when Hooten had confessed what he'd done. He'd been sitting on the side of the bed, staring at the carpet, crying like a schoolboy. She'd put her arm around his shoulder. He shrugged it off.

"Tell it to that worker on life support," Hooten said. The patient had survived the operation, but he did not wake up. A ventilator breathed for him while the Mexican consulate tried to learn the man's identity. The time Hooten wasted opening the wrong side of the head cost both men the rest of their lives. Hooten did not think he deserved affection. He felt a deep rage at how his reputation could be lost in an instant. He was the surgeon who operated on the wrong side of the patient's brain. Everything else he did was now a footnote. Oh, and he worked for more than twenty years to improve the quality of care at Chelsea General.

Hooten would walk out of the hospital and not look back. Martha had been urging Hooten to retire for the last year or two. Martha had lost two of her close friends in quick succession, one with a heart attack and the other to ovarian cancer. She was keenly aware that their time together in the golden years was not guaranteed.

Hooten would get his chance to say good-bye to his friends and coworkers. They'd hold a retirement dinner for him. He was sure of that. They'd probably choose a restaurant rather than one of the hospital's function rooms, at the lawyer's suggestion. And they'd probably hang his portrait in the hospital's main entrance as was customary.

Hooten used the electronic key to unlock the car, and the accompanying beep startled a mourning dove. The bird flew in a straight line from the underbrush into the low branch of a pine, its wings whistling as it flew.

As he drove to the hospital, Hooten thought how this would be his last trip there. The route seemed new. Along one stretch, he saw a law office he'd never noticed before. It was in an old Victorian house. The sign out front said O'BRIEN AND SHEA. Had that been there all along? He must have been thinking about the hospital. Hooten tried to use this observation to cheer himself up. Surely, as one door closed, another opened.

At the hospital, someone had set a stack of flat boxes outside his office. Hooten got to work. He boxed the framed pictures, the diplomas, the honorary degrees, the medals, and the knickknacks. He had an ornate set of chopsticks he'd received when he spoke at Osaka University. There was a Buddha he'd picked up in China, and a beer stein he'd bought in Germany after a conference at the Max Planck Institute. He stared at his Mark Rothko *Untitled 1964* painting for a long time. Despite its mystique, he had always known what it meant for him. A gray rectangle inside a black space. All of his life, he had lived in the smaller, brighter inner box, protected from the blackness that surrounded most people. He worked hard to get there, always knowing that in a split second he could find himself outside, looking in. It had happened. The blackness was now surrounded by gray. He also looked at the picture of the scarlet ibis. Maybe it was time to finally take Martha to South America and find the rare bird for himself. "Bad things happen to good people," he muttered to himself. Hopefully, the people at Chelsea General would learn from his terrible mistake, and it would never happen again. Hooten was always still the teacher, even as he was summarily dismissed from his post as chief.

It was surprising how easy it was to pack a lifetime's memorabilia. He had all his things boxed before seven. J. J. Jerome leaned into the office as though he had just happened by.

"Morning, Dr. Hooten. You need some help carrying boxes?"

"Yes, thank you, Mr. Jerome."

Jerome wheeled in a hand truck and stacked the boxes. One remained.

"I can come back and get that one, Dr. Hooten."

"I can manage."

Hooten bent down, lifted the box, and headed for the door. Jerome started following but stopped.

"You forgot a picture, Dr. Hooten."

Hooten wheeled around. There on the

shelf overlooking the desk was a picture of
Hooten next to Dr. Sydney Saxena. They
were both smiling, standing in identical
poses, hands clasped in front. The hospital
had taken the picture three or four years
earlier after Hooten presented Saxena with
the Julian T. Hoff Outstanding Young Professor Award.

"Thanks, Mr. Jerome. I didn't forget that.
I'm leaving that one. Can you make sure it
doesn't get tossed."

"Sure thing, Dr. Hooten."

With that, Hooten turned for the door.

Villanueva's funeral was as enormous as the
man himself. It brought together the different currents of his life. From his old neighborhood in Detroit, a few middle-aged men
and women whose brown faces had been
either worn or sharpened from a lifetime of
hard work. From his football days, there
were four hulking men with bad knees and
sport coats that no longer fit. From Bloomfield Hills, his ex-wife and several of their
old neighbors, men and women who had
peered out of bow windows to see an enormous man playing catch with their sons.
From his new neighborhood, the bartender
Soupy Campbell and a few of the regulars
at O'Reilly's. From the hospital, doctors,

471

nurses, orderlies, parking attendants. Villanueva had an effect, it seemed, on almost
everyone at Chelsea General who came into
contact with his enormous presence.

Sydney sat next to McManus. Dr. Um-So
and his wife were there. Dr. Smythe sat with
another similar-looking man. Park sat in the
back row with his wife and three children.
Ty sat by himself a few rows up.

Tina had taken news of the Big Cat's
death particularly hard. She was still in the
hospital. She was out of her medically
induced coma. Her brain seemed to be
intact, but she remained heavily sedated.
Even in the painkiller-induced fog, Tina had
this thought: Everything principled in her
life seemed to be falling away.

Nick sat in the front row, next to his
mother. His eyes were red and downcast.
Initially, he had blamed himself for his
father's death. If only he had started the car
on the first try. If only he had convinced his
father not to buy him the car. If only. His
mother had convinced Nick that his father
was a walking time bomb. If it wasn't then,
she said, his heart would have caught up
with him soon. "It's just the way he lived."
As she explained this, she thought about
her ex-husband's passion for life and made

a note to drop the aloof lawyer she had been dating.

The priest said a few words about eternal salvation. The congregation sang "Amazing Grace." Then Dr. Nancy Reid, one of Villanueva's professors from residency, walked up to the stage. Reid was small and bookish, the physical antithesis to the Big Cat. She had to adjust the microphone at the pulpit downward and was so short most of the congregation only saw the top of her head. She coughed a couple of times as she tried to stifle her crying. "Jorge was my friend," she started. "He was a flawed man. But he was deep, he was genuine." Reid came out from behind the pulpit. "I never dared imagine the day Gato would die, but I guess it does not surprise me it happened like this, doing what he loved and trying to make someone's life better and happier."

She gave a compassionate smile to Nick, who wiped his eyes. "I remember my initial skepticism when a former professional football player told me he wanted to become a healer. I thought, *What does this big dumb jock know about medicine?* Boy, was I wrong," she continued. The congregation laughed. "I am sure the people here from Chelsea General will agree that when George was around, everyone was somehow *better.* Patients healed quicker, and doctors performed at a higher level. That was the magic of George. You see, George was not content to be a wonderful doctor himself. He wanted others to follow his high standards, and he was not afraid to rattle a few cages." Many nodded in agreement. "You would never have expected it, but he was the most gifted clinician we have ever trained. He had more clinical acumen in his eyes than a room full of diagnostic equipment. More important, despite his sometimes bombastic ways, he was also the most honorable man I have ever met. You could always count on George to do the right thing. Goodbye my dear friend and student. You left way too soon."

One of Villanueva's old teammates followed. He limped up to the pulpit. He was a former NFL tackle named Vic Warren, whose gut now outreached his barrel chest. Warren rubbed his flat top, gripped the pulpit for support, and then told the story of Villanueva's rookie year. In the NFL, rookies were routinely hazed. They would have to carry the veterans' playbooks or do push-ups or other tasks on command. Some of the hazing was uglier still. A few of the older white veterans on the Lions tried to get a rise out of Villanueva with ethnic slurs,

Warren said.

"I won't repeat them here because we're in a church and all," Warren said. "Another thing rooks would have to do was sing their college fight song in the dining hall. Remember, this was long before hip-hop or rap or any of that crap." Warren looked embarrassed and turned to the priest. "Pardon me, Father.

"George probably got it worse than anyone I had ever seen. I remember once walking into practice seeing a circle of veterans around Gato. They were taunting him while he was doing push-ups. He had done two hundred perfect push-ups while singing the Michigan fight song, 'Hail to the Victors,' at the top of his lungs. They had only asked for a hundred push-ups, but George didn't want to leave any doubt that he could take whatever they threw at him and more." Warren paused. "By doing that, I don't know, George somehow let everyone know he was proud of where he came from but didn't take himself too serious." Warren's eyes clouded with tears. "That was the kinda guy he was."

Nick looked up briefly at the former football player, but tears came and he returned his gaze to the cathedral's stone, his hands over his face.

Hooten followed Warren. This was the first time many of his former colleagues had seen him since his sudden departure from the hospital. Hooten wore his signature bow tie and stood ramrod-straight.

"How do we measure a man?" Hooten asked. He looked out over the congregation and let the question hang the way he might let a question about a surgical decision hang in M&M.

Sydney wondered whether Hooten might be asking the question about himself. She felt sorry that Hooten's career would be marked by a terrible mistake as its final act, the kind of mistake he fought hard to prevent others from making.

Ty thought briefly of Quinn McDaniel and of his own brother, neither of whom lived long enough to become a man. Ty thought of himself. He could only measure himself by the goals he set for himself and the effort he put into them: He would always treat the patient's family as though it were his own, and he would always push his skills to the top of his profession.

"George Villanueva was a man of enormous appetites," Hooten continued. "That was obvious. He devoured life. He jumped in with two feet and invited everyone around him to jump in with him." This brought a few smiles.

"I'm not telling anyone in this church anything he or she doesn't know. I'm sure everyone in this room can think of a story. Some of them should wait until we're outside church." The mourners laughed, grateful for a relief from their grief, and Hooten waited for the laughter to subside.

"George Villanueva was remarkable in one other way. He was a doctor who upheld the highest standards. More than any doctor I've worked with, he did not let anything or anyone get in the way of providing the best care possible." Hooten paused again. He was distracted by thoughts of the white supremacist. That was an aberration for Villanueva. He had let his prejudices — justifiable as they were — get in the way there. Hooten looked up at the packed cathedral.

"George just did not care whose feathers were ruffled. It didn't matter if it was a homeless person who wandered in off the street or one of our civic leaders. George was absolutely passionate about making sure that person got the best care modern medicine has to offer. George was one of the rare doctors who — day in, day out — lived his ideals. So I ask you — all of you — when you walk out of this place. Honor

George. Do your best to live your ideals."

More hymns were sung. The organist played a somber recessional. And the mourners went out, blinking in a bright midday sun.

Driving back to the hospital, pulling into the enormous parking deck, walking across the footbridge into the original Chelsea General building, walking the busy hallways flush with patients, family members, house staff, doctors, administrators, there were no outward signs anything had changed at Chelsea General.

Patients entering the emergency room with a fractured leg or wandering up to the information desk looking for the newborn grandson or heading to radiology to learn if the persistent cough was lung cancer wouldn't notice anything different. The hospital still inhaled the staff and the patients and exhaled the staff, the treated, and the dead.

For the doctors, nurses, and others who had been to Villanueva's memorial service, reentry into Chelsea General came with a sense of emptiness. The Gato Grande's ferocious, funny, and outlandish presence would no longer be there to cure, educate, amuse. They went back to their departments, reviewed charts, checked on patients, sat at monitoring stations but did so without energy. Time would fill this hollowness, and the memory of Villanueva would fade. His presence would be missed less, and his name would not come up as frequently. He would devolve in their collective memories into something of a caricature: a brilliant buffoon in giant scrubs.

Someone at the hospital had videotaped the funeral for the doctors, nurses, and techs who had to work. When Tina watched on a portable DVD player Sydney brought her, Hooten's words stuck with Tina, and she repeated them like a mantra: "Live up to your ideals. Live up to your ideals. Live up to your ideals." The words hung in the air like a dare. She had not been living her ideals, personally or professionally. In a flash, Tina realized what she needed to do, regardless of the personal consequences.

Ty Wilson, Chelsea's greatest natural athlete, was walking down the operating room hallway. He had not a shred of self-doubt as he started washing his hands at the scrub sink. "Live up to your ideals," he said. More than that, Ty knew in his heart that he was human. Medicine was a human profession. He made mistakes. All doctors made mistakes. The lapses arrived unannounced. They came in broad daylight, hidden from view by hubris or pride or ignorance or stubbornness. They arrived in the shadows, creeping behind inattention or distraction or fatigue. The medical errors were always there, waiting for their moment, waiting for human frailty.

After Quinn McDaniel died, Ty wanted to be forgiven for his deadly error in judgment. He thought forgiveness would make things right. If he could receive forgiveness from Quinn's mother and his peers, he thought, that would be the first step to righting his wrong.

More than forgiveness, Ty had wanted to redeem himself. He wanted to do something that would somehow compensate for what he had done. Part of him realized that simply wasn't possible, and he froze. Doubt consumed him. No effort could undo what he had done. All he could do — all anyone could do — was learn from mistakes and move on — becoming a better doctor in the process, and hopefully teaching countless other doctors to do the same.

Sung Park was sitting on the porch telling Pat stories about Villanueva. The rare laughter she displayed during their romantic dinner now occurred almost every day. "He was at all-you-can-eat Chinese buffet," Sung was saying. "He ate so much the owner come from kitchen and kick him out of restaurant." They both started laughing. "But he was very special man. Whenever he go to restaurant, he always look around the room and pay for at least one table of people he didn't know." Pat smiled.

"I love you Sung, and I love that you remember your friend that way."

Sydney walked into her new office and saw the picture Hooten had left behind. She picked it up and dusted it off. She stared hard at Hooten, and mouthed, *Thank you, Boss, for everything.*

CHAPTER 47

Sydney sat down in the chair Harding Hooten had occupied for as long as she had been at the hospital. The cream-colored walls were bare, with nail holes where the framed photographs had hung, each marking a milestone in Hooten's personal and professional life. Hooten as chief resident. Hooten with President Clinton when he had visited the hospital. Hooten with his son in his high school graduation cap and gown. And so on. Where the pictures had been, the paint was a little brighter. The sun hadn't hit those spots, and the effect was odd, almost unsettling. A pattern of rectangles marked the walls on either side of Sydney, like ghosts of Harding Hooten's career. Sydney remembered reading how the atomic bomb dropped on Nagasaki vaporized some of the victims, leaving only a shadow on the wall behind them.

The shadow of Harding Hooten fell over

Sydney Saxena as she occupied his seat. She idolized the man. When she'd first overhead a doctor describing the careless mistake that precipitated his retirement, she did not believe it. She thought it was a joke. Then a malicious rumor. A man with such exacting standards would not, could not make such a colossal blunder. But he had. It was a warning, a cautionary tale to her, to all the surgeons. Everyone was fallible. Even the great Harding Hooten.

When Sydney arrived at the office, maintenance was already there, changing the locks on the desks. They handed her the two shiny keys on a small, round ring and left her with a paint wheel, promising to paint the office as soon as she picked a color. Sydney felt like a traitor, an apostate in the cult of Harding Hooten. As stunned as she was to hear of Hooten's professional fall from grace, she was more surprised she had been chosen as his successor.

The day was full of surprises. On a whim, she had stopped by the playground she usually only frequented on her birthday and felt for the first time in her adult life a pang of desire to have children. This revelation shocked her even more than her being named to succeed Hooten. After all, she fully expected to become chief of surgery.

That was something she was working toward. It was a promotion she saw in her future. She just thought she would have to wait another decade before it became a reality. Wanting to have children was a real stunner, but as she watched the love between the mothers and daughters she realized she wanted that for herself. She pictured herself seated on one of the benches, thrilled for each new accomplishment, consoling after a fall, offering snacks. Out of the blue, Sydney felt that she was ready for the whole package.

Then she thought of McManus. She was picturing him as a father when there was a quiet knock on the outside of her door.

"Your ears must have been burning. I was just thinking about you."

"Really? I thought you had to talk about someone to have their ears burn."

"Don't believe everything you read in the *Archives of Internal Medicine*."

"You'd probably have some sort of surgical solution for ringing ears. Resecting the ear, maybe."

"Very funny."

"I digress. Would you like to have a celebratory dinner tonight? My place?"

"Sounds good," Sydney said, thinking *his place*. The relationship was entering the next stage, and Sydney was looking forward to it.

As he turned to go, McManus pointed to a picture on the shelf above Sydney's desk. In it, she was standing next to Hooten. They almost looked like twins, posing the same way as they did.

"Where'd that picture come from?"

"I don't know."

"Looks like he left it for you."

"Yeah. I'm sure he did. But how could he have possibly known the board would name me?" Sydney's voice trailed off.

It was time for a new era at Chelsea General. On her computer, she typed "Prevalence of Wrong-Sided Craniotomy for Brain Trauma." Then she went to the central paging site and paged everyone in the department.

311. 6.

Even though it was a Thursday, Sung Park decided to take the day off and let the residents take clinic. The chemo hadn't made him overly tired, nor did he feel nauseated. He just wanted to stay home. The girls had started their winter break from school, and he felt a tug to be with them. The day was impossibly warm for December, pushing seventy degrees, and the girls were in the small backyard playing with their brightly colored hula hoops. Sung marveled at how their lithe bodies could keep the hoops spinning seemingly indefinitely above their narrow hips.

The girls smiled when they saw Sung watching them through the kitchen window.

"Daddy, look!" they called.

A month or so earlier, Park might have admonished the girls to do something useful with their time: to read a book or practice their violin or cello. Something that would help them later in life. Something that would prepare them for the future. Now he walked outside with a glass of orange juice, sat down on a deck chair, and watched them.

Park's two-year-old son wandered out of the house and tried to grab the spinning hoop orbiting around his older sister Natalie. She stopped and handed him the hoop. The boy studied it, confused. She put it over his head.

"Like this," Emily said, and demonstrated. He let go of the hoop and gyrated. The plastic disk fell to the flagstones. The girls laughed. He tried again. Once again, the hoop dropped.

Four-year-old Natalie leaned over. "Ready," she said. The boy took on an exaggerated look of concentration. "Go!" She pushed the hoop to start it moving around his small waist. He gyrated wildly. The hoop dropped.

"I did it," he cried out. "I did it."

As Park watched from the chair, he thought there were some things in life you could not prepare for. A brain tumor, for example. Your children idling on a balmy December day, for another. These were the moments to learn from and to savor.

Park tipped his head back to feel the sun. His mind wandered to his language tapes.

"Savor: to taste and enjoy completely."

By Tina's calculation, she had about a twenty-four-hour drive ahead of her and the rest of her life to figure out how everything had gone wrong at Chelsea General. It had been nearly four months since K. C. Ruby had nearly killed her. It turned out he had also assaulted his girlfriend that night — the same one George Villanueva had rescued while his scared son looked on.

Thanks to brain monitors, diuretics, and mechanical ventilation as well as months of cognitive and physical rehabilitation, she was finally back to 50 percent of what she once was. The one thing she was given was a lot of time to think, and she had made some big decisions.

She was looking forward to practicing medicine in a small office in Vermont, the way her grandfather had. The way her father was now practicing medicine in his "retirement."

Tina's plan was to charge fifty dollars cash for basic doctor visits, eliminating the mountain of paperwork, the billing, the insurance companies peering over her shoulder, measuring how many patients she should see in an hour, telling her what she should and should not be doing. Also, despite Vermont's reputation as some sort of green utopia, plenty of people there lived hand-to-mouth and did not have insurance. They were self-employed or day laborers or part-time and needed someplace to go for their basic medical needs.

A wave of excitement ran over Tina at the thought of delivering babies again. She had done an OB rotation in medical school, and she remembered the thrill of bringing new life into the world, messy, squalling, joyful life.

Tina nosed the car onto the highway. She imagined her colleagues' cortisol levels rising steadily, as her own had, every time she entered the hospital in recent months. Tina thought about the competition to get into medical school; the competition to get the best grades and score points with the most influential professors; the competition to get the best residencies; the competition to get the best fellowships; the competition to get a position at a teaching hospital. The competition to become a department head. Always jockeying. Always pushing. Always trying to get ahead. Ambitions. Politics. Egos. She had competed with her peers and, for the most part, she had succeeded, but where was the practice of medicine in all this? Where were "the healing arts," as her grandfather liked to call them?

Tina was on the interstate now, heading toward her future at seventy-five miles per hour.

Maybe, Tina thought with a moment of alarm, her vision of medicine was idealized, infused with the saccharine glow of a child who sees a grandfather and father as fonts of great wisdom and stature in their communities. Maybe they, too, had faced profound disappointment in their professional lives, or concluded that the practice of medicine was not what they'd imagined. She didn't think so. She had never heard them talk about medicine as anything but a noble calling.

At home, they became animated when

their conversations turned to vexing cases. They tossed out possible diagnoses, possible treatments. Tina remembered vividly one of her grandfather's patients, an elderly woman named Violet. Tina was nine and spending the month of July in Vermont. Tina loved the name Violet. She wanted to change her name to Violet when she was old enough, so she paid close attention to the woman's case. Violet complained of aching joints and muscle pain. At first her grandfather thought it was fibromyalgia. He recommended warm compresses and exercise, although Violet walked almost everywhere already. Her aches continued. One day, her grandfather came home with a smug look on his face.

"Did your mother or father ever make you drink cod liver oil as a punishment?"

"Cod liver oil? Sounds gross."

"We made your father drink it when he didn't mind his parents."

"You did?"

"Tastes awful."

"It sounds like it tastes awful."

"Today, I made Violet Olson drink cod liver oil."

"She didn't mind you?" Tina asked.

Her grandfather laughed. "No, it wasn't that. She drank it to make her feel better.

And you know what? She started feeling better. Her problem all along has been a vitamin D deficiency."

Tina remembered her grandfather's pride that he was able to outthink this elderly woman's joint pain and muscle aches. That there was a simple remedy to her symptoms made her case even more satisfying — so satisfying he had to share it with his nine-year-old granddaughter. So many of Tina's colleagues talked about other things. They became animated when they talked about reducing the percentage of costs devoted to overhead or Medicare reimbursement rates or real estate investments.

As she drove south around Lake Erie, Tina again questioned her decision. Before she left, she and Mark had agreed they would split amicably. No lawyers with their cut-throat tactics and exorbitant fees. Ashley was coming with her. The girls would stay with Mark until the school year was out before spending the summer with Tina in Vermont. Tina knew this would not be easy on the girls, but living in a home where Mommy and Daddy are fighting — or, worse, where they simply don't care any-more — that had to be worse, didn't it? Tina certainly hoped so.

Tina heard a keening in the backseat. Ashley had thrown her head back. Tina turned on the car radio, and Ashley happily banged on her tray. Tina welcomed the challenge of caring for Ashley. She didn't consider it a penance but a gift. She knew she could do it well, and she looked forward to connecting with this girl who had been to this point, if Tina was really honest with herself, little more than a responsibility she had accepted.

Tina's father had been reserved when he'd heard the news. He was no doubt excited his daughter would be joining him, but was silent for a long time when Tina told him that she was coming with Ashley and leaving Mark and other girls behind. He and Tina's mother had been married forty-two years before she had died of breast cancer a couple of years earlier. They shared not only love, but a fierce loyalty. Her father felt the same way about his patients. He felt the same way about Tina, for that matter, and even her brother, who had struggled with alcohol and drugs after failing to follow in the footsteps of his father and grandfather. He now worked in a bike shop in Vermont.

Tina was approaching the Ohio state line. *How many more states to go?* Tina wondered idly. Before she could work it out, another thought intruded: She was heading home.

Toward her roots, her birthplace, her family. She was driving toward her past.

CHAPTER 48

Even now, 13 months after the funeral, a pall hung over the Emergency Department. Dr. Kauffman, better known as Dr. Um-So, sat on Villanueva's stool as the docs went about examining a cracked skull, a sprained ankle, an odd rash, a delusional psychotic, a febrile child, a nauseated woman. Kauffman thought he should ease the loss those around him felt by thundering around the room like the Big Cat, roaring profanity, insults, diagnoses. He knew he could no more pull it off than he could wear the size XXXL scrubs.

There was a crackle on the radio behind him. Kauffman didn't quite believe what he'd heard, so he asked the paramedic on the incoming helicopter to repeat. Kauffman went pale.

"Um so, page Dr. Wilson," Kauffman said. "This one will loosen even his sphincter."

When his pager buzzed, Ty Wilson was sitting in the call room, legs crossed, back straight. The lights were out. His eyes were shut. He took in a deep breath through his nose, held it, and released the air slowly through his mouth. The pager buzzed again. Ty took another long, slow breath and stood up. He looked at the pager: *Um-So wants you. Now.* He called the ER then quickly grabbed his coat and made for the roof via the stairwell, two steps at a time. He had never seen a traumatic atlanto-occipital dislocation. This kind of internal decapitation was almost always fatal. The connection between the spinal column and the brain stem would be severed, and the respiratory arrest would follow quickly. Hangmen through the ages counted on this simple equation.

The teenager coming in on the helicopter was incredibly lucky. First, that he had survived the initial ATV accident. Second, that he had survived the trip to the hospital. His father and brother had carefully lifted him into the back of the family's pickup truck. Somehow, they managed to move him there without killing him. To make him comfortable, they had placed his head on a pillow. If they had called 911, and the paramedics had placed him on a standard trauma board, the boy might not have survived. Straightening his cervical spine beyond its natural curve might have been enough to kill him. In the helicopter ride from the county hospital, his head rested on a sandbag.

Ty spoke on his cell phone with the radiologist who had seen the CT scan.

"You got yourself one lucky son of a bitch inbound," he said. "Emailing you the scans now. Possible subluxation at the time of the trauma. When he arrived at the ED, the CT showed a subarachnoid hemorrhage at the craniovertebral junction. Definitely AOD."

"Thanks," Ty said. "AOD is a lot better than DOA."

"Ha! You got that right," the radiologist said. "Kinda spooky, though, the head up there hanging by a thread."

"Appreciate your help," Ty said. He was on the roof now and heard the throbbing of the rotors getting louder. He took a deep breath through his nose and breathed out slowly through his mouth.

Ty could see the helicopter now. It descended slowly toward the roof, its tail twisting in the wind, the sounds of the engine and the rotors echoing off the small landing pad, the prop wash blowing Ty and the ER nurses who had also come up to the roof.

Ty ran through his plan. First, get his own CT of the patient, along with a craniocervical MRI. He wanted to make sure he knew exactly what he was dealing with.

Then Ty planned to put a halo on the boy's head to completely immobilize it. Any movement at all could kill him. Once he had the kid in the OR, he planned a craniocervical fusion.

Ty thought about calling in one of the other neurosurgical attendings, but he was the last one standing. Hooten was gone. Tina was gone. Park was out of the picture. After years of relative stability, the ranks of the neurosurgical unit at Chelsea General had been decimated in a matter of months.

Still, if there was one thing Quinn McDaniel's case told him, he was not an island. He was not the Lone Ranger. His skills alone were not enough. Ty paged chief resident Mac Ryan and told him to bring his best senior.

"This is going to be one for the books," he said. "Oh, and let's make sure we get all his labs checked, especially his coagulation function." *Quinn's protocol* is what Ty called it.

Ty had read basketball great Bill Russell's book when he was a kid and couldn't read enough sports books. He was surprised when Russell said some great players did not want the ball at end of the game. In the timeout before the final shot, they would make themselves scarce, sending the coach the message: *Design a play for someone else.* Now Ty wanted the ball. He wanted to be the one in charge of this boy's case, but he was acutely aware that he was part of the team. Aristotle had said the only person who could live alone was an animal or a saint. He could not do it alone, in the operating room or in life.

Ty scrubbed in, strode into the OR, adjusted the loupes over his eyes, and turned to the scrub nurse: "Scalpel."

The employees of Thorndike Press hope you have enjoyed this Large Print book. All our Thorndike, Wheeler, and Kennebec Large Print titles are designed for easy reading, and all our books are made to last. Other Thorndike Press Large Print books are available at your library, through selected bookstores, or directly from us.

For information about titles, please call:
 (800) 223-1244

or visit our Web site at:
 http://gale.cengage.com/thorndike

To share your comments, please write:
 Publisher
 Thorndike Press
 10 Water St., Suite 310
 Waterville, ME 04901